The Herbalist

The Herbalist

NIAMH BOYCE

PENGUIN
IRELAND

PENGUIN IRELAND

Published by the Penguin Group
Penguin Ireland, 25 St Stephen's Green, Dublin 2, Ireland
(a division of Penguin Books Ltd)
Penguin Books Ltd, 80 Strand, London WC2R ORL, England
Penguin Group (USA) Inc., 375 Hudson Street, New York, New York 10014, USA
Penguin Group (Australia), 707 Collins Street, Melbourne, Victoria 3008, Australia
(a division of Pearson Australia Group Pty Ltd)
Penguin Group (Canada), 90 Eglinton Avenue East, Suite 700, Toronto, Ontario, Canada M4P 2Y3
(a division of Pearson Penguin Canada Inc.)
Penguin Books India Pvt Ltd, 11 Community Centre,
Panchsheel Park, New Delhi – 110 017, India
Penguin Group (NZ), 67 Apollo Drive, Rosedale, Auckland 0632, New Zealand
(a division of Pearson New Zealand Ltd)
Penguin Books (South Africa) (Pty) Ltd, Block D, Rosebank Office Park,
181 Jan Smuts Avenue, Parktown North, Gauteng 2193, South Africa

Penguin Books Ltd, Registered Offices: 80 Strand, London WC2R ORL, England

www.penguin.com

First published 2013
001

Copyright © Niamh Boyce, 2013

The moral right of the author has been asserted

Typeset in 12/14.75pt Dante MT Std by Palimpsest Book Production Ltd, Falkirk, Stirlingshire
Printed in Great Britain by Clays Ltd, St Ives plc

A CIP catalogue record for this book is available from the British Library

ISBN: 978-1-844-88304-2

www.greenpenguin.co.uk

Penguin Books is committed to a sustainable
future for our business, our readers and our planet.
This book is made from Forest Stewardship
Council™ certified paper.

ALWAYS LEARNING   PEARSON

For my daughter, Rosie

Author's Note

Although *The Herbalist* is inspired by real events, it is a work of fiction. The story that unfolds, and every character apart from the herbalist, are products of the author's imagination and any resemblance to any person, living or dead, is entirely coincidental.

He just appeared one morning and set up shop in the market square. It was drizzling. Everything was either a shade of brown or a shade of grey. He was the lightest thing there, the one they called the black doctor. He wore a pale suit, a straw hat and waved his arms like a conductor. The men spat about dark crafts and foreign notions, but the women loved him. Oh, the rubs, potions, tinctures and lotions he had. Unguents, even.

I went to the market the first chance I got. Craned my neck, trying to see past the headscarves, but all I saw was a glimpse of a bottle held high, and the gold-ringed fingers that gripped it. The women crowded around his stall. God, but they'd no sense at all, clucking like hens.

One at a time, ladies, one at a time.

He sounded hoarse, not young. 'Oh, isn't he lovely,' some girl whispered. I nudged my way forward till I got a poke in the back. I turned. It was Mam. She dragged me away by the collar. What did I think I was doing, gaping at some heathen hawker? Gaping indeed: I hadn't even set eyes on the man.

I couldn't get the herbalist out of my head after that. The slightest mention of him made me giddy. I think some part of me believed Aggie. For she had told my fortune at the carnival, the day before the herbalist came to town. And she had sworn that love was coming.

I

It was an Easter Monday, and it was one of those days. Father couldn't bear for anyone to breathe the same air as he did, let alone speak. So Mam and I set out for town, leaving him hunched over his cold dinner, jabbing a finger at us by way of goodbye. Charlie had already made himself scarce; he was getting good at that.

I thought we'd never get to the carnival. I had won two free tickets for the Wall of Death in Kelly's Easter Draw. But Mam wouldn't take the river path; she insisted on keeping to the road. Said she needed time to make herself look normal. Her eyes were a bit red.

It was hot for April; my feet were swollen by the time we got to Nashes' Field. I took off my sandals and cooled my heels on the grass. The carnival people were magic, the way they changed everything. Took what was a plain riverside field and turned it into a foreign land of coloured tents and stands, a land buzzing with people.

All were decked out in their Easter finest. They queued for barge trips and lay about on blankets; some lads had their trousers rolled up to dangle their toes in the river. The ground was scattered with tickets and sweet-papers; I kept my eyes peeled for coins. Mam waved hello to lots of people but kept moving in case anyone noticed she'd been crying.

'Fortunes, fortunes!' The voice made me turn. A fat woman sat in a shabby armchair with a tray of cards on her lap. An orange scarf was tied around her head, and the sign beside her read CARDS AND PALMS – HAVE YOUR FORTUNE TOLD! She made a big show of shuffling the pack. Mam paid her no heed; walked on as fast as she could. I slowed down, couldn't help myself.

The gypsy spotted her catch. 'Come here, young one, come on!'

Mam was far ahead of me. I ventured over. Too late, I recognized the woman as Aggie Reilly, the town you-know-what. I'd never seen a woman of ill repute up close before. Her eyes were grey and friendly, her round face brown, her nose beaky. She looked like a burnt hen. Not quite the face of evil. A bit of a let-down, all in all.

She shuffled cards from one hand to the other and then tapped the pack against the tray. It was lacquered black and showed a golden Eiffel Tower.

'Choose one, only one now, mind.'

She spread the cards in an arc across the Eiffel Tower. Her nails were ridged with earth. I chose one from the centre. It was soft as cloth. Aggie Reilly snatched it from my hand. Her mouth pursed into a small smile.

'Let's see what the future holds. Oh, ghastly, ghastly! I cannot tell thee.'

'What is it?' I asked.

'What does the card say, missus?'

A boy's breath hit my neck. There were three of them, lads that had sneaked up behind me.

'The worst fate of all,' Aggie said, leaning forward.

Her bosom bulged from her dress and her dyed hair straggled out from under her scarf. I hated her then. I wanted to walk away, but I stayed. She held up the Queen of Hearts for all to see.

'What does it mean?' I asked.

'Love is coming,' she said, 'but not from one of these buckos.'

She jabbed a thumb towards the boys. 'Cross my palm with sixpence, sweetie, and I'll tell you more.'

I felt my face heat up. The boys roared with laughter. Pádraig Greaney made the most noise, braying like a donkey.

'Watch out, lads, love's coming for pale-face!' he hooted.

And to think that I'd put my arm around that little snot as he bawled for his mother on our first day of school. The boys held their sides, pretended to collapse with mirth and rolled off across the grass.

Two girls nudged their way in front of me. The Nash sisters – dosed to the high hills with Lily of the Valley. Milkie carried her sunhat, to better show off her long white hair. The skin on her nose and chin was red and peeling. She requested a palm reading, 'a good

3

one', she added. Moll pressed her face into her sister's shoulder and began to giggle. It never took much to set her off.

I edged away from the fortune-telling. I couldn't see Mam anywhere. Midges bit my scalp, and my neck was burning from the sun. I shouldn't have put my hair up. The style I'd copied from *Modern Woman* magazine was falling down. That's what you get for aping hair-dos you can't pronounce. Chignon, my bum.

The carnival people were setting up the main attraction: Daredevil Stanley and his Blonde Bombshell. A motorcycle revved inside a large tent. You could almost taste the petrol. Tanned men in white vests were laying down boards. They were making the ramp to the Wall of Death. The wall was huge, a sky-high wooden stand creaking against the sun. There was already a queue at the bottom of the rickety stairs, with Mam near it, nattering away to Birdie Chase. They were holding each other's elbows, as if they were about to start a two-step. Birdie's lardy upper arms would put you off your supper. It was odd to see her out of the shop; she seldom left the premises since her fall. She wore a faded sequinned number with no sleeves and had wound a white ribbon round the crook of her walking stick.

As I watched, I noticed how thin Mam had become. She used to look like Maureen O'Sullivan, but that day she didn't look like anyone, not even herself. She still pinned her hair away from her forehead, and it still fell in dark kinks to her shoulders, but her face was pinched and her collarbones stood out. We'd left in such a hurry that she hadn't changed out of her yellow housedress. It had been washed so many times it was almost see-through. I felt ashamed of her, and then felt ashamed for feeling that way about my own mother.

I called out, and Mam turned and waved. I ran over and hugged her tight around the waist. She smiled and took my hand. I was dying to tell her that love was coming for me. She liked that kind of talk. But she would have killed me for speaking to Aggie. The thing was, only for the likes of Aggie, our family would have had no one to look down on at all.

A man marched by with a speaker, calling out the same thing

4

over and over again: 'Stanley, a man who dices with death for a living. With death, I tell you! With death! The speed, the danger . . .'

Mam swung my hand and started to sing softly: 'He'd fly through the air with the greatest of ease, that daring young man on the flying trapeze.' She didn't like what the man was saying about death, but she joined the queue anyway. She had to, she'd promised, and Mam always kept her promises. When our turn came, we began to climb towards the top. We had to go real slow: there were a lot of people behind us and in front. Like cattle in their best clothes. The stairs wobbled. There were gaps in the steps, and you could see the ground way down underneath. Every now and again a girl would let out a screech. Mam kept humming the trapeze song. We reached the top. The wall came up to my chest. I looked down on the circle beneath us: the grass was worn away from motorbike wheels. So Stanley had performed already and survived. I had a memory then, a quick one: I was in my father's arms, and mine were tight around his neck; his face felt clean and fresh shaven. He was telling me it was all right, that he had me safe and sound. I was very young and I was proud to be with him.

'I wonder if this is safe,' Mam said.

Probably not, I thought, *seeing as it's called the Wall of Death*, but I didn't say anything. Some young lads started to lean forward, trying to make the wall shake and wobble. Suddenly they stopped and stared into the ring. We looked down.

The Blonde Bombshell was wiggling into the centre. She did a turn and stretched her arm out in different directions to signal the imminent arrival and feats of the Daredevil. She wore a blood-red corset with green fringes on the chest and belly. Her legs looked like they'd been steeped in tea; long and fat, they ended in the highest heels I'd ever seen. Mae West, and well past her best. The lads gave Tarzan cries and started to jump up and down, trying to make the wall shake again. Mam grabbed my arm so tight I nearly yelped.

'Oh, Lord,' she said. 'Blondie must be sixty if she's a day. If she's any sign of things to come, this display won't be up to much. Let's sneak off.'

Mam didn't like showing what she was really afraid of. She always pretended it was something else. I could've cried. As we turned to make our way down the stairs, I got a glimpse of Daredevil Stanley strutting out with his motorcycle. He was tucked into a very snug outfit. A child piped up: 'You can see his nobbly bits!'

Mam yanked me and I followed her down, step by lethal step. We had to get down before the show started or we'd be mincemeat. That's what Mam said.

Though we'd barely arrived at the carnival, she was too tired to see the singers and too broke to afford a ticket for the Arabian Magician, with his flowing black robes and seven child assistants. So we strolled along the riverside to find a nice spot where she could rest. When we found one, I rolled around on the long grass to make it nice and flat for her. She laughed, and then she lay back and closed her eyes.

'I hope this grass isn't damp,' she murmured after a while.

'Do you think it's all right to go home yet?' I asked.

'Not yet.'

She looked sad, and I was sorry for reminding her of home. She soon fell asleep. Her cheek was getting pink from the sun. I pulled some of the flattened grass up till her face was in the shade. I didn't fall asleep, but I lay there as if I was, liking the idea of Mam and me dozing in the long grass while everyone else buzzed around – a world unto ourselves. Special people who didn't need to talk much to know they liked each other.

2

Carmel was all set to wash when the knock came, someone banging on the shop door. Well, whoever it was could knock away. It was a bank holiday and after hours and people should know better. Thank God the back door was bolted. Grettie B would think nothing of barging through it, yodelling her hellos and gabbing away, while Carmel was stooped half naked trying to soap herself behind a towel. She emptied the kettle into the basin and dropped a muslin pouch of dried lavender into the steaming water.

The knocking got louder. Someone who wasn't giving up - a straggler from the carnival maybe? Carmel sighed, rebuttoned her smock dress and carried the basin into the kitchen, out of sight of visitors. She moved slowly; customer or no customer, she wasn't going to rush and slip, not in her condition. She put down the basin and patted her arms dry with a towel. Then she pulled her hair back, put on her spectacles and went to open the shop door.

When she eased back the bolt, it was neither Grettie nor a straggler. It was her brother, Finbar.

'Hello, Carmel.'

'Finbar!'

She wanted to hug him, but he'd always hated 'gushing'. Besides, he was carrying a large cardboard box.

'It's wonderful to see you, Finbar. Come in, come in.'

She locked the door behind him.

'Come into the back. How've you been? How's James? How –'

'Ah, one question at a time, woman.'

He sounded gruff, but he smiled.

She wanted to say how much she had missed him, ask had he got her letters. But knew better: Finbar would interpret that as a rebuke for not having visited her in so long.

He followed her into the living room and set the box on the

sofa. He turned then and gave her a peck on the cheek. His skin smelt of Pear's Soap. He was impeccably attired, as ever.

He looked around the dim room, frowning at the closed curtains. He went over, pulled them open and sighed when, instead of the garden, he got a view of their new kitchen extension. He didn't say anything; Finbar would be loath to acknowledge any of Dan's handi-work. Instead he concentrated on his own reflection, licked a finger and tamed his fringe. He hadn't changed much since she last saw him, at the reading of the will.

'You're looking very well.'

'As are you. I see the child must be due soon?'

'I think it's a boy,' she said, smoothing her smock.

So he'd received *that* letter at least. It would be so nice to share her joy with one of her own. Finbar glanced away from where her hand rested on her swollen belly. Carmel thought she detected a faint shudder. She folded her arms in front of her stomach and adjusted her expectations accordingly. How quickly it came back to her, the code she had developed long ago for dealing with her diffi-cult brother, for staying in his affections.

'How's James – did he pass his exams?' she said.

'Long ago, Carmel. And why wouldn't he? What kind of head-master would I be if my own son were a dunce?'

'Of course, I knew he'd do well – how's he spending his Easter Monday?'

'James can take care of himself. He's not a child.'

He didn't offer any further information on his son, and he didn't ask after Dan. No surprise there. He looked around the room a bit more and then his gaze landed on the box he had brought with him.

'What's in it?' she said.

'Excuse me?'

'The box?'

He went over, sliced the tape with his thumbnail and flipped back the lids. Carmel looked in. It was full of books.

What had she expected? Flowers? A christening gown?

'Books?'

'Banned books,' he corrected; 'a friend in Customs supplies a select few, people who wouldn't let them fall into the wrong hands.'

'Oh, Finbar, thank you!'

She threw her arms out towards him.

'Carmel, will you stop?' He sidestepped away. 'Now you can give old Birdie Chase a run for her money, eh? Though why she rents banned books is beyond me; it's not like she needs the income.'

So he had got all her news and he had been thinking about her – that was something at least.

'You never said how you found out what Birdie was up to. Or were you one of her customers, Carmel?'

'Stop it! Of course not. Seamus Devoy was delivering the papers one day and mentioned Birdie's under-the-counter game – as he called it – in passing. As if it were common knowledge. He knew by me I hadn't a notion what he was talking about. "Renting the filthy books," he said, with a big leer on him. He said she had loads of *Lady Chatterley's Lover*. He thought it was great gas.'

'Well, make sure you're more discreet than Birdie, won't you?'

'Oh, you've no worries on that score.'

Carmel lifted books out of the box. Some were dog-eared already. *Tender is the Night, Bird Alone, Hollywood Cemetery, As I Lay Dying.*

'Is *Lady Chatterley's Lover* in here?'

'Ah, Carmel, how would I know? I wouldn't lower myself to read that lot.'

'I know you wouldn't. You're very good to bring them at all.'

'Make sure you get cash up front. Give no credit.'

'Don't worry your head about the finances.'

'I'm telling you, Carmel – give no credit.'

'And I'm telling you, Finbar – you've no need to worry.'

'Your letters give me cause to.'

'I know, I know, I just worry, that's all.'

She felt guilty. She shouldn't have said anything, imposing her troubles on him. The shop would probably have done better under Finbar. He had a knack for business, an eye for opportunity. Well, it hadn't been her decision.

'Come into the kitchen. I've a nice bit of ham.'

'I've eaten,' he said.

They stood there, momentarily silent. It felt like he was waiting for something, but she couldn't think what.

'You know, you look well, Carmel, and happy.'

'I am happy.'

Finbar laughed. 'Daniel Holohan won't be happy, not when he sees these books. Maybe we should run our scheme by the man of the house?'

How slippery Finbar was – that much hadn't changed. He knew she wouldn't tell Dan, knew it would be their secret.

He closed the box and hoisted it high. His face reddened with the strain.

'Where will we hide the evidence, half-sister dearest?'

She hated it when he called her that.

'In the extension, through the door behind you – there's a long white cupboard. I'll show you.'

He followed her through the door. She opened the cupboard and cleared the rags and polish from the lowest shelf. Her belly made her awkward and slow. When she was done, Finbar eased the box into place and closed the cupboard.

'You won't be stuck for reading material now, Carmel!'

'Between the shop and the baby, there won't be much time for reading.'

'You'll want to be careful not to get worn out. Remember poor Nancy, how frazzled she got trying to manage everything, what it did to her temper?'

'I'm not my mother.'

'Of course, you're very different women, Carmel. You, most likely, are well prepared and have help arranged – some local girl?'

'We don't want everyone in the town knowing our business.'

Finbar's face lit up. 'Do you know, I have just the person. She's of good character but not local to you – an old pupil of mine.'

'I don't know, Finbar – girls can be trouble.'

'Sarah's far from a girl – very pleasant, and very reasonable, if a touch on the plain side.'

'Well, I could probably do with a hand. I'll talk to Dan.'

'As if Dan ever made a decision in his life.'

'Now, Fin.'

'That's settled, then. I'll send her on when the time comes. Just drop me a note.'

He walked back into the shop. Carmel followed. He went behind the counter and ran his hands across its surface.

'That'll be in four weeks, Finbar. Imagine, four weeks and I'll be a mother!'

Carmel went to grasp her miraculous medal, but it wasn't there. Could the chain have snapped and fallen into the basin? She'd have to look later.

Finbar took the stack of ledgers from the shelf behind him. He selected the most recent one and started leafing through it. Without looking up, he waved his hand at her. Carmel took off her glasses and gave them to him.

She looked at the top of his head as he studied the ledger. It was like he had never left. Why had he come now, after two years of no word? Dan said there was always a motive with Finbar. Carmel didn't like it when Dan spoke like that, but he was right. She had adored Finbar since she was a child, but she wasn't blind. She knew how he felt about her.

Finbar had always drawn attention to his status, refusing to call his stepmother by anything other than her first name. That hadn't gone down well. Carmel's mother hated her name, thought it was common. Maybe that was why Nancy took to Dan. He always called her Mrs Kelly and treated her with the upmost respect. And when it came to the end, Dan was the only one who could tolerate her fevered notions. He would sit by her sickbed, letting her ramble on and on long after everyone else had grown tired listening. Such a contrast to Finbar, whose visits felt like assessments to calculate how long she had left and exactly when he could step in and take over.

During her lifetime Nancy treated both children like her own. After she died, however, it was a different matter. At the reading of the will they discovered that Carmel, not Finbar, had inherited the shop. Finbar went white, and stood up and sat down again several times. His hands shook. When Mr Carr, the solicitor, finished reading, he looked over his glasses at Finbar and said quietly that of course Finbar could challenge the terms of his stepmother's will, that many would consider it most irregular to leave a business to a daughter when they had a son.

Carmel was too dazed to respond. Dan rose to his feet and said the only thing that was highly irregular was a solicitor drawing up a will and then encouraging somebody to challenge it. That shut Mr Carr up. Carmel had been proud of her husband at that moment – how quickly he had responded, how calmly he had spoken.

Finbar went over to her when the solicitor left.

'Thank you, Carmel.'

He put his hand on her shoulder.

'I didn't know, I swear.'

'No, I said thanks and I meant it. You've saved me from a life-time of weighing ounces of sugar and listening to woman-talk. Your husband is more suited to that kind of thing. My time will be better spent providing the next generation with an education.'

He left the office, and she hadn't seen him since.

Whatever he had said, Carmel knew Finbar had been devastated. He had wanted the shop. From the minute she had married Dan Holohan, Finbar arrived every Saturday afternoon to check the accounts. When Dan told him there was no need, Finbar said, 'You work for me.' They were barely seen in the same room after that. Grettie B said it was a common state of affairs: 'You can't have two bulls in the one field, Carmel.' Common or not, it hurt. They were a small family but a family all the same. Finbar and his son, James, were all she had in the way of blood relatives.

Now here he was, leaning over her counter as if he had never left, checking accounts that were really none of his concern. The poor man, he must really miss the place. She didn't want to lose touch with him again.

Finbar slapped the ledger shut and smiled as he handed over her glasses.

'You're after going very quiet, Carmel – were you away with the fairies or what?'

'Just wondering, will you visit more often now?'

12

'I've every intention of it,' he said, placing his hand over hers.

That wasn't like Finbar; maybe he was softening with age.

'Would you like to see the baby's bedroom? It won't take a minute – come on.'

He followed her up the stairs, stepping on her hem and sighing at how slowly she moved. She opened the door of the bedroom and let him walk in ahead of her.

'Isn't the room lovely and bright now? Do you recall how dark it was?'

'Of course I recall how dark it was, isn't it mine? Or was. Looks the same as ever to me.'

Carmel bit her lip, didn't point out the brand-new rocking chair where she would nurse her baby and rock him off to sleep, or the soft quilted pillow she had made in a fit of craftiness. She rubbed the side of her thumb: it was still sore from the needle. Finbar went over to the mantelpiece, picked up the old tin monkey and flicked its cymbals. He kept flicking as he spoke: the sound was tinny, small and horrible. Carmel felt uncomfortably warm. Perhaps she should open the window.

'You've unblocked the fireplace,' said Finbar. 'Don't you remember the young blackbirds every June? Flying down the chimney and ruining the walls? How we crouched under the bed with our hands clamped to our ears?'

He came nearer.

'What monkeys?' said Carmel.

'What are you blabbing about? I said birds. Blackbirds.'

Finbar placed a cool palm on her forehead. Suddenly the soapy smell from his skin was sickening.

'You look flushed; you should rest, Carmel.'

Downstairs, she sat at the kitchen table and Finbar set a glass of water in front of her. He watched as she sipped.

'I may go,' he said.

There was sweat on his top lip.

'At least have a drink of something before you leave?'

'I don't have time. I'm calling to the Sergeant's for a quick cup of tea before I head home.'

13

He made his way through the shop, and Carmel followed.

'She can come as soon as you want,' he said as he unbolted the door.

'Who?'

'Sarah.'

'Oh, that. We'll see, we'll see.'

'Goodbye, Carmel, no need to come out.'

The door slammed shut.

'Goodbye, Finbar,' she whispered.

Carmel told herself that her brother's reappearance was a good thing. Look at all he had brought with him? A stock of books that might bring in a few bob and a woman to help when the baby came. All these things, they were good things, weren't they? Yet all she wanted to do was lie down. She felt like she could sleep for years.

3

Sarah was hiding out in her bedroom, settling herself before she went down to face Mai. She couldn't stop thinking about that morning, about the risk she and James had taken and how awful it had all turned out. She was tired of seeing him in secret. James said that his father wouldn't approve. Claimed the well-respected gentleman raised terror under his own roof. God knows what he'd do – he'd flay them. Sarah wasn't sure about that: Master Kelly was especially nice to her, and a frequent visitor to their home. She wasn't so sure that he'd object to them walking out together. It was the lying that bothered her most. It didn't seem to bother James; he almost relished it. It had been his idea to meet up in the town when Sarah mentioned that she was getting a lift to the market with Bernie O'Neill and her uncle Pat.

The second they arrived, Sarah spotted James leaning against the door of the town hall.

Bernie elbowed Sarah. 'I wonder who that fine man is waiting for?'

'Leave the poor girl alone,' said Pat, as he helped them down from the trap; 'she's only mad about him.'

So much for their secret. Sarah walked towards James, and Bernie followed at her heels. James tipped his cap and told Bernie that Sarah wouldn't need a lift back, that he would see her home safely. He linked his arm with hers and they strolled off, leaving poor Bernie gawping.

They sauntered around the market. He looked handsome, manly, and proud to be seen with her. She never knew where she stood: sometimes he would walk past without so much as a hello, other times he couldn't keep his eyes off her. He had tormented Sarah when she was young. Pulled her plaits, threw stones, called her a 'long string of a thing'. And then he changed, went sulky, silent. And then, later, there were gifts, bars of chocolate, sachets of lavender, ribbons, a comb. And then, on and off, they began to keep company. And now this, walking around together in public, almost daring someone they knew to catch them. Maybe it was a good sign, maybe he was ready to tell Master Kelly the truth.

Sarah had worn a peacock-blue shawl with a gold fringe. And earrings: a pair of green glass-droplets a grateful mother had given her aunt. All sorts of things were bestowed on Mai; her bedroom was like a magpie's nest, for few had money to pay, and you couldn't shove a baby back in, as Mai said herself. Sarah felt very grand indeed as she and James walked past farmers selling pigs, chickens, eggs. Stalls selling clothes, shoes, blankets, bed irons. There was even a Shetland pony on offer. Droves of men in dusty suits smoked and bartered by the walls of the huge town hall. James told her that dances and theatrical shows were held there on a regular basis. He said it in a way that implied they might be going soon, together.

Under the town hall clock, a dark man was arranging brown glass jars and bottles of medicines, herbal tonics. His cream suit was slightly loose, sagging at the shoulders, as if it had belonged to a bigger man or maybe he himself had been broader once. Sarah uncorked a short bottle and inhaled. What was it? The hawker watched closely: he had thick lashes and narrow eyes; sniffs of grey edged his forelocks. There was something droopy but alert about his expression. His mouth was wide; an old scar scored a pale line through his bottom lip. James nudged her; he wanted to move on, away from the man who was staring so hard. She read the label: FORTIFICATION TONIC. She smelt it again.

'Ah, borage.'

'You know herbs?' asked the man.

'My aunt knows – she's a midwife.'

'An old wife, with tales, superstitions and lies?'

'No. Not lies.'

He stroked his chin and smiled, waved her closer, as if to whisper a secret. His breath held a hint of peppermint and tobacco. There were rings on his fingers. He wanted a favour; it was his first day in the town, everyone was looking but no one was biting. Sarah wasn't sure; she was no actress. James changed his mind about leaving: she should do it, he said; it would be amusing. He talked like that, *amusing*. So she did.

It came so easy, pretending to be someone else. Exactly who she was pretending to be, she couldn't say. She stood to her full height, straightened her back and squared her shoulders, like Mai was always nagging her to, waited till there were a couple of women at the stall and inquired after the skin cream in a louder voice than she would normally use. She could feel all eyes on her; it was strange but she didn't feel embarrassed or shy at all. How could she, when she wasn't herself, or maybe was more herself than she knew? Within seconds they were buying. She tarried a while, complimenting a lady on her child, praising the dark man's potions to anyone that cared to listen. No one noticed as Sarah dropped the jar into her pocket without paying. She hadn't a bob, and it would ruin the charade to give it back.

The women were pushing forward with enough force to topple the table. They were picking up bottles, trying to match the labels with their ailments. Some had forgotten their spectacles; all had forgotten about Sarah or, as the herbalist had called her, the lovely lady. She slipped through the crowd towards James. He was vexed and didn't hide it.

'Not amusing, then?' Sarah asked.

He didn't answer, just dug his hands into his pockets and started off in the direction of the main road. She had no choice but to follow him. He was fuming. Sarah knew what ailed him: she had been admired by others and he didn't like it. She humoured him till he smiled at her again. After a few minutes he seemed to have recovered. As they strolled along, side by side, they talked about the road being quiet, wondered when a trap would pass in their direction. She took the face cream from her pocket, twisted the lid. She wanted to try some on the back of her hand. James snatched it, threw it into the nearest ditch and grabbed her head to pull her close for a kiss. Sarah struggled free and ran.

How dare he? To treat her like that, so roughly and commonly and at the side of the road where anyone could see. Yet she wasn't good enough to announce to his father. She wasn't going to speak to him, at least not until he apologized and maybe not even then. And who was James codding that his father didn't know what he was up to? Mr Kelly knew everything that went on in the parish. James was fooling himself. And he was fooling himself if he thought their first proper kiss would be snatched at the side of the road.

They walked in silence. It was too early for traps returning from the market. She glanced at the sulky boy behind her and kept wondering how she had mistaken him for a man. Her anger gave her the energy to keep going. It was taking hours. Mai would be worried: Sarah had told her Bernie's uncle would have them back by two. What would she say to her at all?

They parted without a sorry or goodbye. James should've said something then. He had looked like he wanted to. Sarah wondered how anyone could be so stubborn.

There wasn't a sound from the house as Sarah eased open the back door. She stood for a second, and, when there was no familiar call from the kitchen, she crept upstairs to wash her face. That's when she noticed the blood on her earlobe, and the tear. The earring must've caught as she pulled James's hands from her face. Some beau he was. She unhooked the jewellery and wiped it clean before she put it away. She brushed her hair forward to conceal it. Looked at herself in the mirror and didn't like what she saw: a cover-up, a liar. Mai would see it too – Sarah knew she would.

When she went down, the kitchen was sweltering. A pan of water bubbled on the fire. Mai was in her favourite chair at the head of the table: her eyes were closed but she wasn't asleep. Captain Custard was curled purring on her lap. The table was covered with jam jars. A basket of violets was set at her feet. Mai prayed any time or anywhere. Sarah gave her a gentle kiss on the forehead. Her aunt smiled and opened her eyes.

'What happened to you?'

'Bernie and me had to walk all the way home. Her uncle's horse was lame and he told us to try and get a lift with someone else. I'm bushed, that's all.'

'Don't give me that, I'm not a thick. And I had that dream last night –'

'Not that dream again.' Sarah lifted a glass bottle of clear liquid, uncorked it and sniffed. 'How much did this set you back?'

'Nothing.'

'Ah, come on now, nothing?'

'Billy owes me a favour or two.'

'Let me come to Billy's next time you go. You'll need me someday; you won't always be able to make the journey alone. I won't tell a soul.'

'It's only a few miles up the road, young lady. I'm not dead yet.' She stroked the cat on her lap, whispered into its ear, 'Isn't that right, Captain?'

'Which road is it a few miles up?' Sarah jiggled the bottle.

'Whist. Pour that poitín into the jug before the smell knocks us out. And pour me a wee dram. Not too much, mind.'

Sarah let a splash fall into a small glass and handed it over. Mai sipped it and let out a *whoosh* that scared the cat off her lap.

'If anyone could see you knocking back the hard stuff like that –'

'Stop that kind of talk.' Mai frowned. 'I'm just checking the purity; don't want my tinctures going mouldy. And stop standing over me, you lanky lass, lend a hand.'

Sarah put on an apron and sat. She began to break the sweet violet apart while Mai worked with a copybook and scissors to prepare some of the tiny labels she liked to paste on to the undersides of all her jars and bottles. Mai never wrote her name, just the name of the herb – she was modest about her talents.

'Bristly babies, aren't they?' Sarah's fingers were reddening already.

'You always say that – you're just sensitive to sap.'

They lapsed into silence. Mai wasn't fond of chatting when they were preparing cures. Once the jam jars were full of violet, Sarah poured in the mixture of spirit.

'Sarah,' said Mai, 'stop frowning; do it with love.'

'Listen to the old romantic.'

'Sarah!' She pointed her fountain pen in Sarah's direction.

'Yes, Mai, with love, Mai.'

'Or is it, Sarah, that you have no love left? Is it, Sarah, that you've been giving your love all away?'

Mai was imitating the wheedling voice of her older sister Gracie. She was getting a bit too close to the truth for Sarah's comfort.

'Look at that face! You're courting, aren't you?'

'Stop that lovey-dovey talk. An old woman like you.'

'Who is it? Go on, you can tell me.'

'There's nothing to tell.' She looked at Mai. 'Well, not yet.'

They both laughed. Custard climbed back on Mai's lap as she wrote. His fur was the same colour as her cardigan, so he appeared to have become part of her. He purred with satisfaction. They both seemed pleased with themselves.

'A toast' – Mai put down her pen and lifted her empty glass – 'to Sarah's young man!'

'It's early days, don't.'

'How well I knew. It was the gallons of water you've been bringing up to your room. Is she washing herself or an army up there? That's what I was thinking. Then it hit me, Sarah's soaping herself to nothing over some young man. So, who is he?'

'I can't tell, so don't bother your head throwing names at me.'

'Why ever not, Sarah?' Mai's voice became sharp.

'It's like you and Poitín Billy – I just can't. There are no two ways about it.'

'That's different.'

'How's it different?'

'If a girl can't say who her beau is, either he isn't free or she isn't . . . and I know you are.'

'Not free! That's a shocking thing to say, and of me! As if I'd do something so awful, so, so out of the question!'

'It's not as out of the question as all that. I of all people should know – don't I deliver the consequences?'

'You're a filthy old woman for thinking that of me. I feel sick; I think I'm going to get sick.'

'Sit down and stop fussing – I had to ask. You've no one to blame but your own sweet self. Just spill the beans and tell me who your fancy man is.'

'He's not my fancy man!'

'Not a fancy man, then, your . . .' Mai scrunched up her face as if to think of a name. 'Your pal? Your comrade –'

'Please stop. I can't tell yet, but I'll tell soon.'

'You'd better, Sarah, believe me, secrets aren't good. And what's more your lad should be proud of you, beauty and brains in one, he should be shouting it from the rooftops.'

Sarah began to fix the lids on to the jars. She held one up.

'I love when they are like this, so pretty. The green leaves and the tiny purple petals.'

'Don't be tormenting me with your soft talk. If you want to change the subject, pick the weather.'

'Yes, ma'am.' Sarah pretended to tip a hat.

'Make sure the lids are tight.'

'Are these tinctures all for old piss-the-bed up on the hill?'

'Leave be – the poor lonely colonel doesn't have long; he deserves comfort the same as the next man. That reminds me, fetch me a few jars of comfrey cream from the back of the press.'

Sarah got up, opened the press, took down six small jars and set them on the table.

'The poor lonely colonel indeed!' she said as she sat down. 'How lonely can he be with everyone and anyone traipsing up to see him? Strange-looking characters, they say, of every seed and creed.'

'That's not you talking, Sarah – who told you that?'

'Bernie.'

'Tell Bernie she's sounding like an old woman already – she should have more charity.'

'You're very forgiving.'

'Why wouldn't I be? Give and so you shall receive.'

'And what would you need to receive forgiveness for, Mai? Have you ever even hurt a fly?'

Sarah was surprised when Mai didn't respond. She looked up.

'Mai?'

Her aunt was wiping her eyes.

'Did I say something?'

'Nothing, you said nothing.'

They worked in silence for a while, with Sarah glancing over at her aunt every few seconds. Mai stood up and began to sweep some fallen leaves. Suddenly she moved behind Sarah and tapped her.

'So! Is it Paddy Murphy?' Mai's sudden liveliness seemed forced.

'Don't be mad.'

'His cousin Tom?'

'Leave me be.'

'It's not James Kelly, is it?'

'Stop.'

'It had better not be, it had better not.'

The back door opened and Master Kelly strode in. Sarah froze. Had he heard?

'Evening, Mai. My God, it smells like a brewery in here.'

He looked around, but there was nothing suspicious to be seen. Sarah had the bottle under her apron, clamped between her knees. She only hoped it didn't slip. Mai glanced over and looked relieved.

'Cup of tea? Sorry I can't offer you anything stronger, Finbar.'

'A cup of tea is strong enough. Imagine if the headmaster were to be seen indulging!'

He smoothed his sleeve across the table and cleared the remains of the herb on to the floor.

'Well,' he said, 'isn't this a cosy set-up?'

Sarah tried not to stare at his hands; they had always fascinated her. The skin on Master Kelly's fingers and palms was discoloured. When they were infants learning their letters, he told them it was from picking too many blackberries; when they became older, he said it was from a fire, but didn't tell them how it had happened. Said it was a painful memory. Mai reckoned that if it was a painful memory, he was mightily attached to it, for she had offered him a lotion that would improve the appearance, even at this late stage, but he'd refused.

Sarah was dying to excuse herself, but the bottle of poitín was nestling between her knees, so she had to stay and listen to the Master inquire about the colonel's Tropical Disease. Tropical, my eye.

Bernie said the dogs on the street knew it was syphilis. Mai seemed to be enjoying the conversation; it was hard to tell sometimes whether she was fond of Master Kelly or not. They both had firm opinions and liked to exchange them. Mai had known his family well. He liked to hear about them and she liked to talk about them, especially his mother.

Sarah was afraid the bottle was about to slip to the floor. Just in time Master Kelly did something unusual and asked Mai to go for a stroll around her beautiful garden for a chat. As he followed Mai out, he turned and gave Sarah a wink. He had never done that before.

Something about Master Kelly was beginning to unnerve Sarah. She had been in awe of him as a child. He was courteous to the girls in the class, especially quick thinkers like Sarah. The boys, she felt sorry for the boys, even James. How would the Master react when James revealed that he and Sarah were walking out? Would he call her a fine girl then? Well, she'd find out soon – Jamsie couldn't put it off for ever.

Sarah leant out the window to scoop a jug of water from the barrel. Mai and Master Kelly were sitting on the low wall. He was talking nine to the dozen, and Mai seemed thrilled. Sarah poured the water into a bowl; the sap had turned her fingers pink. In fact they looked just like the Master's. She was glad to soap them back to normal.

4

Mam was up the stepladder, painting the kitchen ceiling. She kept giving me jobs to do: fetch this, wipe down that. If Charlie thought he had it hard in the foundry, he was wrong: he wouldn't have lasted five minutes under Mam's watch. For weeks now she had been spring cleaning, like someone was coming. Then she started going on how it was a terrible pity about Birdie and Veronique falling out, said she might get Seamus to take her over to Veronique's shop in his trap, just to have a word, see if she could persuade her to make up with her sister, try to make peace. Father interrupted from his chair, said Mam wouldn't know what peace was if it jumped up and bit her 'on the bum-bum-bum'. She shouted that he only stuttered when it suited him, that perhaps 'that man' was right, and my father was putting it all on, the whole thing, that perhaps he should go into show business. When Mam mentioned 'that man', it was time to leave the kitchen, so I did.

I swung on the rope that was tied to the oak and tried not to hear what they were saying indoors. Mam raced out, took my hand and dragged me through the gate with her. I knew better than to ask where we were going. Lately she had taken to wandering the roads after a flare-up – no coat, no money, just roaming about till it was dark. She let go of my hand, untied her head rag, flung it over the hedge and marched along with her arms crossed. I prayed we'd end up in town, and not walking in circles like the last time. After around twenty minutes she took a lipstick out of her pocket, smeared a bit on her finger and rubbed it over her mouth. Her face and hair were spattered with cream paint. The lipstick made her seem even paler; she looked a fright.

'Do I look all right?'

'Lovely. Really lovely. Like a beautiful –'

'That's enough, Emily.'

She veered down the slip towards the river walk, and I followed. Now that we were going into town, I was dying to ask – could we nip into the market and see if the famous herbal man was there? But I didn't say anything. It made my mother a bit agitated if I sounded too interested in someone. I don't know why, just the way she was.

It seemed the herbalist had been an instant hit. Some beautiful lady had tried to buy him out of face cream; she'd had skin like milk, hair like ebony and jewels in her ears like an Egyptian queen. Of course the rest of them couldn't buy enough after that. They swarmed him. There wasn't a bottle or jar left by midday. He was the talk of the place. Tessie Feeney said he was an ugly man; Milkie Nash said he was divine, and her mother slapped her for blasphemy.

In the days that followed his potions worked a treat: warts, veins and dandruff disappeared overnight. The people wondered where he was lodging. And, more importantly, would he be back? Some said he had sold so much that he was already sailing home to buy a temple. I heard that from Birdie Chase. It got me worried: maybe I'd missed my chance to get a look at him. Mind you, Birdie was no expert: she hadn't seen him either, too short to see over the crowd around his stall and too achy to wait it out.

Birdie was Mam's friend, but she was too old to be making any plans with. You'd be afraid to say, 'Will we go to the pictures next week, Birdie?' in case the thrill killed her. Last time she went to a performance in the town hall, in her eagerness to grab a front-row seat – it had to be the front for the Chases – she got giddy, fell sideways and hurt her hip. So now she was on a stick and couldn't walk out to The Farm. That's what she called our place. 'Never mind the decay, it still has a luscious air to it.' That's what Birdie said.

Birdie could afford to be big-hearted – she owned nearly every house on her terrace and she had stacks of cash. I often wondered why Mam and Birdie were so pally. We weren't exactly Birdie's kind of people. She had two Protestant ladies up for sherry all the time. Miss Murray and Miss Hawkins were single and afflicted with flat shoes, thin voices and no men on the horizon as far as the eye could travel. They played bridge and talked about theatre, the reds and how great things had been when they'd better use of their legs.

They were Birdie's kind of people. She had probably adopted Mam as a charitable case.

Birdie's twin sister Veronique had lived with her until she went and bought an identical shop in a town a few miles away. Veronique used to drive a motorcar and visit every week. Then they fell out. It was shortly after Birdie's fall. Maybe the two were connected. You never knew: old people could be terrible odd.

Months passed and there was no sign of Veronique. Birdie fibbed to save her pride – said she was ill and couldn't visit often. According to Mam she didn't visit at all. They must've had a bruiser. Twins shared the one soul, so they'd have to make up if they fancied having a good time for eternity. I'd often heard Birdie telling Mam that riches in this life didn't matter; it was the reward in the next life that counted. The next-life rule definitely didn't apply to Birdie; anyone who wore yellow stockings like she did wasn't waiting for the next life to have fun.

Anyway, whatever Birdie said, our house wasn't a farm house, it was a shambles. We weren't respectable. Father was well shook, and nobody knew this, but around January Mam began to drink too. It wasn't as simple as that – there were good times as well – but you get the gist: dinnertime, the spuds boiled dry, the bottom of the pan burning and her holding out her skirt, singing, 'Dance with me, daddy, dance with me.' By tea-time, she'd be asleep or hunched on the stool crying over some well-aimed insult from my father's mouth. Mam called them his fits of eloquence; she could be very sarcastic. But I think she preferred them to his other fits.

'Lush.'

'I've never darkened the door of a public house.'

'How-how-how I ask you, Maureen, is that a virtue? Not doing something you can't do anyway. Now, now, if you didn't drink this house dry, you'd have something to boast about. So-so-so you would.'

'Brian, how dare you? I don't drink.'

'Aye,' he said, 'aye, Mrs Medicinal.'

Until she started drinking on the sly, Mam used to try to hold things together, used to put on a brave face and take Charlie and me for long walks with her make-up on, telling us that love was only a cod, a luxury people like us couldn't afford. Something that happened before I was born had left our family unable to hold up their heads in public. Until then Mam'd had a life, friends even.

Before she gave up pretending, she liked to act like we were normal and she would be all about my education. She'd smooth down my hair, look into my eyes and tell me I'd have a future and a good one at that. Of course, that fell by the wayside, and two years ago I was kept home to help out.

I had liked school but nothing much was expected of me. No one checked my homework, but I was first in line when there was a nit scare. Immaculata said I was a daw, like the rest of my lot.

'Who here's going to be a nun?' an inspector asked once.

'The four at the front; we'll leave the rest to the men,' old Immaculata had said with a wave of her hand and a sneer.

So, here I was: spared the convent and the men. I never dreamt that someone would fall in love with me, not someone normal and good living. Maybe Aggie was wrong about love coming my way; maybe I was a fool to believe her.

Mam did love us when she wasn't nervous or in a terrible temper. When she was in a good mood, she forgot everything else. 'I've a great little family,' she would say, ruffling Charlie's hair. We were the best in the world then. Touching our heads, kissing our necks. The rest of the time we gave her a pain in her eye and would have to get out, get out, get out, or the brush would be across our backs.

'Get out or I'll fetch the cruelty man,' she used to shout when we were small.

I used to have nightmares about him, the cruelty man in his shitty brown suit coming to get me, whipping me off in his car. He pulled up into our yard once. Big dusty car, short clean man. He was looking for the Carvers' place. I wish my father hadn't told him how to find the house. My father said he took Kay Carver's baby because she hadn't any sense. Mam said it was because she hadn't any husband. Kay used to jump out from the hedge and shout 'boo' at us when we were walking the road. She still followed us but she didn't jump out any more.

Charlie used to laugh when Mam threatened us with the cruelty man. I just ran like hell. Charlie and I were pals. I fished with him. I loved fishing and loved fried trout. Didn't even mind gutting and cleaning, not when I knew we'd be in for a treat. I didn't have a weak stomach like my mother. We'd have cold spuds and tomatoes with it.

Charlie was in great form of late, getting letters that made him smile. You should've seen him, running to meet the postman like a child, twirling into the barn to lie down and read them. Mooning around, daydreaming. About what, that's what I'd like to know? Sweethearts, I supposed.

Me, I dreamt of staying on in school, imagined years of correct-marks and 'Good work, Emily' written all over my copybook and someone saying, 'We'll make a teacher of you yet.' Birdie said I'd make a fine teacher or dressmaker, that I'd be great at whatever I put my hand to. As if teachers left school at fourteen.

When we got to the town, the market was packed. The chicken and dog man near deafened me as we passed, roaring his prices, half his red hens dead and the other half pecking the ground, and black pups in a barrow, all small and shivering. I leant down and rubbed one: he was the size of my hand.

'Don't ask, Emily – you're not getting a pup and that's that.'

We were at a standstill then; a crowd blocked our path. Mrs Greaney turned and smiled at us, fag limp and brown in the corner of her mouth.

'Keeping well, Mrs Madden?' Her eyes travelled slowly over my mam.

'The best. What is it, Mrs Greaney? What's everyone looking at?'

'The Indian lad – he's put a spell on them. Don something-or-other he calls himself.' She coughed and moved aside. 'Go on, you'd love him, Mrs Madden. Go on, have a gander at The Don.'

'Thanks but I won't, we have an appointment.' Mam yanked me back by the collar. She made me follow her around the edge of the crowd and across the road. A few dicey-looking characters were leaning against the wall of the courthouse. Mam didn't like being near them either, so she turned on her heel. 'Home,' she ordered. I could have cried. We had gotten so close. Was I ever going to see this herbalist, this magician? Why did Mam always have to go the opposite way to everyone else?

'Are you not curious to see the herbalist?'

'A rogue. They're all rogues.'

She was talking about my father again; everything came back to him being a shyster. You'd be sick listening to it.

As we left the square Birdie waved from her doorway.

'Maureen Madden, you look exhausted – come in and rest those feet.'

In we went, out of the sunshine and into the dark dusty shop with not a sinner in it and no craic. My mam sat on the low bench beside the vegetable boxes. I leant on the counter. Birdie pushed a magazine towards me. Greta Garbo was on the cover. Where did Garbo get those eyebrows? I held her up to the light to check if they were pencilled in. The women started to murmur: *mmm* and *haw* and *I know, I know* and *tut, tut, tut*. Then, sobs. I turned. Birdie had her arm around my mother; their heads were close together. Mam was crying and talking real low. *A few weeks, maybe months*. I spotted my chance, tiptoed out of the shop and ran like billy-o towards the market.

The women were still crowded around his stall. His voice was hoarse from all his proclamations about the power of his potions, the strength of his medicine. I stood on tiptoe, glimpsed his hand waving over the sea of headscarves: it held a brown bottle, sported golden rings. *I could love that hand*, I thought then – my first thought as a woman. I pushed forward between the shoulders in front of me; they were hard to part, but I persisted, imagined that they were the tide and I was a magnificent swimmer. Then came a poke, followed by a familiar tug at my collar. 'Got you,' Mam crowed, 'and not a minute too soon.' That's what she thought, but she was wrong. Me, I wasn't thinking. I was in love.

5

Carmel's back ached. In between serving customers she'd taken down all the tins and spent the afternoon dusting and rearranging them, and then she'd cleaned both of the outside windows. Everyone that passed was on about that man. The herbalist this, the herbalist that. Or The Don, as some were calling him. A charlatan, a magician, a fraudster, a saviour, who had appeared in the market to con them or heal them – take your pick – and there wasn't a one that didn't have an opinion and every second opinion was contradictory.

Emily had stopped and offered to help. Carmel wasn't in the mood to listen to her nonsense, the way she repeated other people's news as if she'd seen it first hand, as if she had actually been there. Carmel told the girl she was expecting, not an invalid. She was sorry for her sharpness afterwards. The child hardly got the time of day from anyone; there was no need for Carmel to join in. Emily was only gone when Birdie hobbled across the road, carrying a kitten, and informing Carmel that she must be 'nesting'. What would poor Birdie know of nesting? That woman had never known a man let alone reared a child.

'Would you like a kitten?' she had asked. 'It's a lovely grey one, very unusual.'

'A kitten is the last thing I'd want, Birdie.'

When the shop had finally shut, Dan went out to the pub; he had to 'talk to someone important about something important'. That usually just meant a chin-wag with Mick Murphy. Sometimes she listened to Dan's long explanations of why he had to go out; some-times she didn't, and let her mind drift, thought of her baby's fingers, his toes, and how she would soon hold him and never let him go. She had known it was a boy before Mick's mother divined it. The face on Dan when he saw Carmel stretched on the sofa, with Lizzie crouched over her wielding a pin on a string, and it swinging back and forth madly over her belly. His reaction later had surprised Carmel. He'd called it witchcraft, said he didn't want 'that filthy crone' in his house.

'But she's the mother of your pal?'

'Doesn't mean I have to like her.'

'I don't like her much either,' Carmel said, putting her arms around her husband. 'It was only the once – calm down. Lizzie does smell a bit, but you're a bit salty yourself.'

He smiled then, and gave her one of his bear hugs.

'I just didn't like it.'

'I know, I know.'

Carmel went up to the baby's bedroom and opened the window on to the street. She lifted the monkey off the mantelpiece: the cymbals' edges were rusty and sharp. Sorry, Monkey, she whispered, as she tugged. The cymbals came off easily; she moved the screen and threw them into the fireplace.

As she sat on the rocking chair, she realized the stairs must've made her breathless. She leant back and relaxed. There was a nice breeze. The yellow check curtains flew up, fell down and flew up, over and over. It reminded her of being a girl, of playing rope. She didn't even run nowadays, let alone jump. Or use the bicycle. Being careful had paid off; she'd made it past the dangerous stage this time. Dan called it God's will. He was never keen on giving any credit to Carmel, but she didn't mind, not now. She ran her hand over her stomach: it was smooth and firm. Babies didn't move much in the last few weeks. Doctor B said there just wasn't the space. It was a sign the baby was getting ready to be born.

It was lovely and bright in here, no matter what Finbar said. Completely different to how it was years ago. The walls were papered in pastel stripes and the ceiling was painted ivory. Dan had done a great job, and he'd been thrilled to do it. This baby coming had given him a great lift. Carmel knew Dan had been the subject of jokes for not fathering a child sooner in their marriage, especially as he was such a tall, strong man.

A child a year was no bother to some women, but that hadn't

been the way for Carmel. At least now she could serve them their powdered milk and syrup of figs without feeling an envy that nearly floored her. Something had finally worked – be it prayers, devotions, miraculous medals, feet-up, milk puddings, tonics or blessed ribbons, she didn't care. This time, things had gone as they should have. She went to touch the medal at her throat, forgetting it was missing. A small thing like that, if it wasn't found at once, was usually lost for ever. She felt guilty – it had been her mother's – and she had near worried it away in the early days. Now she hadn't even searched for it, distracted by Finbar's visiting after so long.

How like him not to explain or apologize. Probably felt he was eternally in the right as someone so badly wronged. It wasn't just the will; it stretched back further than that, to the day Nancy had cleared any trace of his mother from the house and shop.

Finbar told Carmel everything he had seen, and everything he had heard, then and after. He'd made it her memory too. Frances had died when her son was five. Cancer, they'd declared. Consumption, they'd whispered. When Nancy came on the scene, all photographs of her predecessor were destroyed. According to Nancy, it wasn't 'the done thing' to mention the past, no exceptions. She had wanted to burn all the bedding, sheets and blankets, to get rid of the germs, even though it was over a year since Frances had passed. Her new husband had let her remove the sickbed mattress, but drew a line at the bed itself.

Nancy had hauled the narrow mattress through the back door, past the vegetable patch, and down to the end of the garden, where the nettles and brambles ran riot. It was early autumn; the sun was setting in a pink sky. Finbar remembered how his mother's mattress had dragged on the ground, making a dark path through the golden leaves, and how Nancy had hummed as she rambled to and fro, building a pyre of dried branches and twigs, blankets, shoes, clothes, books, embroidered tablecloths, paintings, photograph albums and, one by one, the collection of miniature musical boxes. She wound each lacquered box carefully as she set them on the heap, and then she lit a match and dropped it. The music waned as the fire smouldered. It took an age to light up, yet everything was burnt to cinders in minutes. And then there was silence.

Nancy went into the house; Finbar stayed outside shivering, his back against the wall. After a while, he walked over to the dead fire and picked through the blackened remains. He recalled the stench of scorched horse hair, the heat on his face, the search that turned up nothing, but, strangely, he didn't recall any pain as he burnt his fingers.

But Finbar had been only six years of age, so maybe, maybe in his grief, he'd made it all up? Maybe his hands were burnt some ordinary way, like on the stove? Carmel asked her father once. 'The stretch of Finbar's imagination is matched only by his boundless capacity for self-pity.'

What kind of answer was that?

Carmel's mother wasn't much clearer when she eventually dared to ask her.

'Ah, now, pet, use your head. Would it be like me to do such a thing?'

It would be just like her, but Carmel didn't say so.

Finbar had moved into this room, where his mother had died, when Carmel was born. Mother never went into it herself, because of Frances perhaps, not even to tidy. That made it a good place to be, Finbar used to say. Carmel liked the fact that her mother hadn't spent time in here. Was that a bad thing to think? It was a peaceful room, so full of light now and perfect for a baby.

She had no memory of any blackbirds. Finbar had a habit of darkening things. And if there had been blackbirds flying from the chimney every June, she hadn't seen them. No, she hadn't. Carmel had slept in with her mother, snug and tight, most nights. Then where was her father? Oh, yes, in the box room that was supposed to be Carmel's, dying in the company of his dictionary. *May he rest in peace.*

Funny where the mind travels, especially when people return that you thought were lost. Strange what you think, and strange what you see. For, as the soft breeze and the moving curtain lulled Carmel towards sleep, soot marks silently appeared on the walls and ceiling, and wings brushed past her hair, till she heard the frightened trapped beating of something used to freedom. She opened her eyes: there were no soot marks, there was no bird, there was no sound at all except the sound of her heart. No movement except the pain darting through her back. She fumbled around her neck for the medal that wasn't there.

Carmel adjusted the pillow behind her. She felt panicky. From being woken suddenly – by what?

Settle. It's all right.

She rocked gently to ease the back pain. The bloody pain. Was it starting? Was this what it was like?

Carmel didn't know. It felt like the agony of the curse, not like a baby coming. Oh God, oh God, she was alone, and with no breath to shout out. The pain around her waist was like a brace tightening, again, and again, and again.

She was on the floor panting – she couldn't get up. Someone passed outside the window; a high laugh rose up. Birdie. Please. *Please.*

She moaned.

It's too quick, not like this. Oh, Dan!

If only longing could bring a person home.

Don't be afraid – you've waited a long time for this. Don't be afraid.

It was hot, too hot, yet she was shivering. The pain had eased. Everything was still for a second. She took her bearings – she was on the floor by the chair, on her hunkers, rocking back and forth. Her underwear was drenched; she must take it off. She tugged it free.

She never knew it would be like this. The unbearable urge to press down, the soiling. A roar came out of her. And another. She didn't care that she was hunched on the floor, she didn't care. She let instinct guide her and bore down. She screamed.

The baby slithered silently from between her legs. It glistened. A beautiful baby boy, so perfect. His hair sleek and dark, his face round and calm, eyes closed and delicate lashes sweeping over his cheeks. His tiny mouth pursed into a cupid's bow, his fists closed tight, each fingernail a pearl. Carmel held him to her breast. Could a baby be born sleeping?

6

One of the best days of my life was the one when Carmel nearly fainted in the shop and I was the only customer. It got me the part-time job.

'I'll have to close.' She was grey in the face.

I stepped up to the mark.

'No need, Mrs Holohan. I'll take over. You lie down.'

'Can you add and subtract?' she asked, not a bit embarrassed.

'I'm quick at my numbers and can read as well as most.'

I hadn't left school because I was slow. A well-off woman like Carmel Holohan wouldn't understand that. I had been on my way to the market to get a proper look at the herbalist and give him an opportunity to catch sight of me, so I was done up lovely for what turned out to be my first day of work. I wore blue serge with a deep sweetheart neckline, all made from a pattern out of my own head. And what did Carmel do, only tie a big old apron around me? Said my homemade dress was a bit 'showy'. What would she know? Practically living in a shapeless gansey since the previous week when she'd taken badly.

After a while I realized that Carmel wasn't coming back down. No wonder: she looked atrocious. After all her swooning these past months, didn't the babe go and die on her? So much for 'I'm not an invalid, Emily.'

The shop was quiet and I decided I might as well have a good look around. I'd been coming to Kelly's since I was a tot, but I'd never been in the back. I couldn't wait to see the decorating Carmel was always boasting about. 'Dan's a Trojan – he never stops. You should see the kitchen extension he's built.'

A short hall led from the grocery, so thick with cerise wallpaper you could press your thumb into it. There was a wedding photo on a what-not facing into the shop. As if Carmel wanted everyone to accidentally see her looking young and pretty.

'Oh, yes,' I'd heard her say, edging the door shut with her foot, 'that's my husband and me, the day we wed.'

Plums in her mouth, shite on her shoes.

I examined the picture up close. Dan hadn't changed a jot. Carmel had. Her face was heart-shaped then, not square like now. Her hair was waved back as if she was facing a light breeze. But I knew those lovely soft waves were stiff from setting lotion. She wore a dark suit, single breasted, with a cinched-in waist.

The living room was dim and stank of turf and laundry. A clothes-horse laden with sheets hunched over the hearth. The walls were painted olive-green. Good-quality tan lino was laid right to the wall. A plush armchair with wooden arms like paddles had a pile of books slipping out from under it. I sat and sank almost to the ground. The ceiling above me was yellow from nicotine. Carmel's mother had been a wicked smoker. Three embroidered cushions on the settle bed caught my eye: *Home Sweet Home*, *God Bless This House* and *Níl aon tinteán mar do thinteán féin*. The stitching was loose and careless; the colours were dire, browns, mustard and violet. Carmel must've decorated in a fever, or maybe it was her mother before her. There were knick-knacks on every surface; the sideboard and mantelpiece were crowded with china and brass, there wasn't a saint or politician left out.

The big window looked out on to a makeshift kitchen extension. Dan did everything himself, according to Carmel. He suited her so well: neither of them would part with a penny if they could help it. The lace curtains were open. The effect was strange. The window-frame and the curtains seemed to open on to a different world altogether, like one of those Pathé documentaries in the picture house. Beyond the frame was a table set with a big brown teapot and two cups and saucers. And beyond the table was another window, through which I could see hawthorns trembling in the wind.

I stood there for a few seconds, half waiting for something to happen, for something to begin. Then I felt someone watching me.

Of course there was no one, but it gave me a shiver. And the Sacred Heart pictures gave me the creeps. Half a dozen pictures in a row, all those upturned brown eyes, raised hands and poor barbed hearts with blood dripping from them. Lord help us, it was too much; it was like a grand general Jesus convention.

The door that led to the kitchen was so heavily painted it wouldn't close properly. It seemed Dan got his excitement from painting things. The kitchen was a short and wide affair, a black stove, a small table, a dresser full of willow pattern and books. Beneath the window stood a churn of water; next to it was a cluttered sideboard that was none too clean. Three steps across and I was at the window, and looking out at the biggest pig I'd ever seen in my life.

So this was it. I had arrived. I had finally witnessed Dan Holohan's miraculous extension.

The shop bell reminded me why I was there. A craggy voice called out. I ran out to the front and slipped in behind the counter. It was Lizzie Murphy with her yellowed Woodbine fingers. I gave her my best smile.

'Well, Mrs Murphy, aren't you looking splendid? And what can I get for you today?'

'Come out from behind there, Emily Madden – before I have you arrested.'

It didn't get much better than that. Did every single soul that walked through the shop have to be told exactly why I was there instead of Carmel, or count every penny of their change so thoroughly? Did they think I was an amadán, a thief or a bit of both? While the rest of the town were getting themselves healed by an exotic stranger, I was being treated like an imposter just for helping a woman who was weak as water.

After an hour of general interrogation and unpleasantness I was in for a change. Who strolled through the door at half past twelve but the very man himself? The herbalist. The hat, the suit and the pure smoky wonder of his skin – it couldn't be anyone else. He caught the bell to stop it clanging. He was a slim man, not as tall as

I'd imagined. I saw his gold eye tooth when he smiled, oh Lord, he had a wonderful smile. He was as dark as a maharajah from the newspaper, and as strange as anything I'd ever seen. He picked a russet from Nash's apple box, shone it on his sleeve and bit into it with gusto. Then he went and tapped a penny on the counter as if I was busy doing something other than gawking at the wonder of him.

'Is that a sombrero, amigo?' I said.

'A panama hat.' He tipped it. 'Where have they been hiding you?'

'I'm just taking a break from Hollywood. Mr Spencer Tracy writes often. He misses me, the poor thing, he's a broken man.'

He waved my nonsense away; maybe he didn't understand.

'Your name?' he asked.

'It's Emily.'

'Well, it's very nice to meet Emily,' and, with that, he tipped his hat again, smiled and took his leave.

Dan blustered in then, all hot and bothered. Wanting to know where Carmel was, was she all right, what was I doing with the change? He got quite the surprise when he found out I'd been working there the whole morning. He wasn't pleased, but I explained the situation and kept a cheerful face on me. I was still thrilled from meeting the herbalist, no matter that it was only for a minute. I wanted Dan to see me all efficient and think it was a good idea to give me a position. Mam would be proud, and I'd be earning.

Dan checked on madam upstairs, and then got on with doing something in the living room, leaving me behind the counter.

It wasn't long before Carmel joined us. I tried to tell her about the herbalist, but she only half listened. She was too busy being Lady Muck: *Do this, do that . . .*

Dan wasn't too bad, took to a bit of simpering.

'She's not bad, eh, Carmel?' he said to his wife in the middle of the afternoon.

'No, she's good.'

Carmel didn't even crack a smile. They both seemed awfully impressed that I could sell a few groceries without making a hames of it. They laughed when I climbed into the window to rearrange it by colour, putting in only the brightest products. The difference it made was remarkable. I knew that because everyone that came into the shop remarked on it.

Dan said to come in for a few hours on their busy days so Carmel could rest. She didn't contradict him: she looked mighty teary. When Dan left, she checked my neck for tide marks. I had hopes for more than a casual arrangement but quickly realized that a run-for was all Carmel saw me as. *Do this. Do that. Good girl yourself, Emily.* She kept looking me up and down. Got it into her head that I needed a dress that was 'more practical'. She marched me up to Behan Brothers and bought me a dress on tick. Black with a mandarin collar and capped sleeves.

'A tidy brooch would set that off and some clip-on earrings,' Carmel said.

I've landed on my feet, I thought. When we got back, Carmel totted up my wages and then subtracted them from the cost of the dress. She told me that when I'd worked off two and six, the dress would be paid for and I'd get cash wages.

'Now you've something decent to wear next time.'

I marched home with the brown-paper package wrapped in twine. I couldn't seem to explain it so Mam would understand. She thought it was my fault all the money was gone on a dress.

'You vain little witch.' She smacked the table.

I did a lot of bawling before Mam got it into her head that I wanted to see my earnings as much as anyone. I shoved the dress into the corner of the wardrobe in its wrapping. Never liked that smart dress after, too good for work and not fancy enough for a dance.

7

Carmel went upstairs to rest. It was a relief to be away from Emily's chatter. The girl's eyes seemed to take everything in. That was a silly strange thing to think, but Carmel didn't really care. She wanted him back so badly, the boy born sleeping. She could think only of him – the pain in her chest never ceased, and it would never cease, this loss, this cutting of her heart from her. Carmel's arms ached with the emptiness every second of every day. She wanted him back. *Give him back.*

Dan said she'd been hysterical, that she'd clutched the baby for two days, wouldn't hand the child over. She didn't remember hysterical, but she remembered Dan tugging him from her and somehow it felt like her husband was on the side of death and of everything that had conspired to take her baby's breath from his body.

She called him Samuel.

'It's not a Catholic name,' Dan had said.

'It's fucking biblical, just like Daniel!'

The foul language had almost knocked him backwards. Her too.

'May God forgive you,' he kept saying.

God. How could she believe in Him now? Yet she didn't dare say that out loud. As if there were anything else left for Him to take from her. *Do your worst; your worst is done.* Yes, she had adored Christ, his virgin mother and all his saints and angels, but how could she now, how could she now? These were all thoughts, not things she could say to Dan, to anyone. She wrote some of them down, letters to no one, saying over and over, *Why, why, why, my perfect little son.*

Lizzie Murphy said offer it up. Grettie B said he's an angel in heaven. Then she covered her mouth when she realized her mistake. Carmel's unbaptized baby wasn't allowed into heaven, only to limbo. Father Higgins wouldn't give him a blessing. She'd had to beg Dan even to ask.

'The child is not the Church's responsibility.' That's what the priest had said.

You'd think the worst was over, but it wasn't. He couldn't be buried in consecrated ground. He had to be buried in unholy ground with the lost souls, criminals, suicides, with no rites, no blessings. And Carmel wasn't permitted to be present.

She sat at the dressing table and wrote to Finbar. The letter was a rush of anguish that shamed her, and caused her to cry afresh when she reread it. She could never send it. She heard the girl Emily moving downstairs, but didn't care, let her root around all she wanted; there was nothing Carmel cared about down there. Nothing Carmel cared about left anywhere.

Doctor B had had to dope her the night Dan left with her child and a shovel. The medicine was to stop her doing harm to herself. To wipe out the feelings, the loss, the absence. It was all about absence – of breath, of life and now even of dignity and holiness.

She had washed him – she was able to do that, soaped between his toes and fingers – and dried him slowly, patting gently. She had wrapped him in the crocheted blanket. He wore his white christening robe. She could prepare him for it, but she could not part with him, she could not let him out of her arms. She had screamed and called Dan a devil.

After Dan left to bury the baby, he stayed away from their bed for a few nights. He must've slept somewhere else in the house, or maybe in the shed. They passed each other in the shop during daylight hours, frozen solid in their loss. She was told to pray, to get over it, to try to conceive again, to get on with living. Carmel would do none of those things: she had been forced to release Samuel from her arms, but she would not so easily give up her grief – why should she? It was all she had of him, of Samuel. A name Dan would not say.

And where had he buried their baby? That tormented her till Dan took her to the cemetery one evening at dusk. He showed her a ditch that ran alongside its shadow side. She walked behind him, weeping, accusing.

'You don't recall where you buried your son.'

He didn't answer. He wasn't for talking by then; he had begun to say *whist* a lot. 'Whist, woman, whist your crying.' Carmel watched the dirt under her feet as she walked, and all sorts of things passed through her mind: that Samuel was cold, that he was crying somewhere, that his soul would never see the face of God, would never join with hers. That he was lost.

'You can't remember where you put my child.'

She was sobbing now; the sun was low in the sky, turning the fields a golden yellow. She could smell the yew trees, smell spring and death in the earth, or so she thought, so she felt. Dan had stopped.

'It's here.'

'It?'

'The grave.'

'There's no grave – he's buried in a ditch like an animal and you don't know where he is.'

She was sobbing hard. Where did all the tears come from – was there no end to them? Dan took her hand.

'I do know, I marked it. Look.'

Carmel saw a large smooth stone; it had a hole in its centre where rain gathered.

'And see here. I scored the stone, so we'll always know.'

He guided her fingers over the surface as if she were a blind woman. She felt deep, scored letters. She knelt down, and saw the side of the stone where Dan had etched SAMUEL HOLOHAN – R.I.P.

'It must've taken you the whole night.'

She stood to meet his eyes.

'Two nights. It took two.'

Dan's face was wet with tears. 'I'm broken, Carmel, I'm broken too.'

And so they both cried, standing beside the stone that marked their baby's burial place, neither able to comfort the other.

8

Sarah spent the morning weeding; she had received a letter from James. He had copied part of a poem. 'My love is like a red, red rose, that's newly sprung in June. My love is like the melody, that's sweetly played in tune.' She recognized it from their old English reader. Why hadn't he copied the whole poem? He wrote that he was sorry, very sorry. Then he talked about the weather, how good it was. At the end he wrote, 'I want to see you again.' It sounded like an order.

She was trying not to think about James; he confused her. Working the garden was Sarah's cure for ills, but it didn't stop nonsense thoughts rattling in her head. Thoughts like the fact that James had kept other boys away from Sarah all through school and afterwards, whether he was even talking to her or not. Now here she was, twenty-three, and he was still playing cat and mouse.

But did she want her life to be any different than it was? Most of Sarah's classmates were married. Did she want marriage? She certainly didn't want three in nappies like her cousin Mary. Though that would be better than ending up like Annie Mangan. One morning, after years of perfect attendance, Annie just didn't show up. Never came to school again. Her family had her in America, lodging with a second cousin, doing very well for herself. Then they had her as a librarian in New York City. They had her very busy.

Sarah had forgotten about Annie until recently. In February, just after Sarah's birthday, James had said he wanted to go steady. A few days later she was standing at the kitchen window, gazing out at the snowdrops on the slope outside, her hand in her pocket secretly holding the birthday brooch he had given her. He had whispered his love to her. Next time the snowdrops pushed up, it might be an engagement ring she held. She was trying to take in what that might mean when out of nowhere Mai asked if she remembered Annie Mangan.

Of course she did; they'd been good friends. Mai told her Annie hadn't been sent to America; she'd been sent to a laundry and was there yet.

'It was all hushed up at the time.'

'How do you know about it, then?'

'I confirmed the girl's condition.'

'What happened to the child?'

'The nuns that run the laundry took it. They take all the girls' babies –'

'What girls?'

'There are lots like Annie Mangan.'

'Why are you telling me this – why now, after all these years?'

'Poor Annie didn't get there by herself. Do you understand me?'

Sarah recalled Annie's smooth plaits, how they'd hung right down past the bench. How she'd sat stock-still during class. Annie was an example to them all, the Master used to say, attentive, with a wonderful posture. The back of her brown jumper was coated in fair hairs. Sarah was always dying to reach out and brush them off. She tried to imagine Annie fat with child, but couldn't.

'Do you understand me, Sarah?'

'I think so.' Sarah wasn't sure she wanted to. 'So when's Annie coming back?'

'Ah, what do you think?'

Mai looked at Sarah as if she were the biggest eejit ever to walk the planet. Mai flared up sometimes, but it never lasted more than a few seconds. They were opposites like that: Sarah tended to brew. Like now, using weeding as an excuse.

Sarah plucked a cowslip and lay down – the scent was heaven. A cabbage butterfly flitted past, a blackbird sang, Sarah stretched out her arms. Life was fine here, just fine. The shadows of the long grasses played across her skirt. What if all the secrecy was a ruse by James? Only for that, they could get married and set up home, or go off travelling together. Would she like that? Sarah didn't know what she wanted – just knew that when she saw James again, it would be him she wanted.

Mai called her. Sarah stood and waved. Her aunt crooked her finger, which meant *I want a word*. What if someone had seen her and James on the road? Mai sat on the bench and waited for Sarah to climb the slope to the backyard. She patted the space beside her. Sarah sat down.

'Now.'

'Now what, Mai?'

'Now we've something to talk about.'

'We do?'

'We do indeed.'

Mai took Sarah's hand, turned it over as if she were going to read her grass-stained palm and took a deep breath.

'You did very well at school, Sarah; if we'd the money you could've gone on further, but we didn't and that's that. You don't realize it when you're young, but time goes very quickly, one year leads to the next, and before you know it I'll be passed away and you'll be nearing middle age, with all opportunity behind you. Don't think I'm trying to be rid of you –'

'What are you talking about?'

'Don't look so worried: it's good news. Finbar has found you an excellent position in his sister's shop. You'll have heard me mention Kelly's? In my youth it was run by Finbar's mother – she was a Connelly. Very decent people, the Connellys.'

'What exactly is the position?'

'His sister's expecting a child. You'll assist in the house and shop, be a help to the new mother – her name's Carmel Holohan.'

'Ah, Mai, I've no interest in babies or in living in a stranger's house.'

'It's not a million miles away – you'll be home a few times a year, and we'll write.'

'You want me to leave – is it something I've done?'

'Did I not just explain all that to you? Master Kelly's doing us a favour. Don't be ungrateful, Sarah – you'll have a wage, live in a busy town, you'll meet people.'

'I meet people here.'

'Oh, is that so? Your heart's desire is here, is it?'

Sarah didn't know the answer to that one any more.

'Hasn't he two legs whoever he is – can't he cycle to see

you? And if he won't go to the effort, you're better off without him.'

'Do I have to go?'

'Are you not excited? A job in this day and age? And a good one?'

'Why did Master Kelly pick me? Did you ask him?'

'No, it came out of the blue. Last time he was here, do you remember? We came out here for a chat?'

'Yes, you were very cosy. Maybe he wants me out of the way? Maybe he wants to clear a path to your door? He's been a widower a long time now, fine man like him must get lonely.'

'Sarcasm doesn't suit you, Sarah. The opportunity may not present itself again. I've been mulling it over for the last couple of weeks. It's not easy for me either, but I want you to have a few bob in your pocket, to live a little. If I was only thinking of myself, I'd keep you here for ever, my constant companion and helpmate.' Mai squeezed Sarah's hand.

'When do they want me to start?'

'Finbar will let us know. It's likely to be as soon as the baby arrives and it's due shortly.'

'So it's been settled?'

'I suppose it has.'

Mai got up and went into the house. Sarah sat for a while, taking it in. Why would Finbar do her such a favour? She had never hinted that she wanted a job. Perhaps Mai had. Oh, Mai. And what of James? What would he say? Or did he know already?

She sat looking out over the place that had been her home for so long. Who'd keep the garden in order, the vegetable patch, collect the apples from the orchard, bake and take care of the house while Mai worked? Mai was fit but she couldn't do everything. She rarely had two days together without a call. The poorer the people got, the more babies popped out. But obviously Mai thought she could survive very well without Sarah, and she had every intention of trying to do so.

9

I arrived in work looking very swish, if I do say so myself, but all Carmel wanted to know was the whereabouts of the damn shop-bought dress.

'I'm keeping it for a special occasion, seeing as it cost the guts of a week's wages.'

Out came the big ugly apron. I could see by Carmel's face she thought someone like me wasn't ever going to be having any special occasions. Maybe she was right. Michael Ryan used to smile at me. I thought he was gearing up to ask for a walk but nothing came of it, and then he stopped smiling. He must've found out who I came from, that we were not respectable.

As the days went on and people got used to seeing me serve, they began to treat me like I was one of them. They whinged about drenched laundry, swollen ankles and spoilt hams. It was all *end of my tether, one of these days I'll throw myself in the river*. I jumped right in – sighed along with them, threw my eyes up to heaven – and had a grand old time. Time went much quicker once everyone was gabbing. When there was a lull, I swept the floor and polished the counter. Once the place was spick and span, I felt great.

One morning, when it was quiet, Mrs Daly swanned in. She couldn't walk through a door without looking as if she'd earned a round of applause. She was disappointed when she saw I was on my own. It wasn't the same if there were no men around; she got a lot of attention from them. I couldn't see the attraction myself: her cheeks were pockmarked from old acne but seemingly she'd a nice figure. She was wearing widow's weeds. Some said she'd buried her respectability along with her husband. A nappy pin was keeping her side zip together.

'I could fix that for you,' I said, pointing towards her hip.

'Ah, these new zip yokes are a nuisance,' she said. 'I haven't the patience to do it myself, always make a mess of it. Are you sure you could manage?'

She took out her compact, blotted the shine on her forehead and tugged a few curls free from her headscarf. She was very proud of her blue-black hair.

'I can indeed,' I said. 'I'll collect it from the house later today, bring it back and all. I'll be cheap.'

'I've a few others, a waistband or two that need letting out. There'd be no need to come to the house, though, I can get Margery or Joan to drop them here.'

'I'll mend the lot.'

'You won't take too long? I don't want to be caught short.' She smiled at her reflection and snapped her compact shut.

'A day, done in a day.'

She sent her daughter Joan over with the garments later. Joan was still waiting for her good figure to arrive and it made her grumpy. You should've seen the greasy waistbands. Nell Nickety Nackety Daly didn't even launder them before she handed them over. I planned to charge her the price of a zip and a few pence. I'd let on that I'd bought the zip in the drapery. One from a skirt of Mam's would do the trick; she was wearing her old clothes again. Her usual few skirts had been sitting in the airing cupboard for months now. While all the other women her age were getting fatter, Mam was getting thinner. I couldn't credit that people would pay for such small jobs. Perhaps Mrs Daly would recommend me to her friends. I imagined the pennies adding up and me buying yards of silks and satins.

Carmel came down early that afternoon. She seemed happy enough with my work. I told her all about Mrs Daly and my sewing job. Carmel fingered the slack material around her own waist – maybe she'd want the smock altered. She looked fresher than before. I hoped she wasn't getting so well that she didn't need me any more.

Dan came in then. Carmel scooped a few acid drops from a jar, popped them in the pocket of my apron and told me to head off home. Any price for a moment alone with her husband: she was pure mad about her child bridegroom.

I rushed to the market square, worried that the herbalist would be gone already. It was late in the day and had started to rain. I couldn't believe my luck. All the stall-holders except the fishwife had left – she was entertaining her cronies with some yarn or other – but the herbalist was there, packing his wares into a suitcase. His table was folded and set against the wall. Even with the soft rain he took his time. He wore a suede brown hat instead of the white one. Old vegetables and whatnot were strewn on the ground. I felt ashamed, him looking so clean, and that he'd think we were a dirty class of people. I walked over to him. I said nothing, I'd nothing to say. I just smiled, and waited. He didn't seem to notice. Was he going to ignore me altogether? I began to feel stupid. He looked up from his suitcase: his skin was slick with rain, and his eyes crinkled as he flashed a grin.

'Cat got your tongue?'

'Can I give you a hand – carry your case?'

He laughed. The herbalist wouldn't let me carry anything but he let me walk alongside him. He didn't talk much either; he just whistled. We walked across the square, down the lane by the River Inn, and I nearly died then. He didn't live in a house; he lived in a hovel with a tin chimney. It was almost bare inside – rags, an earth floor, hooks on the walls. I wondered how he slept at night. How he kept so clean-looking. For a fancy-looking man, the herbalist had nothing – no possessions beyond his case and folding table and the clothes he stood up in. He had a box of greasy bottles and jars. I stood there looking on as he began to wipe them clean with newspaper. Then I walked across to a small square window. It overlooked a yard of weeds and beyond that was water. The river looked different from there, blacker, higher, faster.

'Well, now,' he said, as if it was time for me to go, but I didn't want to go.

'Do you like it here?' I asked.

'Well enough, but pious people are hard to get to know.'

That was my opening: if there was one thing I knew, it was the people of this town. I informed him who was who, ran quickly through the Greaneys, Nashes and Chases, to the Feeneys, Purcells and Ryans, and of course the Holohans and their recent problems. I told him Grettie Birmingham looked posh but rarely spent a penny and certainly wouldn't come near him, what with her husband being the proper doctor, no offence. 'None taken.' I left my own family out of it. I told him what people were saying about him – that he was a godsend, saved them a fortune in doctor's bills. That he was clean. And that he was an Indian. When I ran out of information, I just sat quietly on a crate while he wiped glass jars.

Then the herbalist took some blankets and old papers from a heap in the corner. I followed him outside and around to the yard, where he piled them up, poured kerosene over the lot and set it alight.

'Hope you're not burning anything that doesn't belong to you, my boy!'

It was Aggie Reilly, shouting from the deck of her shabby black barge, bosoms and dusters flapping.

'Just rubbish, just foul rubbish, madam.' He took off his hat, waved it and bowed low like he was in a play.

She cocked her head to the side, almost smiled. Aggie never moored on this side of the bridge. She must be after something. I didn't wave. The poor herbalist, though, wasn't from around here, he didn't know any different.

'She's a bad woman,' I whispered; 'goes with men.'

'Ah.' His hand felt hot on my waist as we turned towards the shed. 'Like you?'

I stomped off. Regretted it the second I left. I would rather have been with him clearing his shed, making it suitable for human habitation, than facing into Mam's questions, into the hot air of our house.

I mooched around for a day or two, spent most of my time stitching a new sewing bag, dark green, with my name embroidered in red. I was fevered with imaginings: that the herbalist was being seduced by some lecherous widow; that he had run off to greener pastures; that someone had set light to his shed while he slept. I couldn't settle to anything, so I swallowed my pride and went to check on him.

He was letting out Catty Dolan as I arrived. She nodded at me and hurried on by. Then she stopped and turned. 'I'm beating the queues,' she said.

'Are you?'

The herbalist didn't look a bit surprised to see me. He walked on into the shed and left the door open for me to follow. There were shelves there now, filled with brown bottles and jars, pestle and mortars, and tins for tea and sugar that didn't look like they contained tea and sugar. He had a gas-burner. Someone must've given him a kettle, someone else a saucepan. I felt bad that I'd nothing to give him. A dowdy partition curtain stretched from one wall to the other. There were herbs everywhere, tied by string and hanging from the rafters of the shed to dry. Honesty, sorrel, herb Robert, speedwell, and others I didn't recognize.

I sat on the chair, suddenly aware that I'd no biscuits or cake with me.

'Are you ill?' he said.

He looked so concerned, and so kind, that I wanted to fall into his arms.

'No, no, I'm not ill at all, thank you.'

'Well, why are you here?' He looked puzzled.

I didn't know how to answer. For a terrible second I thought he didn't remember me.

'Would you like a quick cup of tea?' he asked.

'I'd love one.'

He gave me the nicest smile then, the herbalist, and I knew I had been right to come. We'd a lovely drop of tea till I had to go: someone else was coming. He told me he was making special tonics now, for people who wanted them. That was why Miss Dolan had called.

'I concoct remedies especially tailored for the individual.'

'Bespoke,' I said.

'Oh, I'm impressed.'

I thought the tea would go to my head.

Dan couldn't pass the hall mirror without admiring himself. He never seemed to age, not like her. It drove Carmel bananas.

'That looking glass,' she said, 'is for lipstick only.'

'Anyone can look in a mirror. It's not the preserve of the ugly.'

'You swine.'

He laughed, held her wrists above her head and gave her neck a quick kiss. She pretended horror but didn't really mind. She went upstairs to change out of her smock. A song wafted up from the kitchen. Dan was listening to the gramophone. Vera Lynn sang 'My Cinderella'. Eliza and Vera, the twin loves of Dan's life. Those records were expensive but how could she begrudge him? He was being so good to her, not saying anything about the state of the house; she hadn't had the energy to lift a finger, fell into bed as soon as Emily arrived. It was great to get the break, but it wasn't enough. Carmel had got weak this morning: she had been trying to wash the damn clothes. The hot water, the steam, standing for that length of time, she just wasn't able. The washing was still soaking. She needed a live-in: she would write to Finbar and tell him to send that girl, for a couple of weeks at least. That was all Carmel needed to recover – a few weeks – she could let her go then, make up some excuse. Emily was a quick learner, but she wanted her gone. The Maddens were unstable. Look at Brian, claiming shell shock, when it turned out that the bombs had been way off in the distance.

Carmel lay on the bed and began another letter to Finbar; she must post this one. It was a hard thing to write down, that her baby was gone. She started off easily, asking him to send the woman, thanking him for the books – she had rented a few already. She thought of Mr Purcell skittering by earlier with his head down. It made her long for a Sweet Afton. She left the real news till last – it took one sentence. She wept then.

She woke to roars. Dan was singing and rattling the grate. She checked her face: it was creased from the pillow. Ink from the words she had written stained the corner of her mouth.

'Carmel, the food's ready!'

She rubbed her mouth. Put her housecoat on. Went down cross.

'Did you fall asleep?'

He wrapped his hand in a tea towel and lifted the lid off the bastible. The stew smelt delicious.

'How could I, with all the noise you're making?'

She set the table while Dan looked out at Eliza. You'd swear he cared more for that hog than he did for his wife, the way he talked to her, calling her a fine girl. They ate in silence, both famished. When the dishes were washed, she joined Dan in the living room, sat by the fire and tried to read. The evenings could be very long. It would have been so different if they'd had children.

Carmel was tired, yet restless. She was meant to stay in bed as much as she could. Doctor B said she had probably lost a lot of blood; then he asked her if she'd visited 'that quack in the square'. He was worried about losing patients to Don Vikram Fernandes. The apple of Emily's eye. Customers were commenting about the girl's carry-on. She was pestering the herbalist, hanging around his stall. And if a certain someone was to be believed, she had visited him alone.

Emily had turned out to be surprisingly efficient. She had done a great job on their window display – people had commented on it – and Carmel was grateful, but there was a shiftiness about the girl. Her gestures were theatrical, unnerving. The constant fiddling and babbling about Harlow, Gilbert and Garbo was very wearing.

But that wasn't the real why of it, why she wanted Emily at a distance. Carmel had visited the herbalist on the sly. She wanted to get strong again, she wanted to have another baby; she was going to give it one last try. If anyone could help her, he could; God knows she had tried everything else. So it didn't do that Emily was around. Not that the herbalist didn't seem discreet – he'd have to be in his line of work, wouldn't he? – but Emily . . . well, Emily had a habit of seeing things you didn't want her to see.

When he first came, she wouldn't have dreamt of seeking him out, but that was before her baby was in the ground. Now she didn't care what she had to do, as long as no one knew. She could do her penance later, after she'd had another child. She felt a change in herself – whether it was a hardening or a softening she wasn't sure. And there was the guilt. All the time the guilt of wanting a living baby when poor Samuel was lost and alone in limbo.

Carmel had waited till it was dark one evening and gone to his door, nervous as a girl. It had opened on the first soft knock. Well, you'd swear she was royalty, he was so welcoming, so understanding. She didn't have to explain. He had just the thing, and wouldn't tell anyone. That's the way Carmel wanted it: she needed the small bulb of dark liquid to remain secret, as secret as her wish. It hadn't taken a second and had cost her one and six.

Dan sat down on the settle bed, crossed his legs and opened the *Sunday Press*.

'I wrote to Finbar,' Carmel said; 'told him that we'll take the girl he was going to send before, when . . . Anyway, we won't need Emily any more – will you tell her?'

'I thought Sad Eyes was a great help?' He straightened up. 'And do you know what she told me? Did you know, Carmel, that Carole Lombard and Clark Gable weren't even properly married?'

'Ah, how would Emily know, she's full of nonsense. Dan, Grettie B says she's besotted with that herbalist person; it's unseemly and reflects badly on us.'

'Emily's no worse than the rest of them – sure isn't every woman in the town lapping up his miracle elixirs? You even.' He winked at his wife.

'What on earth do you mean?'

'Lizzie saw you coming out of that shack he calls a dispensary. Did Mr Sing-Song promise to make you look younger? The things women believe. Only a time machine could do that. Is that what he has in there, Carmel, a time machine!'

'Very funny. Lizzie must've been on the lash because it wasn't me she saw, mark my words.'

She snapped her novel shut. *Brave New World* indeed – she couldn't make head nor tail of it. It vexed Carmel that Dan thought she wanted wrinkle lotion. The whole thing vexed her.

'Look, I'm sorry for laughing. He's only a con man, you know that, don't you?' He reached over and touched her knee.

'What would you know about anything?' Why was there a lump in her throat?

'He's just peddling hope, Carmel.' Dan's tone had softened.

'What have you got against hope?' She gave him a water-eyed glance.

'Nothing.' He held her hand, and dared to say the unmentionable. 'Did you think he could help us have children, is that it?'

She couldn't speak.

'So what now?' he said. 'Bed?'

'Why not.'

She poked the fire while he left the room, didn't want to meet his eye. Followed him up the stairs as if she were in no great hurry. Unbuttoned her dress with her back to Dan, hung it carefully in their wardrobe. Got into bed with her slip on.

'My eyes are sore, Dan.'

He got up and closed the heavy drapes. All light left the room except for bright pins where the curtains didn't meet. It reminded her of when the thread ended on the spool and the needle ran on regardless, puncturing seed holes of light into the seams of the fabric. He pulled up her slip. This was the first time, the first time since she had lost the child. Again, she felt guilty. She tutted and sighed as she allowed him to adjust her clothing, like it was all for him. He was more gentle than usual, went slow. Still, it stung. She winced at first, but then she felt herself move beneath him, in time with him. Mortified that her body had betrayed her. It was greedy, ready and waiting.

Afterwards Carmel had a dream, as mixed up a dream as she'd

ever had. The roots of her hair were bedevilled by care; someone kissed her fingertips with a soft mouth. 'Oh, my dear, you have dancer's hands.' She wasn't sure if it was a woman or a man. They wore a headscarf like a man in a play who acts as a stepmother, who dresses as a witch, who pretends to be a good woman selling an apple to Snow White. 'Be careful what you wish for, it could come true,' whispered this stepmother, as she pressed the apple to Carmel's mouth. It was green and felt hard against her lips. Blood pooled in the loose skin over her front teeth. 'I don't want it!' Carmel screamed.

Dan woke her.

'What is it, kitten?' He always called her silly names after.

'It was Goldilocks's stepmother; she was trying to feed me a poisoned apple.'

He hugged her. 'No, she couldn't,' he said. 'Goldilocks didn't have a stepmother.'

'That doesn't mean she couldn't force an apple down me.'

'It does, because she didn't exist,' he said, pleased with his logic.

He smiled, moved in closer. 'Do you think we've made a baby?' he whispered.

'Stop it. Don't tempt fate.' She pushed him away.

'You're awful contrary, Carmel, you know that?'

'Oh, what happened to "kitten"? Is kitten gone?'

He pulled on his trousers and walked downstairs with his hands in his pockets, trying to whistle.

II

I chanced calling round to the herbalist early one Sunday morning, just after breakfast. Curious to see if he observed the day of rest. He answered the door with his shirt hanging out and his hair all over the place. Asked if I was ill, but he was only joking this time. He looked up and down the lane to see if there was anyone about – there wasn't – so he let me in. The partition curtain was half pulled back. His bed was a stretcher bed. A basin and a jug stood at the end. A golden virgin-and-child calendar was taped over the head of it. He stoked the stove, slipped in a piece of turf and set the kettle on heat.

'Tea?'

'Yes, please.'

I arranged myself on the corner stool with my new mending bag on my lap. He got on with his morning routine as if I wasn't there. Soaped and shaved in front of the mirror taped to the wall above the basin. With his shirtsleeves rolled up past his elbows, I could see he had the muscles of a barrowman. I moved a bit, to get a better view of him and his reflection. As he tapped his razor off the basin, something he did again and again, I kept seeing a flash of green in the crook of his arm. His skin was inked in jade, some sort of tattoo. He caught me staring then, thought I was admiring his muscles and dared me to feel his arms; I did. They were like stone.

'Are you human at all?' I asked.

He liked that. Said he did physical exercises every day in the yard. I made an impressed face, didn't mention the tattoo; maybe he was ashamed of it, maybe that's why he shaved with his shirt on and didn't strip to the waist, like I had hoped he would. He had the cheek then to say that Irish women were square-shaped, when he was no Johnny Weissmuller himself. Told me that I was shaped like a girl from his country. His family, he did not talk about them. All dead.

57

'Your mother too?'

He shook his head. No more talk. He splashed some cologne on to his palm, rubbed his hands together, then patted his jaw and neck. The sweet peppery scent would send you to heaven and back. Oh, he was a proper herbalist, no matter what Mrs B said. He walked the fields collecting weeds and wild flowers most mornings, till his trousers were wet to the knee. I saw him, but he never saw me. At least I hoped he didn't.

The kettle was beginning to steam. The herbalist rushed to take it off the heat. Steam wasn't a good idea, not when he was drying plants. I was surprised at how withered they were. What good was a dried-up old flower head?

'You love them old weeds,' I said.

He got in a huff. Snapped that common didn't mean useless.

'There's often good in bad and bad in good. Poison in the root, medicine in the flower – like you perhaps,' he said, softening.

'Yes, but too much of a good thing will kill you?' I said.

'No, not you.'

I hadn't the faintest notion what we were talking about. He handed me a cup of sugary black tea and lay up on the bed. I took some work out of my bag and unpicked threads from the seams of Birdie Chase's dress. We could hear all the sounds of the square. A horse and trap clattering, children playing swing rope and chanting, 'Call for the doctor, call for the nurse, call for the lady with the alligator purse . . .' I snipped a thread with the tip of my scissors and thought, *Isn't this lovely – don't I have a good life now? Between my new job and my own mending work, I'll soon be able to buy a few yards of fabric and make a brand-new dress of my own. I won't know myself then.*

There were three sharp knocks on the door. I jumped, but the herbalist just smiled.

'I've some business to attend to,' he said, nodding at me.

The nod meant *feck off*. I gathered my things and let myself out, curious to see who was calling on him. I turned to tell the herbalist that there was no one at the door, but he just waved me away with a flick of his hand, like you would a fly.

*

I was going mad in the head from eating rabbits. You'd think on Sunday we'd stretch to one of the old hens. As soon as the dishes were done, I made my escape. Mam was in a strange mood: she hadn't said a word to me, bar calling out 'Don't you dare go far' as I was climbing the stairs. Sure how far could I go in that direction? I went to my room and had a grand time lying on my bed totting up my earnings. I kept track of my few customers in a copybook. There was Birdie Chase, Carmel Holohan, Mrs Daly, the Moriarty sisters, Mary Burke and her mother. I was hoping that the list would get longer and that I'd get to do some real sewing, perhaps for Mrs B's daughter Rose. She wore something different almost every day. Beautifully tailored dresses from Dublin. She got a Jean Harlow white fur for her sixteenth birthday.

For now it was mostly zips. People hated doing zips. I loved them; loved sewing. Would hem a handkerchief just to keep my hands busy, for the pleasure of making rows of neat, even stitches. I was only earning pennies, but in a matter of weeks there might be enough. The problem was, though, that once I'd mended something it was usually mended for good. So my main source of income was Birdie – or Lady Chatterley, as Carmel had taken to calling her. As long as she kept discovering clothes that needed renovating, my dream dress remained a possibility. I never called Birdie by her new nickname. If she knew that I knew, and that the whole town knew, she sold filthy banned books, Birdie would be mortified.

'Emily!' Mam called. 'Emily, come down to the parlour if you please.'

If you please? Why was she talking like that? I went downstairs to see what she was carrying on about. And who should be there, plumb on the sofa of the 'parlour', but only Doctor Birmingham. He had never crossed our threshold before. Not one of our family calamities had ever been great enough to warrant summoning the gracious Doctor B. Not when our father went missing, not when Mam wrung the neck of every single chicken. This must be shocking serious.

'You've been consorting with the peddler.' The doctor spoke to me but looked at Mam.

59

How could he know? Doctor B would never be caught mucking around the square on market days – he'd rather be caught picking his nose. Mam gave him a pinched smile and then walked out of the room, closing the door behind her, real gently. Doctor B seemed to relax then; leant back and let his fat legs fall open. I could see the lump between them. The seams were stretched to breaking. He laid a hand on each knee and cocked his head to the side.

'I came for Grettie's sake, blood being thicker than water and all that, you know yourself. But of course you don't. You don't know anything, you're only a girl. A slip of a thing.'

What family connection was he yammering on about, with the big grey bollocks on him eyeing me from beneath his trousers? I'd swear it moved. He cleared his throat. I was going to be sick.

'Come here like a good girl so I can talk to you properly.' His voice had gone hoarse. 'Come on, closer.'

He raised his hand out towards me. I didn't know what he was going to do and I never got the chance to find out, because right at that moment a scream came out of my mouth. And then I near ran through the door to get away from him.

Mam was just sitting there in the kitchen, at the head of the table; it was set all fancy, with the white and gold teapot. She brushed past me and went into the parlour. The front door slammed. She was back out again in seconds.

'What did you do to the poor man?' she said. 'He's after running past me without so much as a word. What will he think of us at all?'

She sat down at the table.

'Who on earth is going to help me now?' she cried.

'I'm so sorry, but he gave me the heebie-jeebies, and I thought . . .' I rubbed her shoulder.

What had I thought? What was Mam thinking? Why couldn't she talk to me herself? There was always a man being called in to deal with me: it used to be my father, then it was the priest, now it was the doctor. Who next, the plumber?

She shook off my hand and began to clear away the nice crockery and put out the ordinary plates. The silence over tea was hell. Charlie was in a world of his own. The only sounds were our forks and knives, and the odd cough from my father. He didn't ask what was wrong: he'd no curiosity when it came to goings-on under his own roof. We were eating lettuce and tomatoes with cold potatoes; they were waxy, and felt like marbles in my stomach.

I was miserable for making Mam miserable, and for making her call the doctor and bringing her strife – she hated strife. And how dare Doctor B call the herbalist a peddler? How dare he? I hoped Doctor B wasn't coming back. Fancy doctor man or not, I didn't care – something wasn't right. But I'd never be forgiven for scaring him off, and for having done something to have him called here in the first place. And I only befriending a poor stranger. *Consorting.* What a horrible word. And the big fat mouth on him and he saying it.

Mam started to choke – held her hand over her mouth. Father stood up, like that was enough of a help. Just stood there gawking at her. When her hand came down, her face was flushed. Then she started laughing. It was an age before she calmed down, and we just waited in silence as she wiped the tears away.

'The face on poor Doctor Birmingham and he springing out of here like someone had shot him up the arse. Oh, Emily, what am I going to do with you at all?'

She looked sad again when we were doing the dishes after the tea. 'You know I love you,' she said. I knew that. She said that it was coming time for me to leave, leave the house and go somewhere if I was to have a chance of anything better.

But where was a girl like me to go?

Mam never mentioned consorting of any sort again. She also never asked me why I had screamed that afternoon. I suppose she put it down to me being daft.

12

Sarah woke at daybreak and heard Mai pottering around. She wrapped a blanket around her and tiptoed into the room. The kettle was steaming and Mai was sitting on the stool, waving a slice of bread over the fire. She was shivering. Daylight had crawled halfway across the floor.

'What has you up at cock crow, Mai?'

'I'm only home – was in Phil Green's. They sent for me after midnight; I didn't want to wake you.'

'You should've – they're a tough lot. I would've come, no bother.'

'Well, I'm fine, and all's well – a boy, 8 pounds 10 ounces. And they actually paid me.'

'I thought Phil wasn't due till June? Aren't they only wed since Halloween?'

'It was an early delivery. I don't know who the father is, but it's not the string of a thing she married.'

'I pity the men.'

'I do too. I pity them all. Phil looked terrified but she was quick. "It's come terrible early, hasn't it, Mai?" "Indeed it has," said I, looking at the fat-faced leanbh; "the poor craythur is lucky to be alive."'

'How could she?'

'What choice did she have?'

'Plenty.'

'Ah, the innocence of youth.'

Later that morning Willy the Post knocked on the back window. Mai opened the window and took the envelope. The postman stood peering in, as was his habit. Mai took her time fidgeting with the letter before sighing 'Ah, think I'll read it later' and placing it in the pocket of her apron. That was her habit. Willy rarely took a scrap of news from Mai's house. Sarah thought it was uncharitable of her aunt; the old man loved news of any sort and considered it his vocation to spread it.

'Well, hope it's good,' he said, as he loped away.

It was a note from Finbar: Sarah was to start in Kelly's shop the coming Saturday. There would be six weeks' trial.

'Trial sounds about right,' said Sarah.

'No, no, listen to me now.' Mai made her sit down and began to talk.

Sarah felt bad for her cheekiness when she saw how hard Mai was trying. She carried on about what a busy town it was, and how many interesting people Sarah was bound to meet. What a wonderful opportunity, to work in a shop! She remembered when Finbar's mother had run the place, and what a gentle person Frances had been. She reminisced until she wasn't really talking to Sarah any more, till she was talking to herself. 'You always remember the ones that die young the best. She loved flowers. Her watercolours were all over the shop. Maybe you'll see them when you go there, or maybe not, that was a long time ago.' Then she began to talk about a party. Mai, who'd never had a party in her life.

'I want to have a nice supper for you, a send-off.'

She retrieved her big black handbag from the trunk under the stairs, sat in her armchair and began to ease her feet into her best shoes.

'Thursday evening.'

'What about it?' asked Sarah.

'That's when I'll tell them to come, for your send-off.'

'Tell who?'

'Why, everyone.' At that Mai left the house.

That Thursday, Sarah walked in on the preparations. There was steam everywhere. The scent of cinnamon, roast chicken and burnt sugar filled the air.

'What are you doing?'

'A few neighbours, a drop of sherry, no big fuss,' Mai sang as she pierced the roast chicken breast.

The skin crackled and broke under her fork. There were beads of sweat on her upper lip. Her tight bun had feathered askew.

'This is too much, Mai,' Sarah said.

'I want to send you off in style.'

And she did. The table laden to breaking, teacup towers, apple tarts, rock buns, a Victoria sponge with jam *and* cream. The best cloth, white linen, shiny shamrocks embroidered on each corner – finally good enough to eat off, now that Sarah was leaving. A fine spread to celebrate her new position.

There wasn't a neighbour that didn't come. By ten the party was in full swing, and Sarah sat with her cousin Mary and Bernie and the other girls on the bench in the kitchen. The Flanagan boys played a reel, her lemonade was warm and flat, and all she could think was *Is James ever going to ask me to dance at all?* The tune went faster and faster, like the fiddle was fighting the box accordion. They were all trying to outdo each other. So many musicians, there was almost no one left to clap. Feet stamped, the people called for a waltz, a waltz. A chance for couples to take to the floor. Was he ever going to ask her?

It was late, pitch black.

'Dampen that fire, I'm sweltered,' Boom-Bellied Johnny roared.

Aunt Gracie leant in the doorway, arms crossed high and a steely eye on who went where, and who did what. Mai was knocking back the rum and giving the Charleston a go. She declared her knees weren't up to the job any more, and all the old men laughed and laughed. She gripped the beads around her neck and spun them instead. Sarah could almost see how Mai might've been when she was young, her cheeks pink, her skin glowing and her eyes full of devilment.

Finally, James walked over to where Sarah was sitting and asked her to dance. His mouth was fixed in a smile that was more deter-mined than kind. Maybe it was her imagination. Everyone seemed a little strange to Sarah tonight. Perhaps it was because she was leaving them all. James and Sarah danced into the centre of the floor – his hands were sweating and she was afraid of slipping from his grip, of hitting the wall of old ones. She wanted to talk to him, to see what he thought of her leaving, and how often he planned to visit her or if he planned to visit at all. Gracie tugged at her sleeve. James let go of her hand.

'Go on outside, catch up with my Mary. She left a while ago to walk Midge home. Keep her company on her way back.'

Sarah turned. James wasn't there any more – he was chatting to some lads by the door, and they were elbowing each other over some joke. You'd think he was dying to get away from her. Sarah fetched a cardigan from her bedroom; it was lovely and quiet in there. She shut the window. Why did Gracie have to ruin everything?

As soon as Sarah stepped outside, she was pulled by the waist to the side of the house, carried to the far ditch and thrown over it. She only had time to see the moon. *It must be a giant, a mad cruel ogre*, she thought. But it wasn't.

Was it a hard life, Aggie, living on the river? Did you not long for the comforts that other women had? Did you not get lonely? Weren't you ever scared?

I was a hardy annual; I'd survived anything the sweet Lord wanted to throw at me. Why so hardy? I'll tell you why – now, listen to my advice – drink a drop every day; it'll keep the memories away. A drop a day, I used to tell the lads at the bar. That's right, *at the bar*. They were not stuffing me into that cubby-hole; I took my drink with the men.

'Is that right, Ag?' they'd say.

'Oh, yes, a drop a day,' I'd say.

The cheeky yokes always answered back.

'What doctor gave you that advice, Ag?'

'Doctor Me!' I laughed. 'Doctor, me hole. Doctor me good.'

I laughed till I cried, pounded my fist on the counter and roared above the scrawb of the fiddle.

'You without sin throw the first one! That's what Our Lord said to thee,' I told them.

'Ah, Aggie, you've got it all wrong again,' said Ned.

'Give us a miracle, Aggie, give us a miracle!' called Jim.

'The holiest hoor in old God's kingdom!' added a fella still in short pants.

'Let it be, lads, let it lie,' said Seamus.

There was always Seamus to be relied on. Not a penny on him, but a staff you could spend all night climbing, bless his slick little smile. That lad in short pants was too raw to be out. A cheeky pup with a big mouth. Talking Geography. Estuaries. Claimed my river was on its way to the city.

'It's our river. Full stop.' That's what I told him. But no, he knew it all.

'It comes from the mountains and it goes to the sea.'

I squeezed the back of his skinny neck. 'That bloody river goes nowhere, it's always been there, always will be there, it belongs to the town, and it as soon goes to the sea as a terraced house lifts its skirts and walks its grey walls off down to Wicklow.'

'Would you ever shut up,' said Jim; 'wish I'd never let you in.'

'This is my world, boys, and no one – I said no one – is ever going to shut old Aggie up.'

It was dark when I left the laughter behind and headed home. Wobbling away on my heels, clip-clopping like a mare over the flags of the bridge. I stopped like I always did, and leant on the smooth stone ledge, to have a squint through the railings at the moon shimmying over my black river. I loved that river. Couldn't imagine it ever being anywhere but here, no matter what anyone said. A cold hand gripped my arm.

'Would you like me to throw you in, Mollie? Do you think it's cold?' I felt bristles on my forehead but couldn't see his face; he had lodged himself tight agin me.

'Not as cold as your hand, Christy.'

'I'm not fucking Christy.' He slapped my mouth.

'Well, I'm not fucking Mollie.' I spat out the blood.

His knee came up. Bone as hard as a hammer. It knocked the breath from me, collapsed me. He leant over.

'Fuck you.' He sounded winded.

I heard him step, drag, step and drag away across the bridge. A soldier, I'd bet, with a crippled leg. Taking it all out on an old whore. That was my lot – not much lonelier than anyone else and well past being scared of any living thing.

13

Carmel changed towards me so slowly that I couldn't put my finger on when it had started. She just got cooler and cooler, till she wasn't really talking, just giving me stiff nods. Then she spoke to me, as I wiped the counter that Thursday.

'I'm sorry to say, Emily, that we won't be needing you any more.'

Her neck was red in patches, like she had been stung. My mouth went dry. I knew it was my great friendship with the herbalist, but she wasn't going to say that, not outright. Now if they'd said 'Don't see him', I couldn't have obliged them but I could've pretended to, and then we'd all have been happy. Isn't that the way things usually went around here? And she was all about the herbalist herself, swanking in when she heard his voice, sweet as apple drops, wanting a quiet word. Mad for him. They all were.

'I haven't done wrong, Mrs Holohan.'

'I've been told otherwise.' She handed me my mending bag.

'By who?' I clutched it to my chest.

'Never you mind.'

The door was held open and I had to go through it. I went down the alley for a cry. How easy it happened. A snap of the fingers and I was gone, for consorting with a man she would've given her right arm to consort with.

The market was a poor affair when I arrived in the square. The hawkers were packing their traps, rolling up their sheets of shoes and clothes. The whole place smelt of chicken shite and straw. The herbalist wiped rain off a brown bottle with a small cloth in a really slow way, as if it gave him great pleasure.

'Soporific, Emily,' he said; 'today it's been soporific.'

That's how he liked to talk, the swankier the better. That he made any sense was the least of his interests.

'It's all in the first impression,' he'd say, and smooth his lapels with his ringed fingers.

He was the only person who'd liked the first impression he'd got of me. I tried to recall if I'd been in any way spectacular that afternoon but I hadn't, I was just my plain self standing behind the counter, eyes agog.

The herbalist showed an interest in me. It was hard to credit it, but it was the truth. I didn't think then *I lost my job over you.* I didn't see it like that at all.

'No work today?'

'Not ever no more. Have you a cure for that?'

'Come, I'll put a smile on your face, milady.'

I helped him carry his cases back to the shed. He had fixed a bolt on it; he set great store on the value of his potions.

I was starving when I got home. I let myself in the back door; there was no one around. The breakfast things were still on the table. My father's egg cup, Charlie's half-drunk tea, a slice of toast with one bite taken out of it, Mam's frilled-edge porridge bowl, and the pot of honey beside it. Father was probably out, and most likely Mam was lying down. I cut some soda bread, piled it with gooseberry jam and poured a glass of milk. The letterbox clattered, probably the second post. I went into the hall to fetch it.

Mam lay on her stomach, her face to the side, her arms under her like a sleeping child. Her eyes were open and she didn't look at all surprised to be there like that.

I took Charlie's bike, cycled to town and found my father in his local. I couldn't get his attention. The lad beside him nudged him and my father turned around, his expression loose from drink.

'Mam's dead.' He looked at me like he couldn't hear. 'Mam's dead – she collapsed in the hall.'

He didn't answer; just put his old head on the bar. The man beside him patted his back. Word spread: this poor man's just lost his wife, give him a whiskey. There seemed no movement on anyone; no one seemed to think it was their place to offer any assistance. I stood there for a moment, wondering what to do next.

I left the River Inn and cycled on to Father Higgins's house. His stuck-up housekeeper, Mrs Ball, offered me a brandy. She put the drink on the table in front of me.

'Knock it back, you're shivering – it will warm you up.'

That's when I realized I shouldn't have left Mam alone like that. What had got into me? She should be wrapped up snug. I jumped up and left without waiting for the priest; he could follow, he knew where we lived.

They eventually found Charlie, walking some young one down the river. Rita Brennan. By the time he came in, Doctor Birmingham had arrived and was in the front hall with Mam. I was sitting in Father's fireside chair; there were people everywhere, talking and making themselves tea. She'd had cancer, they were all saying, cancer had been killing my mother. But how did they know, how did they know anything? Charlie walked over and put his arms around me.

'Charlie,' I said. 'Mam –'

'I know, they told me. I'm going to the undertaker's, I won't be long. Will you be all right here?'

'Don't you want to see her?' I pointed towards the shut hall door.

'No, not yet. Not like that. Rita will give you a hand.'

Rita stepped forward and hugged me as Charlie left. She had been in my class but we weren't friends, weren't anything. She was just a nice girl who had never seemed to notice me. And here she was holding my hand.

'I'll help you now, Emily.'

'Help me what?'

'Feed the people, of course.'

Someone had already cleared the table of the breakfast dishes. Rita was a great help, rallied other women to bring food, handed out the sandwiches, cigarettes and booze. There was a great ruckus as Mick Murphy and John Dunne carried the bed down the stairs and manoeuvred it into the parlour. Mick came into the kitchen and nodded at two women, who stood up. I got up too, but Rita put her hand on my arm. 'They'll lay her out,' she said. 'They know what to do.'

I wanted everyone to go away then. They were jostling against each other, eating and drinking and talking. Had they all forgotten why they were here? I wanted to scream. Rita gave me a sherry with a wink that should have annoyed me, but it didn't.

I opened the door of the parlour, and I went in to see Mam. The praying had started. The mourners crowded in behind me till I was at Mam's feet.

And still no sign of my father, not a word.

The next night, the boys took it upon themselves to arrive home. Jack and Peter. Grown men now, and like strangers, awkward in how they embraced me. Stayed for one decade of the rosary and went off to drink the town dry with Charlie in tow. No matter that Charlie was a Pioneer and had never touched a drop before. They looked like cowboys, swaggering down the lane with their black handsome heads cocked high and purposeful, all decked out in suits got from God knows where.

'We'll do right by Mam – we'll give her the send-off she deserves.'

I'd visions of them coming in drunk and laying whiskey glasses on her belly. She looked calm, respectable – blank of who she'd been. I'd no picture to prove she'd ever been any different except for the one in my head. Her swinging me around the garden, her hair flying out behind her. Brown-skinned, plump and full of life. 'Hold on tight, Millie – you're in for a ride.'

I'd forgotten she called me Millie. Till I told her to stop. I knew she loved me. Loved Charlie better, but no matter. Loved like she sowed seeds. One for the pigeon, one for the crow, one to rot and one to grow.

Carmel and Dan arrived late on the second night. Gave their sympathies. 'You're very good to come,' I said to them, just like I'd said to everyone. I wore the miserable dress that had caused such a ruckus. They didn't stay long.

Birdie gave me a big hug. Her face was blotchy and she kept blowing her nose. Said maybe it was a blessing that poor Maureen's heart gave out so sudden, that it had saved her from a terrible death. Cancer was cruel. Cruel the way it could drag out for so long. Birdie had witnessed her own mother's demise and you know what, she wouldn't wish it on her worst enemy. She knew it was a poor comfort, but Maureen had been spared, and I had been spared seeing her in such pain that I'd have ended up praying for her last breath to come. She kept stroking my hair, looking at me like her own heart would break. How does a heart give out? How could my mother's heart stop beating and I not even know? Where was I, what was I doing when it beat for the last time? Was I strolling into Kelly's shop, thinking I had a job? Was I crying in the alley beside it? Or was I rushing into the herbalist's shed, thinking about nothing but him and letting my mother down? I was so glad when Mrs B bustled in. Birdie's kindness was too much for me, made me think things I couldn't bear to think.

Mrs B wore a veiled black hat that looked like an upturned bucket and was dragging Rose and Doctor B behind her. The doctor shook my father's hand and nodded at the rest of us. Young Rose stepped forward, pale and blonde in her dark outfit. She didn't say anything; just smiled a sad smile. She kissed me, and her hair smelt like candyfloss. I rubbed my cheek afterwards and sure enough there was lipstick on my knuckle.

Mrs B lingered beside the coffin. She wore her red fox-fur coat. She had let me touch the sleeve once: it was so soft, it melted under my fingers. She blessed herself, reached in and tucked a strand of hair behind Mam's ear. Her face was heavily powdered and baggy from crying. Her husband quickly stepped forward to steer her away. Was it possible that the grand Mrs B and my poor mother had once been friends? Once upon a time, before Mother got mixed up with my father and his lot, before Mrs B had Rose and Mother had us? Doctor B had hinted at some connection that time he called up. Yet Mrs B had never set foot in our house, not in my lifetime.

I felt the herbalist's presence the second he walked in. Who had told him? I hadn't left the house since I'd got the priest.

'Poor Mo was a lonely soul,' someone muttered.

'Her name was Maureen,' I said softly.

I was facing the body, looking at her hands. Beads were woven through the fingers, which were so thick and pale they didn't look like hers. Hers were brown from the garden.

There was consternation by the door behind me. Doctor Birmingham was taking his leave, and signalling as such to Mrs B, who was chatting with Mrs Daly and didn't look like she was going anywhere soon.

'I'll follow you in a while, Albie,' she whispered louder than most people shout.

He had no choice, with all gawking at him. Off he went with Rose in tow. The poor girl was blushing. Someone said to me then, some old drinking friend of my father's, 'It's up to you now, young Emily; it's up to you to keep things going.'

Keep what going – Charlie and my father? A half-arsed yard? I looked at Mam's death-bed: I was almost seventeen years of age and it felt like mine. The herbalist was moving near me, I could feel him. Then, his hand on my shoulder. The heat off him. I looked up. He handed me a holy card with a piece of fabric stuck to it. A relic of St Thérèse, the Little Flower. I smiled, despite myself; it was a piece of blue serge I'd left in his place. I didn't say a word. I was only thinking, God forgive me, *Now he's seen where I live.* I felt ashamed, like something that I'd hid could be hid no more. I was heart-sore.

I took a break from my vigil and went into the kitchen for a drink of water. Three of the women had gathered together around the table, greedy beady-eyed birdies – Mrs B, Mrs Daly and Mrs Nash having a real good root through Mam's box of photographs. I went over and stood there. I put out my hand, but they didn't even notice. Mam liked photos. She didn't have a fancy album or any album, just a small cigar box that she liked to keep to herself, which was fine because no one besides me was interested in pictures, and none had been taken since I was born.

'That's you, Grettie! In a swimming costume!' said Mrs Daly. 'You certainly didn't look like that in school!'

'Oh, Jesus Christ, get that out of there this minute,' squealed – yes, squealed – Mrs B.

The stuck-up biddy mauled Mam's photo and tried to cram it into her pocket.

'That's stealing,' I said.

Mrs B didn't have the decency to look embarrassed, but she handed over the photograph all the same. They sobered up a bit then, started munching on the fruit cake. I lifted the box from the table and left the room. I wanted air. I'd heard people say that before and never known what they'd meant, but I did then.

I found the photo that had caused the shrieks. It was taken on a rocky beach, and a group of seven were wearing dark old-fashioned swimming costumes. Four men, two women and a girl. They seemed to be mostly in their twenties, a bit old to be dressed so friskily. The men's costumes were black vests and shorts; the women wore belted tunics that were edged in white at the neckline and ended above the knee. They seemed to have some sort of bloomers underneath, but still it was all very indecent, to be half dressed in mixed company and probably wet from the sea to boot. They looked kind of ordinary all the same, like there was nothing to be fussed about. A couple sat on the sand, four perched on a rock, and a man stood behind, leaning down. He had his hand on the girl's shoulders. She was the only one not wearing a cloche swimming hat; she was reaching back so her hand lay on his forearm. The standing man was striking and somewhat familiar. He had black hair and muscled shoulders. His face was flushed and very hand-some. Though he was older than the other men, he made them look old, all fuddy duddy in their duds.

Which one was Mrs B? I was searching from face to face, trying to find her, when I suddenly locked on a pair of eyes: Mam's. How had I not seen her? She was the girl reaching back towards the man with the muscles, but she looked so young, so tiny, compared with the others.

And the man on whose arm her fingers lay? I knew the answer as soon as I'd thought of the question – that was the man who had turned into my father.

Let the other women stay at home – I was going to the funeral Mass. They couldn't stop me if they tried. I always felt weak in chapel, but this time was the worst, when we were seated at the top of the church and our mother was in the centre of the aisle in a wooden box and the priest looked straight at me every time he spoke.

The brothers always made a laugh of how afraid I was of that Father Higgins. Whenever I saw his gaunt white face, all I thought of was the first time he'd come to our house. I was only seven but I never forgot it. He came in without knocking. Mam was all about him – *'Father' this, 'Father' that*. I just looked at my plate. It was blue and white. There was a bridge over a stream, and on the bridge was a maiden wearing a round-brimmed hat. Pastures and blue skies – that's all you want underneath your Sunday dinner, under your potatoes, ham and cabbage. The more you eat, the more you see the whole picture. I looked harder. Didn't taste a thing. Tried not to listen to what Mam and the priest were saying. *A blessing . . . a casting out . . . yes, Father . . . of course, Father.* There was a smoking chimney on the roof. The whole picture appeared as I cleared my plate. The woman in the wide-brimmed hat was leading a cow over the bridge to market. When he came back into the kitchen, the priest had a rope.

Charlie carried me out of the church. Said I'd fainted. He didn't make me go back in, said I'd been through enough.

14

Dan was asleep, but Carmel couldn't rest. Yet she was so tired all the time, couldn't manage to stand and wash over the tin, felt ill at the line, kept wanting to curl up in the hedge at the bottom of the garden. The house felt alive with dust, like it was calling her to get up and clean it. So she pulled back the covers and quietly got out of bed. She had already spent the day getting the place ready for the help that was coming. She had intended to put her in the spare room, to leave Samuel's room as it was, ready, in the hope of another chance. Carmel walked down the hall, opened the door and switched on the light.

She sat in the rocking chair. She had been expecting the last time she had done that. There was bird noise from the chimney. She listened carefully: no. No, there was nothing; just the usual night rustling. She would leave this room be; it had witnessed his silent birth. Carmel would use the spare room if she was lucky enough to be blessed. This bedroom would do the woman coming.

Carmel wondered what she was like, this Sarah? Carmel hoped she was strong and able. She felt bad for sacking Emily. With her poor mother passing, it was unfortunate. She must make up a parcel of food for the Maddens next week, that would be the appropriate way to help out. She would send the new help, so she didn't have to go to the house herself. The wake tonight had been bad enough.

And she would find a way to be soft towards her without giving Emily the impression there was any chance of her working in the shop again. She wasn't a bad girl, but she was going the way of her mother before her, besotted with an unsuitable man far too old, making a fool of herself, and look how that had ended for Maureen? Living in poverty with a shell-shocked alcoholic. Everyone had warned her at the time: what would a travelling salesman – if that's what he was at all – know about land? All Brian knew about was drink and women. God, he was lovely in his day, though, had put the *d* into dashing. But Maureen had paid for her silliness, God bless and save her – all her lovely fields were eventually let out to neighbours, and for half nothing at that.

Perhaps Carmel should also take it upon herself to talk to Mr Don Fernandes. He must be mortified by the moony-eyed attentions of a scrawny girl like Emily. Carmel could advise him on how to let her down easy. The direct approach was more effective with some people.

She hoped he had found himself somewhere better to live; she wasn't going back to that place, and being seen at the market stall buying potions wasn't a good idea. People would guess, they would jeer. She had hid her distaste on entering his premises – his shack, really – but he must have noticed, because he immediately told her that it was only temporary, that he was looking for suitable accommodation from which to practise. Come to think of it, the herbalist could give his remedies to Carmel, on a sale or return basis, and Carmel could sell them in the shop. They would seem more reputable then. She would suggest it to him: he'd be delighted. And then she wouldn't have to leave her own premises to get cured at all.

She had taken her tonic this evening before bed; the herbalist said it would take some weeks before it made any difference. Told her that she was still in recovery and had to mind herself – she enjoyed hearing that. It made her feel looked after. She asked him for a month's supply. She wondered if he knew why.

She didn't sleep well any more, walked the house, in and out of every room, checking, tidying, moving things. Sometimes she heard him crying. The first time she had been sleepwalking. That's what Dan said. He had found her here, opening the drawers, pulling out the blankets.

'Where is he?' she had said. 'I hear Samuel crying – he's crying so softly, where is he?'

Grettie B told her to concentrate on other things – the business, the garden, the parish, the community – that there was more to life than babies.

'Should I give up? You know . . . trying?' Carmel had whispered.

'What do you mean, give up? Sure that would be a sin. Hush now; you don't want Rose to hear such indiscretion, do you?'

'God forbid.'

Rose was doing what she always did when her mother was deep in conversation: standing there, daydreaming, pushing back her cuticles. She was well used to waiting for her mother. Carmel was sure she was privy to many indiscretions.

Concentrate on something else. She had cleared some brambles at the back of the garden, cut back the climbing rose on the shed, taken a wire brush to the garden gate so she could give it a lick of paint. But she always ended up in the same place: the back corner of the garden. It was overgrown but got the most sunlight. She'd find herself sitting on her old childhood stool, her eyes closed, the warm sun on her face, feeling close to Samuel, the closest to praying since he had been lost. She kept the soft blanket he had been wrapped in. It smelt of him yet. If she sat there and held the blanket to her, she too felt still-born, suspended, almost at peace.

Theresa Feeney had been in the shop earlier, her brood with her as usual. She had been a few years ahead of Carmel in school, and, though she had been harassed by life, she was always good-natured. Her eldest daughter, Tessie, was carrying the latest addition to the family. Mrs Feeney rubbed its tiny chin and looked towards Carmel, expecting the usual congratulations. Carmel gave her best smile.

'Is that your grandchild?'

'It's my new baby, you know it is.'

'You're at the age to be a granny, not a mammy.'

Carmel left the bewildered woman and ran into the back. She felt a meanness rising up in her, pure hatred for the stupid fat bitch at the counter. She knew it was wrong – that Theresa Feeney couldn't help having all those babies – but it wasn't fair, and until she calmed down Carmel almost wanted to kill her. She had locked the shop when the Feeneys left, and just sat at the counter looking at her hands: they were shaking.

As she rocked, she wondered what was happening to her?

Throwing spite at an exhausted mother? The chair rocked noise-lessly as Carmel stole into a fretful sleep.

When she woke, she was on Dan's lap. They were still in the rocking chair. His arms were around her, and he was fast asleep. His neck was at an awkward angle, and there was sweat on his forehead. His vest was damp where her face had been resting. Had she been crying in her sleep? Had she cried out for him? She inhaled the scent of his warm skin. Her husband. That he had come to her in the middle of the night, that he had lifted her from the chair and set her on his lap without waking her, made her feel a terrible tenderness, gave her hope.

15

Sarah unfolded the softened paper one more time, just to see Mai's familiar round handwriting. A short note and directions to the shop. It was sweltering. She had worn her Sunday coat; it was far too heavy to carry. She found the shop easily: it was just off the market square, perched over a narrow road where the windows of terraced houses glared across the street at each other. Kelly's was a small shop and a dark one at that. Sarah pushed the door. A bell tied to a string gave a half-hearted clang. The place was empty. She put her case on the ground, where it promptly fell on its side. She picked it up again.

The counter was coated in thick cream paint, and she guessed that she'd soon know every crack and dent on its surface. Sarah swung the door back and forth, hoping the bell would alert someone. A section began to separate from the wall at the rear of the shop – a door. It was painted the same pale mushroom as the walls. A man appeared: he was very tall, broad shouldered with dark hair. She glimpsed the pink wallpaper behind him as he turned to link a woman's arm. The woman was fair and short. Her plump face had just passed pretty. Mrs Holohan looked nothing like her brother, Master Finbar. Sarah tried to smile, but her lips were so dry the skin cracked.

'You must be Sarah.' Mr Holohan's voice was jovial.

He patted his wife's shoulder while he told Sarah how welcome she was.

'Isn't that right, Carmel?'

'Yes, Dan.'

'And where's the child?' Sarah managed a smile.

A bead of blood rolled down her chin. They were interrupted by an untidy woman who bustled into the shop carrying a wicker basket.

'Morning, Aggie.' Dan frowned.

His wife turned on her heel and disappeared into the wall, shutting the painted door behind her. Mr Holohan motioned for Sarah to slip behind the counter alongside him.

'Let's get down to business. Watch and learn. Tobacco, Aggie?'

'And tea, a quarter-pound, Danny boy, no more, no less.'

Dan measured out the leaves without introducing Sarah. The woman was mid-aged but wore no headscarf to cover her untidy copper knot and white roots. Her long navy coat was shiny at the cuffs, and its round buttons were tugged to the last across her chest. Her shoes, however, weren't shabby at all: they were the latest in platforms. White, cork heeled. Something a glamorous girl would wear. City shoes. Aggie was studying her too, and not in the most friendly of ways. There was something familiar about the woman.

'Who's this one?' Aggie asked.

'This is Sarah – she's taking over full time.'

'You mean poor Emily's out of a job and her mother not even cold?'

'Bad timing, Aggie, bad timing.'

'Bad timing my backside.'

Dan smiled as if Aggie were joking and hurried her on her way. When she was gone, he shivered.

'Well, I suppose her money's as good as anyone else's.'

The woman's coins went in a box under the counter, instead of in the drawer with the other takings. He didn't explain why.

He took Sarah through the workings of the measuring scoop and the weighing scales as if it were all terribly complicated or she were a terrible fool. He never mentioned the 'other one', the one whose mother had just died.

'Add an extra few ounces on the day they are settling up and make sure they see. Always say, "Here's a bit extra for luck." Encourage them to pay something off every time they buy – God knows money's scarce, but mention it all the same.'

He opened a faded blue ledger and ran his finger down the names and accounts of all the customers. As far as Sarah could see, nearly all the customers were in arrears. There were several more ledgers on the same shelf. He took out one from 1908.

'That's my mother-in-law's handwriting; she passed away some time ago.'

He looked quite chirpy about that. He'd a butt of a pencil and ran it down the lists, telling her which families went back a long time. Good stock, he called them.

'We're making progress.' He didn't look directly at her, but at some place around her ear.

He seemed pleased, yet Sarah had done nothing but nod at him. Her case was still on the floor. A smell was coming from beyond the door, a soapy dank odour. Bacon and cabbage. She realized she was hungry. Mr Holohan stretched his arms out in front of him and cracked his knuckles, as if he'd just completed a hard day's labour.

'Well, sugar is thruppence a pound, potatoes are sevenpence, eggs one shilling and twopence a dozen . . . Don't look so worried, the prices are all in here.' He smiled and handed her a copybook. 'I'll leave you to it. We close at six on Saturdays, and nine the rest of the week. Any trouble, give us a shout.'

Off he bolted through to their living quarters without even offering her a glass of water. There wasn't much to get the hang of. The drawer for the cash was set into the counter: she pulled it out. Either they didn't make much or they didn't trust her. Alongside the tray of coins was a fountain pen, an inkwell, string, a short, sharp knife and a spool of navy thread. The ledger was simple enough: what was bought, what was paid and what was yet to be paid were listed each week for each customer. She was to use the copybook for totting up the sums. She'd a ruler, a pencil.

Sarah leant against the high stool. There was a whole shelf of glass sweet jars to her right. They had red cloves, toffee mints, butterscotch, fruit drops, sherbet lemon, butter mint, bon-bons and acid drops. Again, she wondered where the child was. Maybe they planned on keeping Sarah in the shop. She wanted to wash, to rest.

She kept remembering: his face, the jolt when she'd hit the ground, the waltz being played in the house, her going-away party in full swing, and that horrible cold moon. She wouldn't think about that. She'd put it all behind her, like Mai had said. *Today's a clean slate.*

Everyone that came in that afternoon asked about 'poor Emily'. Her mother's funeral had taken place that morning. It made Sarah feel awkward. She had weighed tea, sugar, biscuits, flour, potatoes, sold bread soda, Reckitt's blue and soap, and twelve times said yes, it was a tragedy. And no, she hadn't known Emily or her mother. Her legs were killing her – she wasn't used to all the standing. Then, just as she thought the day was over, a crowd of young people arrived, asking all at the same time for sweets, toffees, Peggy's Legs, broken chocolate, apples. That's when Mrs Holohan finally came in.

'It's the intermission crowd, Sarah – you'll get used to it.'

'Who?'

'From the Picture Palace up the road – there's a show and a ten-minute intermission on a Saturday. Do you like the pictures?'

'I've never been.'

Mrs Holohan saw her suitcase on the floor then.

'Go on in the back – there's a plate of cold meats and bread laid out in the kitchen. Wait for me there.'

Her case seemed much heavier than it had earlier. The living room she landed in was dark and smoky; a glass door opened on to a brighter room that Sarah guessed must be the kitchen. There was a tea towel over a plate in the middle of the table. She lifted the cloth – sliced ham, a boiled egg, tomatoes and scallions. She was ravenous. There was a jug of milk and a glass set out. She felt shy about eating in a strange kitchen all alone, but she ate every morsel. The kitchen was an odd shape: it was the width of the house. A window on one side looked into the living room, and the two on the other looked out into the garden – it was most peculiar sitting there, like being on display. She could see the man of the house out in the back garden, which was long and narrow and dipped at the end, where the hedging was rather wild and beautiful. He was running back and forth: he seemed to be playing with a dog. She had just finished when Mrs Holohan came in.

'You're not what I was expecting: you were meant to be older and a lot plainer. Ah, well, what can you do? Was the food all right for you?'

'It was very nice, thank you.'

'Did it go well today? Do you have any questions for me?' She took a packet of Sweet Afton and matches from the dresser, then put an ashtray on the table.

'No, Mrs Holohan, it went fine.'

She sat down beside Sarah and looked out on the garden.

'Is that eejit playing fetch with Eliza?'

'Excuse me?'

'Nothing. Never mind.' She lit her cigarette. 'Who are your people, Sarah?'

'Whytes.'

'Yes, but what do they do, for a living?' The smoke rose between them, and Mrs Holohan began coughing.

'My aunt Mai Fox reared me. My mother died having me. Mai was in England at the time and stepped in to take care of me. Then the Spanish flu killed my father . . .'

'Oh, you're an orphan. I'm sorry to hear that.'

'Ah, it's not so bad. Mai's very good to me. When my father died, she gave up her position; we came to Ireland and made our home near her sister Gracie. I never knew any different.'

'It must've been hard, though – how did she manage financially?'

'Well, she's a midwife, Mrs Holohan, so she worked.'

'Oh.'

That seemed to displease Mrs Holohan, and made her cough again. Why did she smoke if it caught in her throat?

'You can sweep the downstairs and upstairs and polish; then your time is your own. And of course you have tomorrow off, except for preparing dinner; we'll be going to the holy well. You can come with us.'

Sarah was exhausted by the time she got to bed. At least she'd been given a bright, freshly painted bedroom. There was a grand brass hook on the back of the door. She hung her coat on it and looked around. There was a bed, a lovely rocking chair in the corner and lemon curtains. She tried the bed: the springs were firm. In front of the fireplace was a screen on which someone had begun to paint a daisy but had given up after a stem and a few petals. There was a tin monkey on the mantelpiece. There must've once been a drum or some other instrument between its arms, the way they were stretched out. She turned the tiny key in its back, and the arms came together and parted over and over again without a sound.

She put her suitcase on to the bed and opened it. She set her hair-brush on the mantelpiece and folded her under-things, blouses and cardigans into a drawer in a small white locker. Sarah lifted out her tin of tricks. She wasn't a magpie, like Mai. The small box contained all of Sarah's treasures: her lipstick, cold cream, a powder compact, toothbrush, a set of linen handkerchiefs, rosary beads, her missal and the green glass-droplet earrings. Left in the suitcase was her fringed peacock shawl, a jam jar containing three and fourpence, and a copybook that held Mai's mother's recipes. She removed the jam jar before shutting the case and shoving it under the bed. No need for fringed shawls in her new life. Sarah set the fire screen to one side, put her hand up the chimney and felt for a ledge, some-where safe for her savings. When she found it, she tested that the lid of the jar was closed tight and then put it in its new hiding place. She was slow moving, taking her time. No matter how strange this place was, she was glad to be here, because home would never be the same again.

16

I was wrecked from crying. The mornings were the worst. There was always that second when I forgot Mam wasn't with us. How could I? I don't know. But I did, every single morning since the day she died. I missed her so much, it was like my heart was cut out. I missed her hands, her voice, her lovely soft hair. I even missed her giving out. Father was around less than ever. He had a wandering soul. If we met of an evening, I couldn't look at him: the skin was near raw under his eyes. A bit late to be showing his feelings.

I called round to the herbalist. Told him it felt like someone had picked me up and wrung me out, asked had he a cure for that? He didn't laugh; he invited me in and sat me down in the chair with the high back. The one for proper visitors.

'There's no cure' – he rubbed my hair, and then he held my chin – 'there's no cure and there never will be.'

I won't tell what he did then. No, I will. He kissed me so hard I thought the chair would topple. And it was wonderful. He called me a goddess, an empress. I started to cry.

'There are so many bad things . . .' I said.

'I'll make them go away.'

He kissed me again. And then we had tea, and a rock bun each from the half dozen he'd exchanged for some remedy. There was no butter, so the bun was a bit dry. I would bring him some later, a present.

I was rightly set up, then, had myself a man. That's what I thought.

But when I went back later with a pat of butter, his door was shut and there was no answer. That doesn't sound like anything much, but here's the thing: I knew he was in there, I just knew it. I was growing myself some women's intuition.

It went from bad to worse. There was a new girl in Kelly's. A live-in help, who worked six whole days a week. Her name was Miss Whyte. A country one. The people were only too delighted to tell me all about her. Seems she wasn't a patch on me, slow and a bit full of herself, as country ones are.

I went straight to the shop, stood by the grocery window, careful not to be seen from inside. Carmel was standing beside a tall, dark girl. They were examining a ledger. Carmel had flour on her jaw, her white apron on; the glass was all steamed up. The girl's head was bent, and her coal-black hair hung in a thick plait that she lifted every now and again. I couldn't see her face. Carmel leant in and it looked like she was about to press her lips to the nape of the girl's neck. I stepped back. What a strange thing. Or did I imagine it?

I entered the shop, and they stopped talking. I didn't care if I was told off or sent on my way. I just wanted to see that girl's face.

'Oh, hello, Emily,' Mrs Holohan said, as if no trouble had passed between us.

The girl looked at me. Her eyebrows were thick and straight and her eyes were blue, a dark blue like you'd see on delph, and slightly slant. There was a lot wrong with her face: a wide mouth, a chin an inch too long, flared nostrils. And yet . . . she was perfectly lovely. What was Mrs Holohan thinking? A barren woman inviting a beauty into her home. That was asking for trouble.

'This is Emily,' she said; 'she was with us for a while.'

'Nice to meet you.' The girl smiled and held out her hand. Her palm was warm.

'I worked here till you came,' I told her.

'That's nice.'

'They sacked me the day Mam died,' I sobbed.

Carmel had me by the shoulders and out the door before I could catch the girl's response.

I went to see what the herbalist had to say about all this. He had nothing to say. He grudgingly let me in – didn't even put the kettle on. Had he forgotten that I was his empress? Had I imagined that kiss? Was everyone against me now?

'Emily, you have to stop loitering at the stall.'

'Why?'

'People are talking.'

'No. They're not.'

'Why, then, did you lose your job? I'm a businessman. I have to be careful.'

'This morning I was queen of everything, now I'm nothing.' I sidled towards him.

'I can't breathe; back away.'

'Why are you talking like that? You hate me!'

'If you don't stop, Emily, I will. Stay away till I tell you otherwise.'

He sighed and kept pasting labels on to his bottles.

'You said you could keep the bad things away, stop them hurting me, but you know doctor shite, you're the bad thing!'

I waited for a reaction, but got none. I slammed the door on my way out, but got no pleasure from it.

17

Carmel felt incredibly well. Maybe it was having the help. More than likely it was the remedy. She would have loved to know what was in it. Of course, the phial of medicine the herbalist gave to Carmel had no label on it. She was eager to ask the doctor about his herbal remedies; she intended to interest him in recording his recipes, and maybe together they could collect them in a book, like Doctor Culpeper. Her talents were wasted in the grocery. In the meantime she would talk to him about selling his wares on her premises.

The next time he appeared in the shop, Carmel pushed past Sarah to attend to him. He set his tin on the counter and took off the lid. Tobacco and sugar were all he wanted, and he seemed quieter than usual, though his smile was ready. Carmel hoped to steer the conversation around to his medicines and the possibility that she, Carmel, might sell them, and perhaps they could eventually record them.

Carmel could see it already: a small cream volume, with the name *Mrs Daniel Holohan* in sweeping script on the title page. And the herbalist's name too of course, *Don Fernandes*, or whatever it was. But everyone would know it was really her work, that his English wouldn't have been up to scratch. She could fill the shop window with books, put some in the library, maybe even write a letter to the Press.

'Those back windows are filthy, Sarah.'

Sarah took the hint and went on into the back. Carmel weighed the sugar and added an extra generous scoop with a wink. He smiled as the hill of white grains grew high. Then she poured the lot into the tin he always brought with him.

'You forgot to drop by?' he said, no longer smiling.

'Drop by?'

'To settle up, for the month's supply of tonic.'

'It slipped my mind.' She had hoped he would give her more time.

'That's understandable; you've been to hell and back.'

'I have, I have . . .' Carmel opened the drawer and counted the coins into her hand.

'By the way, while there are no ears to hear –' she said.

'Yes?'

He seemed so kindly now, the way he looked at her.

'It must be very inconvenient for you, to be pestered so by Emily. It's best not to be too kind to some people; they can be very hard to shake off. And it sets people talking, and the things they say, you would be appalled. So it's best to just cut it off at the root; it would be kinder in the long run. Do you understand my meaning?'

He picked up his money and put it in a leather pouch he had taken from his inside jacket pocket. It didn't look like he was going to answer.

'I'm not inconvenienced by much, Mrs Holohan. In general and nowadays, I suffer no inconvenience at all.'

She wasn't sure what he meant. Felt strangely rebuked, like an old biddy who didn't know what was going on in the world beyond her prayer book.

'I was thinking of doing you a favour, as it happens –'

'Oh?'

'Yes. I would be happy to help you record your remedies for posterity; we could have a fine herbal volume on our hands?'

'Why would I give away my remedies for just anyone to use?' His voice was curt.

Carmel was taken aback. Who was he, to talk to her in such a manner?

'You're a very gracious and generous woman to think so highly of my remedies. I can see you have only good intentions, Mrs Holohan, but my prescriptions are not for everyone; in fact, they could be quite dangerous in the wrong hands.' He had changed his tone.

'I see.' Carmel didn't quite know how to retrieve her dignity.

'Good evening.'

'Good evening.'

She retreated to the living room and sent Sarah back out to the shop. The girl looked confused, but she put away the cleaning rags, took off her apron and returned to the counter. The herbalist had left so abruptly. Carmel had wanted to consult him about her sleeping difficulties. Why did she feel so chastised?

She'd read Mr Corcoran's bible. That would settle her. Dan said she was a fool, having her head turned by the salesman's smart talk. 'What odds?' she told him. 'At least "the salesman" has taste.' The man had admired her hair, in particular the way it was plaited and pinned around her crown. She'd been delighted. Dan used to tease her when they were courting – 'How's Heidi?' he'd ask. Not so Mr Corcoran; no, he had called her plait 'a wheaten halo', said that she reminded him of a German princess. By the time he left, her cheeks were scarlet and she was holding the beautiful leather-bound bible to her chest. Carmel read it all the time nowadays: she liked the stories, and she liked to remind herself a man had once called her a German princess.

She took the book from under her chair, reached down and pulled out the old leather handbag. It contained the Buckfast she kept for times of distress or sleeplessness. She poured herself a generous and much needed mug full. It had been an upsetting week in general. Very upsetting.

This morning, when they were washing the bed linen, Sarah had asked again about the child. 'I was told I'd be minding a baby?' were her exact words, as her elbows moved up and down, crushing fabric against the washboard. Carmel didn't know what to say. She wrung out a pillowcase. Why hadn't Finbar informed Sarah? He'd hardly forget something so important. Well, he hadn't told her, and after a weekend of avoiding the question Carmel had to answer it.

'He's in limbo,' Carmel said, short and sharp. Let her feel the bite too.

Sarah stopped what she was doing, stepped near and put her wet arms around Carmel. Sarah pulled her tight, and Carmel took in her breath. Carmel wasn't going to cry, not in the arms of a shop girl.

'I'm so sorry, Mrs Holohan, sorry for your trouble, I really am.'

'You're grand, you're grand. Take those sheets out to the line while there's still a bit of sun out.'

Sarah did as she was told.

She was the first and only person to have offered Carmel condolence on the loss of her baby. No one else had ever spoken much about the matter. They had followed Carmel's lead in that respect. She wasn't like Grettie B, making a fuss over everything. Grettie would have had Mass said for a splinter in her finger – she talked far too freely about private matters. Carmel didn't do that. It wasn't her way.

Sarah was back. Carmel had left soup and bread in the kitchen for her.

'Would you like a cup of tea, Mrs Holohan?'

'No, thanks – look after yourself.'

The tonic was going down nice and easy. She heard the girl fill the kettle and go about her supper. Carmel half closed her eyes; she liked that the living room was dark. It was like a cave. She must try to shift those Sacred Hearts. They unnerved her. It was a consignment Dan had ordered in that hadn't sold. She could have told him that they wouldn't. Anyone with a few bob spent it on food or fuel.

People used to wonder if Carmel and Dan were up to something anti-Catholic, seeing as no children had come along in the early years of their marriage; or, worse, and more peculiar, were they up to nothing at all?

As it went, neither was true. When they first married, Carmel had been keen. She had wanted to eat Dan up, butter him and smother him in jam. He smiled when she talked like that; it tickled him how different she was in the bedroom, how warm and loving. When did that all change? It was the little things. And the little things had added up, as Carmel said, to a mountain she couldn't bear to look at, let alone climb. 'The smell of your feet alone would wither love in an angel's heart.' He had never asked her what she meant.

'Good evening, Mrs Holohan.' Sarah held a hot-water jar in her arms.

'Sleep well, Sarah.'

Carmel poured another drop of tonic into her mug. She pushed off her shoes. The words in the bible were very small; even with her glasses she found them hard to decipher.

Dan was in the yard, locking the shed and talking to Eliza. Telling her she was a great girl, the best and most beautiful pig in Ireland. All silly lovey dovey. He never used that voice with Carmel. She lit one of her Sweet Aftons and took a drag. Read about Lot, leaving the burning cities of sin, with his wife and daughters behind him. And his wife, though she was told not to, looking back over her shoulder and turning instantly into a pillar of salt.

Carmel always wanted to stop the story just before Lot's wife turned, to stop it and grab Lot's wife's hands in hers, and say 'Look into my eyes' and lead her safely away. As if you could step on to a page, especially a sacred page, and change anything. She knew it was mad, but Carmel couldn't read or hear the story without wanting to do that.

She could hear Dan in the kitchen, cleaning his teeth with baking soda, gargling to beat the band. It was a horrible sound. At least Sarah couldn't hear it; she wouldn't be back down. She tired easily for a young woman. Or maybe not everyone was a night owl like Carmel, that's what Dan said. And then in he came. He swaggered past her to check himself in the hall mirror. It was the same scene six nights of the week now – Dan with his face shaved, looking dapper and smelling of cologne, flying out to the local.

'Oh, they'll love you, Dan. You look wonderful,' Carmel mocked. 'Off to Murphy's done up like a film star. They'll lap you up.'

'Night, night!' And he was gone.

Carmel sat by the stove with her mug of tonic, her closed bible and her dying Sweet Afton. She began to cry.

She went on up to their bedroom, where she changed into her nightgown and got down on her knees. Closing her eyes, she recited aloud her nightly prayer against nightmares.

Anne, mother of Mary, Mary, mother of Christ, Elizabeth, mother of John the Baptist; these three I place between me and the malady of the bed, suffocation, drowning or injury ...

As she prayed she began to feel comforted, protected. On reaching the last line, she heard a sound, a low echo behind her, a voice joining in, whispering the same meaning at the same time, but in the Irish. Her mother's voice.

Carmel wanted to call out for Dan. He was too far away. She blessed herself with shaking hands and slowly turned around. There was no one there. The wardrobe and the dressing table were the only black shapes. She slipped on to the bed and between the sheets. They felt so cold.

It wasn't a voice, she decided; just the memory of a voice. Her mother had taught her that prayer in Irish when she was an infant. Carmel used to call it the 'Anna Maha Mirror' prayer. She didn't understand what the words meant, just that they were good. *Let's say the Anna Maha Mirror and make the bad things go away!* In school, they'd been taught the English version, which vexed her mother. Then Carmel realized the Irish words were 'Áine, mháthair Mhuire' – 'Anne, mother of Mary'.

The prayer didn't seem to be working lately. If anything, the nightmares had become stronger and stronger. That night she felt the cool shadow of a bad dream spread its wings as she closed her eyes.

18

Sarah was smiling to herself over what Mr Holohan had said this morning. 'Sarah, you'd sell sand to the Arabs!' She had persuaded Mr Gogarty to settle his account just by squinting at the ledger with a woefully sad expression on her face. She wondered would it get her a rise in her wages. It was embarrassing having to wear the same few clothes day in, day out. Carmel had gleaming white cuffs on her satin blouse – no rayon for her – but by six o'clock she usually stank to high heaven anyway.

Was Mrs Holohan ever going to get up? Sarah was weak on her feet, had had nothing to eat since breakfast. Sacks of potatoes, flour, sugar and tea surrounded her, crowded her. A woman came in wearing a long cream coat fastened with a belt. She left the door wide open.

'And who,' she asked, 'might you be?'

'I'm Sarah – pleased to meet you.'

The woman ignored her offer of a handshake. So much for Mr Holohan saying how much all the customers were looking forward to meeting their new girl. The women only wanted boiled sweets. On tick. Opening the ledger, Sarah glanced up.

'Your name, ma'am?'

It was as if she had slapped the woman's face.

'Mrs Birmingham! Have you not been taught anything at all? Have you ever worked in a shop before?'

'This is my first time, ma'am.'

A girl swung in on a breeze of perfume.

'Ah, Rose, love, there you are.'

The girl had a painted mouth and blonde waves swept high off her forehead. While Mrs Birmingham was busy tutting and sighing, Rose whispered to Sarah from behind cupped painted fingers: 'You poor thing, stuck in here for the summer!'

The girl looked at Sarah with genuine pity. Sarah made a face, as if the shop were something she'd got landed with rather than a safe haven. Mr Holohan stuck out his head from the living quarters.

'Such lovely ladies loitering in this drab place, when you could be enjoying the sights!'

Rose started to giggle.

'My dear' – he slipped an arm through Mrs Birmingham's – 'let me accompany you.'

He turned and winked at Sarah as he escorted mother and daughter from the shop. But it was all part of his act for them; he had nothing to be winking at her for.

Mrs Holohan appeared then, looking for titbits of gossip. The customers didn't tell Sarah much. She was still 'the new one from the country'. Knew she was from the country without being told. Her hair was the tell-tale sign, she realized, so long and old-fashioned. And the dowdy skirt, almost ankle length, didn't help either. Even if they did talk, she didn't know who they were talking about, except for the stranger in the market. She figured out that he was the same hawker who'd asked her to pretend to be a satisfied customer, the one who'd given her the skin cream that had ended up in a ditch. *Don't think about it.*

'Any news from the great unwashed?' asked Mrs Holohan.

'The herbalist is making a fortune; they say he's going to buy a car.'

'I could do with making a fortune myself.'

'I know, Mrs Holohan.'

Sarah thought she was very well off indeed.

'Don't call me Mrs Holohan – it makes me feel old. Call me Carmel.'

'You're not old at all, Carmel.'

'I certainly feel it. This scrimping and saving life is bearing down on me – I'll be woollen legged and exhausted before I'm thirty-seven.'

Carmel's eyes were baggy, and there were deep lines across her forehead. Her complexion was, as Mai would say, the colour of a

96

boiled shite. She looked well past thirty-seven and in need of some sound beauty advice.

'I cut out the Pond's Cold Cream advertisement and taped it to my mirror; I follow the face-massage instructions every morning.'

'How old are you, Sarah?'

'Twenty-three.'

'It's easy for you, but I don't have time for such nonsense.'

Neither did Sarah, seeing as she now spent every waking hour behind a shop counter. She noted the sag beginning at her employer's jawline and wondered if it would happen to her own. Sarah took care of herself, but sometimes she wondered why she bothered. Brushing her hair a hundred times just to sell groceries to housewives. Sometimes Sarah wished she were a man and could have adventures.

A customer came in and Carmel put on her shop smile. 'Ah, Nora, Nora!'

Nora was a faded woman in a blue coat. Her shoulders were hunched, and her headscarf had slipped over the tops of her glasses. She took her time, pointing out the various boiled sweets and broken chocolates that her nephews liked. Her hands were raw knuckled. She reminded Sarah of her aunt Margaret, Mai's eldest sister, not so much in stature as in her air of worried kindness. The woman had Carmel divide the sweets evenly into three paper bags and pop a gobstopper into each.

'Now,' she said to Carmel, 'will you give one of them bags to that nice new girl?'

Carmel wasn't pleased but she handed Sarah the bag of sweets.

'Thank you very much.' Sarah was touched; she put the bag in her pocket.

'I know what it's like to be a blow-in. And speaking of blow-ins, Carmel, you know, I didn't believe all they were saying about that dark man –'

'The herbalist?'

'Yes, him. I didn't believe what they were saying, but he gave me a remedy for my rheumatism, and it has worked wonders.'

'He knows his trade.'

'It's more than that, Carmel. We've a healer among us now.'

'Indeed.'

'Mark my words,' the woman said as she left.

'I will, Nora, I will.'

Carmel turned to Sarah when she was gone. 'Seems we've a miracle man on our hands.'

'That man's no healer.'

'How would you know, sure you haven't even met him? And that's the least of what they're saying. Mrs Cranny said he's better than any doctor. Mrs Nash claims he knows your heart, can even read your life. Maybe he'll foresee a wedding for you, Sarah? Would you like that?'

'I'd rather join the convent than be a wife.'

Carmel reached out and pinched the top of Sarah's arm. 'That's for your lack of respect for the sacred sacrament of matrimony.'

Shocked, Sarah ran up to her room. She had got the impression that they were becoming friends. *You're not her friend, you're her skivvy.* There was a sharp knock and Carmel walked in. She was carrying a cup of tea, and there was a biscuit on the saucer. She left it on the mantelpiece. She looked and sounded apologetic but didn't say sorry.

'You shouldn't rile me so.'

'Yes, ma'am.'

The following morning Sarah worked alone in the shop. She recognized her first customer – Emily. The girl just stood there without speaking. She seemed jittery. Sarah filled the silence.

'I love your blouse.'

'Oh, thank you. I made it myself; I can draw you a pattern if you like?'

An elderly woman in a mauve beret passed the window, and made no bones about stopping and staring in at Sarah.

'That's Miss Birdie Chase. She owns the shop across the road. Mrs Holohan's not too fond of her, calls her Lady Chatterley. Birdie's all right, really, keeps lodgers sometimes, not that she needs the money. She and her spinster sister own this whole row except Mrs Holohan's shop. They love the theatricals. The sister runs a shop the next town over. Her and Birdie used to go to the shows in the town hall. Sat right up front every time. Frank Taylor said you could smell the excitement off them. Guess what the sister is called, go on.'

'I really wouldn't know.'

'Veronique! Seems they were musical in their youth. Birdie would take out her harmonica if you asked. You should ask; she's not bad. She keeps her harmonica in her trousers pocket. Yes, you heard right. Trousers! She's fond of an old puff too, at her age! And to look at her you'd think she was the plainest driest piece of cake you ever did see.

'She's mad about our Charlie. He's my brother. He's nineteen. Always asking after him. "Tell Charlie to come and see me." Who does she think she is, Mae West? Most lodgers don't stay long. She overcooks everything, a bit forgetful, more money than sense. Her and Veronique are twins, you should see them together, shrivelled peas in a pod. Both wear the same gold and red headscarves knotted at the back of their neck instead of under their chin. Same old bird-ies, down to the voice. Can't abide to live together, get on each other's nerves, you see. That happens when people are too alike, you know. They've had a big bust-up and they're not talking. I don't know why. Are you listening to me at all?'

'I am of course, it's very interesting. You must know everyone.'

'That I do.'

Emily put her elbows on the counter and began to read aloud from the paper without asking Sarah whether she wanted her to or not.

'Get this: Mrs Alfred Gwynne Vanderbilt, a well-known society woman in New York, was selected by the American fashion acad-emy from twelve of the best-dressed women in the United States as *the* fashion trail blazer!' She lifted the page to show Sarah a photo-graph of a gaunt woman in slacks.

'She looks like a man,' Sarah said.

'You're just raging bet she has a dress for every occasion, instead of one-for-all like you.' The girl looked miffed.

A sharp tongue had Emily, and sharp eyes too.

★

That night Sarah shivered under her thin blankets. There was a draught from the fireplace. She heard footsteps on the path outside, the sound of someone coming near, pausing under her window and moving away again. Then nothing except the wind whistling in the chimney. The town was too quiet at night. She was afraid to go asleep. Her nightmares were filled with Hottentots coming after her with spears, and she kept turning into a chicken with no opening and all her eggs were building up inside, going off, cracking. A cat's chorus laughed at the high notions she used to have. *Where are your fine clothes? Where's your jewelleree?*

She thought about the farewell party Mai had prepared. Mai, who'd never had a party in her life. All that food, and drink and music. It was too much, Sarah had said. But she hadn't meant it; she was delighted then. She hadn't known what was to come.

Oh, why didn't Mai let Sarah go quietly, with no fuss, no little sing-song? Before Sarah fell asleep she had the clearest memory of Mai that night: she was laughing and flinging a wishbone in the air. Sarah had caught it neatly. Put it on the back of the stove to dry, so she could make a wish later, when it was all over.

19

When the herbalist banned me, he might as well have cut off my arm, that's how badly I felt. No one in the house but me, Mam in her grave, my father in the pub, Charlie forever gone fishing with Rita instead of with me. And me barred from all that had kept me happy.

Oh, so friendly Sarah was when she met me. Said I was missed by the customers. Well, that was easily remedied. She had taken my place with everyone, blinded them with her charm. Not me, though. She said she'd call in to see me, let on that she felt sorry.

I went to see him, but the herbalist's door stayed locked to me. I pushed a note under it and carried on down the lane towards the river walk, rather than facing the square, rebuked for all to see. Aggie was crouched in the grass beside *Biddy*, her barge. She waved me over. Must've seen me call on the herbalist, but she made no comment about that. A kettle was steaming over a small fire. Aggie stoked it with a stick, made embers crackle up. The tea was nice, black and kind of smoky. I had a pain in my chest. Heart-broke wasn't the word. Aggie was quiet too, worse for wear, I suppose. She must've been worn out doing what she does at her age, especially seeing as she's been doing it for so long. She had a bruise over her eyebrow as big as a marble.

'What happened to you, Miss Reilly?'

'Ach, they torment the cat till she scratches. Look at this and tell me what it says.' She handed me a piece of paper.

'It's a list of names.' I recognized most of them. 'It's a petition to have a person of immoral . . . oh.'

I read on. It was a petition by Doctor Birmingham to have Aggie and her barge removed from the river, or 'local waterway', as it was called in the petition. There were a lot of names on it.

'It was tacked to my hatch – what's it say?' She knew it wasn't good.

'Doctor Birmingham is trying to get *Biddy* off the river.'

'I couldn't live without *Biddy*. My odd-job man mended her from a wreck for me. Without *Biddy*, I'd be nothing, just another old whore.'

She flung her tea into the grass. I did the same. She never offered to read my leaves, just stoked away at the fire. I thanked her for the tea and left her in the glooms.

There was a parcel from Carmel at our house. Barley water, sugar and a Madeira cake. Charlie said that Seamus had delivered it; it wouldn't have killed her to drop it over in person. The Madeira was lovely. Carmel always baked when she was in good form, when things were going her way. Well, she'd got her way. The house-keeping money my father gave me wouldn't keep mice in cheese. I didn't see any way out. Would I end up like Mam, going cracked inside these four walls? I wrote to the herbalist again. 'I'll be good. Let me back, just for a cup of tea and a chin-wag.'

I was like a ghost hanging around the market stall, at the edge of everything. I was dead already. Nothing to get out of bed for. I let everything in the house wait, the floor crying out to be swept. I was waiting for someone to come and save me, or take me away.

I missed him, missed our chats. If I couldn't talk to him, I could talk about him. And there were plenty willing to talk about him. My man, that's how I thought of him. Everyone else called him the herbalist, the doctor, the Indian or The Don, owing to the fact that they couldn't pronounce his name. The people said his name didn't even sound Indian, and the Indians in the films certainly didn't look like him. He had told me that they were different Indians. Said it like he'd said it a hundred times before.

I missed watching him. He had odd tastes, loved his sugar, sprin-kled it on everything, I'm not lying to you, even his meat. He ate with the front of his mouth, as if every morsel was roasting hot, quickly dropping his long fingers back to the plate for more. As if someone was going to snatch it away from him. And all his ablu-tions at the magnifying mirror, tweezing hair from his nostrils, don't get me started on that. Or all the times I was sent packing because he had an appointment coming. Sometimes men, most times women. But still I missed him.

I waited till it was dark and walked into town. There wasn't a soul about. I turned off my torch when I hit the square. It was so dark that I couldn't see my hand in front of my face. The butcher's dog started barking and didn't stop till I was well past. I stopped walking and that was a mistake, for suddenly I didn't know which way I was facing. I stood there for the longest time, shivering. There was a baby crying somewhere in the distance, and a chimney smoking and a smell of porter from the Inn. After a while I heard the river rushing under the bridge to my right side, so knew to move ahead. I walked like a zombie, with my arms stretched out. My palms hit the cold wall, and it gave me a jolt, right into my armpits. I felt my way, one hand over the other, till I met the corner. I was so relieved I could've cried. It was so strange – a lane I'd trod a million times in my life had become an unknown thing. I followed the turn and walked quicker, knowing once I passed a short gap behind the public house I was at the herbalist's shed.

I felt for the metal of his latch and knocked gently on the door. I heard a rat scurry past but swallowed my yelp. There was no sound from within. I began to feel watched; thought of the murderers that lurk in the big cities, and of how they go on the run, roaming the small towns for girls to tear asunder. I was about to start kicking the door when I heard a voice on the other side of it.

'Who's there?'

'It's me, Emily, and I'm scared,' I whispered.

I was whipped inside the shed like a bride on her wedding night, all commotion and examining me for injury. His long shirt lit the darkness. What was it, he wanted to know, what in God's name had happened to me? I hated to let him down with the truth, but for once in my life I couldn't think of a lie.

'I missed you terrible.'

I thought he would kill me then – but there was just silence, and a sigh, and he put his arms around me. Outside, rain began to hit the corrugated roof. It sounded like a tin shield between our heads and an army of arrows. His mouth tasted of whiskey and I wanted to bite it, I wanted to eat him all up. Never in my life had I been pressed so close to another person. He pushed me away.

'You couldn't put me out in this weather?'

'I wouldn't put an animal out in it,' he said.

And that was when he came upon the idea of a compromise. He let me sit up in the bed beside him, and he talked and talked, and as he talked he looped my hair around his finger, and I really wished he wouldn't talk so much, I would've been happier with some more kissing. The compromise was this: I couldn't be seen hanging around him, loitering with ill intent – he laughed when he said that – but maybe, just maybe, I could pop in to see him the odd time at night, if it was late and there was no one around. And as long as he said it was okay first. No more surprises.

The herbalist didn't try any funny stuff; there was nothing like that. Just that one kiss, and talking shoulder to shoulder on his bed – well, it was more him talking and me concentrating on the feel of his body alongside my body. The rain had stopped without us noticing, and he said he'd bring me across the town.

'Bring me to my door?'

But no, I wasn't to be playing the helpless female after showing up at three in the morning at a man's door. It wasn't three in the morning. Sometimes I wondered if we were on the same planet at all. It was one o'clock at the latest.

He walked with me a bit, gave me a hug and said goodbye. I switched on my torch then, and shone it on him as he walked away, his white shirt like a flag moving off down the road. I was exhausted, and I was cold, and I was happy.

20

Carmel rushed in the back door soaking wet, wiped her face with a towel and wrapped it around her head. She had just been to the *Wuthering Heights* matinee at the Picture Palace and was famished. She threw off her damp coat and went to fix herself a cup of hot tea and a few fried tomatoes. The stove had gone low, and the kettle wasn't anywhere near boiling. She threw in a few sods and wiped her hands on her apron – it was only then she realized she must've worn the apron to the Picture Palace. The mortification. Why hadn't Grettie B mentioned it? Maybe she hadn't noticed. Carmel hoped so. The rain was pelting down; it was loud but comforting. It had been raining every evening for days now. She sat at the table and waited for the water to boil.

Carmel had her doubts about that Laurence Olivier – he didn't look a bit like the Heathcliff she'd had in her head all these years, the one with the Irish accent and curly hair – but she had got used to him after a while. She was surprised to be so full of emotion by the end of the picture, but she refused to join ranks with the sniffers. Carmel wasn't showy like that. Grettie B had a particular set of handkerchiefs just for the Picture Palace. Carmel wouldn't mind living on the heath herself, the romance of it, the wildness.

She felt herself getting a bit down. A drop or two of her herbal tonic would do the trick. She took the bottle from her bag; she was never without her handbag, it was the only place safe from Dan's eyes. She was used to the taste by now. The herbalist's tonics were very addictive. This one would have to last a bit longer than the last bottle. A respectable shop owner had to watch herself; couldn't be seen to be knocking on some foreigner's door every second day. But she was desperately in need of something, anything. She stopped the hand of the clock over the stove: it got on her nerves, had a sharp, irritating tick.

Time was against her. She was ageing – even she could see that. Her hands were her mother's hands now. The raised blue veins, the looseness to the skin, freckles that weren't there before. Her hands were often so slippery from Nivea that she couldn't close the tin. Dan hated the way it was always left open and the midges settled in the cream. The sight disgusted him. He went on, and on, about her horrible habits. Carmel had become a creature of habit, bad ones. Late to bed, late to rise, tonic wine and books. The latest one was the Sweet Aftons. If Dan could've glimpsed how his bride would turn out, he would've raced back up the aisle and hopped on to the first boat to England. Carmel was sure of it.

It was very quiet when she went into the grocery. For a second she thought there was no one about. Dan was just standing there, watching Sarah humming as she polished the counter. He was smiling. Carmel sneaked up behind him.

'She won't be such a songbird in a few years, when her teeth have fallen out.'

Dan jumped, and went on about his business. She wondered after if he'd heard her at all. He didn't bring it up that evening. Carmel would have to watch her tongue; it was running away with her these days. It was how her unhappiness seemed to leak out, that and her sleeplessness. She had arranged a river nature walk with the herbalist and Sarah tomorrow, a talk about the health benefits of herbs. Maybe Carmel should procure a stronger dose of that Pick-Me-Up for her nerves, and another bottle of Women's Tonic wouldn't go astray either.

That evening was the same as most evenings since they'd lost the child. She and Dan seemed to be at a loss as to how to pick up their lives again; mostly they just grumbled at each other, especially once Sarah had retired to her room. She was a quiet one, hard to get to know, but at least she kept herself to herself, didn't ask awkward questions, not like Emily. That Madden one had never stopped with the questions, had gone on and on about the 'jumping' Sacred Hearts. Pointed out that one week there were six in a row, the next only five and one higher and to the right. Carmel told her it was all in her head. The next week Emily was at it again, calling Carmel into the living room to show her that there were now four Sacred Hearts in a row, and two on the opposite wall. Carmel laughed it off. The Lord moves in mysterious ways, she told the girl. She wasn't telling anyone that her husband had begun to box the wall when he came home late at night. Not that many would believe her. She looked at Dan sitting across from her, all respectable and indignant over something he was reading.

'Canon Boyle has the right attitude – did you read this?'

'Oh, I did,' said Carmel, though she had no idea what Canon Boyle had said. She just wanted to stop Dan from telling her all about it. But there was no stopping him when he got into his stride.

'He's of the opinion, like myself, that it's more vigilance we need, not less. To keep the – listen to this, Carmel – "filth of modern romance" out of the country. I've said as much myself, haven't I? About them books. Great minds think alike.'

'A great mind, is it, you have now?'

Dan didn't hear her as he folded up the newspaper with grim satisfaction. He acted like everything that was anti-Catholic had in some way contributed to their misfortune, as if not reading would bring them children. He hated Irish writers, hated foreign writers, hated women writers. Nothing was highbrow enough for Dan; yet all he bought were local newspapers and skinny Westerns. They weren't highbrow, they were no brow. Not that he read them much; he was too busy with schemes for the shop. He wanted to put a bench outside on the path to encourage people to stop. Seems they all sat in the street in Paris. He saw it on a postcard. The bench had to be primed first. A great man for solving things with a lick of paint. It couldn't solve everything, though. Couldn't freshen a marriage, cover those cracks.

They were five years married this September. Carmel hadn't paid much attention when Dan first started coming into the shop; he was just some young buck from Tipperary who had palled up with Mick Murphy while they were working in England. Then one day he asked to take her to the pictures. Simple as that. People would talk – he was a good ten years younger – that was her first thought. Her second was: *He's so handsome.* The second thought won.

They saw *Of Human Bondage.* Leslie Howard was a fine actor, but she didn't enjoy one minute of it. Dan winced every time Bette Davis spoke and grumbled all the way through her hysterics. She asked him if he wanted to leave, but no, he didn't. He couldn't tear his eyes off the screen, didn't put his arm around her or say a word till it was over.

'Well, that was a holy disgrace. That woman behaved no better than an animal. It should be reported for indecency.'

That should've told her everything she needed to know about Dan. He had lots of opinions like that, lots of gems. He saved the best till they were married.

'Marital relations are solely for the production of children.'

That became their weekly obligation. No children came, not for four long years, and when one finally did, they lost him. Since that day, Carmel and Dan had passed most evenings tormenting each other.

'When my mother was alive –' Carmel might begin.

And then Dan would say, 'I'm sick of hearing about when your mother was alive.'

Did he have to shout?

'When my mother was alive, she never raised her voice –'

'She could hardly raise it after, could she?'

Dan was such a short-tempered man, though on one of her visits his mother claimed he'd the patience of a saint. Carmel took that at face value till she realized it was meant as a rebuke: that Dan must've had the patience of a saint to put up with Carmel. Flighty, her mother-in-law called her, when Carmel was the one who did the cooking, laundry, cleaning, accounts, dealt with the wholesalers. Or used to. No wonder she needed a glass or two of tonic to get a decent night's sleep.

She looked over at him and noticed a shadow on his lip. She peered more closely and saw it was the beginnings of a 'tache. She couldn't help herself.

'Dan, there's a bit of dirt over your lip. Here, do this' – she licked her finger and rubbed her own lip – 'and see will it come off.'

She roared laughing.

He growled and called her an ignorant old lush.

Old indeed. Just because he was only twenty-six. It wouldn't be worth remarking on if it were the other way around, but people talked. Carmel knew how jealous women could be. *Jeeze*, Carmel thought but didn't say. She wasn't allowed to say that word. Dan said it was 'an abbreviated blasphemy'.

Sometimes Carmel almost missed her mother. A fat ball, rarely kind but always dignified. That's how Carmel remembered her, now that she was gone. She kept some memories, and buried the rest. Tried to forget the venom that had poured hot from her mother's mouth. Dan didn't like her mentioned. It interfered with his notions. They'd barely been married when he seemed to convince himself that he had built the shop, brick upon brick, with his own bare hands. Dan had the happy knack of believing his own bull.

'We're established since 1880. A family business.'

He never added that it had had nothing to do with him. Maybe his brother Harry wasn't the black sheep; maybe it was Dan.

'They should be rounded up, every single last one of them, with their books and films . . .' He was back talking about the writers.

'Ah, live and let live,' Carmel said; 'save your energy for growing your moustache.'

'Carmel, you don't live' – Dan almost hopped off the chair; she had hit the sore spot, his manliness – 'you . . . you wallow. You wallow, you whinge, you nag and you drink.'

'Excuse me, Dan, but I'm the one who –'

'Excuse, excuse nothing.' He grabbed the newspaper and flung it on the floor between them. 'I'm sick of bickering, sick of ending the day like this, sick of us.'

'Well, maybe you should find someone else to round off your day with, Dan Holohan, someone more to your liking?'

'Well, maybe I should. Maybe I will.'

Dan went into the kitchen, slamming the door after him, almost shattering the glass. Then she heard the back door bang shut. He was going into the garden to calm down – to see Eliza no doubt, to call her a great girl, to tell her all. Whispering in the dark to an over-fed hog. How laughable. *Laugh, Carmel, laugh, girl. Now why on earth are you crying?*

21

After arranging the excursion, as she called it, Carmel never even got out of bed to join them. Left Sarah the task of accompanying the herbalist. They walked from the shop in silence. As they turned to take the slip down to the river, he stopped and looked at Sarah's face.

'Ah, it *is* you,' he said, smiling.

Even without her earrings, shawl and lipstick, the herbalist had finally recognized her. He thanked her for her assistance in April, winked at her, claimed kinship.

'We are both outsiders, with an interest in herbs,' he said.

Sarah told him that she had no special interest. They were everywhere. It was as silly as saying you had an interest in air.

'I understand,' he said, 'but I can help you, you can help me. We can help each other.'

Sarah didn't want his help. She said nothing.

They arrived at the river: the hedges were creamy with cow parsley. Setting off in the direction of the lock gates, he called over his shoulder to her: 'Tell me what you see, Sarah – what plants can you name that I may not know of yet? Or are all of these' – the herbalist waved his hand – 'just bothersome . . . weeds?'

He had already told Sarah that he didn't believe in the word 'weeds'; it saddened him, like the term 'itinerant salesman'. She caught up with him reluctantly, listening as he expounded on the importance of a herbalist to a community. How someone with his knowledge of health and botany could treat people using the bounty of nature along with the wonderful formulations he was able to acquire from London and Dublin. *What formulations*, she wondered, but didn't ask. When he talked like that, it felt like a trap. Sarah wished that they weren't alone. He plucked the head of a white blossom twining through the hedge and proffered it towards her for identification.

III

'Bindweed,' Sarah said.

She touched the petal, had always loved how it was shaped like the mouth of a trumpet, and was so fragile, thinner than skin even. A hair's breath. What did that mean? The herbalist picked another flower and brought it to his nose.

'No smell, no use,' he announced.

'Tell that to the hawkmoth.'

A moth was diving from flower to flower collecting nectar.

'Must have a long tongue.'

She blushed. They walked on towards the lock gates. The water was high. He took her basket as she stepped to cross. There was no need. She didn't want him to act like a suitor; he was much too unsuitable. She looked to see if anyone had witnessed it, but there was no one around. The herbalist didn't notice her discomfort; he'd already reached the far bank and was kneeling down beside some plant, whistling. A cone-shaped leaf curled around a thick red anther.

'Can you name it?'

Again, she felt it was a question he must know the answer to. He must; everyone did.

'Lords and ladies,' she said, walking over to him. 'The root's full of starch; it was used for stiffening clothes, collars and cuffs. I wouldn't handle them much if I were you; some say they're poisonous.'

He pulled a handkerchief from his breast pocket.

'So, it's beautiful but dangerous?'

He was trying to flirt. What did poor Emily see in him at all? Playing the woman and she barely grown? He could be charming enough when he wanted, she supposed, but when he looked at Sarah like that, all she wanted to do was get away. She realized that he saw her as a challenge. Any attempts to be cool towards him would only make him more fascinated. He muttered something in a tone of reproof to himself. She felt rude. It embarrassed her; she wished she were somewhere else. Wished Carmel had got out of bed. She heard Dan complain about having to make excuses for her at Mass again.

'What will the people think?'

They couldn't mind their own business around these parts. Tell them nothing, Mai had warned her, too nosy for their own good by half, townspeople. The herbalist wasn't nosy in the same way – more of an inquiring mind. Or so he claimed. He wrapped his handkerchief around the plant and uprooted it.

He carried it carefully as they walked back over the lock gates, not taking her basket this time. The bushes crowded on to the path of the waterway, completely obscuring their view of the town. He could do her harm and nobody would ever see. Sarah began to make haste.

'Late?'

'Just hungry – dinner will be on soon.'

They passed the gushing weir in silence. He stopped and sat on a wooden bench. The plant on his lap looked like a mint-green hand. He seemed tired. Reluctantly, she joined him. The willows behind them rustled and whispered, though there was no wind that she could feel.

'I'll rest a while here. You go on home to your meal. Thank you for the pleasure of your company.'

She rose and he said, 'Miss Whyte,' nodding with mock formality.

'Doctor,' she said, imitating his tone.

As she walked away, relief made Sarah feel generous, and she turned to give him a wave. He was looking at her seriously, carefully. She dropped her hand and walked on under the horse-bridge. The stone path was greasy, smooth as soap. Her steps echoed. Grooves were scored into the arch wall: marks left from when barges were horse-drawn, from years of ropes eating into the stone. A phrase came to mind: *Evil lurks here.* And so it did. Didn't it? When she got home, they asked how it went.

'Lovely,' she said.

But, if she were to tell the truth, though nothing untoward had occurred, it had been a deeply unpleasant experience.

Why did you take such a dislike to Sarah, when you barely knew her?

A lot goes on how you meet a person. Well, when Aggie met Sarah, she met a seductress – that's right, a seductress, weaving sticky traps for all of us. So, to me, she was a spider, she was poisonous. Don't look at me like that! I suppose you think I first met her in Kelly's, like you did? Not a bit. Here's a riddle for you: when I met Sarah, she was a stranger and she was familiar.

It went like this. Aggie never forgets a face, but when I saw that girl behind the counter with Dan Holohan I couldn't put a finger on where I'd seen her before. I was tucked up in bed by the time I realized who she was. It was the way she was dressed that had put me off; she was all dowdy, her hair tightly plaited, not all done up, like it had been in the market. Yes, that's right, the market. That's where I first met Sarah Whyte. It was the very first day the herbalist appeared. *Funny*, thought I, *how she arrived at the same time as the herbalist, funny how no one noticed, distracted by her wares – by her glinting eyes, her sleek dark hair.* 'I rinse it in rainwater; you should try it,' she'd said. Sure we all rinsed our hair in rainwater, but it didn't look like that. Who trawled to the pump for wash water? Didn't the herbalist himself get up at cock-crow to sluice himself at the rain barrel? Didn't I see him with my own eyes? Not a stitch on him. A nice way to start the day, I must say.

Am I going in circles? I like going in circles. Where was I? Yes, it was the first week he arrived and people were standing around his table; they were gawking and listening to his selling talk, but no one was buying, no one wanted to be the first, the amadán, in case it turned out to be a pile of shite. He had face creams for keeping wrinkles at bay, tonics for the sleepless, rubs for sore feet, hair-revival oil, mixtures for dry coughs, wet coughs, itchy throats . . . you name it, he had it, and had it corked and sealed.

'My customers look younger and healthier by the week; by the time I leave they have the health of the wealthy. Sometimes I can hardly recognize them!'

Fine talk, but it was met with silence – and that's when we heard her velvet voice. 'Do you have a special ointment, your own soothing skin cream?'

'Right here, madam.'

'My friend lent me some and it has worked wonders for my complexion. Wonders.'

We all turned to look at the girl who had spoken. She was tall with pearly skin, not one blemish, and healthy pink lips and white teeth like from a beauty advertisement. Her hair was swept back from her forehead and waved down her back. She had rings in her ears: not clip-ons – they went right through, like a gypsy's. She wore a gold-fringed shawl, like one of those exotics from the carnival.

One by one the people bought. She started to talk to the woman beside her, admired her ugly baba. No one doubted her, no one said, 'Sure she's a stranger, we don't listen to strangers. Who are you? Where do you hail from?' No one said boo to the beautiful lady; they just took her cue and started parting with their money. I'd say everyone that heard her speak bought something that day. That was just a taste of her power.

When weeks later I met her in the shop, and put two and two together, I thought that she and the Indian herbalist must've been in cahoots all along. Wouldn't anyone – wouldn't you? Though credit where credit is due – I've a keen eye, and not many would've made the connection. The country girl behind the counter seemed worlds apart from the lovely woman from the market. She'd looked so different that day – made up, glamorous and something else, glowing I suppose, as if she was in love.

22

I was lying in the long grass, catching a bit of sun, reading *Woman's Life* on Sunday afternoon, when who did I see canoodling along together – only Sarah and my herbalist. She had her hair loose and was carrying a basket full of weeds. They passed me on the river path as if I didn't exist and headed towards the town. Alone! Together! And I only permitted to sneak around under moonlight. I banned and she allowed. Had I not seen them part that second, I would've parted them myself.

I went to his place that night to express my grave disappointment. There was no answer. I went around the back, climbed the low wall and threw gravel at the tin roof. Made a hell of a racket, but the herbalist never came out. What did I hear then only someone singing near by and coming nearer? I crept back around to the side of the shed. 'Tea for two, and two for tea, just me for you, and you for me . . .' Charlie. I ducked down as he turned into the lane. What did he want? I heard him knock at the herbalist's door and then him and the herbalist muttering. After a minute he left, no longer singing, his hobnails striking the ground. He crossed the square quickly and was swallowed up into the night. I jumped down and knocked on the herbalist's door. One, two, three. Open sesame.

The herbalist wouldn't let me in. My brother was looking for me, and it upset the herbalist that Charlie had guessed I might be there.

'You told on us!' His fingers were speckled with black.

'I never told Charlie anything.'

'Then how would he know to come here?'

'Someone must've seen me.'

Did he think I was invisible or what? I would've loved a hot cup, but he said I wasn't allowed, that we'd have a real break this time, a holiday from each other.

'Like a siesta?'

'No, longer than that.'

'Why is she allowed? Sarah? I saw her.'

'It's just business.'

'Well, give it up, your business, whatever it is.'

'Don't be silly.'

He shut the door in my face without a by-your-leave. I called and called him. A voice carried clear as anything through the dark.

'Put a sock in it! You'll wake the dead!' Aggie roared.

'Old bitch!' I shouted back.

Something cuffed my head. She was right beside me, oozing gin, filth and sin.

'Think you're above me? You're right next to me and you don't even know it.' She laughed into my face.

The door opened then, and the herbalist, he stepped out and yanked me in by the arm. Anything to avoid a scene. I didn't mind. I was delighted to be let in.

'It's only for a few minutes, till you see sense,' he said.

'Isn't Aggie an ugly old toad?' I said.

'Maybe if someone kisses her she'll turn into a princess?'

'That one, she changes into nothing – she barely changes her clothes!'

'Whist about her.'

He wasn't outraged enough, as far as I was concerned. But at least he forgot for a while about keeping me away, about what the people would say. And I forgot all about Charlie. There was no kissing – it was like the kissing had never happened – it was all him going on about his new concoctions. Of course, I was evicted at first light, and scurried away like a thief, my tongue bitter from all the potions he'd had me test during the night.

Later I dreamt a strong one, heard a crowd cheering me on. I was in a boxing ring with Sarah. Dancing circles around her. Then I knocked her on the flat of her back with a punch, and when she fell her skirt flew up and everyone saw her silly frilly drawers. I ended up with a restless sleep full of night terrors, and in the last dream, the one that shook me awake, I was falling, falling past all that was righteous and good to sit at the right hand of the devil. Our thrones were side by side, red velvet, gilt gold and high. Then someone ousted me from my place: she had blue eyes and a deadly glare. She was there. Then she disappeared. I trusted her absence less than her presence. It filled me with a cold fear. It tore me from my sleep.

No matter what I said, he wouldn't let me back. All I could do was watch the women trooping constantly to and from his door. So on Monday, I told Mrs Holohan exactly where her fine shop girl was tripping to on her Sundays off. Carmel just acted annoyed with me, said that I wasn't in any position to be so pass remarkable, that Sarah was a respectable woman on a nature excursion and to take my elbows off her counter.

I waited by the town hall on the next market day. I was going to make him see sense by acting normal and calm, and showing him that nobody would complain about us being friends. Why would they?

All the stall-holders had set up, but there was only a space where he should have been. I waited for an hour and then I got worried – what if he was sick or in trouble?

When he didn't answer my knock, I let myself in. A towel over the window blocked out the light. The place smelt like wet dog, or worse. The herbalist was on top of the bed-covers, stripped down to his vest, shivering. A woman was tattooed on his shoulder, and he didn't even try to hide her. I cleared my throat. He took his hand from over his eyes, peeked and shooed me away. I wasn't going anywhere and he was in no condition to make me.

'What's wrong with you?'

'I'm tormented, Emily,' he said.

'Can you not cure yourself?'

'Some things have to be sweated out.'

He made a sour face and started to ramble, but at least he let me stay on. I sat on the bed. He didn't seem to care. His breath reeked of alcohol. I couldn't make out what was going on.

He soon told me everything. It turned out that he was tortured by demons. It was a real battle: he got the sweats and the shakes, but he always won in the end. Most times he was as fit as a fiddle, but when the devils came he had to take a few days off. Just to lie low.

He said the devils got in through the skin, so a man had to be very careful. He had to wash, wash, wash his hands. The newly born were closest to clean, but the old were filthy, right next to hell. He tugged my cuff and began to whisper. I leant in: he called me Cleopatra, said I should be bathed in milk. He cried, and said other things, mixed-up things that I didn't understand. I just studied the hula girl on his shoulder. Her lovely long black hair went right down her back. She wore nothing but a grass skirt, a garland and a smile. She wasn't coloured in, so her skin was his skin – dark like treacle. I placed my palm over her body. He sat up.

'Old hula hula's just for fun,' he said; 'wait till you see this – this is the real business.'

He opened out his arm, and on the inside crook was a fat coiled cobra. It was the shape of an *s* and was patterned with jade-green triangles. I had glimpsed its tail that morning I saw him shave. The fanged mouth opened wide to let a forked tongue shoot out.

'I call her Ruby. Go on, touch her.'

I placed my fingertip on the threads of red that were her tongue. I put my tongue between my teeth and let out a little hiss. I didn't know why I did that.

'Ruby has the power to make the devils go away.'

I giggled. I shouldn't have. He jumped up from the bed as if he was on fire, leant against the wall, held his snaked arm out straight and roared towards the darkened window. 'Off with you!

'That's one less devil in the room.' He looked at me, as if for a round of applause.

'Which one was it?' I asked, going along with him.

'Beelzebub – but he's gone now, the black-tongued demon!'

He leant back on the bed, rootled under his pillow and brought out a bottle to uncork with his front teeth.

'Why did you get tattooed?' I asked.

'To put terror into the heart of the enemy.' He smiled, without really smiling.

'I thought only jailbirds and sailors had them.'

'You'd be surprised. I met a well-off woman once who had a swallow.'

'Where?' I asked. He smiled properly then, but wouldn't tell.

Then he wanted for me to go home, but I explained that I couldn't, that there were demons in my house too: they lived in my father's hands. He was an old man and evil, pure evil. He had medals for killing. The herbalist told me my father couldn't be wholly evil because I was his issue.

'His blood runs through you.'

'I want him out of me!'

I screamed, and screamed. Sick with the thought. If I could have, I would've bled him out of me. It's funny, but my being so frightened seemed to calm him. He comforted me, soothed me down. He gave me a mug of strong tonic. It tasted of liquorice.

Then somehow I was standing in a tub. Warm water was being poured over my head. There was a beautiful humming. I felt strange – the room swayed.

'Emily, for the first time in your young life you are clean.'

He put me on the bed then and pressed love and goodness into me. It hurt at first. Afterwards he popped a boiled sweet into my mouth and called me Cleopatra again. It was a lemon drop, with sherbet in the centre, my favourite.

23

Sarah loved opening shop, loved the way the light lit the silence first thing in the morning. But this morning wasn't so peaceful. As soon as Sarah unlocked the door, Mr Gogarty burst through it, brimming with vim and vitriol. The solicitor was a short stout man who walked as if hurled forward by his own importance.

'Where's the missus?'

'Not here at the moment.'

Mr Gogarty was one of the 'come on through to the living room' people, those who came often but bought nothing. Those who were escorted into the back by Carmel with the small smile, secretive air and fluttering hand movements that she obviously mistook for discretion.

'Well, give her this from me' – he whacked a novel on to the counter – 'and tell her she can keep her old penny books, they're only a waste of time. There's nothing' – he jabbed the novel with his finger – 'nothing at all in that.'

And off he went. Sarah held the book on her lap under the counter. The cover was brown with a long and convoluted title: *The Fortunes and Misfortunes of the Famous Moll Flanders; also, The Fortunate Mistress, or The Lady Roxana.*

A lot of titles for so plain a book. The word 'mistress' caught her eye. This couldn't be a book from the library. You'd never find that word in there. It opened on a much-thumbed page. 'We had not sat long, but he got up, and, stopping my very breath with kisses, threw me upon the bed again; but then being both well warmed, he went farther with me than decency permits me to mention, nor had it been in my power to have denied him at that moment, had he offered much more than he did.'

It wasn't something Sarah felt easy handing over, so she just left it on the shelf under the counter, as if she had forgotten it. 'Stopping my very breath with kisses' indeed.

Carmel came into the shop looking harassed.

'I had the misfortune to meet Mr Gogarty on the road. That man is always complaining about something. Was he in here . . . complaining to you, Sarah?'

'I'm afraid so.'

'Was he talking about a certain book by any chance?'

'He was.'

'Look, Sarah,' Carmel asked, 'are you a reader?'

Without waiting for an answer, she continued, 'Well, I'm a great reader, all my family are great readers, and I suppose that's how this started.'

Carmel's eyes were sleepy, but she was talking lively enough, whispering and gesticulating and the like.

'My brother Finbar's an educated man, with contacts in Customs, and the gardaí. He's a great friend to the clergy too. And through all those connections he found himself with a certain amount of literature that was seized, so to speak . . .'

She paused, as if waiting for some reaction from Sarah, but Sarah wasn't sure what she was talking about.

'. . . and now he has a whole, a whole room full of books still in their dust jackets.'

Carmel said this as if her brother possessed a room crammed with gold bars. It was the first time Sarah saw a resemblance between Carmel and her brother. The way she was smiling and saying one thing, yet you felt there was something else behind it, something darker. She seemed to have forgotten that it was Finbar, as she called him, who had arranged Sarah's position with them. And that as well as the gardaí and the clergy, he also counted amongst his great friends her aunt Mai, humble midwife.

'Sure it was Master Kelly who put me forward for this position – he's a friend of the family.'

'Yes. Well, it pains Finbar to see good books wasted, so he gave them to me. Of course I read them before I rent them out – I'm obliged to. I have to be very particular about who I lend them to;

not everyone would be able to understand them as works of literature. Now you see why I'm too busy for the shop and everything?'

Sarah didn't see how eating apples up in bed and reading books
could be a terrible cross to bear.

'He'd be in awful trouble for giving me such books, corrupting
my mind.' She laughed a short bitter *hah*. 'I rent them to discreet
people, and, as long as they're returned, I'm all right. We all have to
be discreet – do you know what I mean?'

Sarah knew what she meant. Carmel was running a sideline renting out racy books. Carmel brought her to the kitchen, took a narrow
black key from her pocket and unlocked the cupboard.

'I run a respectable establishment.' She poked Sarah with the key,
as if Sarah had rebuked her instead of nodding obediently.

There were three deep shelves, and on the bottom was a large
box of books. Some were bound together with thick elastic bands;
some were loose.

'There's little in that lot for the government to be worrying
about. Mr Holohan isn't aware of the extent of my part-time work.
He wouldn't approve – he's overly fond of Mr de Valera. He thinks
this press is for female hygiene products.'

She didn't blush. Sarah wondered if she used to be a nurse.

'I carry a wide range, not like your one across the road, Lady
Chatterley, who only deals in notoriety. A few copies of the same
filthy book pawed to pieces.'

'Miss Chase?'

Sarah was surprised; the shopkeeper didn't strike her as someone
who would be involved in anything so shabby.

'She thinks it's a secret, but I'm on to her – the whole town is on
to her. Swanking around like butter wouldn't melt in her mouth.
How she got copies of that book I'll never know.'

'Have you read it?'

'No, I haven't.' Carmel couldn't keep the disappointment out of
her voice.

Carmel warned Sarah not to breathe a word about it to anyone.
Surely she knew Sarah hadn't a single friend to tell, even if she were
the telling type, which she wasn't?

The shop bell rang. Carmel closed the door of the cupboard and turned the key.

'Not a word to Mr Holohan. He cares not a whit for the running of the household, thank God.'

When they returned to the shop, there was a woman leaning on the counter, sobbing. It was Mrs Birmingham, dressed in an old cardigan. Carmel linked her into the back. Sarah heard the rise and fall of Mrs Birmingham's woes and Carmel's murmurs of sympathy. Her brother Patrick had died. Mr Birmingham wouldn't give her the fare to England for his funeral. And that wasn't all: there was Rose, 'telling lies again, saying awful things'.

The door closed gently between the living area and the shop.

Sarah wondered what the trouble could be with Rose. The girl was always so fresh, so bubbly, so squeaky clean. She hadn't been around much these past few days. Busy with her studies, they were told. 'A studious girl is my daughter.' How did Mrs Birmingham keep a straight face? Studious? Rose would sell her soul for a bar of Yardley soap.

The women trooped back into the shop, Mrs Birmingham sniffing up her sorrow, Carmel padding behind her like the cat that had got the cream.

'Wait, I almost forgot.' Mrs Birmingham began to rifle through her massive handbag.

'Oh, no, really –' Carmel started.

'Ah, found it.' She tucked a small card into Carmel's hand. 'I bought this for you. May it bring you and Mr Holohan the luck you so richly deserve.' She added, lowering her voice, 'You know yourself what I mean. It's a grade two.'

'Bless your heart, thank you, Grettie.'

Carmel opened the door for the woman. Went out on to the path after her and waved her off down the road. When she returned, Carmel looked towards the ceiling and addressed the Lord.

'And there was me thinking she was finally going to settle her bill. Feck her, and feck her bloody dead brother! She's as mean today as she was in school.'

She threw the card on to the counter and trotted off. Sarah picked it up: a prayer to St Thérèse, the Little Flower, on thin, almost transparent paper with a relic stuck on – a smidgen of raw-edged blue cloth. Grade two. Did that mean it had touched the cloth that had touched the cloth that had touched the saint? Or was that a grade three? Sarah couldn't remember. It was pretty. A wreath of red roses circled the face of a beautiful young nun whose lips were drawn in a cupid's bow. Sarah put it in her pocket.

From then on, when she took her naps, Carmel trusted Sarah with the key to the banned-novels cupboard. At first, Sarah was flattered. Later she realized that Mr Gogarty's outburst had left Carmel no choice. Sarah flicked through the books. Most were long-winded explorations of gritty lives and nothing to get excited about. The opposite in fact. They pulsed with grisly loneliness, destitution and poverty. Nothing at all threatening. It didn't occur to Sarah that one day Master Finbar might come by to collect them.

24

Lo and behold, didn't I have a swanky customer first thing on Saturday morning? Rose of all people, and without her mother. A rare happening. I don't think Mrs B knew where she was. Don't ask me why, it was just a feeling. I hinted that we should do the fitting in her house next time. I'd never seen past their fancy tiled hallway, always wondered what was behind the door that led to their living quarters. I could hint all I liked, but Rose didn't bite – said she preferred to come to me. I knew why too. The looks she threw at Charlie when she came in! And my poor brother beaming back like dark clouds had parted to let the light of God shine down on him and him alone. You should've heard her.

'All the boys have grown as brown as Indians – it makes some of them look like Errol Flynn.'

'Ah, everyone is better looking under the sun,' I said; 'come on upstairs.'

Rose skipped up the stairs after me, and then she did a funny thing: she stopped at my bedroom door and began to examine it.

'This is a very hardy door. You've a lock, and a latch?'

'Aye, it's the old shed door. Charlie hung it for me. Are you fond of carpentry?'

She laughed like that was the funniest thing ever. Rose was harmless enough, even if her mother was a horror. But I liked things as they were for Charlie. Rita was good to him. I didn't want Rose toying with him, passing time until her father selected some upstanding bachelor to pair her off with.

I took her measurements – wasn't a pick on her. I'd the vital statistics of quite a lot of ladies in my copybook. I lifted Rose's hem out of the way as I knelt to take her length. She moved to stop me but was too late. I saw them. Her knees.

'Jesus Christ, what happened to your knees?'

They were destroyed. Criss-crossed with white and purple scars. Covered in thick, cracked scabs. The flesh was pulpy, red raw in places. And there were cuts going up her thighs.

'I want a pretty light cotton dress. Long, if you please.'

'But what happened to your knees?'

'Blue, a pale blue, with buttons all the way down the front, and flowers.'

I looked up from where I was crouched. She stared towards the window. The rope swing was moving back and forth in the breeze. One fat tear ran down her jaw, along her neck and into the hollow of her collarbone. I rolled up my tape.

'Rose, what happened to your poor knees?'

'Nothing. I'm just a very clumsy girl.' Her voice was chirpy, broken.

'Did you hear Charlie? He said summer suits me. Whatever does that mean?' She laughed, tugged one of her crisp platinum curls.

There was no talking to her. No getting an answer.

We said our goodbyes downstairs. Rose stuck her slight chest out and swivelled her hips as she waltzed out of the door. Charlie just stared with a really stupid smile on his face. When she was gone, he started singing that stupid song, 'Tea for two, and two for tea, just me for you and you for me . . . alone.'

He had changed his tune. He used to tease me over John Gilbert. Told me romance had brought on the Great Lover's early death, that he'd been a fatal victim of the kissing disease. Even one kiss could wither the healthy. That kind of talk tormented me, for I had seen him with my own two eyes, Mr Gilbert. It wasn't long before he died, and no one had known that death was imminent then, not even him, the poor lamb. They were showing a matinee of *Queen Christina* and the queue was atrocious. I was itching to see what all the fuss was about but knew I wouldn't be let in; I was too young.

I hung about, waiting to sneak through. A posh woman was kicking up a fuss at the door. Only room in the pit, Beardie Billy told her, only room in the pit. He shone his lamp back into the full picture house so she could see for herself. It was like a blue moon jigging over the rows of heads.

127

The woman wanted to go in, I could tell – was only dying to run in to see the Great Lover – but she was too posh for the pit.

'The picture is starting, madam.'

That's when I squeezed by, the invisible girl. I couldn't see the steps in front of me. I tripped and burnt my knee but scuffled on towards the first bench in the pit. Didn't care if I was pulled out by the scruff of my neck as long as I got a glance at John Gilbert. The usher shut the doors and pitched us into complete darkness.

I don't remember what the funnies were that day; I only remember *Queen Christina*. The queen was a reckless spirit – you wouldn't know if she was a man or a woman till she swept her hat off. You should've seen Garbo, leaping from her horse, taking her castle steps two at a time, dismissing her noble advisers with a wave of her hand and falling into John Gilbert's arms. It would make you swoon. You should've seen Gilbert; you should've seen the eyes on him, dark as ink, as chocolate, as sin. He ruined me for anyone else. That afternoon filled me for ever with the longing for my own great lover. I ran home and was so excited that I forgot to hide my sin, told everyone that John Gilbert was like God made man. *Emily, what a thing to say!*

A while afterwards I was in the dispensary, waiting for the nurse to be finished with Mam. The doctor was running late again; maybe someone rich was sick. The women were grumbling. They were always grumbling.

'His mother ruined him.'

'Who'd blame her? I'd ruin him.'

'Died of a heart attack.'

'The doctor's dead?' I asked.

'Whist, child. It's John Gilbert, Gilbert's dead.'

'Children should be seen and not heard.' Mrs Brennan reached out and slapped my hand.

'He had an operation and got an infection.'

'Did not – he had a heart attack.'

'He died of an infection, I tell you!'

'He would've died of old age waiting to be seen here.'

I got some dirty looks then, because it was Mam holding some of

128

them up. I was crying snots from being smacked and the shock of John Gilbert's death.

'Women swooned at his funeral.'

'Poor Garbo will kill herself.'

'Don't be sacrilegious in front of the child.'

'I saw him once,' I said, heartbroken.

'Will you stop, you're only a baba!'

No one paid any heed to my grief at home. They thought it funny when I lit a few candles for him, hilarious when I asked for money to get a Mass said for the repose of the soul of John Gilbert. That's what too much kissing gets you, Charlie said. Heartless. They hadn't seen him. They didn't know.

25

Carmel went into the shop to collect the tin of Aggie's coins. Dan had insisted they rinse her money. Expected the notes to be washed too, but she'd rather be damned than hang up pounds to dry. It was a bit of a fuss, but Aggie was their only customer who didn't owe a small fortune.

Dan was tightening a hinge on the shutters. Sarah was on the ladder, taking down a box of caramel creams from the shelf above the window. She tripped as she put her foot to the floor and Dan reached out and held her elbow to steady her. Carmel could've sworn she saw something pass between them. Sarah's stupid smile and that glance from Dan. If anything happened to Carmel, that Sarah would be quick as lightning into her house, her kitchen, her bed. Pictures of them together came to her, smiling into each other's eyes, whispering hot I love yous, full of that early sweetness. It made her feel pinched and angry. Carmel wanted to turn around and slap Dan. He was beaming. Had he the same picture in his head as she had?

It felt so real – more real than Carmel standing there beside him, or these past few weeks of tiresome arguing. Or those long stretches alone while he'd worked across the water. Dan hinted that he might go again; a lot of the men were. He might be trying to keep her on her toes, or maybe he was serious. Money was as scarce now as it had been then.

She hadn't wanted her husband labouring in England, mixing with all sorts. 'My year as a widow', Carmel called it; eleven months, Dan always corrected her. As if there was a big difference, though there was. She worried that he'd get more than his hands dirty. 'It's only for a few months,' he had said. It was all Mick Murphy's idea. That gobshite was full of great ideas. Though only for Mick, Carmel mightn't be married at all. It was he who had met Dan working on a big job in England and brought him to the town when it finished up. Carmel and Dan had been married for only three months when Mick announced there was more work for them over there.

Every day he was away Carmel missed him sorely. She couldn't warm up in bed on her own. She couldn't find a book to settle into. The wireless was a poor substitute. Dan sent a few bob, but there was no sign of him coming home. Carmel wrote she was going over. He wrote back, 'Don't be daft.'

She went so far as to go to the chemist's to get her photo taken for a Travel Identity card. Stood stiffly in front of the hump-backed tripod with her hair coiffed, trying to look jolly in case people started to talk.

'A holiday, Carmel?'

'That's right, Mr Martin.'

As she left, she heard him laughing to his assistant – another one off to bring the husband home from England. Dan must've got wind of her activities, because he was back within a fortnight.

She'd never forget the sight of him in the doorway. His hair was shorn and his nose was sunburnt; he dropped his case and opened his arms. He smelt of a soap she didn't own. 'My little wren,' he whispered into her neck, as he squeezed her and lifted her high. Then, as if caught unawares by his own affection, he started to cry.

It was through Lizzie that Carmel heard about the lodgings the men had shared in London. Mick, the big eejit, told her everything. Seemed the landlady had mixed lodgings, men and women. Mick's rip of a mother could barely conceal her excitement.

'Delia was her name. And get this, Mrs Holohan, she allowed women to lodge under the same roof as our fine men.'

'Who on earth are you talking about?'

'The landlady across the water. Where my Mick and your Dan and half the town stayed, stayed with fallen women, and their off-spring to boot. Widows, Mick said they called themselves. Aye, tin rings and imaginary husbands.'

'I highly doubt it,' Carmel replied; 'my Dan wouldn't stay a second in such a place.'

'Ah, when in Rome . . .' Lizzie Murphy flashed a gummy grin.

Carmel had quizzed Dan.

'Old gummy-face told me all about that blowzy British bitch.'

'Stop it,' Dan said, looking wounded. 'She was a decent woman, and charged very reasonable rates.'

That infuriated Carmel.

'There were female lodgers! Did you meet them over breakfast? Oh, I can just see it: "Pass the buttermilk, you trollop." You wouldn't tolerate the carry-on of that here!'

'The rules are different over there.'

'Decency is decency, no matter where you are.'

She tortured Dan and herself with questions for months after. She'd say 'Go back to London' or 'You're not in London now', sounding just like her mother.

'You deserted me.'

'I sent a wage. Lots of men do it.'

He would stand up and leave the room before she could really get going.

Carmel thought she should tread easily this time round. Maybe the glance between her husband and the shop girl was a figment of her imagination. She didn't want Dan scooting off to London.

'Come into the back, Mr Holohan,' she said softly.

Dan looked up and smiled; she led him into the kitchen and sat him down at the table. She took her husband's hand.

'Are you happy with me, Dan?'

'Don't talk like that. Sure isn't everything grand? Aren't we as happy as anyone else, on the pig's back?'

What pig's back? How were they grand? He bore her moodiness, the tears and the odd night sucking from the bottle. And she bore him daily, for nearly everything he said nowadays chilled her.

'Look, Carmel, aren't we glad enough? We're moving towards happy, no different to anyone else.' Dan rubbed her hand and glanced towards the window.

'I nearly forgot poor Eliza; she'll be wanting her feed.'

Carmel watched him leave. Maybe he was right. Who'd be completely happy living like church mice all waiting to have fun in the next life?

She called Sarah in, gave her a few bob and sent her off to buy some stamps and envelopes at the post office – told her to take her time. She hoped there was a queue. Carmel didn't want stamps but she wanted the time. She went into the shop to take over. The place wasn't empty for more than a second. The constant clattering of the bell as customers came in and out began to get on her nerves. She wedged the shop door open, unhooked the bell and placed it on the counter. Dan appeared, mentioned getting some timber for a bookshelf and went out on to the street. Every now and then Dan would talk about building her a bookshelf; he would even make drawings and ask her where she'd like him to put it; but the bookshelf itself never materialized, probably never would. Time flew by – it was busy but Carmel could do it in her sleep. Maybe her health was returning.

It was nice to work alone again. There was something about Sarah. The air changed when she was about. The girl was a good worker and people had taken to her, though they still asked after Emily – who would have thought it? There were two old ones in today, wanting to drop off clothes for mending. Carmel sent them on their way. Even Grettie B, the biggest snob in town, said she missed her, even missed her inane chattering.

Carmel had begun to tot up the afternoon's takings when she felt, rather than saw, Sarah come back in. She was radiant from being outdoors. Carmel excused herself and went through to the kitchen, half hoping that one day soon Sarah would slip out the back door with the silverware like serving girls were meant to.

It was chilly despite the evening sun, so Carmel threw on her mother's ancient brown fur. It had hung for decades on the back door. By now the pocket had torn from the weight of her trowel. She must mend it. She carried the small stool out into the garden. There were so many noises – blackbirds, thrushes and a pigeon's low cooing. The carrots were doing well, their ferny fronds upright and shy. Eliza trotted over, expecting a treat, nudging a damp nose into Carmel's empty palm. She circled her feet like an excited puppy. Dan should sell Eliza before she forgot she was a pig altogether. Carmel led the animal to her pen and tied the gate before strolling towards the end of the garden.

She set her stool in the long grass by the back hedge and sat down. Her back and belly ached. The rosebush was bare of flowers, except for one stem that leant to the ground with the weight of two pink roses. A bumble bee sailed from lavender stem to lavender stem, till one by one they nodded from its attentions. She thought of her baby, his body in the earth, his soul in limbo – all she wanted to do was to wrap some warmth around him. She recited Hail Marys through her tears. She recited the Guardian Angel prayer. Then she sat in silence and listened to the birds.

A dream returned from last night. Dan had something to tell her, something important. She was at the basin rinsing dishes; he had walked into the room and was watching her. He was preserving the seconds before he told her something, something that would make her whole world come crashing down. So the Carmel in the dream didn't turn around; she just washed and washed the one white plate, squeezing the sudsy dishcloth around its rim, circling in towards the centre and out again, determined to wash that plate for ever. That was all she could remember.

Was this all there was going to be of their marriage? A life half lived, love half given? She thought of all the foul words that had been hurled relentlessly back and forth between them, of having nothing worth holding close to her heart. Except for hope. She felt a sharp pain then, the pain that came with every blood time, every month. It was back. She would go to the herbalist that night.

Carmel hurried along. The moon moved behind clouds till the houses, bridge and river flushed dark and melted into the blackness. Rain washed her eyes, her cheeks, dripped from her hair on to the back of her neck. She had left Dan dozing by the fire and would have to be home before he woke. As she walked, she tried to loosen the stopper on the small glass bulb, to save time, but the rain ran over her hands till they were blue knuckled and numb. She stopped at the entrance to the alleyway to check that no one was around. Carmel realized that she was still wearing her slippers, down at heel and sodden. Thank God for the dark. Suddenly she felt old – old and desperate.

She ducked into the alley, ran to his doorway. Gave it two short raps. Waited. Knocked again. As her eyes grew accustomed to the dark, she saw that there'd be no answer; there was a padlock on the grey door. She yanked it, but it wouldn't budge. Where was he? What about her, what about her treatment?

As she shoved the empty bottle back into her pocket, her fingers touched a wet handkerchief – she was soaked through. Carmel walked back the way she had come, her heart pacing, her teeth chattering, ashamed and in naked torment for all to see. In the depths of her pocket, she clutched the empty bottle – it felt like a tiny skull.

You found the herbalist, didn't you, Aggie, after he was beaten? They said he was barely breathing, and that his own cures brought him back from the brink.

Not a bit of it: he wasn't next nor near death. That lad never missed an opportunity to advertise his own wares. But it was me who found him all right. Curled up on his own doorstep. His face drenched red. It took a while to find his key in the pool of blood, but I did and then I dragged him inside. Do you know what he said as I wiped his face? 'Who did it, Aggie?' As if I would know. Wink, wink, nudge, nudge.

'I saw nothing,' said I, taking a snort of snuff. 'I heard a racket, looked out and saw you lying in the gutter. Your old head's sliced. A bottle, I'd say. Why would anyone do that?'

'Ah,' he said, 'they're just jealous.'

I smiled. That was my saying, the one I used to account for my unpopularity with the ladies of the town.

'That well may be.'

The Don didn't recall much except that an ugly mouth came close to his face and snarled. Couldn't recount what happened next. He passed out, woke with a cut in his head. He told me that there had been a few of them, that he'd fought tooth and nail.

I wasn't going to tell him that I'd seen everything, that there'd been only one, a boy less than half his age. I had a soft spot for young Charlie, as well you know – all us ladies did. Whatever 'it' was, Charlie Madden had it in spades. Got it from his father. Brian Madden was a vision in his day.

I ran my nail down the back of his bloodied white shirt.

'It has the look of a map, red, white and dust. What country would that be?'

'What country? It would be mine,' he said.

Ha! I should've known. All about the love of himself.

The herbalist took off his shirt, wrapped it in a sheet of news-paper and went out to the backyard. Burnt it in the bin. Watched it blacken till it was ashes.

'Well, aren't you a strange man?'

'What would you have me do with it?' he asked. 'It could never be worn again.'

'You'd have a duster out of it at worst.'

'Allow my own blood to be rubbed in grime! I should think not.'

He had to bring his fresh split head to old Doctor Birmingham. That near killed him. Pride was a big thing for him. He told me later that Doctor B didn't ask how he'd got the wound, but he didn't go easy on The Don.

'Are you,' the doctor asked, 'are you intoxicated?'

'No,' The Don told him, smart as anything, 'I was set upon by some of your fellow Irishmen.'

'And what did you do to upset them?'

'Nothing.'

Doctor B poured something foul and burning on the wound, let it drip over his forehead and then began to stitch it in the hall of the house, without any ceremony.

'I'm surprised . . .' Doctor B said.

'Surprised at what?'

'That such a great and wonderful doctor as yourself couldn't do the sewing on your own head.'

'I've many things in many places,' The Don told him, 'but I don't have eyes there.'

At that, there had been movement on the stairs. And out of sight of Doctor B, wasn't there pale hair trailing over the banister, as his wife listened to every word?

'All done,' said Doctor B. 'Three and six. I'll send you the bill.'

'Night night, Grettie!' The Don waved towards the staircase and legged it out of there. That was probably the most civilized meeting him and the good doctor ever had. I wondered at The Don being on first-name terms with the doctor's wife; I bet the doctor did too. I'd say the conversation they had when he left was far from civilized, wouldn't you?

The Don wasn't floored for long. One day he was on the ground stinking of piss and blood, and the next standing at his doorway, chipped tooth and all, waving to the women with open arms. 'Ladies, ladies, come on in!' His white shirt opened at the chest, a necklace with a blue stone pendant shining from across the street. Could you be up to him?

Could you be up to anyone in this town? You know, I thought Charlie was protecting his sister's virtue when I saw him leap on the herbalist. Wasn't I a terrible innocent? It wasn't Emily he was fighting for at all, was it? No, it wasn't her.

Is that a smile I see?

26

The Adventures of Robin Hood had returned to the Picture Palace due to popular demand. It was Charlie's day off and I really wanted him to take me. I asked him at breakfast while he was still fuzzy.

'They say Errol Flynn wears no underpants,' I said, joining him at the table.

'Will you shut up saying that? Anyway, I'm busy today. You can come the next time I'm going with a gang.'

Gang my bum, Charlie never went with a gang; Charlie always had a girl. He had started late and was making up for it. No wonder he ate like a horse.

'Are you not going to bring Rita?'

'No, not this time. Pass the marmalade.'

'Will you ask Rose perhaps?' I said. 'You can bring Mrs B too; cuddle up to her fox-fur. Have an old nuzzle-nuzzle.'

'Stop it. You'd need to grow up.' He let on to smack my shoulder; it didn't hurt – Charlie couldn't hurt me if he tried.

'I am grown up,' I said. 'I've got a beau.'

'Ah, will you stop. Don't talk nonsense.'

'I do, he's John Gilbert and Clark Gable all rolled into one. Before Gable grew that fat moustache, I mean. I really don't like that moustache, I hope he trims it . . .'

'That herbalist is a pauper who thinks he's a prince. And if he doesn't stay away from you, I'll make him.' Charlie touched my arm. 'Everyone is laughing at you, Emily.'

He said the last bit softly. I didn't like Charlie saying that so gentle, making it sound almost true.

'I'll keep to my love life; you keep to yours.'

He sighed, and chewed away on his bread.

'How is poor Rita?'

'She's fine, busy enough nowadays. We're just pals.'

'I'd say that suits you. So, who are you seeing on the sly?'

'No one.' He knocked back the rest of his tea.

'You'd like to, though, wouldn't you? Go to the flicks with Rose? Pity, he'd have your guts for garters.'

'Who's *he* when he's at home?'

'Her father of course, the eminent Doctor B.'

'That man's a brute,' he said, shoving his plate away and standing up. 'Cows. I'm off.'

There was no picture house for anyone that afternoon. There was me at home drawing water from the well, carrying bucket after bucket into the kitchen to fill the kettle to put on the fire, because our lad Charlie had decided to wash the windows of the parlour and needed hot water. Then more turf had to be brought in to keep the fire going to heat the water to clean the tiles.

And for what? He said he just wanted it ship-shape.

Well, I wanted to feed the hens and bring in the eggs and clean them. But I had to take out the ashes that had built up from keeping the water boiling hot for Charlie, the new lover of sparkling windows.

I'd have much rather been holding my breath in the picture house, watching the ever so dashing Errol Flynn robbing rich folk. I loved it there. The sticky Highland Toffee, the wait for the picture to begin, the music, the suspense. Oh, there was nothing like it. I even loved the smell of tobacco and brilliantine. The stink of piddle from the flea pit. It was so good to be there in the dark, in a packed smoky picture house, with the stars on the big screen. Watching a man stretch his arm around his girl's shoulder and trying to look casual about it. It was pity to come out again, out of the dark into the bright shining daylight of the same plain town you were born into.

Charlie had the windows wide open to help the tiles dry; he'd even wiped down the walls. He was fierce busy tidying a parlour that no one ever went into, the room Mam kept for good use. The one we'd laid her out in. Poor woman. I didn't like to think about that, of her keeping the room clean for visitors when no visitors did she get, not a one. Not till she had passed on.

It was the coldest room in the house; never got any sun, never would. I stored the butter box in there. Not that anyone noticed or cared. My father was in the pub or visiting, hardly ever came home. Visiting, mind. Who would bother with him at all? I could never fathom it. Some old biddy must've been feeding him. He almost never showed for dinner but, as far as I could tell, he hadn't starved to death yet. Who'd think that he'd be the one widowed when he married Mam all those years ago, she twenty and he thirty-five? And there he was, a vagabond thriving on a regime of drink and tobacco. 'Never marry muscle.' That's what Mam used to say, amongst other things.

I tiptoed across the tiles and sat on the windowsill, watching Charlie sweep a damp rag across the floor and wring it out in the basin. If Father had been here, he'd have been telling him off for doing women's work. His pals in the foundry would have been laughing their heads off.

'Charlie,' I asked, 'why are you cleaning up in here?'

'Might have a friend coming, just for a short time.'

'Who is it?'

'I can't tell you. But this person needs somewhere safe.'

'A sanctuary?' I loved secrets.

'Exactly,' he said. 'You're not to tell anybody, Emily. Not even your man from the market.'

'He has a name.'

'Promise?'

'Who's this friend, Charlie?'

'I can't say, Emily, I really can't. Someone who desperately needs help.'

'Oh, how exciting. I'll help. I'll cook extra and bring it to him. Does he like eggs?'

'Doesn't everyone like eggs? You're a good one, Emily.'

'Ah, feck off,' I told him.

Charlie looked like he was going to say something else, but he didn't. He just wrung out the cloth and brought the basin back into the kitchen. I stayed on the window-ledge, imagining Charlie's desperate friend. How grateful he'd be for the kindness of Charlie's sister. I'd crimp my hair and swan around in a gauzy gown with fur cuffs. Sit with my elbows on the table and say things like, 'Now wait a minute, fella. You have to eat, you have to keep your strength up.' I was a terrible eejit, really, when you think of it. I should've guessed when Charlie came waltzing in with a vase full of poppies and set it on the sideboard that this desperate friend of his didn't wear trousers.

27

'It says here, it says here that this wine restores normal vitality when reserves of strength have been depleted. A glassful taken three times a day will key up the appetite, bring refreshing sleep and build up energy and bodily strength with gratifying rapidity.'

Dan didn't answer; he just growled and stretched his legs. Carmel loved to read in the evening, relished the combination of tonic wine, a thick novel and a dying fire. And when she could no longer fix her eyes on the page, she'd resort to reading the label on her tonic wine for convalescents.

'And it also says that it contains medicinal ingredients *not* to be found in any other tonic wine. What do you think of that?'

'It would want to, at six shillings a bottle,' Dan said.

'It's made by monks, I'll have you know.'

She liked to read and read – she was mad for it. That night it was *Madame Bovary*. Dan went in search of something that needed painting, or fixing, or both. He was back in a breath.

'Look what our shop girl's been gobbling up – *The Fortunate Mistress*! How did she get her hands on that? I found it beside the ledger – anyone could've seen it.'

'It's not hers. It's ours.' Wine made Carmel brave. 'You know Finbar does great work on behalf of the Catholic Truth people. Well, I was giving him a hand, checking a few suspect novels that might have to be reported to the censorship board. You can't be vigilant enough nowadays, can you, Dan?'

She hoped Dan wouldn't spot the lie.

'Underlining dirty bits in foreign books?'

'Most of them are Irish, I'll have you know. And he'd no choice the way things are, the way the government is coming down on all of us. Do you think he could have said no? Well? Said no to the

Catholic Truth people and he the master of a Catholic national school? An overseer of the innocent?'

'But *you* could've said no! And what kind of man would give his sister questionable books to read?'

She hadn't an answer for that.

Carmel watched her husband fume as he flicked through *Moll Flanders*. Such a big man – his thighs were as hard now as they'd been on the day they married. He was so righteous, sturdy and stern. Dan had a real soft spot for the sacrament of confession, for those fleeting seconds when his soul was officially declared sin-free and pure. *Go in peace to love and serve the Lord.*

Half an hour later he was still spitting fire over the damn book. Opening it and letting out exclamations of outrage at whatever offending sentence he happened to pounce on.

'This has to be reported. Brought to the gardaí; it's the only thing. You can't have this sort of smut around a girl like Sarah, it will contaminate her mind! Listen to this: "'Mrs Betty,' said he, 'I fancied before somebody was coming upstairs, but it was not so; however,' adds he, 'if they find me in the room with you, they shan't catch me a-kissing of you.'"'

He slammed it shut, glared at his wife. Opened it again . . . read a section, snapped it shut. Glared. Opened it . . . on he went, over and over again, with the same exaggerated expression of wide-eyed horror. It reminded Carmel of a Charlie Chaplin film. She just wished it were a silent one. Was this the same man who'd whispered once a week like clockwork, 'Do you want to go to bed, love?' Like his own lust was a meek weekly cuckoo.

If that's shocking you, Dan darling, thought Carmel, *I could say something that would really get your cuckoo hopping.* She smiled but couldn't keep her eyes open and dozed off by the fire. Maybe she should've listened more carefully.

28

One Saturday after work, when Sarah was looking forward to collapsing in a heap, Carmel asked her to take a message to Emily's. She set sheets of brown paper on the counter, parcelled up some bacon and then a fruit soda.

'That should be enough, for what's left of the Maddens now.'

She cut a piece of string with her teeth. Sarah really wished she wouldn't do that, nibble on string like a rat. The bacon grease darkened the paper as soon as it was wrapped.

'Used to be, let me see, Mo, Brian, the four young ones, and the lad that helped. That's seven altogether. Now look what's left: just Emily, Charlie and their father. How things change. The house is well in off the road, on the right, behind hedges let grow high. A run-down house with a madman's garden. You'll know it when you see it.'

Carmel gave her a sharp look and handed over the parcels.

'Now don't dally.'

How like Carmel to forget that Sarah's working day had ended an hour earlier.

Sarah began to wonder if she had passed the house when the hedges began to swallow the road and she saw a narrow gap where an open gate leant back. There was fuchsia on either side: Sarah popped open a red bud and stepped through. The house was a large square two storey. It must've been a fine building at some stage, but now the stone was smothered in ivy, and the window-frames were rotten. The garden was overgrown with nettles, poppies and foxglove. It felt lush and heavy. It made her notice things, like the smell of lilacs after rain. It made her want to lie down.

A hammer tapped on tin. A young man sat on the ground at the side of the house, his back against the wall, a bucket between his legs. It must be the brother, Charlie. Sarah was shocked at how handsome he was. Dark and well built, nothing like Emily. Tarzan with his clothes on. She walked towards him, but he didn't look up. She even coughed but still he didn't look up. Sarah's shadow crossed him. He jumped to his feet, let his hammer fall. Frowned at her. God, he was gorgeous.

'Mrs Holohan sent me with this.' She raised her greasy parcels. 'Is Emily about?'

'She's in her room – go on in. It's at the top of the stairs. Mind you don't frighten *her* to death.'

The front door was open; the cracked red-and-black hall tiles were gleaming. The stairs were bare and scuffed. At the top, something touched Sarah's shoulder: a wilting piece of flowered wallpaper. Sarah gave a gentle knock on Emily's weather-beaten door and lifted the latch.

Emily was kneeling on the ground. If she was surprised, she didn't show it. She nodded hello. A dress pattern fluttered on the floor in front of her, with cotton fabric tacked to it. The draught created as Sarah shut the door set pins rolling across the carpet and made the paper flap. Emily sighed. Scattered on the floor were coloured spools, scraps of fabric, a pin cushion full of needles, cards of darning cotton, skeins of embroidery cottons, a jar of buttons, another full of hooks and eyes. Emily had huge shears in her hand.

'Wait a tick.'

Sarah sat on a chair. Despite the disorder on the floor, Emily's room was beautiful. The white bed-cover was embroidered with a border of bluebells and violets. The pale grey curtains were also embroidered at the edges and held back with swathes of blue velvet. Miniature patchwork dolls lined the windowsill, perfectly attired, and each with a different felt hat. She watched as Emily began to tack together the pieces she had cut out. She worked quickly. There was a treadle sewing machine sitting beside her bed in the way other people had nightstands.

'Where did you learn to sew?'

'I learnt in school, and from Mam. Didn't you?'

'Only to hand sew.'

'Sure what's the difference?'

Not the welcome that Sarah had expected.

'What's the occasion?'

'Oh, I don't have an occasion yet. This is the kind of dress I would wear to a dance. Only then I'd make it from satin. A bias-cut of the darkest blue, with a row of tiny pearl buttons.'

The fabric on the floor was yellow cotton. The colour of a duckling. Poor thing – as if she'd be invited to a dinner dance. Emily lifted the whole ensemble on to the bed as carefully as if it were a baby.

'The leg-of-mutton sleeves are fabulous,' she murmured to herself.

Emily turned then and looked at Sarah as if she had only just noticed that she was a real live visitor. She seemed at a loss as to what to say. Sarah handed over Carmel's parcels.

'Would you like a cup of tea?' Emily asked.

'I would.'

They went downstairs. Charlie was at the kitchen table having his own tea amidst the debris. Sarah gobbled the generous slab of buttered fruitcake that Emily set before her. Charlie looked over at her.

'In some sort of trouble, Em?'

'No, I'm not, Charlie. This is my good friend Sarah.'

'The one who took your job?'

'Yes, the very one.'

On the walk home, Sarah realized that she and Emily had something in common. They had both lost their mothers. Sarah didn't feel the loss the way Emily must; didn't know any way different. When she was a child, she had often pestered Mai about her mother, asking where she was buried and why they couldn't visit her grave. Mai didn't like to talk about her sister; she just stayed silent and then would get fired up and point up towards the main road.

'That's the way, that's the road to the town where your mother's buried. Now skedaddle down it if I'm not good enough for you.'

She had meant to look before this, but almost every daylight hour was spent doing Carmel's bidding. Well, she was on her own time now. Sarah set out to find her mother's grave.

The cemetery was set across the railway bridge, around a falling-down church whose stonework seemed knitted together with ivy. She walked the narrow paving towards the back, where it was wilder, where the headstones were older. The graves of the wealthier families were marked with big granite crosses set behind ornate railings. The smaller iron crosses were less imposing but had more flowers: pansies that looked like a bunch of butterflies, ox-eye daisies and pale blue forget-me-nots. Inside the walls of the derelict church were graves of heavy slabs set flat into the ground. Sarah sat on one, resting herself. Wondered if the stone slabs were there to keep the dead in, or the living out.

She'd heard a story once about a woman who'd been buried alive. Her grave was opened by two men intent on robbing her of any jewels. One of the grave-robbers tried to cut off her finger. He was after her wedding ring. She woke screaming and the thieves ran off in fright. What a way to wake up. Though only for the robber she would've woken to a much more horrible fate. She could've died scratching the lid of her own coffin. So sometimes bad brings good along with it. Sometimes.

Sarah was consoling herself and she knew it. She was growing something. There was the sickness, the tears and then the getting fatter despite eating nothing. How hard the ground had felt beneath her that night. *Get up, do what you came to do, Sarah Whyte.* Sarah rose and began to read the names on the gravestones.

She had no luck finding anyone with her surname. Why wasn't she surprised? And she had spent too long among the headstones; it was nearly dark. Perhaps she was wrong to be searching for her mother's grave. Mai was the only mother Sarah had known. She had delivered Sarah. Delivered lots of babies but had never married and had one of her own.

That night Sarah dreamt she was dancing in high shoes, handed down, black. Her best, which someone else had broken in. The pied piper of Hamelin played the Walls of Limerick. How she hated the Walls of Limerick. Tapping feet, open sesame, abracadabra. *He* reached in and took a plastic bunch of roses from her stomach. A clown, a circus. Some carnival. She heard the crunch of steps on gravel.

'We must learn about solid matter.'

Who said that? Whoever it was, he woke her up. She lifted back the bed-covers and went to look out of the window. There was no one there.

Sarah wondered what Mai was doing. Was she also awake? Mai was often called upon at odd hours, to go to odd places. Seldom said much when she returned; was never a one for telling stories. As a midwife Mai dealt quietly with whatever the sins of the flesh brought her way. A woman of few words, *Sleep well . . . Morning, child.* Kind – you never met kinder – but she wasn't popular. Men didn't know what to make of where she put her hands. And she didn't gossip enough to get on with women. When Sarah got that bit older, Mai often brought her along but never introduced her by name, always said *This is my sister's child, God rest her.* Sarah once heard a gangly widow imitate Mai. 'My sister's child, God bloody rest her!' And she'd roared with laughter.

Why so mean?

Sarah's mother died giving birth. The grave far off, down that road, the next town over. That's all Sarah was told. Was it a different road, a different town? Sarah tried to remember.

Pray for her in your head. You don't need a grave. Enough said.

And, after making sure his wife's final resting place was in Ireland, Sarah's father ended up buried with strangers in Staffordshire. All Sarah had were Mai and Gracie and her cousins. And now she was going to bring shame on them.

Sarah got back into bed. She was getting wider. There was no getting away from it: she was expecting. She had drunk Mai's raspberry tea till it came out of her ears, taken every remedy she could think of, but she had still ended up with this beautiful secret, a sweet one. A time bomb.

She slipped her hand beneath the blankets, over the new hard warmth of her stomach, and sang a lullaby for the child, the hidden child.

'Hush a bye,' she whispered, 'bide your time. You're safe inside.'

In truth, she was terrified. She couldn't stop time. Redcurrants ripened, the washing line was full of whites, and the sky was a heat blasted blue.

Sarah felt a rising panic. *Think of something else.* She thought of school, of inkwells – who could have known she'd miss those inkwells? White chipped inkwells sitting into her desk. The Master standing over her. A stain spreading across her copybook. Her name in Irish. *Sorcha.* Strange in her mouth. Like the word 'blotter'.

She drifted off and dreamt a mixed-up dream. There were kiss curls, jars of Vaseline in a row, red ants and black ants. Someone rubbed her cheek as she fell from her dream to oblivion, and she heard a whisper, Mai's voice: *It'll be all right. It'll be all right, a leanbh.*

29

Mrs B was in a terrible way – came into Kelly's when I was there and said she couldn't find Rose.

'But it's only two o'clock in the day,' said Mrs Holohan.

'Why so worried – isn't she all of sixteen?' I added.

'Ach, what would either of you two know about good mothering?'

Mrs B had tried to be nice to me since Mam died, but she kept forgetting.

'You see,' said Mrs B to Carmel, 'she's not that well; she's rather frail, not able for much sun.'

'I'm sure one afternoon of warmth won't kill her.'

Mrs Holohan was even grouchier than usual. Maybe Dan was casting his eye over their shop girl's big bum. She should've kept me on. I'd have been less of a temptation, seeing as I had a man of my own, and no behind to speak of. Think of the devil and he shall appear. Dan arrived in wearing his sermonizing face. He shook out the newspaper.

'You're not going to believe this propaganda!'

Mrs Holohan set her head on her arms, so she could at least be bored in comfort. Mrs B suddenly had something important to do, so I scarpered too.

It was one of those days when I just felt homely on our road, glad to know every bump and turn. The hedges were alive with butterflies, berries and bindweed. The sun was like a warm hand on my neck. It felt like Mam was reaching down from heaven, touching me with her love.

I didn't wait for the gate. I squeezed through our hideout hedge and into our garden. When I was small I used to crawl through it on my belly, with my elbows walking me through the grass like a red injun. Mam used to tie feathers in my hair and draw stripes across my cheeks with her lipstick.

I heard a laugh. A girl's laugh. I put my hand to my eyes to block the glare of the sun. Sitting on our parlour window-ledge, swinging her feet, was the fragile Rose. Charlie was inside, leaning out of the open window with his elbows on the sill. She looked very small, sitting there, very young. She wore a red-and-white floral dress with a narrow white belt. I was most put out. Didn't she have a big fine house of her own without coming to our run-down one?

Charlie was talking away, his head to the side, looking up at her face. And she was smiling. Was he telling her about the desperado coming to hide out in our parlour? Was he telling her everything about us? She pulled a branch from the tea-rose bush, twisted off a small flower and handed it to Charlie. Charlie put it behind his ear. He looked funny. It made me smile.

I started walking towards them. Rose saw me first: she stopped laughing and hung her head, as if I was a mean person who didn't want people to have fun. Charlie hopped out on to the gravel.

'Hey, Em,' he said before I could ask any question. 'Rose came to see you, to see about that dress you're making up.'

'Come back next week,' I told her. 'I'm a very busy woman.'

I watched her walk to the gate with Charlie; she seemed in a terrible hurry all of a sudden. She must've remembered she'd a mother. What was Mrs B so afraid of, that she couldn't let her daughter out of her sight for more than a second?

Charlie was all for sweetening me up when he came back – gave me a hug and a penknife. It wasn't new or anything. Better than that, it was his favourite penknife altogether. Our father got it for him, years ago, when he'd had some sober days. It had a screwdriver, a corkscrew and a good sharp blade. The blades and handle were polished. It looked like a glinting fish, and it was heavy and smooth to hold.

'I can't take that, Charlie.'

'Oh, yes, you can.'

'Give me your second best one.'

'It wouldn't be a gift then. It would be a hand-me-down. You've enough of them.'

That's how I became the proud owner of a blade that would take the eye out of you. All so's I wouldn't ask too many questions. Charlie seemed so touchy about that girl. Jumping up when he saw me in the garden, when all I wanted to do was join them; it would've been nice to have had a bit of fun around here, a bit of chatter.

'I near forgot about the present I have for you.'

I got my mending bag, fished out the sausages Birdie had given me and put them on a saucer.

'You'd never be short if you married Birdie.' I punched his arm and he went brick red.

'Oh!' I said. 'Have I hit the spot? Have you finally fallen for Birdie's charms? You'll make a lovely couple walking up the aisle.'

He laughed then. 'Ah, feck off.'

Birdie had been mad about Charlie since he was a child – always had a sweet or a broken biscuit for him. 'Sugar face' was the name she had for him. Since Mam died she'd taken to calling me in from the street to give me cold sausages or sliced ham or rashers for 'poor Charlie'. As if I'd no stomach. I liked her, though. She was gentle, and so very small. And she missed Mam something terrible.

There was news for me when I got to the herbalist's that evening. It had all been fixed up. He was getting a proper roof over his head. A small house on the road out of the town. A 'friend' had assisted him in finding this new abode. No one I knew. And in exchange for what? He tapped his nose, to indicate it was a secret. He did that a bit too often for my liking. There would be two rooms, a lavatory out the back and a water pump outside the front door, and best of all he still had his river behind him. His river? Sometimes I wondered who he thought he was. But the herbalist had no doubts: he was moving up in the world. He would be able to treat people in his house now, it would be like a proper surgery. And between them and his regulars in the market, he wouldn't know himself. He had already started to pack. There were crates of glass bottles and jars stacked up in the middle of the room. I would miss the shed, even the mice clanking against the bottles at night. Aggie knocked on the door. Handed him something wrapped in newspaper.

'Don't forget your old friends.' She turned to me then. 'Did you hear that this fella got a hiding?'

I looked at the herbalist and he smiled – was his tooth chipped?

'Did someone hurt you?' I suddenly felt like crying.

'Miss Reilly's talking nonsense as usual – don't mind her.'

I gave Aggie the dirtiest look I could muster up.

'Are you a stray or what, girl?' she said. 'Does no one care whether you go home or not?'

'No, I'm me own woman,' I told her.

'She hasn't a clue,' I said to him when Aggie had gone.

'Not a notion.' He locked the door.

We had our lives mapped out. As soon as he was all fixed up and everything was settled and he had saved a few more bob, him and me were going to up and move to Brighton; he'd run a practice and I'd be his empress on a full-time basis. That's what he called me, his empress, his goddess, his queen. How can I serve thee tonight, my gracious one? He loved all sorts of gabbing. Liked talking about it as much as doing it. He showered me with affection, took clippings from my skirt lining, my hair, my fingernails, put them in a little box. 'Offerings, tokens, lucky amulets!' he cried, as if he was selling them to the public. 'Your body is a lucky rabbit's foot all by itself.' In Brighton, we would be one, but until then I had to settle for being his mystery woman, rapping at the back window of his new home, till I heard him whisper, *Who goes there?*

30

Carmel was slicing soda bread for their supper. Sarah was gone for a walk. Dan was doing the crossword at the table, pretending not to watch her movements, as she sawed into the loaf. She tried to calm her hands. Carmel was upset. Was always upset these days, always in need of a drink.

Something was haunting – no, tormenting, her. It was Mother. It wasn't like Mother was a ghost or anything so tawdry. But she heard her voice. She heard it when she sat in her chair and looked in the dressing-table mirror. It was sharp, a sharp whisper, a cold breath on the back of her neck. Saying horrible things, things she used to say years ago. Always giving out, always complaining. The way, Carmel realized, that she herself did now.

She was thirty-six years of age and felt withered, on the way out. Felt so sad about herself and Dan. Were they going to have a lonely, barren marriage? What about love? Where had it gone? Silly thoughts for a woman who was finding grey hairs amongst the blonde.

At the same time, Sarah had acquired the glow of someone in love. Carmel had asked her about it – not in a pushy way, just a friendly inquiry from one woman to another, 'Is there anyone special?' Sarah had denied it, given a small dry laugh. This disappointed Carmel. Sarah could've taken her into her confidence. It would've been nice to be asked for advice, to chat about romance.

The handle of the butter knife came off in her hand. How did that happen? Dan's hand covered hers – it was warm.

'Let me finish this – you sit down and read a book.'

She pulled a volume from the dresser and took her place at the table. *Tristram Shandy*. Even her books gave little comfort. The stories were all getting mixed up in her mind, giving her headaches. Even her bible stories. Oh, sacred holy mother, if only her baby wasn't in limbo. No matter where Carmel went when she died, heaven or hell, she would never meet her baby. Get on with things, keep busy, Grettie said. Most women, they just got on with it. Lived week to week, day to day, were grateful to have turf for the fire, a roof over their heads and children to pray for. But most women she knew had children to spare. Even Carmel's one true faith meant nothing to her now. Dan sat and began pouring the tea.

'Maybe,' he said, looking at her sad face, 'maybe we should get some hens.'

As if hens were aspirin. Instead of the age gap closing, it seemed to be getting wider – with him not ageing and her, well, going to the dogs. She took a bite of bread and excused herself.

Carmel was at the dressing table in her bedroom, leaning into the mirror and hearing all the bad things again. She wasn't sure if it was memory, if it was her own mind talking to itself or if it was as real as it felt.

You're as pale as a ghost when you wear dark clothes. Have you not got a nice blouse or something to go next to your skin? Those glasses do nothing for you.

'Well, I have to wear them or I can't see.'

What are you going to do about that complexion – would you put a bit of rouge on? Not there! Not there! Oh, God, and your poor thin hair, could you not do something with it, a trim might thicken it up. Have you not got the shillings for a trim?

'A trim isn't going to give me a head of thick hair I've never had. After all these years, would you leave it – have you nothing good to say about me?'

Well, look at yourself!

'Oh!'

Dan came in, said there was a racket, that Carmel was making a racket. Grabbed her by the shoulders and made her look at the woman in the mirror. Her face was patched with make-up: the rouge on her cheeks looked like a clown's, her mouth was dark and sticky. She was making sounds; there were words in there somewhere.

'Were you eating lipstick?'

'I want my baby back.'

The woman in the mirror started crying.

'You're having a bad dream.'

Dan guided her away from the mirror as if she were a sleep-walker, led her towards their bed, made her lie down and smoothed the sheets, and then her hair. He closed the bedroom door as though he were trying not to waken her. But Carmel didn't sleep: she wept, and wept. Later he brought her a cup of strong sweet tea.

'What in God's name is wrong with you, Carmel?'

'I don't know.'

How does it happen, Carmel wondered; *how do you become an embarrassment to yourself? Is anything ever going to be good again?*

31

Sarah was doodling on the previous day's paper, pencilling an angry moustache on a millionaire's daughter who had just flown her first aeroplane – THE SKY'S THE LIMIT said the headline – when she smelt a whiff of cedar and saw a shadow move over the paper. Master Finbar was standing there. How had he got in without the bell ringing? Her mouth went dry.

'Is my sister on the premises?'

'She's lying down – will I wake her?'

'No, no need. It's a flying visit. I was in the locality.'

She resisted the urge to cover her stomach with her hand. *He couldn't know*, she thought. *Of course not. See how prim he is, how clean his collar is. He knows nothing except for book learning.* His eyes, when they found hers, said otherwise.

'How are you fitting in, Sarah?'

'Very well, thank you.'

'Nothing untoward to report?' He smiled with his mouth shut.

He talked like that – nonsensical, sarcastic but gentle. She never knew what he really meant, even though he spoke plainly enough. His shirt was the whitest she'd ever seen. He was wearing a black tie, neatly knotted. Who did all that for him, kept the widow man so spick and span?

'I see you're filling out.'

'Thank you.'

'It wasn't a compliment. It wouldn't do to put on too much condition. Not at your age.'

He tapped the counter absent-mindedly. He was treating her coolly. It hurt. From the time Sarah was four and started school, the Master made no attempt to hide the fact that he'd a soft spot for her. Was especially kind, attentive. Now he was icy. Suspicious. Angry in a calm way. He held his fingertips to his temple as if he had a terrible headache. Sighed, as if there were nothing left to say.

'Have you seen Mai, Master Kelly?'

'For what?'

Sarah pressed against the counter, the wood smooth on her stomach, shielding her from his gaze.

'I'll be off – give Carmel my regards.'

'I'll do that.'

His cologne lingered after he had left; it was pungent. There was too much alcohol in the mix.

Sarah felt chilled. Finbar Kelly knew. Or maybe he just suspected and had come to confirm his suspicions. But how had he guessed? Had Mai told him? No, of course not, Mai knew he'd have Sarah locked up, hidden. Buried alive, if he could. She saw it in his eyes.

That Saturday afternoon, when Sarah met the herbalist and he doffed his cap and asked her if she could assist him, she listened. She needed extra money and sooner rather than later. Carmel paid her a pittance. Subtracted bread and board from her wages, and left her with hardly anything. As if a girl had no future, no need of money, as if they were doing her a favour. Sarah needed the price of her fare, a ticket to somewhere.

It was very simple. It seemed the herbalist couldn't keep up with demand. Sarah would write the labels for his remedies. There might be other small chores to do around the making of the ointments and such, but not to worry, she wouldn't get her pretty hands too dirty. He proudly gave her the directions to his new address.

When she arrived the next day, the herbalist was at his kitchen table, rubbing leaves off stems. The leaves crumbled easily between his fingers. They were too dry and brittle; they should still have been green. She said nothing. Fine herbalist he was. Aunt Mai would be disgusted. His new place was a simple two-roomed house, but there was plenty of light in it. He tapped at a child's school-desk; his latest acquisition, he told her. This was where Sarah was to work, to write out the labels. There was black ink in the inkwell, a fine narrow nib to work with, a blotter, gum and sheets of thin paper. Sarah was to write ten labels for a 'Warming Chest Rub' for starters. She watched him work as she practised her strokes on a scrap of paper.

The herbs he had picked that morning were pulpy. He must have gathered them too late. She could see that he overhandled the leaves, bruised them, took too long. Sarah considered not telling him, letting him go on making that mistake. She didn't know why – other than that he was so high and mighty when he obviously didn't know half as much as he let on.

'You should pick before the plant flowers, on the morning of a finer day than this, after the dew has been burnt off.'

'Is that so?'

'Yes.'

'And who says?'

'My aunt Mai.'

'Well, tell her the herbalist sends his regards.'

What a funny way of saying thank you. There were a dozen sealed glass jars on the mantelpiece. Sarah wondered if they had any potency at all. When she finished her work, he handed her a slip of paper, an 'I owe you', he called it.

'I'll have cash next time.'

Sarah hoped that the herbalist would pay her sooner rather than later. She had less and less time to save her skin and that of the child that was coming.

It had occurred to her, to her shame, that there might be time to meet a man, to get herself safely wed. However, the men she met in the shop were either very young, or married, or widowed and decrepit. The older and uglier they were, the more freely they flirted. Her only offer had come from Jackie, a fifteen-year-old who had wanted to take her to the latest Andy Hardy picture. It was laughable. Pitiful.

'Well, if no one else comes along, he's not the worst,' Carmel said.

They started roaring laughing then, her and Dan; it cheered their night up no end.

'You're too good-looking, Sarah, you scare them,' said Dan when Carmel had left the room.

Then a new man began to come to the shop. Shy, with high cheekbones and dark slant eyes, a full mouth in a sunburnt face. Matt was his name. He was much older than her, lines winging from the corner of his eyes, grey cutting through his hair. He got his paper and tobacco every second day. Tuesdays, Thursdays and Saturdays.

'He comes three times a week,' Dan would say. 'Sarah has a shine for three times.'

It was true that Sarah lived for when he came in. She could see that he liked her too. And it grew on her that he could be her ticket – her way out. But, for some reason, she found herself lost for words when she was serving Matt.

32

I waited till Charlie had gone to bed before sneaking out to see the herbalist's new house. Charlie was starting to quiz me on my whereabouts. It was a bit late for anyone to be giving a toss about my whereabouts. I sneaked down the stairs, carrying my shoes. My father was crumpled in the armchair. The curtains were still open, the fire was dead. A saucer of cigarette butts had fallen from the arm of his chair on to his lap. He never so much as stirred as I tip-toed past him to open the back door.

I kept my torch aimed at the ground in front of me. There were strange shapes in the fields, looming and sinking, like pirate ships in high winds. The moon looked brittle. The breeze bit at my ears; my own steps sounded like those of someone close behind me, my own breath like that of a twin chasing me down. *Turn back*, she was saying, *you're sinning. Turn back. Turn back.*

I began to run and run, my arms pumping the air like pistons, like when I was a child and we were playing catch in the fields and I wanted to be the fastest and to never, ever get caught. Sweat covered my back in seconds, but I felt better, felt wonderful. Even the ache in my calves seemed to sing. *Soon, soon, soon*, they said, *soon you'll see him.*

Light glimmered between the curtains at the back window. I gave my secret tap. He swung open the back door as if he was welcoming the sweet Lord home to Jerusalem. Oh, he was in the best of form: he rubbed me all over, to make me warm. He was wearing the loose white cotton shirt that I liked so much. He smelt good.

I got the grand tour; it took half a minute. He had two rooms. The kitchen had a nice fire going and a gas-lamp glowed on the narrow table. He had new furniture, a school-desk, a cupboard for his potions, a big armchair by the front window. The curtains were a beautiful cornflower-blue. In the bedroom, his bed was done up all nice, with fresh pillows and a cover. His knick-knacks, ointments and boxes were all neatly arranged on shelves.

'Isn't it wonderful?'

He was excited, full of plans. Now that he had a proper house, he would attract a better class of customer. Those who weren't too keen on queuing in the market could call round here instead. He was making a sign for over the door: HERBAL SURGERY, it would say. Once he had an idea, he put it into action immediately. The wood, he told me, was outside. For, ta da da da, he had a yard and all . . . He flung open the back door to show me: the river was silvery and swollen in the moonlight. The place would flood in a bad winter, but I didn't say anything, didn't want to spoil his fun.

The herbalist's brand-new house wasn't that much of a step up. It was bigger than the shed, but not by the miles that he had said. Two rooms that you could just about swing a cat in, if it was a kitten. Of course, nothing would do me but to tell him that. He was not amused. As far as he was concerned, he was nearly on par with Doctor Birmingham.

His golden Holy Mary calendar hung on a nail on the back door. There were lines through the days that had passed, and I felt a sting of hurt.

'What are you counting off the days till?'

'Till we can leave this place and be together in Brighton by the sea, a double act, a team. "The herbalist and his lady".'

'Are you asking me for marriage?'

'You'll just have to wait and see.' He nipped at my neck.

'Dracula!' I fell back in a swoon.

'Casanova,' he corrected, catching me and turning me towards the bedroom door.

The new house was less draughty than the shed, I had to give it that. But I was heart-sore for the shed. I always felt sad when worn-out things were abandoned.

Then I suddenly thought of Father. But he was no one to be feeling sorry for, not him. No, it was poor Mam. Then I thought, *Why did she leave us?* And I felt like going all the way back home and waking my father and shaking him and asking, *Why, why did she leave us like that, when we needed her so much?* Before I knew it, I was weeping.

The herbalist put his arms around me, pulled me to his chest and whispered, 'I know, Emily, I know.' He made me feel better for a bit, but what did he know? How could he know, when he never asked why I was crying? How could he know, when he just clamped his mouth over mine?

He took off his shirt and told me to wait in his new bed while he shaved his face smooth. It wouldn't do for me to have a beard rash; it wouldn't do for me to have a mark on me. What would the people say? I took off my dusty shoes and sat high up on the pillows. I still felt shaky, so I told myself things that would make me feel better, hearty things like *No more manky curtain walls for us!* I told myself that we were like Gable and Colbert in *It Happened One Night*. They'd had a blanket too. It hung between their bachelor beds to preserve their modesty when they were forced by circumstances beyond their control to share a motel room. 'The walls of Jericho', Gable had called it. And, in the end, when they got hitched, he brought a trumpet into the motel, and when we heard the trumpet sound we knew that the walls of Jericho had come tumbling down. I told the herbalist all this while he shaved. But he had no interest in films, and pointed out that we didn't have any curtain now. The gas-lamp by the bed spooned light upon the wall. I made shadow shapes with my hands while he tackled the awkward bit around his Adam's apple. I made a dog with slit eyes, no, it was a wolf. 'Ahwooo!' I called out. The herbalist looked at me funny.

'Have you forgotten that you're a secret?'

I bunched my other hand to create a rabbit with two twitching ears and watched the wolf chase it away, but I didn't make any more animal noises.

I liked being a secret, being there in my special place, night-time queen of a two-roomed castle. The herbalist's new pillows were high and full of feathers. He was a funny man that way: took as much care of himself as a woman would, better than a woman. Mam had never cared where she slept; I used to find her out cold on the armchair with a coat thrown over her. Not so my man. He was meticulous. He taught me that word. *Meticulous.* He spoke English better than most. He had a dictionary that he consulted when thinking up good names for his medicines. That navy book with its skin-thin pages was with him at all times. The right words were important to him. Precision. He tried to rename me once.

'The name is very important. I think they got your name wrong. Cleopatra suits you nicely or maybe Boadicea . . .'

'I'm called after one of the Brontë sisters.'

'And who are they?'

'English writers, very famous. Mam was romantic back then, said she'd waited too long for a daughter to name her anything other than a name she'd picked herself. There was war about it in our house. You see the first girl is meant to be named after her mother's mother.'

'And what name would that have been?'

'Peggie.'

The herbalist found that hilarious for some reason; he laughed till he was wheezing. I waited till he had calmed down a bit.

'And, after all that, my mother ended up calling me Millie.'

'Millie?'

'When I was a child.'

'That doesn't suit you either.'

'She thought it did.'

There was a sharp rap on the door. Not giving up or going away or getting fainter but instead becoming louder and louder. He dropped his razor in the bowl. He'd cut himself. The towel he held to his face had a growing stain. He met my eyes in the mirror.

'Turn down the lamp. You're not here,' he whispered.

He put on his shirt and closed the bedroom door softly with a look that meant it must stay closed. I lowered the gas-lamp. Imagined some jealous man come to kill him. Men weren't mad for him. Women and children took to him, the market men too, but ordinary husbands were suspicious. They liked to refer to him as a dandy. A fop. Made jokes that he was a doctor in name only. Trying to take the magic off him.

I would act quickly, overpower his attacker. But with what?

With the lamp, one knock to the crown.

I heard whispering and a low hum and *hmmm*. It was Mrs B: she was talking and crying. The herbalist said nothing. Then he said, 'No.' A very definite no. Mrs B got upset again. I heard him soothe her, go into the kitchen and rummage. Then the front door shut and there was silence for a few seconds. The herbalist came in swinging a red fox-fur.

'A present for my lady.'

'For me?'

'Well, *I* can hardly swan about in it.'

'You swan about enough. Did Mrs B give you this?'

'You shouldn't have been listening – you're a terrible girl.'

As if I wouldn't recognize Mrs B's fur anywhere. I hadn't heard a word of what had passed between them, but he didn't know that. Why did she give the herbalist her best coat? What was it in exchange for?

'Is the fur a bribe to keep me quiet?'

I slipped my arms into the silk-lined sleeves.

'No. It's just because you are here and it's pretty on you.'

'I can't wear this about the place either. Mrs B would go mad.'

'It's just for here, for when you're the lady of the lamp.' He stroked my neck, looked at me different.

'You're a strangely lovely pointy-faced beast by times.'

He always said my chin could cut diamonds. He ruffled my hair. The fur smelt musky. I recognized Mrs B's perfume. Shalimar. Named after a garden a shah had built for his beautiful wife. Mrs B liked to tell stories like that, back when I worked in the shop. So she had parted with her famous fox-fur. I made a guess.

'Why didn't she just give you money?'

'She has to account for every penny of her weekly allowance and it's hardly a cost she can put in her housekeeping book, now is it?'

'No,' I said, 'no, of course not.'

I wondered what he had given her in exchange for the coat, and in the middle of the night. A woman like that, to come here, to lower herself – as she would have said – when she lorded over us in the shop. Mrs High and Mighty. I snuggled into him.

'All women are equal in that respect. The Birminghams are no different.'

All women get the curse, but Grettie B hardly gave him a fur coat after midnight for a dose of iron tonic or a bottle of pain relief. He was measuring me with his eyes. If he realized I'd heard nothing, he would tell me nothing. Might even get mad at me for stringing him along. I snuggled into the fur – it was soft as sin.

33

It was nearly eleven o'clock when Carmel heard the latch lift on the back door. What was the girl doing out so late? Sarah strolled into the living room, shrugging off her coat, cool as you like, unaware of Carmel curled up in the armchair with her tonic wine. Carmel waited till she had her hand on the banister.

'What time do you call this!'

Sarah let out a cry of surprise. She turned around; her face was pale and tired.

'I'm so sorry, I –'

'Who was courting you till this hour?'

'No one, there's no one.'

'I'm not an ogre, you know, Sarah. I know what it's like to be young, I've been there myself.'

'It won't happen again, Mrs Holohan.' Sarah turned on her heel and skipped upstairs.

Carmel stoked the grate. Embers flew out on to the rug – what matter, it was singed already. The girl must have a young man. She could've said. Carmel would've understood. Why did everyone treat her as if she were about to bite their heads off? Like she was some kind of harridan? Carmel remembered what it was like to be young and in love, didn't she? She tried to summon up the excitement of her own courtship but couldn't remember much. Ach, if she still had notions about love at her age, she'd be a very unhappy woman indeed, wouldn't she?

Dan came home a few minutes later, a bit earlier than usual and irritable. Maybe the teasing had started up again. 'Go forth and multiply,' the men used to call when he was leaving the pub. Lizzie Murphy had told Carmel this when she was expecting, when it was safe to mention it. He was used to the ribbing he got for not being a big drinker – Mr Mineral they called him – but that was different – they should mind their own business about more private matters.

'Are you okay, Dan?'

'Of course I am. Why are you swigging that tonic stuff again?'

'For my nerves, Dan, for my nerves. The bloody washing line snapped today, and all the clean sheets ended up on the grass. I should have brought them in last night. A day's work down the drain, and there's no point getting Sarah to wash them all again, not till the line is fixed. Will you see to it, and get a good strong rope this time? Don't be scrimping.'

'I will,' he said. He took up the small brush and knelt to sweep the hearth rug. 'Speaking of our young Miss Whyte, do you know what I found out tonight, Carmel?'

'Go on.'

'She's been seen coming out of the herbalist's house at all hours, on Sundays.'

'Who said?'

'Mick, and all of them that were in the pub tonight. They were saying things. You know men, seeing as Sarah is young and single.'

'So that's where she was! Annoying the poor herbalist, just like her pale-faced predecessor. The poor man.'

'Mick said he wouldn't find Sarah's attentions too tiresome.' Dan laughed.

Carmel leant over and gave her husband's ear a tug. 'She's nothing to write home about.'

'Ah, that's it, I'm off to bed.' Dan got to his feet and disappeared upstairs.

'I'm off' seemed to be Dan's favourite words lately. Carmel would have to take matters into her own hands; she couldn't sit by and let carelessness ruin anyone's reputation. She went upstairs and knocked on the girl's bedroom door. Sarah was sitting up reading some yellow booklet; she looked as innocent as if she had come from Mass. Carmel got straight to the point.

'I know where you've been, Sarah. I don't know what kind of house you came from, but when you're under this roof you'll keep your dealings with men to the minimum, especially that man.'

'I need the few bob, Mrs Holohan.'

'He pays you!' Carmel clasped her hand over her mouth.

'Is that what you think of me? And with an itinerant hawker?' Sarah looked like she didn't know whether to laugh or cry. 'I write labels for his medicines, we talk herbs and sometimes we play rummy.'

'Talk herbs my backside.'

'It's true. I'm a good girl: you can't take that away from me.'

Sarah was very convincing. She seemed so offended that it made Carmel feel guilty, bad-minded even.

'Well, no more late nights. The odd bit of work would do you no harm; it would get you out of the shop. I might drop down to make sure everything's above board, though, if I've the time. But no more socializing of an evening in that man's house, do you hear?'

Carmel closed the door before the girl could answer. Sarah didn't look chastened enough for her liking; in fact she looked annoyed. And what had Carmel been thinking? A woman of her standing couldn't frequent that man's house. It just wasn't done. Why, then, did Carmel want to? And why did she have to stop herself from putting on her coat, walking through the town with her half-empty medicine bottle in her pocket, knocking on his door and crying 'Let me in, let me in, I need help'?

Carmel was swimming in the river: the water was black and viscous. Someone was waving at her from the bridge. Signalling at her to get out of the water, but she didn't want to: she felt too drowsy, it was nice and warm in there.

'Carmel, wake up,' Dan whispered.

A door banged; bare feet slapped the hall floor. She sat up in the bed. The soft light told her it was almost dawn. Her headache was immediate.

'Did you hear that?' asked Dan.

'You go look.'

Dan left the bed, and Carmel drifted in and out of sleep till he returned. When he came back, he was chatting as if it were the middle of the day.

'There'll be some cleaning up after that.'

'Just come straight out and tell me, Dan, I'm tired.'

'A bloody blackbird! It came out of the chimney, Sarah said, flew around the room, flapped against the glass, and when she ran out, the damn thing followed. It knocked itself dead in the stairwell, made a pretty mess.'

'Did you clean it up?'

'Give me time to get dressed, won't you? Maybe we should block up that fireplace again. I knew there was a reason why your mother had sealed it.'

Carmel pulled the blankets over her head till he had gone. She could hear the two of them now, Sarah and Dan, running up and down the stairs as if the house were on fire. It was a bad omen, a bird in the house. Carmel would stay in bed until the place was cleaned up; she didn't want to see the marks on the walls, didn't want to see the soot on the stairs.

34

Sarah decided to ignore Carmel's warning. She did the herbalist's labels in batches of ten on Sunday evenings, and stayed late if she had to. Sometimes it was very late, but what choice did she have? She needed the money. She tried to come and go discreetly, so as not to provoke Carmel again. The woman could be very unpredictable.

The herbalist hadn't paid her yet. He said he would soon; it was adding up, he told her. 'Think on it as saving.' She worked carefully, never smudged the ink. Kept all her letters flowing and even. She got immense satisfaction from the odd flourish.

The herbalist would often consult with her on names for the tonics; he liked to change them every now and then. People thought it was a new formula if it had a new name.

'Emily came up with some choice ones.'

He always spoke of Emily in the past tense, in a careful way that made Sarah wonder.

'What would you call a tonic to grow hair back?'

She thought for a minute.

'Root Reviving Lotion?'

'More respectable than Bald Bastard Balm,' he laughed.

'What about for ladies whose hair is thinning?'

'Crowning Glory?'

'Miss Whyte, you're a natural at this.'

He handed her a well-thumbed navy dictionary. 'All you ever need to say is in that book.'

He was proud of his vocabulary, his enunciation. Used his teeth for his *th*'s.

Sarah was glad to be getting a break from the shop. She was tired of Dan's roving religious eyes and Carmel's fevers. Fevers of excitement, fevers of accusation . . . the term 'highly strung' was invented for that one. It was a relief to be away from them, even for a short while.

'We're good to you, Sarah, are we not?' Carmel had asked crossly, as if aware that Sarah was getting weary of a life full of snipes and challenges she didn't quite grasp. And of their night-time arguments – over money, over the shop and sometimes even over her.

'You think the sun shines out of her fat arse!'

Dan mumbled some low denial.

Sarah wanted to scream: 'I've got two ears as well as a fat arse!'

The niceties were over. Their only concession to her presence was to move to other rooms. But not always.

When she had finished work at the herbalist's, she sometimes stayed on for a game of cards. If he didn't have a customer, he had a visitor. They played gin rummy, twenty-five and poker. Sarah won the first hand of poker she ever played. Aggie called her a right shark, said she'd take the eye straight out of your head. Sarah just smiled; it was a welcome few bob. When the cards fell by the wayside and there was a sing-song, the herbalist wasn't as free with her as with the other women. They said some awful things and, depending on his mood, sometimes he'd laugh and sometimes he'd wince. But when he talked to Sarah, he kept to herbs. He often quizzed her about plants, about Mai's tonics. Sarah only joined in the cards or the singing a few times. She was afraid of what would get back to Carmel. She was such a bad-minded woman.

Tuesday was a Matt day. Sarah was trying to think of a topic of conversation, something that could help them strike up a friendship. She was writing out a price list for the window display. Carmel looked over her shoulder.

'Suppose that'll do,' she muttered.

That irked Sarah. She was doing an excellent job and knew it. The herbalist was more than happy with her work, said she had a beautiful copperplate script. Sarah had once won a certificate for handwriting. Master Finbar presented it to her himself while the children did a drum roll on their desks.

173

As Sarah slipped the price list into the window of the shop, she waved at Birdie, who was sitting on the windowsill of her own place, as she did every market day. Matt was due in for his paper any minute, and Sarah still hadn't thought of anything to say. Then she opened the newspaper and there it was: a full-page notice for the summer carnival. Everyone was talking about the carnival. It stayed in town for the whole month. She would say, 'Are you going to the carnival? I hear it's great.' That would give him a chance to ask her out.

She made sure to have the paper opened casually on that page when he came in. He couldn't miss it. Her nerves were killing her.

Matt was pleasant but quiet as usual. Sarah held back his change so she would have his full attention.

'I see there's a carnival on – are you going to it yourself?'

'I don't know.'

'Have you ever been?' This was hard work.

'Oh, yes, I went last year; it was great gas altogether.' He smiled at the memory.

'I've never been to a carnival.'

'Really? You're missing out. You should go.'

He said it so encouragingly it nearly broke her heart. The opportunity would slip through her fingers if she didn't act fast.

'To be honest I don't know many people . . . I can't think of anyone to go with.' She held out his change and he took it.

'Well, Sarah . . .' He had never said her name before.

She felt an arm slip around her shoulder. Dan beamed down.

'You poor thing, why didn't you say so before? It would be a pleasure to take you to see the big carnival, girl, we'd only be delighted.'

'Good luck now.' Matt was off, his paper tucked under his arm.

What was wrong with her at all? She was raging with Dan, raging. He had spoilt her chances.

'He was going to ask me out! How am I ever going to meet anyone? Why did you do that, Dan?'

'Just protecting your honour,' he laughed.

'Do you think it's funny? Do you think I want to be serving here till my hair has fallen out?'

He looked startled, as if it had only just dawned on him that Sarah might have dreams of her own, dreams that didn't involve the shop, or him and Carmel.

Of course Dan never did take her to the carnival; she knew he wouldn't. Carmel wouldn't like it. So the opportunity came and went and was never mentioned again. Sometimes when she served him, Matt's fingers touched hers as he took his change. It made her sad. *I wanted you*, she told him in her mind, *but you wouldn't even walk me out*. She couldn't understand it. He seemed to like the look of her, but he never said anything.

Carmel said that he was a strange man, a widower, that he'd known plenty of women, all sorts. Though what they saw in him was a mystery to Carmel, with him so rough from working the river. River people were odd anyway.

Sarah stopped being nice to him or making conversation – it was too painful. She just said 'Grand day' or 'Wet day' as suited the occasion and kept her feelings to herself. Pretty soon he became brusque too, and it seemed to give him more confidence, make him easier with her. He even made a few throwaway remarks every now and again.

Their dealings became flavoured with resentment. Sarah felt the lost opportunity – the waste – and came to despise herself, and him, for their blushing awkwardness. It showed in how curt she became towards him. He responded by adopting a careless manner, began to call her 'sourpuss'. She followed suit, called him an amadán, or a buffoon, and would often tell him to hurry up, that she hadn't a whole day to waste while he rooted round for his change. And soon all hope of him being tender, of saving her with kisses and a ring on her finger, was locked away and buried for ever. *A girl like you*. He sometimes referred to her like that. 'Sure what would you know, a girl like you?'

35

There'd been a fortune-telling session by accident, and the herbalist had drunk enough rum to blacken his teeth for life. A shindig to mark the hanging of the sign over his front door: HERBAL SURGERY.

At around eight o'clock that night I had knocked, and he had pretended to be awfully surprised to see me, to have had no choice but to let me join the party.

'A one-off, Miss Madden,' he said with a wink, and let me in.

I was surprised to see Miss Goodie-Two-Shoes Harvey standing inside the door, clutching a small sherry and looking as if she didn't know whether to stay or flee. He must've pulled her in off the street on her way to evening Mass. The house was packed. Aggie's pals Lila and Judy were already tipsy and trying to start a sing-song.

'*Down by the River Saile* . . .' Lila belted out.

She grabbed Frank Taylor's arms, and started to wave them up and down in time to the song, like he was a puppet or something. He plucked them back and readjusted his silly satin bow tie. What was Mr Taylor doing there? The town hall caretaker hated market people, called them the bane of his life. Lila and Judy had opened their top buttons to give all and sundry a free sampler. Their fat cleavages glistened with sweat; it was the ale and the excitement – there weren't many places that let them in. They were shameful women, worse than Aggie.

Nell Daly was by the back door, waving her handkerchief around her face as if the herbalist's kitchen was the Sahara Desert. She was still wearing her widow's weeds and was surrounded by rapt men – Billy from the Picture Palace, River Inn Jim and Short Arse Smith – lapping up her every word. She saw me and raised her voice over the din.

'I was abducted from the footpath, Emily,' she laughed, 'abducted!'

That's when I caught a glimpse of Aggie in the yard outside. She was stumbling past the kitchen window, eating the face off Ned, the road sweep, like he was her long-lost sailor love. And it not yet dark! I should've known not to stay. People weren't in full control of themselves. I should've gone there and then, before it got worse.

Milkie Nash was carrying a plate of goodies and wore shining silver bracelets. She offered me a slice of fruit cake. I wondered if her mother knew that she was there. The herbalist handed me a glass of lemonade; I didn't realize the thirst I had on me till then and downed it in one. The fruit cake was delicious, crumbly and moist, with loads of cherries and almonds. It had been a while since I had eaten anything so good.

Lizzie Murphy, perched on the biggest chair, began to warm up her old fiddle; she was all elbows and knees, like a brown spider weaving. John the Jobber was standing beside her, braced for the nod to squeeze a tune out of his accordion. Between the ladies of the night roaring *a-weile weile weile* and Lizzie's fiddle, it was a cats' chorus in there. I felt like putting my hands over my ears. Then a fat man walked into the middle of the room and began to sing.

He was what they'd call a baritone, and he left all other contenders for centre stage in the ha'penny place. There was silence around his voice, even in the spaces he left between verses; nobody filled them with whispers or talk. He had a mighty broad chest, and he sang from somewhere inside it that must've been bottomless. Whatever the opposite of lowering the tone was, he did it. There was a huge round of applause when he was done, and a polite chatter of approval from all corners of the room.

The herbalist strutted over and shook the man's hand. The fat man was suddenly the guest of honour and offered the best of everything.

Aggie came back in after the performance. She set herself up at the kitchen table and started to ply her other trade. She did it all – palms, tea leaves, cured warts too, or so she claimed. I sat at the end of the table and listened. Miss Harvey put down her sherry, muttered some excuse and left. The herbalist ignored me in favour of the fat man. They were deep in conversation, facing each other, legs akimbo and arms crossed. Milkie said that the fat man was the herbalist's new landlord, and that if the herbalist played his cards right, there was a chance of an even bigger residence somewhere down the line. The fat man was loaded: he drove a big black motorcar. It was Lizzie told Milkie, and she'd heard it from the herbalist himself. Milkie was looking very heated and very pretty. I wished she'd just go home.

'I sincerely doubt that a word of that is true,' I told her.

'*Miaow*,' she answered and flicked her hair.

I watched her tour the room with her baking and gulped back the rest of Miss Harvey's sherry. Aggie read fortunes well, with just the right amount of lies and truth. How excited I'd been the day she told me love was coming. She may have hit the nail on the head, but she'd hit it by accident. There was brandy on the table, so I gave myself a refill as Aggie predicted a windfall for Judy. The liquid burnt my tongue and throat but filled my belly with warmth. She turned over a Jack of Spades, let out a low *ohhh* and told Judy that meant false friends and quarrels. Judy scratched her diddy and said she could stand a quarrel if the few bob came first. She roared laughing and I looked away: the woman hadn't a tooth in her mouth, it was as black as a bog hole.

The time flew watching Aggie rake it in. She must've done everyone that wanted to be done, because at some stage she turned to me.

'Well, petal?'

I looked around the room – where had everyone gone? Lila and Judy chatted by the fireplace; the herbalist lay back in his armchair with his legs stretched out and crossed, his eyes half closed. The singing fat man was at the other end of the kitchen table. He lit the cigarette in his mouth with a candle, and winked. He was within arm's reach of me, yet he seemed very, very far away, very misty.

'Why not,' my voice droned, like a record played at the wrong speed.

Aggie laid out a card then but kept it covered. I tried to lift it, but she kept moving it around the table real quick, grinning and spiteful-looking. Then she lifted it close to her face and made a great show of letting on she saw something horrible, like old Nick.

'I can't tell you, oh, no, I daren't!' she crowed.

Then she pushed it towards my face.

It was a Joker. A horrible laughing one in a tight red and yellow costume, with golden bells on his toes, knees and elbows. His tongue stuck out and his big white eyes bulged under a ferocious pair of black brows.

'What does it mean?' I whispered.

'A terrible end . . .'

That drove me into one of my fits. I got up and stamped my feet. And shame on them, the three women – Aggie, Judy and Lila – copied me as if it was a dance step I was teaching.

'Witches! Make them stop! Make them go away!' I screamed at the herbalist.

He opened his eyes but he didn't move from his chair. The fat man egged them on, beating out a rhythm, faster and faster, on the table, and then they took on the attitude of fine ladies at a ball, circled me, raised their fingers into dainty crooks and jigged around. Aggie sang a tune.

'Daisy, Daisy, give me your answer do.'

'Make them go away.' I tugged at the herbalist's arm.

He pulled me on to his lap and whispered, 'They're gone. They're not really here. It's just you and me.' He rocked back and forth. 'It's just you and me. You and me.'

36

Carmel took Grettie B's invitation down from the mantelpiece. She wanted to look at it again. It was quite lovely: a square of thick, creamy card requesting her company for supper on Sunday. She had never been to anything formal at the Birminghams'. It had been an ambition of hers once, to get something like this, but not so much now. The invitation was for her alone. It must be a woman's thing, one of Grettie B's do-good groups.

Carmel plonked herself into the armchair. It was so nice to put up her feet after a long day. Sarah was taking in the washing. Dan had fixed the line at the weekend, so Sarah had been catching up on laundry all week. Of course Dan went and bought enough rope for every washing line on the street. Just to annoy her – *You want rope? Here's rope for you* – but she refused to take the bait and saw him throw it into the shed after it had sat out on the grass for a few days.

When Sarah finished, she would offer her a tipple and they could have a bit of a chat; she must miss her aunt's company. Sarah had received post too, probably from home, but she didn't say. It annoyed Carmel the way Sarah tucked her letters into the waist of her skirt and patted them like they held top secrets. Today's missive was peeking out of Sarah's belt as she rushed in and out, draping sheets on the clothes horse in front of the fire.

'Sit down and join me, Sarah,' Carmel said, when the sheets were all in.

'Thank you but I have to be elsewhere.' Sarah went straight towards the coat stand. Just who did she think she was?

'Hold on. Where do you think you're going?' Carmel jumped up and walked over to her.

'The herbalist's, for cards.'

'First I heard of it. Are Sundays not enough for you? Well, you're not going and that's that.' Carmel had had enough of Sarah suiting herself. She knew she'd been staying late at the herbalist's despite her strict instructions. She took the coat from her and hung it back up.

'What's this all about?' Dan said. She hadn't heard him come in. The sympathetic look he gave Sarah irked her.

'I'm informing madam here that under no circumstances is she waltzing off to the herbalist's.'

'Sure Sarah wouldn't want to, would you?'

'No, I'd rather stay home; it's so much *nicer* here.'

'Enough!' Carmel's hand flew at Sarah, just missed slapping her face.

'Carmel, what's wrong with you?' Dan grabbed her wrists. 'What are you doing?'

'Did you hear her, the spiteful witch, did you hear what she said?'

Sarah backed away from them; she had one foot on the bottom of the stairs.

'Go on, Sarah, go on . . .' Dan said.

He let go of Carmel's wrists when the girl had gone upstairs.

'You can't be doing that, you can't be hitting out like that. Do you hear me? Do you hear me, Carmel?'

'I feel weak.' Carmel sank on to the sofa and put her hands over her face. 'Did you not hear the insolence of her?'

'Ah, Carmel, just leave it, leave it be.'

Dan lifted his own coat from the stand.

'Don't dare say you're going down to the pub. Don't dare put on your coat.'

'Why not?'

'Can't you see I'm upset, that I'm not myself?'

'You're always upset; you're never yourself lately. It doesn't mean the world has to stop going about its business.'

'God forbid. Look, Dan, look.' She beckoned him over to her. 'I'd like us to try again. We can't do that if you're not even in the same premises of an evening, can we?'

'Shush. The girl will hear.'

Carmel put out her arms towards him. 'Sit with me tonight – stay home, let's try again for a child.'

'Will you speak quietly? Do you want the whole world to know? And besides, there's tomorrow night – Sunday – for that.'

'For that,' Carmel began to weep. 'Ah, Dan.'

'Stop, please.' He sat down beside her. 'Please stop. Don't.'

'I never knew marriage was going to be so lonely.'

'That's because you don't have children like other women.'

'Well, give me one, please. Tonight give me one.'

'Stop, she'll hear. Hush, don't cry, don't. I'll tell you what, I'll be home early, how about that?'

She didn't bother answering; just put her hands back over her face. He was gone by the time she looked up. The room looked different, gauzy with hurt.

Carmel hadn't really expected him to stay. She shouldn't have asked, humiliating herself, begging for her husband to make love to her. His voice, humouring her. Carmel was tired of being humoured. Tired of watering down what she really wanted to say just because that girl might hear them. She was tired of the sounds of their voices, of all their voices, knocking around this small house, saying the same things, day in day out.

And what about her medicinal tonic? There was hardly any left again. The herbalist had told her to call round to the shed, said he kept some items locked up there, but he'd never showed. Offered no real explanation, no apology either. She had queued at the market stall, asked for hand cream and whispered her complaint as she handed over the money.

'I forgot,' was all he had said; 'will you take a bottle now?'

She nodded. He had tossed her a small glass bottle with no label on it. Carmel was mortified; anyone with eyes could see that it wasn't a hand cream. And it was tiny. She was too proud to ask for a larger bottle while so many people were listening. So she took what she was given and now she was caught short again. The room was getting dark. Carmel felt a chill. Could have done with something to warm her up.

The floorboards creaked upstairs. The girl. Carmel should let her have a few days off, arrange a ride home for her with Seamus. It would give Dan and Carmel a bit of breathing space. Time alone together, without any distractions. She felt bad about lashing out at Sarah. It was her tone, that haughty tone of voice – *It's so much nicer here.* That's what had made Carmel snap. The insinuation that life with her and Dan was far from nice. Maybe poor harmless Emily wasn't so bad after all.

There was a clatter and a thump from Sarah's room. She'd better go up and talk to her – what if all that toing and froing was the sound of her packing her bags? She was the type, unpredictable, sneaky. They all were, that class of girl.

Carmel went up the stairs, taking it nice and slow and not making a sound. There was movement coming from the bedroom; the door was closed. Carmel put her ear to the wood. It sounded like someone was jumping around in there. She was about to turn the brass door knob when it turned all by itself and the door flew open. Sarah was standing there: the belly of her nightdress was all puffed out and blackened with soot, and in her hand was a dead bird.

Carmel screamed. A silly woman scream that made her angry at herself. The girl was holding the bird as casually as if it were a purse. Carmel gathered herself.

'Another one?' she asked.

'Yes.'

'I thought Dan had blocked the chimney?'

'He jammed newspapers up it; they must've fallen down.'

Sarah shrugged her shoulders, looked uncomfortable. She was trying to get past. Carmel moved aside, watched her go down to dispose of the bird. Heard the back door open. She was going out to the garden – don't say she was burying the thing? Carmel would have flung it out of the window and been done with it.

The room was in disarray, Sarah had probably tried to catch the bird before it knocked itself out. The fire screen was toppled over; there was soot sprinkled all over the floor. The walls weren't too bad – it must've headed straight for the window, for the opened curtains. Carmel looked at the rocking chair: there was a bright blue shawl hanging over it, beautiful gold fringes trailing over the floorboards. The stain wasn't there any more; Dan had washed the blood clean away. She knelt and looked more closely and found where the grain of the wood was much darker. Once you saw it, you couldn't un-see it: a round shadow. The only sign that there had ever been a baby.

So Finbar had been right about the birds coming down the chimney – but why only that chimney? Why not the one in her and Dan's room? Oh, what did it matter? It was only the girl's room now and it hadn't caused any damage. She would instruct Dan to block it properly and that would be the end of it.

She wanted to get out of there before Sarah came back; there was something distasteful about talking to her in her nightclothes. Come to think of it, she was wandering around outside now in nothing more than a nightdress. Anyone could see her. Sarah must've guessed that Dan was out. Maybe she'd heard their conversation earlier? Carmel blushed. Nonsense. She didn't need to eavesdrop to know that Dan went out almost every evening. She felt a pain unfurl deep in her womb, the familiar wretched kick. It was back again, the curse. She went to the press to fetch her rags.

37

Sarah's hands were shaking; she got into bed as quickly as she could. There was something wrong with that woman. She wondered how Dan put up with her. She had slapped Sarah, or tried to, and in front of her husband. And what business was it of hers where Sarah went on her time off? Sarah could have done with winning a few bob. There was no guarantee but so far she had been lucky at the card-playing sessions, and a good bluffer. Every penny counted. She would have loved to tell Mrs Holohan she could keep her old job, but she needed the position for just a little longer.

Sarah lit her bedside candle; it wouldn't do to be wasting electricity, or drawing Carmel's attention back to the room. She could hear Carmel uncapping a tonic in the living room. She'd be up all night now, wandering around the house. Once or twice Sarah had heard her stop and listen outside her bedroom door. Dan mentioned in confidence that Carmel had been a sleepwalker since that time. *That time* was the way he'd put it. He meant when she lost the child.

It came into Sarah's mind that maybe the child was sleepwalking somewhere too, and that maybe some night they would meet each other. She didn't say that, though, in case it shocked Dan, in case he thought she was a heathen. It wasn't like Mai's house here; in Mai's they used to spend long afternoons discussing dreams and their meanings. Here it was very different: there were no warm conversations. Carmel gossiped with Mrs Birmingham and didn't include Sarah. They tended to turn their backs to her and blab only about people they knew between them. Sarah said nothing; it was better than most jobs a single girl could get.

She took a piece of chocolate from her side table. Broke a fraction off and put it in her mouth. Rose had given it to her earlier when she'd popped in with her mother; they were collecting Carmel for some picture or other. Mrs Birmingham and Carmel had gabbed in the shop doorway, half in and half out, for almost half an hour.

'Come on, Mother, we'll miss the funnies!' Rose had eventually said.

Taking the usual bar of chocolate from her blouse pocket, she broke off half and passed it to Sarah with a wink as they left. That wink seemed to say 'I wish you were coming too', or at least that's what Sarah thought. Rose was a nice girl, but they never had the opportunity to chat. Mrs Birmingham hung on as tight to her gorgeous daughter as she did to her purse strings. It wouldn't cost them a penny to ask Sarah to join them. The door had barely closed before they were out on the pavement, buttoning up their coats and laughing. It gave Sarah a roaring headache. A tear had run down her cheek. Lately the slightest thing made her weep. She had turned into an old cry-baby, she who used to be such a tomboy. At least if she'd been home, she could have roamed the field and blubbed in privacy. As it was, she took a deep breath, stood tall and worked on. Some people stood straight through grace; some people were holding themselves up against something – people like Sarah.

She sank down under the covers. She heard Carmel sobbing downstairs – was that part of the reason why Emily had left, this miserable atmosphere? But no – Emily was annoyed to have been let go, wasn't she? Ah, yes, it was her obsession with the herbalist – her 'inappropriate behaviour', as Carmel had called it – that had led to those final marching orders. The poor girl thought she was in love.

Early on, some customers had called her by Emily's name. It was simpler to answer to it than to explain, so they stayed doing it. She didn't mind. The townspeople weren't so bad when you got to know them. Once she got past being nervous, Sarah learnt people liked to be coddled, to be made fun of. A Peggy's Leg for the children, sympathy for the wives, and a laugh at their jokes for the men. Dan had noticed last Wednesday.

'Why, Sarah,' he had said, 'silver-tongued Sarah.'

'Yes,' his wife added, 'silver-tongued Sarah, sly as a fox.'

That had hurt, though Carmel had laughed when she'd said it.

However, it didn't hurt Sarah now; her expectations had fallen considerably since then. She felt under her mattress for Mai's letter, opened it out into her lap and popped the last of Rose's chocolate into her mouth as she read.

Dearest Sarah,

Are they being good to you? I hope so. We are all grand here T. G. Sarah, did you hear? That James Kelly has got engaged to Helen Mahon of the drapery Mahons'. It has only dawned on me what Master Finbar was up to putting you forward as a candidate for his sister's shop. He wanted you out of the way. He wanted someone better-off for his James. You know there's no one better than you in my eyes, Sarah, but to a schoolmaster like Finbar, who thinks he's a cut above, an orphan living with her old aunt wouldn't be high up enough.

I'm heart-broke. He expected us to fall for it and we did. Or I did. It's all my fault. I jumped at the chance. Thought it was a golden opportunity for you to better yourself, get a few bob in a respectable position and be able to have nice things, meet nice people. I didn't think twice. A start for you, that's all I wanted. Me and my pride, I was hot-headed with it, hot-headed with excitement that you were getting out, doing things. And Big Notions Mai goes and has a do, a send-off, and look what it did to you. Look what it did.

Are you drinking the tea? Is there any sign? Please write soon and let me know, I'm out of my mind.

Bless you always,
Mai

James was engaged to Helen Mahon. Sarah couldn't recall him ever saying two words to Helen Mahon, or one word even. And poor Mai, blaming herself. The sound of birds started up from the chimney breast again. If another bloody bird flew into the room tonight, she'd strangle it.

38

I woke alone in the herbalist's bed the morning after the fortune-telling. My head hurt. Everything hurt. I closed my eyes again. Whatever had happened the night before was mixed up with the leavings of a bad dream.

Voices washed over me, some more real than others; those ones had a bite in them. I didn't want to go to the ball, but they dragged me anyway, dragged me and left me lying in the middle of the floor. Laughter bubbled in the throats of the ugly sisters, Lila and Judy. *Fine girl you are!* They stepped back to allow someone else to step forward. The bogeyman was invisible and he had a thousand hands. Fat, cold and pinching. Those fingers never let up their pawing. It was a dream, it was a nightmare, and it was real. First, I was safe on his lap. *My laudanum whore.* Then I was sore and torn beneath the glinting laughter. And then, *bam!* The door opened and cold and rain and a wild woman all rushed in. Aggie's voice, and Aggie's foul tongue. *Leave the fucking child alone!*

It was daylight. The bells were ringing for Mass. I stung down there. That was the worst of it. I peeked. There were bloody scratches on my thighs. What had happened? Had the herbalist been overcome? He wouldn't have hurt me like this, not him. He had given me a potion, I remembered that. Someone had tied a scarf around my head; it was too tight. Some of my hair caught in the knot but eventually it broke free.

The door opened. It was the herbalist, rubbing his head and looking rough. The fat baritone peeped in behind him: one eye was swollen and purple. He sneered at me.

'A right little earner!'

The herbalist slammed the door in his face. I was well pleased by his abruptness, the way he sent that horrible man packing.

'What happened to that fella's eye? Who hit him?'

'Old Aggie.'

'Why?'

'Never you mind.'

I drifted in and out of sleep. After a while the herbalist shook me awake. He was holding out a lovely slippery nightgown. Red satin, could you credit it? Ankle length and all.

'I'll look like a starlet.'

'A skinny starlet.'

There he went again, making me feel great just so he could move me back down to second place. He liked doing that. I wondered where he'd found the gown. I felt cold all over, couldn't get warm. 'A chill in your kidneys' was his diagnosis. I put on the nightdress and slipped around the bed, shivering. The tea he brought was cold and greasy, so he lay on top of the covers and shared his tipple with me.

The herbalist drifted off. I gazed at the smiling face of the hula girl on his shoulder, traced my finger along her sweeping black hair, and thought of the jade snake curled up unseen beneath the covers. I became sleepy, but, afraid of the bad things sleep would bring, I rose and tried to use the chamber pot. No luck, only pain. A shoe-box stuck out from under the bed. I helped it on its way. Lifted the lid. Amongst beads of dried lavender lay a photograph. A white woman – tanned, wide-faced and thin-lipped, her hair swept back from a severe middle parting into a bun, making black wings each side of her head. She was wearing an old-style striped blouse and a dark floor-length skirt. Her stoutness and clothes made her seem middle aged, but when I looked closely there wasn't a line on her face. She held a dark-skinned baby dressed in a sailor suit. The woman looked at whoever held the camera with real fondness and pride. The infant smiled, and his eyes were wide, as if someone out-side the picture was making funny faces at him. One of the baby's feet was a blur. I turned the photograph over to see what names were written on the back. *Vikram* . . .

'Nosy!' It was snatched from my hand.

Once you had offended him, there was no talking, no use in try-ing to explain.

'Get dressed. Get out.'

There were pinpricks of sweat over the bridge of his nose. He hadn't shaved; his lips were dry. His demons were here again; he didn't have to tell me this time. As I took off the nightgown and put back on my own things, he laid a bottle, a napkin and a cup on the bedside table. The ceremony soothed him. He began to breathe easier. He smiled when he lied – I'd learnt that much. So when I was fully dressed, I asked him: 'Did you come into the bed with me last night?'

He knew what I meant.

'Maybe I did.' He smiled a peculiar smile that bleached the skin around his mouth.

What a funny way to run your lies, towards sin. But maybe he was telling the truth. I'd been touched, that much I knew. I remembered my dream – thick fingers pulling at me, the sneering face of the fat man. Did he come in here? Into the bedroom with me?

No. The herbalist wouldn't let anyone hurt me, he never would. Funny how real some dreams can be.

I folded up the red nightgown and wrapped it in a sheet of newspaper. Part of me wanted to put it back on, run over the bridge and swan through the town in it. Let them talk, let them laugh. They did anyway. There was no more talk to be had here; I could tell by his bent back, and the way his shoulders touched his ears, that the demons were climbing on top of the herbalist, one by one. I went over to say goodbye, rubbed his neck.

'Disappear,' he hissed, 'disappear.'

Aggie, why did you pal with the herbalist? Didn't you know he was bad?

The way I look at it, we're all a bit bad inside. We just have different ways of dressing it up. But, Lord help me, when I saw what happened to poor Emily, I did get a quare shock. I should've stepped in then. It would've saved an awful lot of suffering.

I had been outside with one of my paramours, and returned to be greeted by a terrible commotion. Emily was crying from the next room. The Don was stretched bleary-eyed, out of his mind in the kitchen. In I went to the bedroom, and what did I see but only those two witches crowded around the bed, laughing and clapping. I pushed them back to see that big fat bastard moving on top of her. You wouldn't know to look at me, but I've a fist like concrete. You should've seen the fat lad reel. I split the skin beneath his eye wide open. That put a stop to their shenanigans. Emily seemed drugged or something, fevered – I couldn't wake her, so I covered her up with blankets.

Cursing like a demon, the fat man staggered over to the table and collapsed on to a chair. Then he began to fall forward, really slowly, till his face lay among the plates, bottles and glasses. Blood trickled from his cut. That big head of his looked just like an ugly joint of meat. Lila and Judy were nowhere to be seen; they must've abandoned him, not that he cared, he was busy snoring. I shook The Don, tried to tell him. 'Aye,' was all he said. 'Aye.' He waved me away and went back to his drunken sleep. He smiled to himself then, content with wherever he was in his head. The hate set in there and then. But I bided my time and kept close to his side. You catch more flies with honey, and I wanted this fly.

I called round to him soon after, hinted that he should pack up, move on. That people were talking. Did he listen? Not a hope. The Don was too brimful of pride and Jameson's to take one blind bit of notice.

'I'm a professional and a successful one; my travelling days are over.'

He fixed another drink. Then he whipped out a small black notebook from the inner pocket of his jacket. Licked an inky finger and flicked through the pages. Put on a high and mighty voice, like I'd never seen him on his hands and knees crying with the horrors for his mammy.

'This log records patients, illnesses, treatments, all the ups and the downs, comings and goings, and of course what works and what doesn't. What is efficient in the system of things.'

'There's many would pay a pretty penny to read that.'

I reached out to take the notebook, but he snapped it shut and tucked it away again. The big cold smile on his greasy smig annoyed me.

'I'm just telling what the people are saying,' I said, 'and they're not nice things. You'd want to be careful. Maybe cut your ties with a certain young lady; it's doing you no favours.'

'What they say is up to them. What they see is up to them. Not my doing. I'm anything they want me to be, from Lucifer to the guardian angels at the gates of heaven. I was needed here, Aggie, welcomed. I've had offers of help from all quarters – wealthy quarters. You would be surprised, I think. Wanting to advise me on the ways of the place and who's who. As if here were any different to all the other places. The same pinched faces, but who can blame them? It's a tight corner we're all in, yet the market is livelier now, is it not? And not just with farmers and their vegetables, eggs and chickens. Are you listening? Are you listening to me?'

'You're too full of yourself. People don't like that.'

'Why wouldn't I be? I walked home today with a case bereft of potions and pockets packed with money. Children, three or four, skipped alongside me, across and in front of me, circling in great excitement. "What's in those bottles, mister?" asked the smallest and boldest.

'"Magic," I said. "Pure money-making magic."

'"Can you cure leprosy? Can you cure TB? Are you a miracle worker?"

'"What do you think!" I bent down and took a penny from behind his ear, hoping I didn't pick up lice.

'"Are you from Africa?"

'"Are *you* from Africa?'

'"Of course not, mister, I'm from the lane, you know that!"

'So why wouldn't I be full of myself, as you put it? There's magic at the tips of these fingers, pure money-making magic. I'm getting myself a motor-bicycle as soon as I've enough stacked up. Are you listening, Aggie?'

There was no talking to him. But, I suppose more than anyone, I knew how that lad operated. We were in the same kind of business. The same fake How Great Thou Art. And afterwards the exact same 'I have your few bob, now feck off'. His ladies liked a comment, a little flattery. They may have huffed it off, but they always came back. Like my lads.

I left the herbalist's place and got Seamus to stand me a round at the bar. It took a hell of a lot of porter to wash the bad taste out of my mouth. Seamus didn't mind coughing up; he was mad about me. I was his first love. I was a serious looker in my day. Like Vivien Leigh, but with more meat. You'll have to take my word for it, child. I've no photographs to show you in this place, no evidence. Just memories. Lots of memories, though sometimes I only have one – the sound of a short sharp cry, the red hands of a hysterical nun. What's done can't be undone.

39

The river was high; it shimmered like the crystals off a Hollywood chandelier. Aggie was half asleep in her armchair with a squishy velour cushion behind her head and a crocheted white shawl on her lap. I was painting her toenails a colour the spit of Schiaparelli's new Shocking Pink. Birdie's magazines kept me up to date on the latest trends. Aggie thought it was mad that colours could have names. We were having a grand old time, lapping up the sun. Aggie's boat was moored further back behind us, on the stretch of river that ran by the courthouse.

'I park in the shade,' she said, 'so me butter won't melt nor me milk sour.'

Mad as a hatter but she knew her knots better than any sailor, and the bloody big strong arms on her! Aggie loved that boat. I'd seen her kiss it, I swear to God. Some paint had flaked from its name, so it read IDDY, instead of BIDDY. I kept quiet. If I passed any remark, Aggie would summon Seamus to fix it, have him slaving away in the heat. He'd do anything for Aggie; he was the only man in this town that gave her the time of day. It was quite a different story come the night-time, though. Else we wouldn't have the Schiaparelli, would we?

Seamus was a quare man. Shy, yet brazen when it came to doing Aggie's bidding. Only last week he'd mended her cabin door and painted it pillar-box red as a surprise. She wasn't a bit pleased, roaring that he was making a fool of her and forcing him to redo it in black before it had even dried. Wasn't a bit grateful. She didn't talk much about Seamus, and when she did she never used his name. 'My odd-job man', that's what she called him.

Aggie had taken me under her wing since our shindig at the herbalist's had gone so strangely. She was good company, and she'd been feeding me sugared whiskey to aid my recovery. Announced that I was in dire need of womanly guidance. Open your ears now, or learn the hard way, Emily.

'It's all in the dreams. The dreams tell you everything, mark my words,' Aggie said, all of a sudden.

'What does *he* dream of?'

'Let me see, let me see.' Aggie tapped her forehead. 'He dreams of Indian boys, a ball of sun and dry earth in a place where everyone looks just like him. He has to make this place up, for he has never been.'

'What Indian boys?'

'I don't know – why don't you go and ask him?'

I had hoped she might see me waltzing through the herbalist's dreams in a white fur stole and a lamé dress.

'What about me, then?'

'Oh, you're easy: your dreams are full of white mice, they run all over your room, skid down the banisters and waltz in the cupboard.'

'That's not true and you know it, and we don't have that many mice. What about her, then?'

'Who?'

'You know, your one, Lady Muck the shop assistant.'

'Oh, Sarah.' Aggie shut her eyes, waited a while and smiled. 'Sarah dreams of a man: he's a stranger and he's rowing her down the river, rowing her to a nicer place than this.'

'I wish someone would.'

'Now, now.'

'What about you?'

'My dreams are no one's concern.'

'Ah, Aggie . . .'

'All right, have it your way. If Aggie dreams good, she dreams of the farmhouse she was born to, the warm straw, heavy porridge, being held. If she dreams bad, then she dreams of being sent into service, and of all the grey roofs she could see from her window.'

'What does that mean?'

'It means nothing.'

Dan Holohan walked by, and let on he didn't see either of us.

'What about his lordship there?'

'Oh, Dan, he's easy: he dreams of making love to that dark woman we saw in the paper who wasn't permitted to sing for Mrs Roosevelt, then he dreams of making love to Mrs Roosevelt. He wakes up woeful tired.'

'You're a terrible woman!'

'I know.'

'There, all done. Now don't wiggle those toes! They'll be dry in no time.'

'Thank you, madam.'

'You're very welcome.'

I screwed the nail varnish closed, lay back on the grass and talked about the beautiful dresses I could make with silk or satin. Imagine, satin. The gathers, the drapes, the tucked-in waists. How I would sway into a concert at the town hall and no one would recognize me. And I would be danced all night.

Aggie sat up and pointed to a woman pumping water near by: she was expecting a child and the six around her were barely dressed.

'See her? Her poor ankles, her baggy tired body? She hasn't many years on you. You want dancing, you want glamour, you want men? Mouths to feed, that's what men will get you!'

She nudged a wee naggin of whiskey from her cleavage and took a sip.

'Ah, Aggie, stop, you were young once yourself!'

'Agnes. Agnes Marian. I've got a proper name, just like you.' She waved her finger.

'Don't you like children; did you never want some for yourself?'

'Don't be daft, girl, want children? I'm well past all that.'

'But did you ever . . .' I let there be silence. Aggie hated silence.

'I had a child, a long time ago.' She tugged the fringes of her shawl.

'Where's it now? Did it pass on?'

'Don't know. End of story.'

'Ah, Aggie, please . . . ?'

She rooted her cigarettes from her skirt pocket, lit one and took a hard pull. Looked at me.

'I was very young, engaged but not wed. They said I had to go into one of those places. I wouldn't agree to go. In the end I was carried through the big gates, kicking and screaming and seven months gone.'

Aggie let out a long breath, and sighed before she continued.

'Soon as the cord was cut, a pretty nun by the name of Sister Angela bent over me and snatched the child from between my legs. It slipped from her hands, fell back on to the bed. "Oh, sacred heart of Jesus," she said. I lifted my head, but couldn't see past her veil. And then she was gone. Never knew if it was a boy or if it was a girl. Never saw the baby again at all. Just heard it cry. When Sister Angela returned an hour later, she was empty-handed.'

'Go on, don't stop.'

'Next day I was moved to a women's prison in Galway, served eight months and was released. That part was lucky, getting jail time; otherwise I'd still be in there, wouldn't I? Locked behind those high gates with all the other unweds.'

'Why did they send you to prison, Aggie?' I whispered.

'Didn't I say? I was sent to prison for breaking Sister Angela's lovely face.'

I tried to picture all those things happening to Aggie, but could no more picture her young than I could picture myself old.

'Nothing else came out of there alive.' She pointed to you-know-where. 'Bad luck or silver lining, who knows?'

'I'm sorry.'

'Heed my advice, Emily. Don't fuss about dances, wooing or finery. That just leads to yearning, and yearning is another way of doing nothing. Ask yourself every day – how can I make a few bob? You have a sewing machine and a good pair of hands; get them busy. Sure you're all set up.'

'Set up to make dresses for other girls to go to dances in?'

'Ah, don't be so sour – a woman can't rely on others, she has to be her own boss. Like me, answering to no one.'

'You couldn't keep going without the men. If they gave you nothing, you'd have nothing.'

'How dare you! I'm me own sewing machine!' She was raging, ran her hands down her front. 'You hussy.'

Then she started laughing. If Aggie liked anything as much as cheap gin, it was being given out to.

'You're a holy disgrace,' I chanced.

'A terror,' she said.

'A blight on the country.'

'Coming apart at the seams.'

'A boil on the face of humanity.'

'The scourge of the earth.'

She closed her eyes and smiled, her squishy big cushion like a dirty old halo.

'A terrible woman,' she said softly.

I wondered who Aggie had been engaged to all those years ago? Who was her young man? And where had he been when she'd needed him?

There was no sign of the herbalist that day. Moving on up in the world, Aggie had said, leaving the rest of us well behind. Moving on up in the world. He might want another girl. Poor Emily and Aggie would be left in the dark nowhere space. Aggie yawned and stretched her legs; it was as if she had read my thoughts.

'When the herbalist leaves,' she said, 'he won't look back, not once. Kiss me arse, nothing. Remember that and don't follow him.'

I covered my ears and hummed.

'It's the truth. What do you want from me, warm milk and fairy-tales?'

Aggie was warning me, always warning me, about the darker side to things. And I should've listened. I didn't listen, but I did the next best thing. I made Aggie a dress.

It was smart, just past the knees. Olive-green and V-necked. It was a lovely shape but not so sleek when cut for a 46" bust. Aggie said she was terribly pleased, for ever in my debt. But she paid me. Not much but all it had cost me was my time.

She invited me to her next spiritual night in the boat. 'Free of charge! And you can make a skirt for yourself with the leftover fabric.'

Leftovers. Did the woman not know how broad she was at all? It fitted her perfectly, and was more sober and neat than most of her clothes. She wore it so much it became her second skin, shiny in the seat and the elbows.

'My dressmaker, Emily, put this together for me,' she'd say.

There couldn't be a worse advertisement for a dressmaker than to have Aggie strutting around in one of your creations. I decided that she wasn't smelly, really; just a bit salty. 'Salt of the earth,' they said, when she was dead.

40

Carmel took some care getting ready for her Sunday supper at the Birminghams'. She chose her cream wool cardigan and her spotted bottle-green dress, splashed a bit of Dan's cologne on her wrists and arranged her plait extra carefully about her head. Her hair had darkened since she'd married. It used to resemble wheat; now it was more of a biscuit colour. She lay on the bed to hoist on her stockings. Thank God her damn monthlies were over. She felt such hell when they were due, and such heartbreak at their arrival. *Barren, barren, barren*, announced the red blood.

Stop! Think nice thoughts. Chocolate. Lilies. Madame Bovary. Just look at that dust on the ceiling!

Now for the face. She dabbed on some powder and a touch of lipstick. It wouldn't do to look too done up, too eager. She pulled the green dress from the hanger and put it on. It was tight around the waist; the buttons on the chest gaped. When had she become so busty? Well, it would have to do. It was her best frock and the ones Emily had altered were too plain, too humdrum. She buttoned up the cardigan. Wore her mother's marcasite necklace to jazz things up a bit.

She had taken great pleasure in telling Dan she wouldn't be home that evening. He was glad for her, said that she deserved a bit of fun. He wrapped his arms around her waist and gave her a lovely squeeze. Then he went and spoilt it all by saying, 'I wonder what Grettie is after?'

The house was so silent. Sarah was at her other job, labelling medicines, pickling plants. She should be home soon. Carmel hadn't yet said anything to the girl about what had happened. Several times she'd begun to, but her apology had got caught in her craw, or she had changed her mind and decided it was Sarah who should be apologizing for casting aspersions on the niceness or otherwise of

Carmel's family home. Not that there was any family in it. *Now, now, don't get cross again.*

Carmel's form had improved by the time she reached the top of the Birminghams' avenue. It was nice to be away from her own four walls; she should go places more often. A dour girl took her coat and left her shivering in the hall. 'The missus will be with you shortly,' she said. The girl looked familiar. It took Carmel a moment to place her – with that dark complexion and the dramatic widow's peak, she was a Daly. But which of them had got the job in the Birminghams'? Oh, yes, Margery.

There was no sign of Grettie. Was Carmel early? Her answer came from a blue cuckoo. He sprang from his house over her head: *cuckoo, cuckoo* . . . Lord, would he ever stop? She counted his cries. It was eight o'clock. She was on time. She sat on the long oak bench. A tall brass lamp stood like a sentry beside it, casting a pool of honey-coloured light. The walls were newly painted a clean pale green, no botched wallpaper for Grettie B.

The doctor's door faced her. It was a heavy black door, a bit battered-looking and at odds with the white roses in a crystal vase on the ornate hallstand beside it. It was nice to be here when the place wasn't full of patients moaning and sneezing and noticing everything about everybody else. Carmel had only been twice that she could remember. At least she was healthy in that way; not everyone could say that. She should count her blessings. The stairs were steep, and situated to the right of the doctor's room. The handrail and balusters were plain, simply painted white. Carmel would have loved to wander up those stairs. She could imagine the luxury on the second floor: the thick carpets, heavy drapes, antique heirlooms, the four-poster beds.

A muttering came from beyond the panelled door at the end of the hall. The living quarters. Carmel got up quickly to check her face in the mirror behind the roses, but it was impossible to see beyond the blooms. Their dusky sweetness tickled her nose, made her throat itch. She began to pace. She noticed a split in the wall beneath the upper section of the stairs, ran her finger along it and felt a draught. She stepped back. It was a door, flush with the wall and painted the same green as everywhere else. Grettie B's voice came from somewhere and was coming nearer. Carmel had reached the bench by the time she entered the hallway.

'Forgive me, Carmel, the silly girl just told me you were here!'

The inner sanctum was threadbare compared with the harem of luxury in Carmel's imagination. Still, it was nice, spare but very elegant. There was a long table, at which the surly Daly girl sat polishing some silver cutlery. Her eyebrows were black and furious; she practically glared at Carmel. It was a bit strange to be polishing on a Sunday. Was Grettie B making her maid work late just to show off?

She was led to a smaller room; it had the look of a ladies' drawing room. Now, this was everything that Carmel had imagined. The pale yellow floor-length curtains on the bay window, soft furnishings covered in a cream fabric blushing with rose patterns and trimmed in gold. A low round table was set for two. Carmel's heart sank – it was just the two of them. She took a low chair and was sucked into its softness. Grettie B swished past in her long plum gown. It was dated but suited the room.

The evening began pleasantly enough. Supper was cold meats, stuffing and pickled onions, then plum jelly, cream and scones. And sherry, and a few Irish coffees and then more sherries. The fire was kept topped up with log after log by the sour-faced girl. All Grettie B had to do was ring a small bell and she came running. Carmel relaxed in no time; she even shed her cardigan.

'Oh, dear.' She had forgotten the gaping buttons. 'I must get Emily to let this dress out. The poor motherless girl. Who would've thought that Mo would die so young?'

'I bet Brian didn't; bet he thought he was set up for life.'

'Poor man.'

'Nothing poor about him, Carmel.'

'Do you remember you wanted to marry him?'

Carmel couldn't believe she had spoken so out of turn – it must be the drink – but she ploughed on. 'Aren't you lucky you didn't get what you wanted?'

'Did I? I don't think so, but maybe my memory isn't as good as yours.' Grettie B topped up Carmel's glass.

'Yes, wasn't that when the coolness set in between you and Maureen? You were very close, even for cousins. Remember? You had your eye on Brian –'

'It was the other way round!'

'You had to look out for Mo that day, and you had set up a date with Brian so you brought her along, remember? And he fell in love with her on the spot.'

'That's not what happened at all! The only one I had my eye on was Doctor Birmingham. Do you think I'd choose a travelling salesman over a doctor?'

'They were just men then, and we were just women.'

'You weren't a woman; you were a child of ten!'

'I know, but children see and hear things.'

Carmel knew she should stop, but she couldn't. Grettie B's face was a sight. It was almost fascinating to watch her contain her rage.

'How would you have known what was going on either way? You were such a long time on the shelf yourself, Carmel; you didn't know one end of a man from another.'

'Excuse me. I was fussy!'

'Do you mean I wasn't?' Grettie B leant forward to reveal a splendid powdered bosom.

'No, I don't mean that at all. You were very pretty, Grettie, almost as lovely as Rose. And you were very fussy – you could've had your pick of the men in this town.'

'Almost as lovely? Well, you were a nice-looking girl too, Carmel.' She tapped her spoon off her cup. 'But may I be honest? That weight does you no favours. You're too small-boned to carry extra baby weight.'

'Maybe I want to carry it? Maybe I don't want to lose my baby weight?' Her hand trembled as she set down her glass.

'You know, Carmel, losing that child might've been for the best – have you ever considered that? Not everyone is able for motherhood. Not everyone has the . . . stamina.'

Silence. Tinkle. Sherry.

'How could you?'

Carmel lost interest in the conversation – or in correcting Grettie's versions of everything; she just wanted to go home to her husband. But Grettie B wasn't finished.

'We – well, myself and the doctor – we often wondered what was going on with you, Carmel. You know, you weren't exactly interested in men, then you went and married a kid like Dan. We wondered was it because your mother wanted someone to edge old Finbar out. We wondered . . .'

What? Wondered what? Don't ask.

'You know' – Grettie forced a laugh – 'we wondered if you liked men at all, or were you one of those inverts?'

'An invert.'

'Isn't that funny? Doctor B thinking that about you! Isn't it silly?'

'Oh, yes.'

Laugh, you must laugh.

Carmel laughed. Her throat was dry. A whole reel of film unwound on to the floor. The back of Sarah's neck, warm and brown like an egg. And that girl, that girl when she was twelve. But nobody knew about those things, those nothings. She felt herself redden. It wasn't true, it couldn't be. She liked that part of being married. She liked Dan's body.

She was being punished for something she had said earlier, but she couldn't remember exactly what.

'I must go now. Dan will worry if I'm late.'

Carmel began to put on her cardigan. Her elbow got stuck.

'Will he?'

'Yes, he will, Grettie. Dan loves me, and I love him.'

Oh, no, not tears.

Grettie rose up, leant towards Carmel and wrapped her arms around her. Carmel's nose began to run; she wiped it with the back of her hand. Grettie hugged her tightly. Carmel sniffled.

'I've upset you – I'm sorry.' Grettie handed her a napkin from the supper platter. 'Carmel, I'm sorry, I've been an old meanie.'

Grettie walked over to the fireplace; she hoisted up her dress to warm her legs.

'Carmel, if I've been a bit catty, it's because I feel so wretched myself. I'm in a dreadful situation.'

'I'd no idea.'

'Yes, I've been caught short. I don't want to worry Doctor Birmingham, but, frankly, I need a small loan to tide me over. I had to pawn something of value and I need it back.'

'Oh.'

'We're friends, aren't we? We've been friends a long time?'

'A long time, Grettie.'

'I've never asked you for anything before . . .'

'Oh, you mean me?'

'I've never –'

'But I don't have any money.'

'Of course you don't.' Grettie pursed her lips.

'I really don't.'

'No, really, forget about it, Carmel. I'm embarrassed to have asked.'

She didn't look embarrassed; she looked disappointed.

'Can I ask what –'

'A private matter.'

Carmel tried to stand. She wobbled.

'Grettie, I think I'm drunk.'

'Sit down and let's get you drunker.'

41

Each week Sarah would decide not to go to the herbalist's. She didn't want to go. She never, ever, wanted to. Yet, each Sunday after dinner, when faced with an afternoon of Dan and Carmel, she rose, washed her face and left. Carmel had been sorry-looking since trying to smack her, but there was no sign of an apology, just an extra helping of chicken breast at dinner.

The herbalist looked dreadful and was very quiet. The place was spotless, but it stank of alcohol. He must've had a late night. He waved her towards the desk in the corner; the bottles were in a box on top.

'I wrote a list for you.'

He handed her a page: ten foot rubs, ten back oils, and so forth. Sarah looked at the box of unmarked potions.

'How will I know which is which?'

'Just have an old sniff; you know yourself by now. I'll be out in a bit.'

With that he closed the door of his bedroom. It was a quiet afternoon, and she took her time. It was a gentle quietness, not edgy like in the shop, where you knew it could be broken at any minute. People would call, but not till later. They'd play poker, old maid, rummy, twenty-five. Drink tea. Some had a tipple, port, brandy – respectable drinks. Sarah hoped Aggie wouldn't come today. She knew Aggie was of the opinion that she had swiped the job in Kelly's from under Emily's nose. Made it obvious that she thought it was too smooth a replacement, that Sarah was too clever for her own good, not as soft as Emily. She had said as much at the last game of cards.

'Emily would've given her right arm to be here having the crack. Whereas Miss Sarah' – Aggie raised her voice so Sarah wouldn't miss a word – 'I don't know why she comes at all. Sitting up so straight, saying nothing, taking it all in.'

The herbalist seemed to have gone to sleep; there wasn't a sound from the room. She put the kettle on the stove and hoped that maybe by the time it boiled a visitor would have arrived to play a round of rummy with her. Maybe John the Jobber, Seamus or even Lizzie. She didn't want to leave without talking to the herbalist; he still hadn't paid her a penny. He must have the money: his business was thriving, and now he had this place. Sarah wanted to be well out of the town before she started showing; she needed to get the boat and fast. Mai had written to Sarah again. She said she had appealed again to her sister Margaret in London, implied that Sarah had married badly, was having a baby and needed a safe place to live temporarily. *Please believe or pretend to believe* was the prayer that Sarah repeated to herself when she thought of her aunt Margaret reading that letter. She hadn't seen her since she was twelve years of age.

How quickly a room can change character as one person, then another, walks into it. Within an hour the herbalist was up and chatting to his first caller, a large man unknown to Sarah. Then Lizzie came, and after a while Ned the road sweep arrived, looking sheepish. Young Michael Ryan soon followed. There were more, later, that she couldn't rightly remember. Things became bleary and fun and not real, and the herbalist's kitchen transformed into a party palace. And she was pealing with laughter – even sour old Lizzie was warm to her; they held each other's arms and laughed with their heads back at something outrageous Lizzie had said. Sarah had shocked her by replying back in kind and everyone roared, and there was singing. Some sort of nursery-rhyme song they all chanted and chanted; the table was pushed back and they pranced around the room, mobbing against the wall. She felt dizzy, unbalanced. Realized that someone had slipped something stronger than orange into her orange. She must vomit, she must get the alcohol out of her system.

She fumbled towards the outhouse. By the door a woman was moving in the shadows, moving her hips in a slow, circular motion. Someone was pressed against her – another woman. They stopped embracing and looked at Sarah, mouths wet and slack.

'Good evening,' Sarah said, as if she had met them in the street.

What a stupid thing to say. She almost tripped, and then a man appeared out of nowhere, and she rested her head on his shoulder, till his fingers strayed where they weren't wanted. She shred the skin of his groping hand with her nails and wrestled free. She didn't go back into the house to collect her things, she just stumbled home to the Holohans'.

She expected Carmel to be standing guard, but she was nowhere to be seen. Dan was home. He stood up when she came in. His hair was tousled – had he been dozing? Sarah focused on the stairs, tried walking towards them without wobbling. If she could get her hand on to the banister, she'd be grand.

Dan was having none of that. He said he smelt alcohol off her. Sarah tried to interrupt him, but he wouldn't stop talking and accusing, accusing her of entertaining notions about the herbalist, of being up to no good at all hours. He had it all wrong if he thought Sarah was pining after the herbalist. She didn't even like him; he frightened her almost. She just desperately needed the money he would pay her. But she couldn't tell Dan that, couldn't tell that to anyone.

'You're not going back to that place.'

'I'm not a child; you can't tell me what to do.'

'I can let you go.'

That gave her a fright. She took a step back.

'I'm disappointed in you. Visiting a man like that, consorting.'

'Like what, Dan, like what?'

'Immoral . . .'

'What makes you think he's immoral?'

'Just look at who he consorts with – bad women who –'

'It takes men too.'

'Stop that. All I'm saying is, adult or not, no more of those visits.'

'What else will I do? Sit and listen to you and Carmel argue all night?'

She shouldn't have mentioned their arguments.

'You disgust me, Sarah.'

'No, I don't.'

She took his hand and placed it over her heart. Held it there. Saw him redden. He was so big and tall. She would have liked him to collapse, to have held him in the palm of her hand. To have had his naked body cover hers. Where this desire came from she didn't know; she hadn't known she had it in her.

'I think you'd better call it a night,' he said, turning away.

42

I had sewn in my bedroom all day. My eyes were sore and my elbow ached from feeding fabric to the sewing machine, but I was happy. I got through a pile of mending and then drew out a pattern for my new satin – yes, satin – dress. I had paid for and collected the fabric that very morning. It was only divine, slippery and shiny, and the most beautiful blue I'd ever set eyes on. 'Are you making curtains?' the shop girl had asked when I bought it. Some people have no class. I asked Charlie over supper if he wanted to come along to Aggie's spiritual session. Charlie thought it was a load of silly codswallop. So I decided to clear up and go to bed instead. I was wrecked by that time anyway.

I was drifting off to sleep, warm and lovely, in my own world, when I felt someone was there in the room with me, someone who was looking down on me. I froze, afraid to open my eyes or even to let my breath out. A finger pressed against my lips. I bit down. The yowl put my mind at rest. I recognized his voice.

The herbalist was standing over me. He was holding his finger and looking mad as hell. He placed his hat on the chair and sat on the bed alongside me. He was unshaven; it made his face look thinner, meaner.

'You frightened me!'

'You frightened me too.' He held up his marked finger.

'What do you want – has something happened?'

'I just want to talk.'

'All you do is talk. You said you'd build me a boat, that we'd float down the river all the way to the ocean. Oh, I was to be the queen of the river, the love of your life . . .'

'We will, we'll go down the river.'

He pulled back the bed-covers and turned me over, on to my belly. He undid the string at the neck of my nightdress and slipped it off my shoulders. I felt his jaw against my skin: the bristles felt like a shoe brush.

'When, when will we?'

'Some night soon. Where did you put the fox-fur, Emily?'

'You can't take it back; it was a present.'

He pressed his fingers against my neck and then he spread them wide till he was holding my throat, real gentle, not so it hurt.

'It will all come to pass, I promise you. We'll drift along the river in a cascade of flowers. You will be queen.'

'And we'll have a feast?' I was glad he'd forgotten about the fox-fur.

'Everything we want and more, wine, women and –'

'And what about that other one, writing your labels?'

'Sarah can barely spell. I gave her the sack today. "Get out!" I told her.'

He tightened his fingers on my throat, pressed himself against me. Then a sound came from outside: the honking of a motorcar.

He jumped up and just left the room. I heard his steps on the stairs and then nothing. The herbalist had never come here before. I should've liked it better. I pulled back the curtains and looked out of the window. There was no sign of him. Why had he left without so much as a word? Was he afraid of my father? As if my father would notice anything I did. I could have the whole army up here and there wouldn't be a word about it.

I eased the cloth bag from between the bed and the wall, opened the drawstring and pulled out the fox-fur. It was funny, but there in the moonlight, as I tugged it from the mouth of the blue bag, it looked like an animal being born. I slipped it on and lit one of my father's cigarettes and smoked with my elbows on the windowsill. Maybe the herbalist had been lured all the way out here by my womanly mystique. I blew the smoke out into the dark and spent a few minutes being sultry. After that I couldn't sleep a wink, so I hid the fur, made myself respectable, and decided to take Aggie up on her offer and drop in on her spiritual session.

★

I might've been better off in bed. It was roasting on the boat, and only one sod in the stove. I was sweating. It didn't bother Ag; I suppose she was used to it. There were great sopping patches under the arms of her new dress, and yet she threw a black crocheted shawl across her shoulders.

'Will you not boil up in that yoke?'

'I always wear this – it adds to the magic.'

There were three women due that night. Aggie told me it would be great sport, and Sally Heaney coming made it an easy one. Aggie knew Sally's recently deceased fairly well – well enough to know what he'd say if he was summoned from the grave for a chin-wag. He liked a fine wide arse on a woman, and Bisto in his tea. That's what Aggie told me. The trick, according to her, was not to say too much too quickly.

'Let them wait, whet the appetite, like a striptease. The Gypsy Rose of the tea leaves, that's me.'

Aggie had set up her stow-away table with four stools around. We heard the women making their way on to the boat, the clip-clopping of heels and squeals, as if they were stepping on to the high seas. Aggie stood by the hatch to welcome them and take their sixpence admission. There was Mrs Heaney, Mrs James and Miss Fortune.

Mrs Heaney tried to bring her cat. No moggies on my boat, said Aggie, and she fecked it back to dry land by the tail. Aggie hated cats. The women sat around the table with their hands flat and fingers touching. There were dozens of candles on the table. It made their faces look paler, and the shadows under their eyes darker. I knelt in the corner on a cushion like a squaw.

'There are things that do happen, ladies,' Aggie said, 'that there's no earthly explanation for. As you know I was born with the caul, so I see what others do not . . .'

There was a sharp rap on the door. Miss Fortune leapt. Hot wax spilled across Mrs Heaney's wrist, and she roared like a banshee. A narrow face peeped in – it was Ned. He never missed a thing.

'Come on, come on in,' Aggie shouted, red-faced with impatience.

Ned had a dusty old job sweeping the roads but was always neat as a pin. Lived in one of the worst terraces for rats and muck, but to see him on a Sunday in his good suit and gleaming shoes you'd swear he lived in a manor. He tucked himself on to the step by the door. Mrs Heaney wanted a word with her Raymond; Mrs James wanted to talk to one of her dead children, it didn't matter which one. Miss Fortune just wanted to listen; it was her first time, she didn't want to 'rush things'. Her fiancé had been killed in the war and it had left her very fragile. Twenty years later and she still wasn't over it.

When Aggie spoke on behalf of the departed, her voice went very deep and she pressed her chin on to her chest. The women were delighted to hear their relatives were having great craic in the ever after. I had nearly drifted off when they began to stretch their legs and take out the gin. Aggie was relaxed, now she was done conning them out of their sixpences. Miss Fortune started humming and I could feel a sing-song coming on. The hatch was opened to let some night air in.

'I can feel them, out there.'

'Who, Aggie?'

'The restless ones.'

'Oh, God, don't say that,' said Miss Fortune.

'It's all right – they often come. They come when I'm half dozing – when I'm sitting out on the deck in my chair, snug with all my coats on, and a blanket up to my chin. Once you've seen them, you can't go back to when you didn't – you can't do that.'

'What do they look like?' I asked. She turned sharply, as if she'd forgotten I was there.

'Like wisps of smoke rising from the river. It goes real quiet, like the whole river is holding its breath. It's always around three in the morning.'

'The time of death,' whispered Ned.

'My living heat pulls them, draws them.'

'The way a poultice draws the poison,' said Ned.

'The very same.'

'I'm frightened,' said Mrs Heaney.

'They're the frightened ones, poor things. They come close to me, then closer again. The air cools. I hear them, but mostly I don't understand what it is they're whispering . . . but they'd break your heart.'

'Whimpering like a shivering pup of a winter's evening?' said Ned.

'The exact and the same. Poor divils.'

'What do you do, Aggie – are you terrified?' I asked.

'Nope. I go shush, shush, it'll be all right. And I might sing an old rhyme.' Aggie began to sing:

> *See saw Margery Daw*
> *Sold her bed to lie on the straw*
> *Wasn't she a dirty old pup*
> *To sell her bed to lie in the muck?*

'You'd want to be careful. What if you fell asleep with your mouth open? And one of the ghosts got in?' said Mrs Heaney.

'Who do you think they are, Aggie?' I asked.

'Us. Townspeople. Townspeople that didn't get a proper burial or met death when they weren't ready for it.'

'Who's ready for death?' said Mrs James in a cross voice.

'I am!' Aggie stood up and puffed her chest out, held up her fists. 'Come and get me, old son.' She jabbed the air. 'Come and get me, old son. I'll pull the first punch and you can pull the last one.'

43

Grettie B had dropped into the shop quite a few times, on her own for a change. She was over-solicitous. Probably to show that there was no ill-feeling. And to make sure Carmel didn't blab. Carmel hadn't blabbed: she wasn't going to give Dan the satisfaction of knowing he'd been right, that the fine Mrs Birmingham had wanted more from Carmel than the pleasure of her company.

It had been a strange evening. Grettie really seemed to think that she had money to spare – but no matter how much sherry she fed Carmel, it wasn't going to make her any the richer. It was true that Carmel had a nest egg – the money she had tucked away for the baby – but she didn't think of it as her money any more. No, that was the baby's money, and she wouldn't have dreamt of touching it; it might bring bad luck. If Carmel had had any other money, she would have lent it in a blink. Grettie B would have been good for it. Just look at the style they lived in – all those rooms and only the three of them?

There was no sign of Rose lately. Her mother said she had turned into a homebody, that she always had her nose in a book. That sounded nothing like the girl Carmel knew. She wondered if they were related – Grettie B's request for a loan and her daughter's sudden desire to stay home? Carmel had a vague memory of Rose putting her head into the drawing room that night; just a quick hello. How had she looked? Had she seemed a bit peaky? Did Rose have an incurable disease that needed expensive treatment? Did Rose have consumption?

She shook herself. What a thing to think. All the old rumour-mongers in the shop must be rubbing off on her.

The town was fevered with gossip about a certain herbalist and his women. Carmel wasn't a bit surprised: everyone had been too free and easy with him for too long – it was like they were all half in love. He had given her a new mixture to help her have a child; this one had mugwort as well as whatever else was usually in it. 'Fresh and especially potent, you do the business and this will do the rest.' Carmel wondered had the man lost the run of himself, talking to her like that – 'do the business' indeed.

He seemed less dependable these days, less well turned out. Though trade stayed brisk enough, Carmel noticed that his queues were down a bit. Success, it appeared, didn't suit him; the tide was turning and the townsfolk were suspicious. That's how it went with people. Everyone had wanted to mind him at first, own a piece of him. Not that you'd invite him to dinner.

In a way she felt sorry for him. She supposed the tide would turn back just as quickly. But, still, the things they were saying about him – that he had a roving eye, a taste for swanky sweethearts and a grá for exchanging favours. Maybe it was wishful thinking. Their need for him made the townsfolk uneasy.

Garda Molloy had been in too, asking questions. Nothing in particular but enough to cast aspersions. Asking what was said about the man? What exactly was he selling? Had there been any complaints against him? He had called round to lots of other premises. Carmel told him nothing; she intended to warn Dan also to say nothing. The last thing she needed was an abrupt end to her treatment.

She suspected the garda was more concerned about immorality than the herbalist's medical credentials. The way Emily had made such a fool of herself over him, and her so young and witless, was the talk of the town. The herbalist had to learn that you could be too nice sometimes. It didn't wash well with the people, encouraging a girl like Emily. Customers would say to Carmel, 'Wasn't she pitiful – offering to carry his bags, hanging around the lane?' His business had picked up no end when he shunned her.

Others weren't as harsh – said he must have a piece of ice in his heart, to be so cold to the young Madden one. Didn't her eyes light up at the sight of him? It was just girlish infatuation – a silly little thing, mooning over a man old enough to be her father – and anyone could see that nothing untoward had been going on.

Another thing – that Aggie was in and out of there with her cronies on a regular basis. Seems she did the herbalist's washing. That he collected it from her with a big golden smile and often tarried for a sup of poitín. That couldn't be good for him. Would he be able for it? She had no shame, that one, the big ginger head on her. And she had a big mouth. Maybe she was the one gabbing?

Carmel couldn't imagine Aggie talking to the law, but someone was – someone was letting cats out of the bag, and once they were out you couldn't get them back in again.

Doctor Birmingham, of course, had been suspicious from early on. Carmel knew why – it was no secret that he had been losing patients since the herbalist came to town. 'The herbalist works wonders,' his patients had chimed as they waited on Doctor B's oak pew in the tiled hall of his fine cold house. Doctor B, it was said, had overheard. He'd thrown open the door of his surgery. He ran them all out, every single one. 'Even Noreen Cassidy, and we know how fond he is of her.' Titter, titter.

'Off with you, then. Back to that quack. He's no doctor. Where's his papers? His surgery? On the street, that's where.'

As soon as the townsfolk had had the herbalist hung, drawn and quartered, they changed their minds and put him together again.

His fingernails are clean, spotless.

Ah, he's your man. Whatever is up, he's your man.

Gives great relief from chest pain.

But that never lasted long. There was always someone to bring the tone back down.

The devil takes care of his own.

Things aren't what they seem.

The truth will out.

Carmel sometimes wondered at the delight they all took in the rise and fall, and rise and fall again, of the herbalist. As if all the things they reported with hot scandalized lips were all the things they'd ever wanted.

She nodded and agreed with every contradictory comment. Increasingly her sympathy lay with poor Emily, but she knew not to say so. She missed Emily in the shop; she'd been easier to be around than Sarah. She remembered the way she'd chat, her elbows either side of some newspaper article, telling all about some royal. It didn't take much to make Emily happy – a few kind words, a trip to the picture house, sweets, a postcard of Merle Oberon. So when the herbalist first tipped his hat at her, Emily got her very own living, breathing maharajah.

'Who could blame her,' said Carmel once, 'who could blame her for having her head turned?'

The reply came swift and harsh. 'Ach, easy turn a head that has nothing in it.'

Carmel didn't think she could take another word about the whole thing. She was fed up with them, with their talk and shenanigans. All she wanted was an evening alone with her husband. She would speak to Sarah, tell her to take the next weekend off to go home. It might give the girl a scare, make her think her position wasn't secure.

44

Sarah knew something would happen: it was like she was outside herself, watching the scenes of a film and unable to change anything, just waiting and watching with a lurid fascination, with impatience. They were both annoyed with her after the night she was late home from the herbalist's smelling of alcohol. A confrontation was brewing. Sarah had overheard them. Carmel had been tippling and constantly discussing it with Dan. Sarah's goings-on had livened up her life no end.

Then, one Sunday after supper, Carmel called a meeting of the three of them in the living room. Carmel walked over to where Sarah was sitting, knelt before her and placed a hand on her knee. Carmel's eyes were swollen; there were purple shadows underneath. She patted Sarah's leg and looked ready to speak, when a hammering started on the shop door. They all jumped up to get it. Carmel got there first. It was Mrs Birmingham.

'Oh, dear, are you okay?' they heard Carmel ask.

Mrs Birmingham waited for a second and then released a long sob. Carmel took her hand and led her through to the back room.

'Come into the kitchen, it's warmer.'

Carmel grabbed a bottle of Buckfast and urged the doctor's wife to ensconce herself in the stove-side chair.

'You don't mind, Dan, do you?' she said. 'I'm needed.' She closed the door between them. Sarah got up. They both just stood there then, looking at each other. Dan blushed. Crying and consternation came from the kitchen. Sarah looked towards the window, but Carmel was leaning against the glass, so she could see nothing. She felt like weeping herself. Everything was a mess.

'Are you going to send me back?' she said.

'The place wouldn't be the same without you.'

'It's hardly happy as it is.' She wiped a tear with the back of her hand.

'I'm sorry, Sarah.'

'I'm a good person; I don't mean any harm.'

'I know that.' He put his hand on her shoulder. 'I know.'

She wouldn't look up at him.

'Sarah, do you believe me?' He leant in closer than he should have.

She raised her face, put her hand either side of Dan's head and pulled him towards her. She kissed him, and he kissed her back, every nerve in her face and mouth alive, sensing his smell, his taste, his texture – all of him – in a new way. He pulled back and looked anxiously towards the window into the kitchen. Sarah left him standing there and went upstairs to bed.

The kiss changed everything. The kiss told her why he'd sabotaged her chances with Matt. Why he was so full of praise she hadn't earned.

She ran her fingers over where their lips had touched. She had once hoped for romance but not like this. Maybe she'd had feelings for him but hadn't admitted it, even to herself. It was like an artificial light: one switch and it was on, just like that.

She wondered what to do. Her sensible voice said, *That's the end of it now. It's time to look elsewhere for employment. That was a very nice kiss. Think no more about it. It must not happen again.* The right thing would have been to pack her bags and head away, not spend another night under his wife's roof. But she knew she wasn't going anywhere.

She wondered how he felt about it, being so near to her. She touched the paper on the wall between her room and theirs. She tried to feel guilty, to think about what Carmel would go through if she knew. Lonely superior Carmel – she couldn't be any more miserable. Yet it would give her something to cling to . . . *Here's some news for you.* Sarah never knew she could be so cruel.

She slept well. Dreamt that Dan undid every stitch she wore in every room of his wife's house.

*

The next morning Dan sat and poured himself some tea from the pot Sarah had just made. She looked at his hands and couldn't think of anything to say. Dan cleared his throat.

'We were all a bit upset and said, eh . . . and did things perhaps we ought not to, that were out of character and not for the general good.'

He rubbed the back of his head and licked his lips before continuing. She knew he was remembering how that kiss felt. What's he trying to do, she wondered; does he even know? She rose and went over to him.

'I won't say a word; I wouldn't upset you for the world.'

He turned his hands palm up on the table in front of him, about to say something bland to smooth things over. It was all he ever did. Sarah sat on his lap. Carmel would rise at eleven at the earliest. She put her arms around his neck and kissed him at her leisure. His eyes were closed but his breathing was rapid. He wrapped those arms around Sarah and pushed her further into his lap, pressed his thumbs into her wrist. They clung at each other till the chimes of the clock told them to open shop.

'I'll do it, Sarah. You need time to get yourself together.'

He wasn't as upset as earlier, more in control. But could he deceive Carmel? They killed each other but at the same time they were close. Sarah went to her room. She poured some water from her jug into the basin. Washed her face with a damp face cloth. Laid the cool cloth over her face, and stretched out on the bed, imagining her own cooling hands were Dan's, running over her hips, her belly. There was a creak from the hall.

Carmel's bedroom door had opened. Sarah couldn't believe it; it took a miracle for Carmel to rise so early on a tonic-wine morning. She peeled off the face cloth. Carmel opened her door and came in. She looked terrible. She hadn't even got round to being the worse for wear yet. She walked in and stood over Sarah.

'Why aren't you in the shop?'

'I'm all swollen from crying.'

'I'm not stupid, Sarah, you don't even have to admit what's

going on, I can tell for myself. It's written all over your face, you poor fool – you think you're in love.'

'No,' Sarah said, 'I don't.'

'Don't deny it. No more cavorting, no more alcohol. While you're working for me, you'll stay home in the evenings and behave like a lady.'

Sarah looked at her employer. The stink of drink. The same clothes she had worn yesterday, all sleep creased.

'I'll try, Carmel.'

You were a long way from home, Aggie. Did you miss your family, your mother, your father?

Aggie had a lovely father. Thank God he's long dead and can't see me now. I hope he can't, dirty bitch that I am.

You're kind, Aggie.

You didn't always think that, you snotty thing, did you? Turned your nose up, you and your lot. Old Aggie was to be sniffed at.

I thought you were a tinker.

They'd be too religious to end up like me, a river bird, a sinner, a woman of ill repute. Why do women hold on so fierce to their good reputations? All a reputation does is stop you doing as you please.

Would you not have liked a husband, children?

Long past it, but that doesn't mean I didn't want to, or didn't ever. See that river? Once I crossed that river I became Aggie. There's a time in everyone's life when you leave behind who you were born to be and become what life makes of you, or you of it. I first crossed that bridge at twenty-three years of age, and never crossed back to who I was that first time. And I don't bloody care to. Why would I? Why would I change anything about my life, or the way I lived it? I would never swap my cosy barge, where I did as I pleased when I pleased, for that big house you grew up in. To be shown around town like a china doll, only to be taken apart within the privacy of your own four walls?

I disremember. I don't like talking about things like that.

45

Birdie Chase was slathering on hand cream. Her rings were piled on the counter beside the usual saucer of cold sausages for Charlie. Worried the fine lad would starve. She wore two headscarves, one on top of the other.

'It's on the back of the door, ducky – will you get it yourself, my hands are greasy.'

I did as she asked. The weight of the old nut-brown coat! I folded it across my arm carefully, as if it was the height of fashion. It was the only coat she wore. Winter and summer. Rumour had it that she had thousands of fine coats, robes, costumes and curtains from all her travels when she was younger, that Birdie could wear a different dress every day for the rest of her life and still not run out. Yet all we ever saw her wear was the same serviceable wool. It seemed the only thing Birdie ever changed was her mind and her gold and red headscarves.

'You'll let that out, Emily; I've gained around the middle.'

'I will. I can give you a good half-inch or do you want to be measured?'

'No, no, a half-inch will do.'

I knew she wouldn't permit me to measure her; she never did. Birdie hadn't gained an ounce as far as I could see. But who was I to argue with a woman who wanted to part with her money? Especially one who had so much of it. I picked up her jar of hand cream and had a sniff.

'It's one of the herbalist's. A gift! I didn't buy it,' she said. 'Ah, no, I did. I bought a few items this week. In truth I was hoping he might have something suitable for Veronique. She has been suffering terribly, with her chest.' She thumped her own as if I didn't know where chests were situated. 'I got a letter last week to say she was coughing all night and all day – it has her worn out. She hasn't opened the shop in over a fortnight, and, knowing Veronique like I know Veronique, that means it's serious, much more serious than she's letting on.'

'Maybe it's to be expected, Miss Chase – isn't V getting on a bit?'

'Not a bit, sure isn't she my twin?' Her face scrunched up.

'I always forget you're twins; it must be because I think of you as being so much younger in years than Veronique.'

'Ah, how quick you can be, young Millie.' Birdie laughed and gave me a wink.

The only person who had ever called me Millie was Mam, but somehow I didn't mind Birdie saying it; it made me feel sad and warm at the same time. Daft or not, she was a kind woman, one who never meant to upset. She must've been very worried about Veronique, for Birdie didn't approve of the herbalist; she called him a corrupt charlatan.

So V hadn't fallen out with her – she really was too ill to visit. But why would Birdie go to the herbalist? With her money she could bring in a doctor from anywhere in the world to cure her twin. Her mattress was so stuffed with cash that her little nose touched the ceiling when she snored, or so it was said.

I rubbed a bit of the hand lotion across my knuckle, recognized the concoction as lard and lavender. 'Ladies' Hand Lotion': the label was fancier than before, fancier than what was inside. I said my goodbyes to Miss Chase.

'Don't forget your sausages.'

Birdie waved as I left. She seemed a bit disappointed; maybe I should have stayed longer, let her tell me how beautiful Mam was when she was young, how they'd expected great things from her, how I had her eyes, how I had her hair. All lies, but nice things to hear. But I was too vexed with the herbalist and his hand-lotion label to stay and listen. It wasn't his handwriting on the label; it was a woman's. And I knew who – Lady Muck, my good friend Sarah. He had told me he had sacked her, that she couldn't spell her name if you paid her.

I popped across to Kelly's. Let on I was passing the time of day. I was about to get to the point when Sarah slipped out from behind the counter.

'I feel ill. Will you hold the fort?' She looked marvellous.

'I will.'

Dan came in, looking around him.

'If you're looking for the spinster, she's in the outhouse.'

'Haven't you the sharp tongue?'

When there was no sign of Sarah returning, I decided to go else-where for my information – to go straight to the herbalist himself. I dropped Birdie's coat and sausages off home, so I could confront him without looking too mad in the head.

Charlie was out but Father was there. He was sitting in Mam's corner on the súgán stool, staring into a dead fire. He looked wretched, and I felt sorry for him, but there was no point in talking, never had been. We never got on, never would. He had stopped throwing his fists around far too late. There was nothing left to break.

The herbalist was distracted, so distracted that he let me in. He was in a hurry to get going. Barely noticed what I said about Sarah and him being in cahoots, and didn't seem to have the energy to remind me that I was barred in the day-time. He was packing his boxes and bag. His hands were shaking.

'You haven't even made me a cup of tea.'

'You shouldn't be here – let yourself out.'

At that he was gone, flying off on his new motorcycle. It was the blue-black of a horsefly, had big wide ugly wheels, made a racket and left a cloud of smoke behind it. But my God he loved it – thought he was a warrior on a steed.

I didn't let myself out; I had a good root around. The black sur-gery notebook was on the table. He was usually so careful with it, usually carried it in his pocket. Smudged on the left-hand corner of every written page were the clouds of his thumb prints. I kissed them.

He had it all written down, every pound, shilling and pence, paid and owed. Every patient had a page, where their name, address and complaints were listed – lumbago, nerves or blood, take your pick. There were people I didn't think even knew the herbalist. People too upstanding even to speak of him let alone to him. Sergeant Deegan for one, and Mr Joe Nash for another. His writing slanted to the right, which meant, according to Aggie, that he took after his mother; if it went to the left, it's the father.

His script was neat. Some words were underlined. Like 'next visit'. There was always a 'next visit'. A lot of women in the town suffered from their nerves. Catty Dolan was one of them. She must suffer terrible, the poor thing. Had been in near eight times in the past few weeks. And Miss Annie Brady, nine times she'd been. I got to wondering were they all in love with him? It was a bit expensive for love, at one and six a go.

The pages went back to January, to names I didn't recognize. What town was he operating from back then? He wasn't here. It was all written in a smooth, calm hand. Nerves. Bronchitis. Skin trouble. Examination. Stomach. Blood and Nerves. A leg ulcer. Examination. Blood and Nerves. Nerves. Nerves. Nerves. All those women, all those nerves. Not so many lately – was his star fading? Or was he just too good at his job?

And the most recent entry, in shaky writing, was Miss Rose Birmingham: 'Examination. Paid 1/6'. There were brown marks on that page; they looked like dried blood. The ink was smudged and a line ran under the entry, a scratched, scraggly wave. Sparks of ink had flown from the nib of his pen to collect and dry in the central fold between the pages. No address, no further details. No 'next visit'.

I shut the notebook and put it back where I'd found it. What ailed Rose? Why did it upset me? And not in a jealous way, but in an afraid way, an afraid-for-Rose way. I checked under his bed, wanting to look in the shoebox for the photograph he had snatched out of my hands. I wanted to see if there was something written on the back that would tell me who he really was. Instead I found a wooden box. It was full of implements. A strange-looking collection, things that made my stomach turn. A syringe. A bulb with a nozzle. Two shoehorns screwed together. A piece of stiff wire. A rod with a dark stain on one end. It was the sight of the rod that made me run for the back door and vomit.

46

Carmel walked briskly up the road to Doctor B's house. It was a dull morning; the rain was a soft mist, and there weren't many people out and about. Carmel had a five-pound note in her purse for Grettie. Only it wasn't just a five-pound note – it was a perambulator, it was stuffed toys for her baby boy. It was a loan, not a gift, she had to make sure Grettie understood that. Birdie was sweeping the path in front of her shop. Seamus was painting the Nashes' window-frames. Carmel waved across the road at them but kept going; she didn't want to delay.

You never knew who had trouble and who didn't. Grettie of all people, and everyone had thought she had done so well for herself and that Rose was a saint. It was true what they said: street angel, house devil. It had all been revealed the other night in Carmel's kitchen, when Grettie kept her up till the early hours, pouring out her troubles.

Rose had her father wrapped around her little finger. He bought her anything her heart desired – jewellery, perfumes, trinkets, expensive clothes, a whole new wardrobe. He'd hired someone to paint her portrait, for God's sake, when she was only eleven. And all she wanted was more, more, more. Doctor B kept his wife on a tight budget, yet lavished money on their daughter. And was Rose grateful? No, she was not. She was the opposite to grateful. Nowadays she hardly spoke, and when she did she said awful things. 'Obscenities,' Grettie said. Carmel was dying to know what the obscenities were, but Grettie wouldn't say.

There was ivy twisting around the Birminghams' heavy iron gates. They would want to get it cut back. They had the hired help, hadn't they? This time Carmel didn't wait to be admitted. The surgery was packed anyway. She walked on through to the living quarters without asking whether she could or couldn't. Grettie was in her drawing room, swathed in a green kimono, her face all puffed out from crying. It really was a terrible sight. She lounged on one of the big chairs by the fire, which was smouldering – the room was smoky.

'You'd need to get that chimney cleaned.'

'Albie slammed the door; that always draws smoke into the room. He did it on purpose, the devil.'

It wasn't like Grettie to be calling the doctor by his first name. Things were worse than they'd seemed. Carmel pulled a stool over to where she was sitting.

'I have that money for you,' she whispered.

'Oh, thank God.' The tears that were welling up flowed over.

'But I'll need it back in a month, Grettie.'

'Of course, of course.'

'I've drawn up a docket.'

Grettie took the paper from her, read it. Carmel had set out the amount of the loan and the repayment date.

'You really are a shopkeeper, Carmel.'

'It's money I can't afford to lose; you must know that.'

'Of course, of course.'

Grettie called out for Rose, who appeared in seconds. Evidently she had been waiting in the dining room. Rose smiled at Carmel. She looked wan. Her skin was always pale, but today it was practically translucent. Carmel could see the blue veins in her neck. She was dressed beautifully, as usual. Today she wore a white brocade dress, with gold buttons down the front. The grip pinning her hair back was ruby. Only the best for Daddy's girl. You never really knew, did you?

'How are you, Rose?'

'Good, thank you, Carmel – would you like a tea or a mineral?'

'A cup of tea would be nice.' Carmel was parched.

When Rose brought in the tray, Grettie ordered her to sit down and join them.

'I've very good news, Rose. Mrs Holohan has been kind enough to give us a loan, so we can get by now; we can pay that bill for another week or two.'

Rose fled the room without excusing herself.

'See what I mean?' Grettie sighed.

It was shocking, Carmel agreed; the girl had been thoroughly spoilt.

Carmel went home with her docket signed and tucked into her purse. Helping Grettie had put a spring in her step. Maybe, she thought, it was a mistake to be so focused on her own troubles, maybe it would be best to try to be more outward-looking, more charitable towards others. She waved cheerily at Sarah as she walked through the shop, picking up an apple from the basket on the way. She unlocked the cupboard door in the kitchen and removed three random novels. It was work, really. How could she recommend them, if she hadn't read them?

Tucked up nicely in bed, crunching away on the hard green apple, she began the first novel without even reading the title. She'd do that till it was time to make dinner and then she'd start up again. It was nice to feel industrious while you were lying down.

47

Sarah now woke with excitement for the coming day, for the thrill of seeing Dan. She was no longer afraid of being caught, had no more concerns about Carmel, his witch of a wife. It was so much easier to think of Carmel like that now.

Even though she was sick every morning, the mirror told her she had a glow. Carmel would be puzzled about why she looked so radiant – or at least she would be, if she were able to get out of bed. *While the cat's away, the mice will play.* And play they did. Their fingers touching on the counter.

He whispered to her when the shop was empty.

'I respect you, Sarah. Please don't think that I want to take advantage.'

'Well, what do you want to do, then? Marry me?'

'I can't do that, I'm married already.'

'No, really? Why didn't you say?'

'Look, Sarah, I don't want to spoil you for anyone else. We're going to have to do something about our little problem.'

It was still little then.

Anyone could tell that Dan and Carmel weren't happy together. They must've been once. Sarah looked again at that wedding photo. Carmel so serious but pleased with herself. Pleased wasn't the same as love. Sarah looked closer at the bride. *She doesn't even love him.*

After that, Sarah paid more attention than before to the goings-on between them, which weren't much. One night she heard what she hadn't heard in a while: the bed squeaking, the movement of the headboards against the wall, whispering that had nothing to do with fighting. Then she thought to herself, *I'm imagining things.*

In the shop, alone, Dan smoothed imaginary fluff from her blouse. She needed to talk to him properly, to confirm that something really was happening, but Carmel was always in the house; she never went out.

One evening over supper Carmel suggested that Sarah might like to go home 'to the country' for a few days. 'You'd like to see your people' was how Carmel put it. As if they were a whole tribe different to herself and Dan. 'I'll have Seamus Devoy come and collect you in his trap. There's no need to thank me.'

Did Carmel suspect something? If so, she would hardly be standing there talking normally. There was something up, though. Dan hadn't so much as caught her eye this evening. Was it a game to him? Was he that kind of man? No, he couldn't be; he was always so gentle in his dealings with her.

Sarah would be glad to see Mai – the thought itself almost made her cry. But what if she was seen by the neighbours? There was no counter to hide behind; and folk at home would know she wasn't the kind to put on an ounce. Not 'Skinny Sarah', long drink of water that she was, not for no reason at all.

Sarah couldn't sleep that night; she lay there listening to the house creak. She turned on to her back; it was easier to lie like that. Her breasts had grown fuller, and they prickled. It was unpleasant, made her queasy. With every signal that her body was changing, Sarah wished it was a dream, that it wasn't so. This was something that happened to others, to poor unfortunates, not to girls like her.

Time was against her. Every day brought her closer to being exposed, to being locked up. In the mornings her mouth filled with saliva and her stomach heaved. By the time Carmel came down, it had settled somewhat. Dan looked like someone was going to take him out and shoot him. He went to confession every single morning, to the new priest, because he was wet behind the ears and didn't know the family. So Dan would be absolved of sin till sometime in the afternoon, when she'd turn around to find his mouth crushed against her own. She pitied the young priest and dreaded passing him in the street.

There was something else. All in her imagination, she knew – probably to do with the changes in her body – but it was nerve-racking. It always happened when she was alone, maybe sweeping out front at the end of the day, or strolling back from an evening walk. She'd feel someone watching her, feel a cool shadow fall across her back, smell cedar and turn around to find that no one was there. Sometimes she'd hear footsteps in the distance, which she took for the unmistakable sound of Master Finbar's heavy shoes hitting the dusty road.

She ran her hand across her belly. Her stomach was swollen. That much was real. Sarah imagined soft baby skin and the child safe in her arms. What in God's name would become of them if she did nothing? She'd be put away and the baby would be taken; she'd be placed in a home, or a laundry, like Annie Mangan. There was no word from her aunt Margaret in London. What would she do?

She had almost enough for her fare, for a ring and for widow's weeds. She would have to leave. It was as simple and as hard as that. Because no one was getting their hands on her child.

She thought about what Dan would think if he knew she was in trouble. He wouldn't look at her that way any more. No, he wouldn't.

But what if he thought the child was his?

He would come with her, and they could start a new life together, away from all this. Couldn't they?

What a terrible thing to think. How could that even cross her mind, to be so deceptive, to sink so low? She could never do that. It was wrong, there could be no excuse for a lie like that.

Not even to save an innocent child?

There were movements in her belly lately, like butterflies. The softest, almost unnoticeable flutters. Safe. For the moment. When Sarah thought of these flutters, she knew that for the sake of the child she could become someone else, someone who would do such a thing, someone who could swallow her virtue and get Dan to lie with her. Who could trick him into thinking she was carrying his child. She'd be safe then, they'd both be safe. Wouldn't they?

The house was silent. No voices from the living room. It was well past midnight. Sarah knew she wouldn't sleep. She knew he was awake too. She just knew. Before she could think too much about it, she slipped out of bed and padded down the stairs as softly as a cat and unbolted the door that separated the house from the shop. She felt her way to the counter. The darkness tasted of nutmeg.

She decided to count to a hundred. If he hadn't joined her by then, she would go back to bed and consider her choice made.

By the time she got to ten, he was inside her.

Sarah leant against a stack of newspapers on Seamus's trap and looked up at the sky. The clouds tumbled past like puffy circus clowns and the sun toasted her face, giving her respite, a little peace. She was grateful that Seamus seemed as preoccupied as she was. The weather was warm, and there was a good clean light, but there was something else too, a feeling of summer winding down. Though it was bright till late, that would change soon. Soon there would be dark and rain, soon she would be showing. But for the moment she wasn't, and the fields were like spun gold.

She thought again of Rumpelstiltskin. *What's my name? What's my name?* Jumping up and down in front of some poor mother. Why on earth would he want a baby? Children had a hard time in all the tales Mai had told Sarah when she was young: they were either left in the woods to die or swapped for a head of lettuce. But that was all once upon a time. Nowadays they had no need for witches. They'd had their very own demon, the cruelty man in his brown suit. Well, he wouldn't be getting his hands on Sarah's son. Her son. She hadn't realized it till that very second but she was sure her child was a boy.

Seamus began to talk and once he started there was no stopping him. On and on he went, about some maharajah of Indore who had, would you believe it, married some American divorcée he'd met on a health voyage. 'Them Americans, they'd turn the head of the Pope himself.'

Sarah hadn't a notion what he was on about, didn't want to know. Seamus got the hint and gave up. Instead he began a song about a gypsy. It was very soothing. Sarah felt happy, almost carefree, by the time the trap pulled up alongside Mai's. She waved Seamus off, not daring to ask him in for tea. She opened the latch and called out hello.

48

I donned Mrs B's red fox-fur coat and headed in for the market. I was roasting and people stared. I didn't care. I couldn't stop thinking about the box under the herbalist's bed. Birdie was sitting on a stool in her doorway as I marched past.

'Emily, a minute.' She waved her stick.

What is it about people that no one minds you one bit till you're too busy to stop and talk to them?

'Charlie's grand, in great form.'

I answered the question before she could ask it. Birdie didn't laugh. She was wearing a black headscarf and hadn't bothered with her rouge.

'Who died?' I asked.

'Veronique.' Her voice was hoarse and weak.

'I had no idea, I'm so sorry, Birdie.' I rubbed her knee. Stupid Emily.

'There were so few at her funeral – she should never have moved to that town. This here' – she banged her walking stick off the ground – 'this here was her town.'

'That's terrible. Is it like half of you has died, like you're missing an arm?'

That made her smile. Death does strange things to people.

'I'll never lose my appetite for life, Emily, but it is terrible, and a terrible shock. In a way she feels closer now than when she was alive. Do you understand?'

'Not really.'

'You will one day. Veronique had a few things you'd like, silken fabrics, and such; when the dust has settled maybe we could take a drive over, have a look at the place. Deciding what to do with the Emporium will be a headache.'

'The Emporium?'

'Her pokey hole of a shop, that's what she called it. Veronique was beautifully bananas.'

There was the pot calling the kettle black. All the same, I pitied poor Birdie, left to clean everything up at her age.

'I don't mind helping out, but not today, I have something to do today.'

'Come back to me about it, Emily.'

'I will.' I patted her knee again.

Jesus, what was it with me and old ones' knees? Poor Birdie. I'd call back when I had more time, send Charlie down, that would cheer her up. For now I had to move fast enough not to be waylaid by anyone else.

The market was sparse; the herbalist hadn't any customers yet. He watched as I wove towards him, but as I got near he studied his array of bottles. I stood where I had the first day I'd got up the courage to present myself to him: in front of his table, a little away. He knew I was there, but he didn't look up and smile this time. Instead he growled.

'Get that fox-fur off you this minute.'

'What do you really do to the women that go to you?'

He looked this way and that, then stepped out from behind the stall and cupped my face in his hand, as if to examine me. Then he pressed a thumb underneath my eye and dragged the skin down. Looked in one eye and then the other in this manner. I saw the dark pores on his face, the stubble that was too deep for the razor, smelt the musky salt of his armpits.

'What do you really do?'

'Nothing they don't ask for,' he said. ' "Jesus help me." That's what they all say, every one of them. And does he? No. But I do. I save the day.'

He pinched my chin, raised his voice. 'If you are very constipated, I suggest salts, young lady; now, if you don't mind –'

'A bit of lady trouble, Doctor?' the chicken and dog man shouted over.

'Some people get the wrong idea altogether,' said the herbalist.

He was trying to mortify me into leaving, but I stood my ground. I wasn't going to be shaken off so easily.

'Take off that fur now!' He tugged the neck of the coat.

'I saw your box of tricks, Don Fernandes.'

He dropped his hand and just stood there. We looked at each other: it was like there was no one else alive in the whole town but us two and I was terrified of what he was going to do. I had gone too far. When he spoke, I expected him to roar, not to whisper, which was what he did. He whispered so softly that I could barely hear him.

'Do you think Doctor Birmingham works without tools, Emily?'

'He never took out a rod to examine me.'

He held his belly and started laughing then. His eyes were very angry. I worried that he might lash out and hit me.

'Emily, you are funny. The rod, as you call it, is a door stop. It jams the door closed when I'm treating someone. Now get that fox-fur off you this minute.'

He stepped towards me, but I ran, ran as fast as I could away from the man I'd been running towards all summer.

49

Carmel felt more at ease with Sarah gone home for a few days. Or maybe the new medicine was working. The herbalist had tweaked the mixture again: it was now a stronger pick-me-up. He was very good at listening to a woman, at understanding the importance of this treatment without its being pointed out to him. At first she had been shy about asking for a greater strength, but the herbalist was fine about it, said she could have anything her heart desired. It made her feel ashamed of having entertained the gossips and the inflammatory things they'd had to say. The other tonic didn't seem to have worked, not yet, not this month.

A new laziness came with the ending of summer, and with Sarah out of the way Carmel and Dan were able to loll around and savour it. Carmel was well advanced in her reading of the banned novels. There had been no word from Grettie B since she had given her the money. There were no more unexpected visits and crying episodes. She concluded that things must have sorted themselves out.

They relaxed on the Sunday. Dozed most of the day, had their dinner at teatime and went for a walk down by the river. Carmel had held Dan's hand once they passed the lock gates. It was so peaceful that they were both reluctant to turn back. She had given him a kiss when no one was looking.

Carmel decided that she should be happy with her husband and not envious of their shop girl's comings and goings. When Sarah had started to come home late from the herbalist's place on a Sunday, Carmel had been so resentful. How she would have liked to be part of something lively, a sing-song or story-telling. But when she'd heard it was just card-playing, she wasn't too upset about being left out, and didn't really mind Sarah partaking. It was nice to have the house to themselves for an hour or two.

Dan had minded; he had minded a lot. Gambling on Our Lord's

Day? Their shop girl, ingratiating herself with ne'er-do-wells? He was fuming.

But now that she'd had time to think about it, Carmel had it all in perspective. She just wasn't as free as Sarah. She was a respectable married woman. She had had her fun and should be content with her world as it was.

The next morning she was up to open the shop. Carmel had forgotten how much she enjoyed working the counter by herself. Liked the news, hearing what everyone was up to. It wasn't the same hearing it second-hand. She had been so weak after she lost the child that she needed to be away from it all for a while, because in those days she was the news.

Sometime that afternoon, as they looked through the ledger together, Dan mentioned that he thought Sarah should get a rise soon. The meanest man in the Western world putting his hands in his pockets? He frazzled her nerves when he said things like that.

Carmel tried to get back that soft satisfied feeling they'd had on their stroll down the river, that feeling of completeness in each other. But she couldn't. The nice time was over. Carmel was beginning to think that an apple and a good book in her bed – once he'd got out of it – was the closest thing she'd be getting to heaven in this life.

50

There hadn't been the warm reunion that Sarah had expected. Mai's face had fallen when she saw her at the door. Thought she had lost her job. Her next concern was if anyone had seen her, any of the neighbours. When did Mai ever care about neighbours? She had actually stuck her head out of the door and looked up and down to see if there was anyone around, anyone that might have seen.

'Look at the big chest on you,' she said; 'the whole place will know.'

'I'll stay inside.'

She didn't of course. She spent most of her time in the back garden, weeding. It was good to be out in the sun, moving around instead of standing in the one place in a stuffy shop. The days flew, and Mai was kind enough to let her enjoy them and keep her worries, as much as she could, to herself. On the last evening, the Sunday, Mai made Sarah her supper and got down to business.

'He's been here.'

'Who? James?' It hurt Sarah to say his name out loud.

'No, of course not. He wouldn't dare. It was the father, Master Finbar. He invited himself for tea, and in not so many words said you're not to show your face around here. He didn't say it quite like that. You know the way he talks. Polite but in a way that would scare the bejesus out of you. "Sarah has a good job now," he said. "Yes," I said, "and we're grateful to you for that." "There's nothing for her here, Mai. Her life is elsewhere now."'

'That's not anything odd. Sure you said the same yourself, Mai.'

'No, Sarah – it's the way he said it. He was at your send-off; he must've seen what went on. He was outside that night smoking those foul fancy cigars of his. Then he rushed in and fetched his hat and coat. Not a goodbye or a thank you. And the face on him. Then you came in crying. I never put two and two together till he came here with his message. And it was a message, make no bones about it. A warning.'

Sarah covered her face. He saw. Then he must've seen that it wasn't her fault – but did men understand such things? Oh, the shame.

'You're in a dangerous situation.'

'Do you not think I know that?'

'I don't think you know much. Coming here. Remember what I told you about Annie Mangan?'

'Yes.'

'It was Jamsie boy put her in the family way, and his father who had her locked up. He never had any control over that son of his. I warned you against him. I warned you, but you wouldn't listen.'

'No, it was only me. It was always only me with him.'

'No, it wasn't, Sarah. It was never only you.'

'Why didn't you tell me the full truth before this, warn me properly? I thought you were fussing.'

'It was rumour then, just rumour. What's happened since has made me know that the rumour was true. I've asked around; there are many here who owe me a favour. It seems Finbar had her committed. Took her to the place himself, all the way to Galway. Now I wonder if she got there at all?'

'Mai, don't! You're getting carried away.'

'If you're seen here in that condition, you'll be the one to get carried away. Oh, why did you ever let that buffoon near you?'

'How could you, Mai? You know what happened.'

'Ah, henny, don't cry. I know. I know, my girl.'

'You could keep me here till my time.'

'If he wasn't sniffing about.'

'He has no right to barge into your home.'

'Aye, but barge he will. A curse on him and a curse on his son who did this to you. Still no word from London. I was sure Margaret would take you in.'

'Maybe she will – wouldn't that be wonderful? And then after a couple of years we'd come back home to you, me and my baby.'

'Won't be a baby then, will be a toddler.'

Sarah smiled and hugged herself.

'Would you be able to do it?' Mai asked. 'Love something that was forced into you? Love something that came from him?'

'Good comes from bad all the time. You know that, Mai.'

'You're quare, Sarah.'

'It's the way you reared me, Mai. Was my mother quare?'

'Mad as a hatter, Sarah.'

'Was she?' Sarah said gently, looking into Mai's eyes and holding her gaze.

A soft *oh* slipped from Mai's lips and a tear ran down her face. She clasped her hand over her mouth. Sarah stood up and began to clear their cups away.

'Do you have any cake?'

'I do,' said Mai. 'Madeira, made fresh today.'

51

I was cutting out my dress. The kind I'd dreamt of, not the kind I used to settle for. I was not thinking about the herbalist. I was not. I was cutting out my scoop-necked, bias-cut, royal-blue, ankle-length dress, being extra careful with the fabric, using a tracing from my very own pattern. It took me a long time to afford such a decent length of satin. I wasn't going to rush it now. No such thing, I cut it one steady slice at a time, in good light, with my sharpest scissors and a clean mind. I wouldn't think about him. One wrong move would make a hames of the job. You can't be fussed and shape something beautiful. You just can't.

I shut out the sounds of Charlie and Rita downstairs in the kitchen. Arguing again. Over golden-haired Rose and her Hollywood face, I'd put any money on it. Charlie was smitten with Rose, but he would never come straight out and say it. Instead he was cooling things with Rita, pretending to be a very busy man with his foundry work, his few cows and his yard of chucks. 'Letting her down easy,' he called it. The cows in the back field bayed to be milked and there was a gale brewing, but still no sign of a move on busy Charlie.

I was soon lost in cutting, like I was the blade slicing against the garment's grain. Till, all of a sudden, I was done. I removed the pins from the satin and stretched my arms. Lifted the pieces from the sheet on the floor and placed them on the bed. Admired the wide sleeves and long bodice, the way they pooled like blue liquid. Branches tapped and scraped the window. Then came a slow scratch, and with it a silvery flicker of memory, like a caught reel of film.

The herbalist was standing in the corner of a dark room, wearing a white vest. He grinned at me and turned his head to the side, stretched out his tongue and gave the hula lady on his arm a long,

244

slow lick. And I was there, just watching, numb, dumb and falling slowly forward into his wink.

Blood and nerves. Nerves, nerves . . . all those nerves. A syringe, a piece of wire, a rod. I held my breath, I would not think of him, or of what any of it meant. I would not.

I practised a hair-do for my new dress, settled on a smooth pleat, a swept-back fringe. My skin looked dingy in the mirror, but once I was all done up my complexion would glow and my satin gown would shimmer and I would be invited to dance. Several times. I would nod politely and step forward into a daring tango. So elegant I wouldn't even have to speak. But when? Soon. It had to be soon. No good making a dress if you're not going to show it off. I wasn't going to end up like Carmel Holohan, creeping around the garden gathering small spuds for Eliza's mush in her tatty fur from better days. Back when I was her shop girl and fit to peg her sheets on the line, she used to parade around the vegetable patch with a trowel and shovel, letting on to be industrious. 'I'd say that coat could tell some stories, Mrs H,' said I. Carmel just gave a tinkly laugh as if her stories were too juicy for words. Then she turned up her collar and flew past the cabbages like a bear on its hind legs. She could be a terrible eejit sometimes.

I'd a bad dream that night and I thought it was because of the herbalist. I thought it was a premonition. I was back on Aggie's boat, sitting at her table. Rain pitter-pattered against the window. The lamp was down to a glimmer; long shadows licked the ceiling. Across from me Aggie shuffled a deck of cards and the flab on her arm jiggled. She was dressed in her slip and her skin was the colour of lard. The fat man was tied up in the corner. *His nibs won't get next nor near you now*, Aggie said. *I cut out his tongue too for the hell of it.* Delighted with herself, she dealt a row of cards face down, *snap, snap, snap*, and leant towards me. *Pick one, my love*, she said, her breath cold. She had turned into the old Aggie, the one who teased me so, but I did as I was bid, eased a card from the centre and handed it back to her. She grinned and held it up.

It was a Joker, the same leering, hopping jester as before, wearing slippers with bells on them. He was still waving a stick puppet that looked just like him. The ugly divil came right up to me then, and it wasn't a puppet at the end of his stick; it wasn't a puppet. It was a child.

Aggie gripped my chin, the way my mammy did when she wanted to wipe my face clean. *See chicken, chicken sees everything.* And the fat man in the chair smiled and his mouth was all bloody. *Make it go away*, I wanted to say, but the words had no proper sound. *Your wish is my command*, said Aggie, and she ripped the card right down the middle. The trickster gave a small cry as he was split in two.

I didn't mean for her to hurt him like that.

You talk about everything, Aggie. As if there's no shame.

Tell it and tell it and there'll be no shame, only the facts of the matter and the question of who's to blame. And it wasn't you, child, it wasn't you.

Let me begin. It was dusk. I heard a woeful screech from the herbalist's old shed. I'll never forget the sound. Don't cover your ears, pet, don't. It's your tale, but we all own it.

I raced across the grass with my lantern. The door was locked from the outside, but the wood was rotten. A few kicks and it shattered open. Inside a young girl lay on the filthy stretcher bed. She looked at me, but didn't speak.

'What on earth ails you?'

'My tummy hurts. It feels so pulled apart and all the blood, it keeps coming and it's so hot and high smelling. Did you smell it – is that why you came?'

'Of course not.'

I felt around and began to light the candles on the shelf.

'Am I going to die?' The child started to blub.

'You won't – you're in good hands now.' I saw the bucket beside her and retched.

'I'll never get into heaven, or my baby . . .' The girl began mewling.

'It was only the makings of a baby – look.' I tilted the bucket towards her. 'Look! There's no baby there.'

She vomited bile on to the grey towel that covered her.

There was a knock on the door. It was sharp, a *rat-tat-tat* knuckle rap. A woman's knock.

I shoved a chair against the door and put my finger to my mouth, warning the girl to be quiet. We held our breath and listened. A

247

mouse dropped from the roof into the bucket of blood, and the girl screamed. The shed shuddered as the door was pushed.

'Hello? Are you all right in there?'

If I kept silent someone with a tougher elbow might be called to investigate. So I wiped my hands on my skirt and opened the door slightly, keeping one foot wedged against it. Who was it only Lady Chatterley herself, Birdie Chase?

'Is everything all right?'

'A mouse, bedad, a mouse ran over my foot – can't abide them.'

'May I come in?' she asked.

'It's not my place. Sorry, madam. Tra laa.'

I shut the door and listened carefully, heard silence and then a sigh before the steps on the other side faded away.

'Madam never asked after you, but she wouldn't be here otherwise. She must know something.'

'Oh God, oh God.' The girl scrambled off the bed, held her stomach, bent over.

'No, no, stand over the bucket.'

I let the girl put her arms around my neck and hang there, over the bloody bucket.

'Is it nearly over?'

'How the hell would I know?'

The girl rocked on her heels, crying low.

'Help me, help me, ah, Mam,' she said.

The girl stayed rocking, all modesty forgotten. Her shift bloodied and rucked up around her back. She stilled as red lumps slid out of her and into the bucket.

'Oh, God.'

We waited.

'I think that's all.'

The girl got on to the bed.

'I'll fetch water as soon as I tidy this up a bit.'

The young one looked exhausted. Soon she was dozing restlessly, gripping her belly in her sleep.

Then muggins here had to wipe the floor with rags. The whole business made me sick. I covered the bucket with straw; it quickly seeped up. I went out, made my way down the side alley, through the hedging and on to the wasteland that edged the river. When I was sure that no one could see, I emptied my burden into the reeds. River life moved towards the dark patch, and old Aggie here walked back as quickly as she had come.

The herbalist's deserted handiwork was asleep and whimpering. I collected the bloodied rags and went into the yard behind the shed. The moon was full. The rags took to light slowly in the tin barrel where the doctor burned everything he no longer held in favour. I threw in some twigs, stoked the flames with a blackened stick and sat in the old armchair. Remembered how I'd laughed and called the chair his throne, called him lord of the river, king of all he surveyed. The low flame slowly ate the fabric. I had a slug of gin and fell into a daydream in which the leaves chattered from the trees and talked to the reeds, till the whole town was babbling that Agnes Reilly was a murderer of unborn children. I could just hear them. *She flings remains into the river, feeds changelings to the trout. Don't fish there; you don't know what you'll catch, or what will catch you. Hear that? That's not the wind; it's a poor unbaptized soul crying for its mother. It's a river of tears. A weeping welt. And she's the queen of it. Queen of the dumb suck.*

The girl's moans interrupted my reverie. I twisted my numb foot as I hobbled towards the shed to quieten her.

She was sitting up, naked from the waist down, her fingers covered in red, screaming.

'Where's my baby!'

'Hush, hush, it's over now. It's over now. There was no baby; it's all in your head, there was no baby.'

Eventually she slept again, or maybe she had passed out. How thin she was: I could see the pearled row of her spine. *We're no better than animals*, I thought, *losing our offspring in straw, like cattle.*

After an hour I checked the lane for any sign of life, and then lifted the girl from the bed.

'Put your arms around my neck.' She did as she was told.

An obedient thing, she let herself be carried on to the boat and laid on the settle bed. Seemed to curl up, seemed at last ready to rest. I sat on my stool outside while my kettle simmered. What would the herbalist think when he found his birdie had flown? It was all only a shambles. Everything was strange and yet felt like the realest of dreams. I felt old and of little use to anyone except for that girl. I didn't often think like that. I knew how wise I was, how I knew men and their women too. How when you weighed up my bodily sinning against my adoration for the holy virgin I came out even. Just look at the love Jesus showed for Mary Magdalene over everyone else. Washing his feet with her tears. Oh, I'd give my right arm to dry the saviour's feet with my hair. Sure Jesus died for our sins; if we committed none, the poor man would've died for nothing.

The girl wasn't happy when she woke, fretting. Her skin was like fire. I opened the hatch.

'Why did his lordship leave you there all alone?'

'He said I'd be all right, that it was over, and when I wasn't looking he slipped out.'

'Was he meeting someone?'

'I don't know; he said it was a matter of extreme urgency.'

'Must be Emily up to her tricks. She's mad for him. She stops short of wrapping herself in butcher's paper and delivering herself to him.'

'She's too soft.'

'You're too good-natured. And now you have to go home. Are you listening to me? We have to take you home and tell your father and mother what happened. They can help you. You're fevered; you might have an infection. We have to get proper help for you.'

The girl wouldn't meet my eye, wouldn't answer. I went back to the shed and gathered her clothes. I began to help her dress, and went about it slowly, as you would with a child, raising one arm and then the other, slipping her back into her beautifully cut garments. Her pale blue finely tailored skirt and jacket. I cleaned the girl's hands with a damp cloth, her palms first and then between each finger, over and over, rinsing the cloth many times in a bowl as she tried to rub the last of the dried blood from her nails. She just watched, as if they were someone else's hands, as if none of this was happening to her. Her blonde curls were flat to her neck with sweat. She was so thin, like a fledgling fallen from the nest. Raw boned, fragile. Helpless.

'Stay there. I'm going to get my odd-job man to take us in the trap. Don't worry – he won't ask any questions. He's not the type.'

I half expected her to have run off when I arrived back with Seamus in tow, still wiping the sleep from his eyes. But she hadn't; she was curled in a ball, crying. Seamus carried her to the trap without a word. Thank God it wasn't day-time or the whole town would have been out gawking, asking questions. The streets were raw with silence. The clatter of the horses' hooves was the only sound. Crouched between us, the girl winced at every knock of the gig but never said a word. I held her hand, gave it a squeeze.

'You're a good girl,' I murmured, 'a good girl.'

She looked at me strangely, as if I was speaking foreign. It didn't dawn on me till afterwards, but I never asked the girl the big question. I never asked who the father was. At the gates to her home, she spoke up.

'I'll go in on my own. My father would blame you, you and Seamus. He would have your boat destroyed, Aggie.'

Between us, we helped the child out of the trap. She hugged me then with a strange fierceness. Whispered into my ear.

'What did she say, Ag?' Seamus asked as the girl made her way inside.

' "I love you." That's what she said. Can you credit that? Such a strange poor craythur.'

My voice went a bit hoarse but I contained myself. No tears for Aggie. That was my rule. Always my rule, from way back. I watched as the girl hobbled along the tree-lined avenue, watched as she approached the dark house and became a shadow. No tears.

'Gee up, Seamus,' I told him; 'get this old filly home.'

52

I spent the afternoon looking for the herbalist. Maybe I was wrong in what I was thinking about him. Maybe he could explain it all away nicely. I called to his house, but he wasn't there. There was no sign of him anywhere else. I wondered had he up and left the town. I wondered had I accused him in the wrong. *Nothing they don't ask for.* That's what he had said. Nothing they don't ask for. What did they ask for? What did he do? He saved the day. I asked around, asked had anyone seen him; I got laughed at, I felt like a fool.

I never went to bed. I just sat by the window in my bedroom. Had he run off? Had I offended an innocent man? It was past midnight when I decided to go to see him again. After all, he wouldn't have expected me during the day. I was his night woman. I took Charlie's bicycle.

There wasn't a soul in the square; even the corner boys had deserted the place. When I got to the herbalist, his door was locked, and there wasn't a stir from inside. I waited for a while and then decided I might as well head for home. I cycled by the river way, glad of my lamp. You could hardly tell the water from the path. The moon was a big one, and it seemed to float in the river.

When I saw her, she was gleaming in the dark reeds. It was Rose, half in, half out of the water. I knelt on the river edge and tugged at her lapels, dragged her up on to the verge. I felt uneasy about touching her without permission. She weighed nothing. Her baby blue jacket felt scratchy and opened out as I tugged at it. The silk of her white blouse clung to her like a second skin. Her curls were flat and darkened. The mud spatters on her cheek looked like tea leaves. Her eyes were half closed, like she was swooning in the moonlight, but she wasn't. She couldn't. There wasn't a breath in her body.

I went to close her jacket over her, when I saw something white peeking from the inside pocket. I slid it out. A card envelope, addressed to her mother. It was stamped and everything. I shoved it into my own pocket. The centre of her skirt was black with blood. What kind of monster had Rose run into? Had I heard the grass rustle? Was someone moving through the fields behind me? I wasn't sure.

It was terrible peaceful then: just the reeds swishing in the brown water, the weir running. I wanted to stay there, hating the idea that someone else might come upon her. Her bloodless face was whiter than the moon, than chalk, than bone. Her expression was smooth, her mouth relaxed. She looked calm, almost pleased, like the last thing she had seen was something nice.

I wanted to shout for help but couldn't make a sound, couldn't remember the last rites. I whispered into her ear, 'Oh blessed Virgin Mary, that never was it known that anyone who sought thy help was left unaided. Inspired by this confidence, I fly unto thee, virgin of virgins, my mother.' Then I started to cry. She needed the rites, the last sacrament, she wasn't long passed. I kissed her cold forehead, made the sign of the cross and cycled back towards town.

The place was dead, black except for a glimmer between the curtains of the River Inn, and I wasn't going in there for help. Not again. A trap rattled in the distance but didn't hear my calls. So I hurried to the Birminghams'. How was I going to tell them? The avenue to their house had never seemed so long. I banged on the brass knocker, but no one came. I kept hammering, heard it echo inside. The door opened slowly and Margery Daly peeked out.

'I need to speak to Mrs B or Doctor B. It's very important. It's about Rose. It's bad.'

She let me into the hallway, didn't ask any questions; just signalled me towards a small door. It seemed to be a storeroom of sorts. I was about to turn when she pushed me. It went black and I heard the key turn. Was she completely mad? I knocked and knocked on the inside of the door. I began to shiver. My sleeves and skirt were sopping wet. I stank of river.

Seconds, then minutes passed, until I had no more sense of time. I heard a commotion, people arguing, a knocking sound. I banged and banged on the door – had Margery forgotten about me? I didn't know what to do. I called out. No one answered. And all the time Rose was lying on the ground for anyone to see, all lonely under the moon. A voice said, real soft, *Rose won't be lonely any more*. But there was no one there.

I thumped the door again; it swung outwards. It had been unlocked. The hall was empty. There was no sign of crazy Margery. The door to the living quarters, however, stood open. I walked through. There in her dressing gown was Mrs B, just sitting in a big green velvet chair with her hands in her lap, staring at the pink-flowered carpet like it was talking to her. She didn't seem to see me, let alone worry about why I was there. I knelt in front of her.

'Mrs B, I'm so sorry, a terrible thing . . .'

She looked past me, towards the middle of the room, and in the middle of the room was a bed with Rose laid out in it. I must've fainted, for next thing it was me on the green velvet chair, with my head between my knees and smelling salts under my nose. The salts were held by Margery. Her pretty face was sulky, tear-stained.

'I found Rose by the river. She was dead, by the river.' I was so cold, my teeth chattered.

Margery pressed her lips tight and shook her head very slowly from side to side. Then she walked over to Mrs B, crossed her arms and stood behind her. Mrs B's mouth was slack; her hands were wrapped in a rosary beads.

I approached the bed. Rose had been on the river bank, wearing a blue suit. Now she was lying in a bed wearing a black dress with a white Peter Pan collar. The curls around her face were dry, but the white satin pillow underneath her head was water stained. How had she got from there to here? How had Rose died? Why had Rose died?

Her father came in and looped beads through her fingers. The stiff way he nodded at me made me realize that I was an intruder. That all three of them, Margery, Rose's mother and father, were looking at me with disgust.

'I'm sorry for your trouble,' I stuttered and left.

The hall was empty and the front door hung open. I stood for a second. The house was silent. There was no priest, no prayers, no mourners. Maybe someone in the family had found Rose before I came upon her and, like me, had gone to get help. Maybe they were on their way to get her while I was running towards the house. The horse and trap I'd heard, that must've been them. That was it. But why hadn't they moved her out of the reeds, as I had? I left the Birminghams' and shut the door behind me. My bicycle wasn't where I'd left it, and I couldn't see it anywhere. Turning out of their avenue, I put my hands in my pockets to keep them warm. That's when I felt the letter. I hadn't the heart to go back. It felt wrong to pester them. Also, I wanted to read it for myself.

Poor Rose. I'd known her all my life, who hadn't? She was well known but no one's friend. Always smiling, always perfectly beautiful, but hardly ever had much to say. She was a bit silly maybe, but in a way that didn't mean harm. I couldn't stop crying. I felt a pain in my heart for her, just like I did for Mam. But Rose wasn't close to me, wasn't close to anyone. She was just a nice girl who looked like she'd love to have a chin-wag, but her mother was always pulling her away from people. I thought of the wounds on her knees, the cuts up her legs. I'd forgotten about them. What happened to her at all?

I walked quickly. The shapes and sounds on the road to our house didn't seem so nice and familiar any more. Even my own footsteps were putting the heart crossways in me.

And there was something else. Rose's name was in the herbalist's notebook. But lots of people's names were and they weren't dead. Whoever had hurt Rose could be out there yet, roaming the town, waiting for another victim. I screamed the rest of the way home, swear to God I did.

Charlie was asleep in the kitchen. Head down, his arms on the table, coat still on, the lamp left burning as if he was waiting on me to come home. I watched him sleep. Wanted to put my hand out and ruffle his hair, wake him and tell him everything. But I didn't. He'd be heartbroken soon enough. Charlie didn't take things well; when Mam died he'd hauled her old armchair out into the yard, hatcheted it to pieces and burnt it. I quenched the lamp and went up to my room, unpeeled my wet clothes, took an extra blanket from the wardrobe and slipped into bed with it wrapped around me.

Wishing Mam was there to hold me safe and sound. I bawled myself to sleep.

Rose walked through my dreams all night. She wore blue serge and carried a case like a schoolchild's. The blue she wore was like nothing in nature, bluer than a hot summer's sky; it was a blue I could nearly reach, nearly grasp, but never would. Her voice, when it came, came from somewhere outside my dream, a soft crying. *Save me, Emily, save me.*

53

On the third morning in a row that Carmel heard Sarah vomit into her chamber pot, the penny dropped. The way she was putting on a bit of condition. The way her skin gleamed. The stupid girl had got herself in trouble. Well, she could go back home, let her country aunt take care of her. And all the trust they'd put in her. A wretch like Sarah having a child, when a respectable woman like Carmel was crying out for one. Who on earth had fathered it? And under their watch! The girl had to go.

Carmel threw on her dressing gown, ran downstairs and signalled Dan into the kitchen. Sarah had already made it to the shop counter, looking very green around the gills.

'That Sarah one is expecting. She's been getting sick every morning. She can't stay here, the stupid girl.'

Carmel awaited his outraged response. Men didn't notice these things the way a woman did, so he wasn't quite taking it in. He looked at her blankly.

'She may go back where she came from. God knows we tried. I knew, I just knew something was going on.'

She babbled on and on, her heart missing beats, fear infusing her, knowing she was skipping something right under her nose.

'That's the thanks we get, Dan, isn't it, for giving her a start?'

He opened his mouth but said nothing. He stared at the clock on the mantel.

'Well, say something.'

He didn't look at her. More was wrong than Carmel knew, and still it was eluding her. She looked around. There were two cups and a packet of biscuits on the table. A funny old breakfast. But Carmel wasn't usually up for breakfast, so how could she know what they ate? The chairs were together, the cups were together.

They had been sitting talking. Sarah's place was always set at the far end of the table. That's where Carmel always put her.

She walked over to the table and threw one of the chairs to the floor. Dan stood as loose as a hanging man. Her throat was dry and her heart seemed to be fluttering inside it.

'It was you?' Her hands shook.

'Don't be so ridiculous,' he said, his voice unsteady.

'It was you!' She pulled at his shirt. 'You bastard, look at me.'

He wouldn't.

'Get out! Get out! Get out!'

She screamed at him till she was bent in two, till her voice ran out. When she stopped, he was gone. And Sarah, she had run off too. The shop was empty.

Where did he go? Where did she go? Everything they owned was here under Carmel's roof except for the clothes they walked in and their unborn child. She locked all the doors. As she secured the kitchen window, she saw Eliza. The pig had got huge. It backed into the far corner of the pen, as if it knew what Carmel was thinking.

Carmel sat on the last step of the stairs and cut Dan's face out of the wedding snap with her nail scissors.

Looked in the hall mirror. Old poached face.

Carmel scored the scissors on the clouded grey-and-green-speckled glass till the blades bent backwards and sliced into her palm. Blood on the mirror. The shelter for her madness, for her ugly, tear-stained, blood-smeared countenance.

Mirror, mirror, on the wall.

If Carmel had a hunter to do her bidding, she would've ordered him to bring her the lying, cheating heart of Sarah Whyte.

54

Sarah was serving Miss Dolan when she heard Carmel begin to shout. The shop was packed. Silence descended as Carmel's hysteria rose. The women looked at each other, and at Sarah. She could feel, rather than see, their smirks and raised eyebrows. She walked the length of the counter and past them with her head held high. When she reached the living room, she could see Dan's silhouette through the bubbled glass. She raced up the stairs like a redshank, pulled her suitcase from under the bed and flung in anything that came to hand. She pulled the wooden panel from the front of the fireplace, put her hand up the chimney and felt around until she found her jar of savings. She emptied the money into her purse, grabbed her suitcase and raced down the stairs. Carmel's screaming grew louder all the time. The crowd parted as she went through the shop. Surely there weren't that many people when she had been there a minute before?

She walked as fast as she could without running, walked along the main street with no idea which direction to take. She couldn't go to Mai's; it was too risky, with Finbar lurking there. She almost had the price of the fare to London, but where would she stay? What would she do? She needed more money. The herbalist owed her for all that time labelling; he hadn't paid her a penny. So she turned on her heel and headed for his house.

It was an age before he answered the door. When he did, he was wearing a soft leather motorcycle helmet and brown jacket. He was impatient to get going, told her that he had no money in the house.

'Come back in an hour or two,' was all he said.

But she had nowhere to go till then. She began to weep.

'Can I wait here, till you come back?'

'No, you can't.' The herbalist was jumpy, irritated.

'Then you must give me my money now.'

'I don't have it.'

'I've waited long enough; I need it now.'

'Look, come back in an hour, then you'll get it.'

He shut and locked his door, mounted his motorcycle, started it up and buzzed off. What would she do for the hour, where could she wait? Trust the herbalist to be the only person in the town who locked his door. She walked around the back of the house, to find somewhere to sit while she waited. The back window was open slightly, just two or so inches. Enough for her to get a good grip and shove it upwards. It made a horrible grinding sound, but it opened. Sarah took a quick look around to make sure no one could see and then climbed up on to the sill and in. The window was harder to close than it had been to open, but she tried to leave it as she'd found it.

She moved a chair to the front window, buttoned up her coat and sat waiting. He'd go mad when he saw her here, but what choice did she have? She had nowhere else to go.

She wondered what Dan would do. He would probably go to his pal Mick Murphy's and Mick would keep him there. They were both hiding like children; it was laughable. Since Carmel thought the child was Dan's, perhaps Dan did too? As far as she could make out, he hadn't denied it to Carmel. Maybe he believed he had got Sarah in trouble. The whole town would think it was Dan's child after Carmel's theatrics anyway. Maybe Dan and Sarah could run off together? Could start somewhere else, where the people weren't so narrow-minded.

An unwelcome thought popped up – Dan was narrow-minded. She wasn't even sure if she could go to him.

Panic set in. What would Mai do? What would Mai say?

One step at a time, that's what she'd say. Just concentrate on getting your money, and getting the six o'clock train to Dublin. In Dublin, worry about getting to London. In London, worry about getting to your aunt Margaret. Then worry about her turning you away.

One step at a time. *Just like she had managed.*

The thick greying plaster on the herbalist's walls made her queasy. When was he coming back with her money?

55

Charlie was inconsolable. He had gone into town and heard of Rose's death even before I'd got up that morning. The news had spread quickly. He told me she was found dead in her own bed after a brief illness.

'But she wasn't even sick,' he cried; 'she wasn't even sick!'

He wouldn't let me fix him anything; he went around the house opening doors and slamming them. He was beside himself. He said that he had been waiting up for Rose all night, that she was his desperate friend, that the parlour had been prepared for her. He stopped short of getting down on his knees and howling.

I went back up to my bedroom to dress. I lifted my pillow and looked at the envelope I had taken from Rose's jacket the night before. I eased the envelope open without tearing it and took out the letter. I knew I shouldn't, and at the same time I really knew I should. I thought of Rose's knees, of her never, ever being out of her mother's company. I thought of her parents in that room where her body was laid out, the way they'd said nothing to me or to each other. And the way they'd lied. The way they had already told everyone that she'd died at home after a short illness. Why would they do that when there could be a raving lunatic out there, ready to kill again?

The envelope was barely wet. Rose can't have been there long. The hair on the top of her head had been flat and darkened. Had I come along in the middle of something? It was my duty to find out.

Ah, I was codding no one – I opened the poor dead girl's letter because I was a nosy cow.

Dear Mother,

The baby's gone. I'm sorry. It's what you wanted but not what I wanted. I would've loved that baby. And all the rooms in our house that are so empty.

It would've only taken up a small space. Now it's taking up no space at all.

I have to go. I know someone kind and he's going to mind me. I've got to go, because if I don't leave another baby will come and we'll all be hurt all over again. As long as I live in that house, babies will keep coming. Are you putting your hands over your ears now, Mother? Please listen this time. I'm not lying.

I don't think you know what it was like, what was really done. If you'd known, you wouldn't have made me do it, I know that. You thought it was all flowers and tinctures, isn't that right? A spoon of something. If you knew the truth, you'd know why I have to leave now. I'm not going because I don't love you. That's why I want you to know these things, and when I've gone away, you can tell people and they can stop it happening to another girl, even a bad one, because no one deserves to have their baby hurt out of them, no one.

He always offered me syrup in a small glass first. It was dark and bitter. I got sick afterwards, into a bucket that he kept there. He made me remove my underclothes. He examined me, with his hands. Do you know what I mean? I cried so much it vexed him. Then he picked up a long instrument and forced it into my private parts. He did this every time.

You said to him, 'My little girl is in trouble, help her,' and you paid him. And now there is no baby for me. Maybe there never will be again. God forgive us, Mother.

I don't want you to worry: I'm safe now. No more of that for me, don't ever worry.

Love,
Rose

He did that. The herbalist did that. *Nothing they don't ask for.* That was what he said. And who gave Rose a baby? I ran down and said out straight to Charlie: 'Did you get Rose in trouble, did you?'

He was crying so much I couldn't make out what he said. I felt awful for distressing him when I did finally make it out. He had kissed her once, on the hand. He loved her; he was helping her to escape. Yes, she was in some trouble, but it was another man who had got her in it, someone she couldn't stand up against, someone who'd locked her under the stairs. That wouldn't have made sense to most people, but it made horrible sense to me.

56

Sarah had almost dozed off. The chair was well stuffed and her feet rested comfortably on her suitcase. She leant forward and peeped through the crack in the curtains. Young girls were gathered around the pump outside. One with fair hair to her waist worked the handle; it took all her strength to push it down and release the water. Her feet left the ground every time the handle rose up again. Her two friends held their dusty toes under the gushing water and squealed with pleasure. Sarah smiled. A dark stout woman appeared and the children quietened as she passed. The woman was marching towards the herbalist's house. Sarah moved back from the window and listened to the footsteps approach. Even though she knew it was coming, the knock gave her a fright. She sank back into the soft chair and closed her eyes. She felt the woman waiting on the other side, waiting and listening for any sign of life. 'He's not there, missus,' a girl shouted. 'He's gone off on his motorbike.' Sarah heard the woman walk away. The children began squealing again.

Sarah realized then that she was starving. All she'd eaten for breakfast was a biscuit. She went to the cupboard. The deep shelves were full, but not with food. They were crammed with jars. Some contained dried matter and were labelled – 'Speedwell', 'Red Clover', 'Eyebright', 'Sage' – but most weren't. The unlabelled jars were packed with tablets, some large and brown, others small and white. Sarah uncorked a tall slim bottle that looked like it might be a tincture. It smelt of nothing she recognized. It smelt wrong. She put it back. There were hunks of beeswax on the bottom shelf, sitting alongside bottles of rose water, lavender water, witch hazel and a dozen small jars. She unscrewed the lid of one of them, dabbed her finger into a white cream and rubbed it on the back of her hand. It melted into her skin. She massaged a dollop into her hands. It felt wonderful. Sarah turned the jar upside down, saw a tab and read the familiar round handwriting: 'Comfrey'. It was Mai's cream, the one the colonel loved so much that he had her make it for him in batches. He obviously loved it so much that he was selling it on. She remembered Mai's 'Sarah . . . do it with love.' Sarah took the jars, opened her suitcase and packed them away.

Never mind waiting for him to come back. If the herbalist had any money here, she would find it herself. A two-roomed house wouldn't take long to search.

She checked the cupboard first, in behind the bottles and jars, and then the various tins over the mantelpiece. They contained sugar, tea leaves, dried herbs and biscuits. She looked under the narrow stretcher bed he had shoved against the wall – nothing. She searched beneath the seat of the armchair by the window, in the turf basket by the fire, under the table, the school-desk. She found no money.

She didn't fancy going back into the room he slept in, but there was nowhere left. She went into his room and lifted the mattress. Nothing there. Under the pillow she found an envelope. A picture fell out, a tattered photo of a mother and child. She didn't care who they were. She put the picture back in the envelope and returned it to where she'd found it. She looked in his jug and basin. Still nothing. She got down on her knees, lifted the heavy fringed bed-cover and looked under the bed. She tugged out a box from underneath.

The last time Sarah had seen tools like these was in a doctor's bag. Once, when Mai was attending a breech delivery, the woman's husband had panicked and sent for the doctor. He arrived with a huge black case that he plonked on a sideboard by the window and yanked open. The instruments inside glinted as he prepared to go into action. But before he could do anything the baby slipped out on to the bed – Mai had turned it with her hands. The husband brought the doctor into the kitchen for a drink while the mother nursed her child. Mai took her time tidying up the room. As she waited, Sarah stared into the doctor's open case, fascinated that he needed all those tools when her aunt could birth a child with her bare hands.

Unlike the instruments in the doctor's bag, those in the herbalist's box were worn and dull. He had other bits and pieces in there too. It all looked very shabby. She pulled the lid down on the box and shoved it back under the bed with her foot. Was the herbalist moonlighting delivering children? Who in their right mind would let him near them? It didn't make sense.

There was nowhere else to search. Sarah would have to wait till he came back. He owed her almost twelve shillings and she needed every penny. She also needed a drink of water and something to eat. She left the herbalist's bedroom and closed the door behind her.

She grabbed the biscuit tin from the mantelpiece and went over to the back window, daring to pull the curtains slightly open. The sun shone in as if it were the middle of summer instead of nearly autumn. She spotted Aggie's boat moored just up the river. Aggie moved around a lot. Afraid someone might evict her if she ever stayed too long in the one part of the river.

Sarah ate every ginger nut in the tin. If the herbalist didn't come back soon, she was going to miss the train.

It was growing cooler and darker; the six o'clock to Dublin had left without her. There was only one sod in the fuel basket. She couldn't even light the stove. Sarah took her winter coat out of her suitcase, moved to the armchair by the front window and pulled the coat over her. She wasn't going to use the stretcher bed – she dreaded to think who had been up on it. She felt drained. What if the herbalist never came back? What would she do then? What *could* she do then? Her mouth was dry, her feet and hands were chilled.

She sat there for what seemed like hours, but she didn't know how much time had passed – there was no clock. The herbalist wore a watch, a gold one. She thought of the bed and the fancy bedspread in the other room, but she couldn't bear the idea of lying in it either. She couldn't get the box under the bed out of her head. One day, she knew, the child in her belly would have to come out, but she didn't quite believe it ever would.

Sarah woke with a crick in her neck. It took a second to realize where she was. The morning light showed up all the strands of hair that clung to her coat; she shrugged it off and stood to stretch her aching legs. She shouldn't have eaten all the biscuits the night before;

she was weak with hunger. She glimpsed through the curtains to check the road outside. All quiet.

There was no sign that the herbalist had been back. She didn't think he could have come in and left again. Maybe he had gone on one of his trips to Dublin. In that case he had purposely lied about being back in an hour – which meant he had no intention of ever paying her what he owed. He would get some shock when he walked in and saw Sarah sitting in his armchair. He'd have to pay up then, wouldn't he?

She guessed it was mid-morning, but, if so, why was the road still so quiet? Finally, after what seemed like hours, a funeral came along. It was a huge procession, slow-moving. A person of some consequence, if the crowds were anything to go by, or the pomp. It was almost beautiful: the hazy blue sky, the black horses with the huge plumes, the shining hearse with the closed velvet curtains, the top hat on the undertaker with his straight back. She eased forward to see the chief mourners, to see if she could work out who had died.

Mrs Birmingham and the Doctor were first in line behind the hearse. There was no sign of Rose. Mrs Birmingham wore a veil over her face and held a black hankie to her nose. The mourners spread out as they passed, almost touching the window of the herbalist's house. Sarah couldn't bear it any longer: she slipped out of the front door and put her hand to the elbow of the nearest woman. It was old Nora.

'Excuse me,' she said, 'but whose funeral is this?'

'It's Miss Rose Birmingham, the poor girl.'

'I don't understand. What happened to her?'

A look of recognition crossed the woman's face; she shook off Sarah's hand.

'Go back to where you came from, adulteress.'

Sarah returned to the herbalist's house. What had happened to Rose? She couldn't imagine her lying in that hearse. She was so young. Perhaps that was what was keeping the herbalist. Perhaps he was at the funeral paying his respects. In that case it would be some time until he returned. She might as well make herself comfortable.

It would seem crass now to demand money from him, but she had no choice, and if she had to tell him her predicament she would.

What was she thinking? There would be no need to tell him anything; he would be quite well informed by the time he returned.

She moved away from the window, sat down and pulled her coat around her again. She was nervous that Carmel might turn up. She thought her capable of anything. She might very well report her and have her carted off to the laundry. The important thing was to stay calm and get her money from the herbalist. Just wait it out for now and refuse to leave without her wages. He had plenty to spare: just look at the brand-new motorbike he was flying around in.

If the worst came to the worst, Sarah could hop on the motorbike and make her escape. That made her smile. She could put Dan on the back.

Would he come?

She felt a pain in her heart. No, he wouldn't have the guts. She wished it were different, but it wasn't.

Did she love him?

No. She had wanted him. And she had wanted to love him. But she didn't.

You're too soft, Sarah. You're too soft. If loving him can save your skin, love him.

She didn't know what to do. She just needed to get away. She shouldn't have asked the woman about the funeral. Now everyone would know where she was.

57

Emily knocked at the door before noon, her eyes red-rimmed and as mad as ever. Carmel was surprised that she felt glad to see her. How strange it was that, of all people, Emily would be the only one she could bear? She had always been queasy around the girl's neediness, but at least with her Carmel didn't have to keep up appearances.

'I've come from the funeral.'

Emily rambled on. She was jittery, waved her hands this way and that. Carmel brought her into the back and put a bit of rum in the tea and biscuits on a plate. Once there, Emily's expression changed. She became still.

'You didn't go to Rose's funeral?'

'I couldn't face the whole town like that.'

'Now, don't be offended, Mrs Holohan, but there's more going on than you and your husband's troubles. Terrible things. You should've gone, for Rose's sake. The whole town showed up. They came in droves. We were elbow to elbow behind the hearse. You should've seen the feathered plumes and the young girls carrying white flowers. The horses kicked up so much dust that the chief mourners had to hold handkerchiefs over their mouths. Mrs B's suit was destroyed.'

'It's not over yet surely?' Who was Emily to reprimand Carmel for anything?

'I slipped from the procession before it got to the church. Didn't want to hear the service. It's all lies.'

Emily poured more rum into her mug.

'All lies? Whatever do you mean?'

'Passed away peacefully in the bosom of her family, pah!'

'Emily, stop!'

'I saw her with my own eyes. She died by the river, the poor creature, with blood all over her skirt. That's why I left the funeral and paid my respects at the place where she really passed.'

'Where was that?'

The girl was mad.

'I told you already, by the river. When I closed my eyes to say a prayer, I could almost see her walking down the river path the night she died, wearing her blue serge suit, thinking she was on her way to somewhere better.'

'What are you saying, girl? You're talking nonsense.'

'Do I have to spell it out? I found Rose the night she died. I went to the doctor's house to tell her family. The maid locked me under the stairs to keep me out of the way. And when I went into the parlour, they already had her there – laid out. Someone had brought her home. At first I thought she'd been set upon by a mad man, but I was wrong. Rose wasn't sick at all – she died by the river after losing a child and the parents wanted to hush it up.'

Carmel couldn't believe her ears. Had Emily finally gone cracked?

'Who else did you tell this to?'

'No one but Charlie. And now you. Sure who'd believe the likes of me against moneyed people?'

'To say such a shabby thing about Rose of all people, Rose who never kept company in her short life with any boy, let alone . . .'

'I have proof. A letter Rose wrote. And her name was in the herbalist's surgery book too. Hers is the last entry.'

'The herbalist?'

'I know, it's hard to believe that it was my fine man who did the deed, my fine man who gave her such an awful time. The rumours are true. He gets rid of children from the bellies of unfortunate women.'

Emily started to cry then.

Carmel was stunned into silence. She sat and mulled over what Emily had said. Rumours. The herbalist could get rid of an unwanted baby.

'Have you gone to him with this?'

'His door is shut to me, but I won't give up.'

'Can I see this letter?'

'Don't you believe me, Mrs Holohan?'

'I do but . . .'

'Well, then, you don't need to see it, do you? Besides it's personal, shameful. Rose has been through enough.'

'But she's dead.'

'You're hard.'

Emily stood up, and walked past her to leave.

'I have to be,' Carmel said.

The shop bell clattered as the door shut. Carmel was talking to no one but herself again.

58

I sat on the bench in the cold tiled hall, waiting for my turn with the good Doctor. It was straight back to work for Doctor B. Wasn't he a right Trojan? Wasn't he a cold one? That Carmel was a cold woman; hadn't a jot of feeling for Rose. 'Show me the letter,' she had ordered, as if I would. Rose deserved to keep some dignity in the end. Carmel was all about herself, not even going to the funeral. I know it wasn't a great time for her, what with Sarah and Dan falling in love and leaving her to run the shop on her own. She was always complaining about either one or the other of them. You'd think it would be a relief to have both of them gone.

Maybe older women lacked feeling. I watched Mrs B at the funeral: she was weeping delicately. But I knew the real Mrs B. I knew the woman who had sent her daughter to hell and kept her there. And I knew the real Doctor B. The two of them shuffling in all their glory behind the glossy beast that carried Rose to her place of eternal rest. Did they care? How could they walk straight if they cared?

I knew the real herbalist too, the one who hurt and took, hurt and took, and could laugh and party and live the good life. Who wanted a car, who wanted gold, who said first impressions were all that mattered. I knew all this. And I was the kind of girl that no one listened to, or believed if they did.

Charlie wanted to kill. Charlie cared. I didn't show him the letter; I was afraid he would go out and catch the herbalist – God knows what he would have done to him. So I didn't tell Charlie the full truth of the matter. I'd think about all that later. For now, I was in Doctor B's surgery and I was next in line, and this time I wasn't going to be shoved under the stairs.

When he popped his head out and saw me, he froze. I walked by him into the surgery. I didn't have the kind of money seeing him cost and I didn't care. He tapped his pen, and I told him how I had found his daughter, that I knew she had bled to death. I told him I knew he had hurt her. I was still talking when he interrupted me. He smiled. Had he heard a word I'd said? What he said next made me understand that he had.

'You're a very disturbed young lady. It'll be no bother having you committed.'

I got out of there as fast as my legs could carry me. I was out of my depth. I needed help. I hadn't thought it through properly. I had forgotten who they were, and I had forgotten who I was.

59

So Sarah had fled, and taken her belongings with her. Well might she run – if Carmel ever got her hands on her, she would be beyond conceiving once and for all. Yes, Carmel was tormenting herself, saying aloud again and again, 'Another woman is carrying my husband's child. A mere girl, a whipper-snapper whore.' It wasn't simple jealousy. The colour of Carmel's feeling wasn't green; it was black, it had teeth, and the howl of something ripped from her belly and torn asunder. Her heart roared like the last wolf. She pressed her forehead to the mirror, told it everything.

'I'll get that Sarah. I'll get her and take her kicking and screaming into this abyss. "Hell hath no fury"? She doesn't know the half of it. I don't care what gets upturned, dashed down or destroyed on the way; she will not have that child.'

The baby Sarah carried, when Carmel paused long enough to consider it, would be round and beautiful like her son. It would have that little fold of heaven on the back of its neck, those tiny gripping fists, it would smell of love. Just like her baby should have. She could almost feel it then, touch its skin. That rippled through her anger, softening it. Then she heard her mother's voice.

Wise up.

That child in your mind's eye's no baby. That child gives form to the adultery committed against you. Stupid woman. Fool. Old fool. And under your own roof. An old, old story, Carmel. There's nothing new under the sun.

How long had it been going on? She had shut the shop and it would stay shut for as long as it took. Let them talk; let them speculate. About her, about Sarah and Dan. Their coupling. What had he done to them? And why? She thought about what Emily had said. What that meant.

★

She approached the herbalist as he was crossing the market square. She stepped into his path, her purse held up high on her chest. She mentioned corruption, indecent behaviour, murder . . . all the things that Emily had told her.

'We're talking hard labour,' Carmel said to him, after mouthing 'Rose' soundlessly.

He didn't laugh or wave his hand away. He just nodded. Maybe this kind of thing had come his way before.

'So what can I do for you?'

At least he understood that there was something she wanted, and it was something that she was going to get.

'Give Sarah Whyte a dose of something, and make sure she loses that child. If she has it, I'll make sure you hang for Rose.'

60

A stone pestle was grinding seeds. Sarah couldn't move: her arms were bound to her sides; a thin brown rope went twice across her chest, and another tied her ankles. Tears of tiredness ran and she couldn't rub them away. Her hair stuck to her face. She began to feel more awake, more scared. She tried to remember.

The herbalist had finally returned. She remembered hearing his bike, the way he unlocked the door. Then he backed in with a cardboard box in his arms. He laid it on the table and turned around to face Sarah. Of course, he wasn't surprised to see her. He said he had heard what had happened with the Holohans, heard Sarah was in trouble. He said he could help her, make things easier. He poured water into a cup. Sarah didn't want help, she told him. Told him she wanted her money.

He paced, started talking about her own good. Then suddenly he locked her head in his arm and jerked her face upwards. After that her memory started to get hazy. She knew a wet rag was clamped over her mouth. Then later – it could've been seconds, it could've been minutes – someone yanked open her jaw, dropped hard tablets into her mouth and shoved them down. Water was poured down her throat – a slow steady trickle so she couldn't help but swallow. She was heaving, trying to push the tablets out with her tongue. But she couldn't do it. There was the smell of Sweet Afton and the sound of a woman's voice. After that, she had no memory.

Sarah flexed her feet: the welts stung every time the rope bit. The herbalist had his back to her. He was grubby; she'd never seen him grubby before. He was drinking alcohol from a mug, wiping his forehead with his sleeve; the room felt like it was sealed. That couldn't be good. He came over to the bed, carrying a tonic of some sort. She smelt aniseed, but there was something else, something cloying underneath.

'What's this? What will it do?'

'Put an end to your pain.'

'But I'm not unwell.'

'You are, look at you, you were hysterical. You've been screaming, breaking things.'

He pushed her pillow up so she could see the broken crockery on the floor.

'I don't believe you.'

'You were out of your mind. Angry, accusing me.'

'I came here for my money.'

'You became hysterical; a danger to yourself. That's why . . .' He pointed to the ropes.

'Let me go – this can't be good for the baby.'

'It was all in your head – there's no baby.'

'There is – a woman knows. Who was here earlier? I heard someone talking.'

'No one. My abode is my own. At least for now. It's nobody's concern.'

'But I heard a woman.'

He didn't care what she had to say. She saw it in his expression.

'Untie me.'

'So you can scratch and scream?'

'I wouldn't hurt you – you've been so nice to me.'

She played like a little cat in her voice.

'This is for your own good.'

'I feel sick – let me up. I feel sick.'

He put a bowl by her face; it already held a trace of vomit. She threw up. Her belly ached. How many times had she been sick, how many times had they had this conversation? Had she said all those things already? Is that why he looked so weary, so weary of her? He wiped her face with the sheet; it was filthy.

'Let me go or I'll scream the house down.'

'Is that a fact.'

What are you going to do to me? she thought but didn't say, for it might remind him, hasten him. She thought of the box he kept under the bed.

'Don't hurt me, please.'

'You are beyond hurting, you who cause so much trouble for everyone, so much trouble.'

The room was shuttered, hot, dusty; she smelt the sourness of his body and her own. She must have been there longer than she knew.

'I won't do anything – just let me lie free of the ropes for a while.'

'I've no choice. It's Mrs Holohan. This is her doing.'

'What can happen? What can she do to you?'

'Hard labour. The end of all this.' He waved his hand about the room.

'I don't understand. I won't come here again – let me go.'

'You can't go till we are finished.'

'Finished with what?'

'You'll see.'

She started to shiver.

'You'll be punished.'

'You asked for an examination; I've your signature on a docket. But, as you never told me you were in the family way, how was I to know there would be consequences?'

There was a taste in her mouth, behind her teeth.

'Did Carmel Holohan blackmail you? That's a thing I would never do.'

She knew by the way he looked at her that it was true. He sat on a chair beside her bed and began to untie the rope that bound her ankles together. Being released hurt – she felt a warm drop of blood run down over her ankle bone. She looked at her captor; he glanced back at her. Then he just stared at the wall, and there was silence.

61

The curtains of the herbalist's house were drawn, but I knew there was someone home. I knocked on the front window and kept knocking; I had no intention of giving up. He opened the door like a flash, the face of a demon on him.

'Not now!' He slammed the door shut.

I wanted to have it out with him for what he'd done to Rose, to make him own up, to make him be sorry, to make him pay. I couldn't rest till I did something; I had even thought of going to the gardaí barracks. I couldn't get my head around any of it: that the herbalist could do that to the girl, that Mrs B would force Rose to have it done. Mam would never have let that happen to me. And Carmel was so wrapped up in her own affairs she didn't know anything about that side of things, even with Mrs B being her very good friend. You should've seen her eyes when I told her.

I sat on the wall across the road. Saluted Ned when he passed. That was a mistake, because he came over.

'Isn't it terrible sad? Poor Rose.'

'It's awful, it really is.'

'This town has gone to the dogs altogether. Did you hear about his lordship?' Ned waved a thumb towards the herbalist's house.

'He's harbouring Miss Whyte, the adulteress. Seems she was carrying on with her mistress's husband.'

'Was she now!'

'Yes, she's in there now, hiding from the wrath of Mrs Holohan.'

'Terrible,' I said.

'Shocking. I wonder what the next thing will be?'

'Next thing?'

'Well, you know what they say: bad things happen in threes.'

Ned was walking away as he spoke. He mustn't have cared for an answer.

So she was in there, hiding. How the mighty had fallen. I went back across the road and peeked in the window. There wasn't anything to see. I listened and everything was very quiet, too quiet. If Sarah was in there, she must be desperate. What was she going to do with her baby? She could give it to Carmel, seeing as her own didn't make it. It was in limbo, bless it, with the rest of the poor souls. Did Carmel miss her baby? She'd never said. For a mouthy woman, she never managed to say a word about that baby. But maybe she would like a child, even if it was Sarah's.

I crept around the house and looked in the back window. It was open a couple of inches, and the curtains there were too short, so I had an inch or so of a gap. That's when I saw a terrible sight and knew I was facing something I couldn't tackle on my own.

62

Someone at the herbalist's door seemed intent on kicking it in. He had no choice but to answer it. Sarah recognized Aggie's voice; she was making a terrible racket. 'Not another one – no more mopping up after Doctor Death!' Hearing that frightened Sarah as much as anything else that had happened.

Someone touched her hand then. It was Emily. She placed a finger over Sarah's mouth and took a penknife from her pocket. It sliced through the ropes around Sarah's wrists and ankles. Sarah tried to get up but fell back down again. Emily hooked her arm around Sarah's waist and half dragged, half led her towards the back door. At the front door, Aggie roared on and on, and the herbalist tried to hush her. Emily unbolted the door and, with Sarah leaning on her shoulder, they stepped out of the house.

The light was blinding for a second. And all Sarah saw was the river, the sunshine making it look like a band of diamonds across the horizon. And there was *Biddy*, waiting to take them away. Emily helped Sarah aboard and eased her on to a bench. They didn't have to wait long for Aggie to trundle across the grass. She signalled for Emily to start up the boat. She was holding the side of her head.

'Jesus, Aggie, what happened?' said Emily.

'The bugger jumped up and hit me.'

'Will he come after us?' Sarah said, as Aggie sat beside her.

'He won't give chase. It's the other one who's baying for blood – Carmel. She's the one to run from, seeing as you're up the pole with her husband's child.'

'It's not his,' said Sarah. 'It's not his.'

In that second Sarah knew she was never going to pretend any different – and perhaps had never really intended to. She shut her eyes and cupped the curve that was just beginning to show beneath her dress.

The boat began to move. She didn't even ask where they were going. None of them seemed inclined to talk. Sarah imagined they were sailing a river that went all the way to paradise. Somewhere warm, somewhere unfettered by all the rules of civilization. The wind stirred the riverside willows. They made a clean, shushing sound. It began to rain, but it was soft – none of them minded it.

After a half an hour of peace, the barge bumped against the river bank, and Aggie began roaring at Emily for her steering. The boat came to a standstill against the ridge. They had reached the first lock gate. There was a cottage by the water, and signs of work in the front garden. The lock gatekeeper came out from around the side of his house, pushing a wheelbarrow of soil. It was him, it was Matt.

He dropped his barrow and went over to them, caught the rope Emily had thrown and knotted it around the pillar. Aggie limped off to talk to him. Told the others to stay put as she linked his arm and walked through the open door of his house. They were in there an awful long time before they came out. Aggie got on board and put her hands on her hips.

'We'll be leaving you here,' she said to Sarah, 'to rest for a bit.'

Matt put out a hand to help her step ashore. She took it.

You saved the day, Aggie, didn't you?

I did. I did. Emily didn't have to tell me much. I nearly knocked his door down. The face on The Don. He was careful to block my view into the room behind him. His fists were bunched so tight that his knuckles were white. That wasn't scaring Aggie off, not this time, bucko.

'Who have you now? Have you no conscience?' I said.

'Whist, woman – you don't know what you're saying.'

There was a noise from inside – young Emily climbing in the window. The herbalist made to look over his shoulder. I slapped his chest.

'You're nothing but a dirty bastard,' I said, 'and I'll be telling the gardaí everything you done. And everything you told me, do you understand?'

'You don't have a leg to stand on. Who'd believe a word from your mouth?'

Then came a scraping noise, and a door creaking. I put a hand on his shoulder.

'Have you someone in there? Someone I'll be cleaning up after? Like Rose?'

He turned right quick. Didn't he know there were eyes everywhere in this town?

I stepped forward, he didn't move, we were chest to chest. His eyes were bloodshot; he looked frightened, trapped. I don't recall what happened next. Don't even know what he hit me with, just know I was on the ground. He dragged me off his doorstep, knelt and held my head so tight to his that I felt his jawbone move.

'Get out of here, you old hoor, or I'll kill you.'

He shut the door. I felt my skull; there was a lump as big as a half-crown but no cut. I hobbled away, holding my head. Miss Harvey stepped back as I passed, as if I was a bad smell. Off she went hot-trotting to Mass. I crossed the grass towards *Biddy*, then hobbled on board with a hand from Emily.

Sarah was on the bench, looking half stunned. I sat beside her. We moved away upriver. Emily quit her sobbing for long enough to listen to my instructions. I felt woozy, like vomiting, but I had a suck of whiskey, and when I sat back and watched Emily steer I began to feel better. I knew exactly the place for Sarah to recover.

She had a steady hand, young Emily, kept us in the middle of the river right easy. The reeds bowed before the boat as we passed. It was then I saw the broad woman walking the barrow path in a green dress and my black shawl. She didn't stall to wave as we passed; she just kept on walking, looking straight ahead. She was the spitting image of me, from her auburn hair to her white shoes. A fetch. I'd seen a fetch. I knew then that I wasn't long for this world, that I'd better be readying myself for the next.

So I'll tell your tale, henny penny, if no one else will, I'll tell your tale. Are you listening? We can tell it again and again till it no longer hurts you. That's our medicine.

A beautiful girl went to him. She had nowhere else to go. Had no money, only beautiful clothes and a mother who kept her on a short leash. She was respectable. And he had something that kept respectable girls respectable. Medicine man gave her something, put his cold clean fingers between her legs and made her weep. She believed he could help her, would help her. It hurt but she thought she deserved to be hurt. Aggie knows that feeling, child. It's the very soil that grew me.

The girl grew paler and paler. Her appearance altered like someone had rinsed all around her. The hurt was rubbing her out.

Her mother noticed.

'You're more beautiful every day,' that blind witch said, 'radiant even.'

The beautiful girl bit her lips, chewed her nails till they bled, flushed with shame and became more beautiful.

That's me you're talking about, isn't it, Aggie? I was lovely, wasn't I? Is that why he did it? Is that why it's okay that I'm wiped clean away?

Hush, craythur, hush a bye. While Aggie's here, you'll never die.

63

Carmel knew where her husband would be. There were very few doors Dan would risk his pride knocking on. Mick's was the first place she tried, and she knew by the silence that her husband was there. She opened the letterbox and called Dan's name. Saw a shadow move across the hallway.

'Let me in or I'll stay here all day.'

Mick opened the door and tried to pretend he didn't know anything. She stepped inside; she wouldn't be conducting her business in the street, not like some.

'Get Dan for me.'

'I swear to God –'

She walked past him and into the kitchen. His mother was in her usual spot by the fire, a tartan blanket on her knees and a sly smile on her old yellow face.

'Good afternoon, Lizzie. I'm looking for my husband.'

Dan stepped into the room from the back hall. He kept his back to the wall and waited.

'Your murderess is gone, gone to get rid of your child.'

'Who are you talking about?'

'Sarah.' She spat the name. 'She went to him. The abortionist.'

'What bloody abortionist!'

'Who do you think? The herbalist is who. Our very own. Didn't you know? He's doing it right now. Chop, chop, choppity-chop.'

Lizzie cackled with laughter. Dan ran past Carmel. Not to the scene of the crime. Oh, no, that wasn't Dan's style. Dan went to Sergeant Deegan. Let the law do the dirty work.

The light was fading. Dogs barked at each other, brave in the dark, safe behind fences, small dogs that felt like big dogs as they growled and yapped. The two gardaí stood before Carmel and Dan, awaiting a revelation.

'Will one of you for God's sake speak up? Look at youse, sitting together in your cold empty room like schoolchildren.' Deegan was dying to be home for his supper.

Garda Molloy tried a different approach. 'By all accounts and purposes you seem like a nice, good-living family. It would help . . .' He paused. 'It would help if we knew about the events leading up to this, to the girl getting into difficulty.'

Silence.

'Do you know who the father is? Take your time.'

More silence.

'Mrs Holohan, how well did you know the girl, Sarah?'

'I didn't know her from Adam,' said Carmel. 'My brother, Finbar, recommended her. I trusted his judgement: he's a schoolmaster. She was brought up in the country with an old midwife aunt of hers.'

'What of her parents?'

'The mother died in childbirth.'

'Father?' Molloy took out his notebook.

'Don't know – he must've died in childbirth too.' Carmel sniggered.

'Dan said that you told him, that your shop girl has gone to procure a miscarriage?'

'Yes.'

'How do you know?'

'She told me. Told me she was in trouble, that it wasn't the first time and he, the herbalist, had taken care of it before for her.'

'My God. Will she testify as to that?'

'I doubt it – these girls are very sly.' Her gaze slid towards her husband.

'Did she have any friends we could talk to?'

'No, not a soul.'

64

I was stopped by Lizzie Murphy. 'Emily! Emily!' she crowed. Oh, she couldn't wait to tell me the news. A complaint had been made against the herbalist, made by Mrs Dan Holohan. It was the talk of the town. Everyone agreed something very odd was going on. There was no sign of Sarah, who, or so Mrs Holohan claimed, had procured a miscarriage from the herbalist. And there wasn't a jot of evidence against him either. What a thing to say about the man! A woman scorned has an evil tongue. Lizzie said Molloy and Deegan had searched the herbalist's place and there was no sign of anything untoward on his premises – the opposite in fact, the place was spotless. They had brought the herbalist to the barracks anyway. 'More of a formality really,' she explained, as if she knew formality from hot tea. 'He's there now,' she added, pure twinkling with malice.

I went home and prepared for the occasion. My satin gown fitted perfectly, and so it should, it had been made for me, by me, ever so carefully.

Once I got back into town, I strolled slowly towards the bridge. I wanted everyone around to get a good look at the girl in the long blue dress. At the railings of the bridge I held out the small card envelope, the one with a dead girl's letter in it – a letter I knew every word of by heart – opened my hand and let it fall towards the water, sure that it would never be read again, for the river, the river eats everything.

I stood just inside the station door and saw through to the interview room. There were just the three of them: him and Deegan at a table; Molloy was at a small desk doing paperwork. The herbalist was denying everything, espousing natural medicines. They seemed to be almost finished. I heard Deegan: 'You're very gracious in the face of what are evidently the spiteful suspicions of a temperamental woman. No evidence. No witness. Just one wild accusation. And, with all due respect, what kind of girl would do such a thing? And, with all due respect, what kind of girl would come forward and admit it? I'm in need of a cup of tea – do you fancy one yourself?'

'Four sugars, no milk.'

As the herbalist and the sergeant consoled each other about time-wasters and gossips, I stepped in. They both looked up: the herbalist looked like he was about to laugh; the sergeant frowned.

'What is it?'

'I'm a witness.'

'The investigation is over.' Deegan kicked the interview-room door shut.

I wondered what to do, tried not to cry. Then Molloy came out. He was holding a sandwich.

'I've time – come on.'

He showed me into another room. Once we were both sitting, he took out a notebook, licked the nib of his pencil and looked up at me expectantly. He didn't seem unkind. That gave me courage.

'Off you go, in your own words, take your time.'

'He always offered me syrup in a small glass first. It was dark and bitter. I got sick afterwards, into a bucket that he kept there. Then he made me remove my underclothes. Examined me, with his hands. Do you know what I mean?'

65

Carmel opened the shop – what else could she do? People were in shock, white-faced. *Did you hear? Did you hear?* Milkie and Moll Nash, Tessie Feeney, Lizzie Murphy and Mrs Purcell all arrived in more or less together. They crowded the counter. She filled a threepenny bag with toffees for Milkie. When she looked up, the floor was full. More had come in: she could see the heads of Miss Murray and Miss Hawkins, Nell Daly, Miss Harvey, Catty Dolan, Miss Fortune, Sally Heaney and was that Rita Brennan in the doorway?

Carmel sat on the stool. They were chattering together, and they were all glancing at her, feasting their eyes. Being careful not to mention her husband, or the shop girl, or adultery. They were just there to take note of her condition, complexion, demeanour. Notes they could compare later, expand upon in comfort. For now, in here, they would pick over other carcasses. Like Mrs Birmingham, who had lost everything. Didn't she think the world of Rose! It was so sudden and there were terrible rumours! People said poor Rose was in the family way. Nonsense and tommy-rot, that girl never went anywhere without her mother. She had no men friends anyway; that was just jealous people making gossip for a good family in their time of trouble. And so it went . . .

I've never seen a couple in such a state of despair.
They loved that girl so. She was the apple of her father's eye.
What sort of illness was it at all?
No such thing. She died in childbirth. Blood soaked the earth.
Don't believe a word. The poor innocent died from an infection.
The mother's suicidal.
Don't say that.

The father upped and left, went to America or Cork, or somewhere equally remote.

The mother is drinking herself into a puddle of piss.

Emily Madden made a complaint against the herbalist.

Emily?

Yes, Emily.

Are you sure?

Of course we're sure. He tried to abscond.

Must be guilty, then!

They caught him; he had gone to his house for something.

Must've been something valuable.

Not at all. It was a photo. A woman with a baby.

Ah, his mother. He can't be all bad, then.

He was no innocent.

Rose was an innocent. Yes, a living, breathing angel.

There's no smoke without fire.

Her mother has gone to the dogs, nursing rum in a public lounge.

Can she not fall apart in the luxury of her own fine house?

Lonely, I suppose, with her husband gone.

How did she manage that one? I'd have to put a bomb under my lad to be rid of him.

Oh, that Mrs Birmingham, she was always one big disaster.

A big-boned famine cow.

Rose told someone.

Really?

Shush, yes, before it happened.

It?

Her death.

No.

Yes, I heard it straight from the horse's mouth. 'I'm in deep trouble,' Rose said, 'but I'm keeping it and I'm going away.' It was a reliable source, not someone given to gossip.

Who?

I can't say, I swore.

Ah, go on.

It was Charlie, Charlie told us. He was sweet on Rose; he's fit to kill.

'Get out, every last living rotting one of you. Get out,' shouted Carmel.

She pushed and shoved at the women's backs till she had herded them on to the street. Then she locked the doors of Kelly's shop.

66

His house was neat if a little bare. They were both awkward, Matt less so since they were on his home turf. He went outside to finish his work, and she rested by the fire. Her limbs still ached from having been tied up. Her head didn't feel that great either. There was a faded photo of a stern woman over the mantelpiece. Sarah was examining it when he returned.

'That's my late wife.'

He stoked the fire, took down a heavy black pan and greased it with lard. It was relaxing to watch him: he moved slowly and with deliberation. The door on to the garden was open; the only sounds were the starlings. It was another world here – even the air seemed fresher.

'My sister was taken away for the same thing.' He nodded towards her stomach. 'So I don't mind marrying you, keeping you respectable. A favour.'

'Don't get notions.'

'I've no notions left; I'm not a young man. I was born alone and I'll die alone and I'm happiest alone.'

'Oh, Jesus!' said Sarah. A dark shape had flitted by the window.

'What?' He nearly dropped the pan, nearly lost an egg.

'It's him, oh God, it's the herbalist. He's come to get me!'

'It's only your imagination.'

He handed her a mug of warmed brandy.

'Lock the doors.'

'There's only one door and there's no one near it.'

'Do you have a gun?'

'Just for hunting. Aw, the bloody eggs are burning with all this fussing. You've had a shock, you need to rest. Go into the back room. I'll make you a fresh egg.'

She checked that the window was shut and sat up on the bed

beside it. She pulled the rough blankets up around her and sipped her brandy. The river was out there, the same river. The herbalist could come down it at any time, come after her.

He said his sister was sent away for the same thing.

The same thing.

She remembered Jamsie; how he had pinned her down. Was Matt's sister pinned down too? Jamsie had laughed, imitated her expression and made an O-shape with his mouth. Then he heaved on top of her, pressed the air from her lungs. Tore at her like a greedy piglet, the heel of his hands on her collarbone. She was afraid it would snap. She thought of the wishbone drying on the stove, imagined she was still inside the house holding warm lemonade, safe and sound instead of being on the ground. When he stopped, he was puce. He looked at her.

'You stupid bitch,' he whispered.

The Walls of Limerick gathered momentum as she stumbled up the stairs to her room. Mai followed, shut the door. Sarah told her.

'May the Lord have mercy on your soul.'

Mai crossed herself, as if Sarah had died. Gracie said Sarah would have to be sent away. There was a place.

'You led him on. These lads aren't in full control. Everyone saw youse dancing like lunatics. Enough said.' Gracie was furious.

The two women fought like cats when everyone was gone. Sarah had sluiced herself with cold water from the jug and dried off with a towel, rubbing her skin so hard it almost bled. Then she put on her nightdress and a cardigan. She picked up her dress – muck and blood on gingham – and wrapped it up for burning. She prayed to the Little Flower, promised her all the roses in the world if they didn't send her to the place, the place where Annie Mangan had gone.

Divine intervention prevailed. She was to begin her new position with the Holohans. She was to pretend nothing had happened, to work hard, and to wait and see if the Lord would have mercy.

Sarah finished her brandy and looked out on the river. Maybe mercy was a lock gatekeeper.

Aggie, what did they say? Did they believe all that was said about him?

Look here, my dear.

30 August 1939

CHARGE AGAINST HERBALIST

Don Vikram Fernandes, a middle-aged coloured man with an address in Black Walk, will appear in Court on Friday, 1 September, charged with an offence against a girl.

Does that ring any bells for you? It's a poor article, barely the length of my thumb. Middle aged. Oh, he wouldn't like that, no siree, he would not!

You'd miss it, if you weren't looking for it, but there were plenty looking for it, plenty with an interest. And not who you'd expect. 'Go away, Aggie, you're only a gossip . . .' That's what was said to me, even when it was there in black and white, hidden amongst those other ink-worthy events: Byrne's tot thrown to Daingean for robbing a plank, young Greaney caught for no light on his bloody bicycle, and that lone sentence in memory of you, poor Rose.

You wouldn't know it, but it's my story. You won't find me in the column inches. You won't find me in the newsprint. You'll find me in the gaps, the commas, the full stops – the small dark spaces where one thing led to another. I was afraid to speak, but now I'm not, for who'll hurt me now? I'm past that, past touch. Isn't that right, Aggie?

Shush, a leanbh, that's enough. See how it rains and rains; see how the river breaks its banks? As I speak, mothers are warning their daughters to never, ever, go near strange men. And to always stay away from *that* lane. Bad things happened in that lane, and now it's haunted by the ghost of an unfortunate girl. Oh, yes, they say, there's a crack in the centre of town where young girls slip down. And among themselves, the women talk of matters they'll never tell their children or husbands. Late-night confessions. *He performed unmentionable acts. Put a spell on my daughter, my sister, my neighbour. And on me . . . on me . . . on me.*

Doctor Sin, with his herbs, lotions and potions, creeps into their dreams. And what, they wonder – tiptoeing downstairs to their cupboards to select one of his brown glass bottles and hold it up – just what, they wonder, really swims therein? What sort of herbs, what breed of medicine?

Ladies, the herbs were his fingertips, his quiet lips, his dry hands cooling you down, cooling you down. Now what will you do without him?

The day the black maria came, he let the gardaí lead him away. He looked at no one. The women of the town hung around. 'Let us at him, let us at him!' Crows cawed from the wires, as sharp and determined soapy arms rose. They drove him off in a puff of smoke. I went over to his house. The rooms were empty, dull. The rows of bottles that were its only ornaments, gone. The stretcher bed, gone. The space where it used to be looked different to the rest of the floor; more dust motes seemed to gather over that space. Maybe it was just the morning light through the boxy windows. God preserve us, but who'd call it a surgery – only a mad man.

There was a scent of wood burning. He was up to his old tricks: a tin barrel was smoking, and he'd set light to bits of wood from the bed, the curtains. What else, I could not see. Ancient things burning, a sad smell indeed. There wasn't hide nor hair of him anywhere, no sign of who had lived there. He was a great man for covering his tracks. He'd led everyone on a merry dance.

'I converse with the dead. Does that scare you?' I said.

'Not as much as the strength of this whiskey,' he said.

'You don't believe me? Let me look at your palm . . . your mother loved you –'

'Only a mother could.' He laughed. 'Let's dance.'

And so the first night went like that, a world away from the last.

67

The market was quiet: a few stalls, almost no customers. It was my first day in town since the herbalist was arrested, since the newspaper article, but the hawkers barely raised their heads as we walked by. The air was cool. You could feel autumn coming and autumn felt like a good clean thing.

We were the first to arrive at the courthouse, me and Charlie. It was to be a special sitting, just for me and the herbalist. We sat on the side steps and waited for the clerk and everyone else to arrive. The river was misty; it looked soft, romantic even.

'Maybe everyone has forgotten,' I said; 'maybe it's all blown over.'

'You should tell it was Rose, not you, who had those things done to her.'

'Whist, what are you saying? The Birminghams would never admit such a thing. And then what would there be against the herbalist? Who would give evidence?'

'I want to throttle him.'

We heard a bolt drawing back, the click of a lock. The door opened. Clerk Roberts let us in with a quiet smile, before setting off with a duster. Had he heard Charlie? Would he know what he meant?

We stood like fools in the hall. Then Carty, the solicitor, filled the doorway; lifted my elbow and veered me into a small room. He left the door open.

'Well now, Miss Madden.' He seemed half asleep. 'Any questions?'

I was worried about swearing on the bible and then telling so many lies. But they weren't really lies, they were the truth. They were just somebody else's truth.

'No, sir.'

Mr Carty stood there, looking up at the ceiling. It was a high one, cream and dressed in webs. He was famous for daydreaming, the side effect, they said, of too much education. People began to file by outside, talking and laughing.

'Well, what are you waiting for?' He signalled for me to go in.

I had never been in court before. It was a plain half-moon-shaped room, with high, long windows so the sky could look down on us. The pews were full of people of all ages, and many were standing at the back wall. So much for it all blowing over. The whole town must've taken the day off. Mr Carty showed me to a seat to the left of the judge. I felt the women eat up every detail of me, from the stitching in my hem to the pins in my hair. I kept my eyes on the floor; it gleamed like treacle. The jury were huddled to my right. Ordinary townsmen, who looked a bit alarmed to be hearing this particular case. I sat and folded my hands into my lap; I knew if I looked up that I would see the herbalist, so I didn't.

The clerk stood. There was a sudden shuffle as everyone moved forward. He cleared his throat. How much like church it was then – the way the light hung dusty, the smell of wood polish, the held breath, the sweat.

'The people of Éire versus Don Vikram Fernandes!' roared the clerk.

He sounded ecstatic; as if announcing the arrival of a Bengalese tiger come to perform daring feats. The whispers began.

I put my hand on a bible, not a special book, no gilt inscription, no soft leather, just an ordinary-looking dog-eared thing. Aggie said it was a Protestant bible, so it wouldn't matter a jot. I crossed my fingers behind my back anyway and sent a silent wish for strength to the holy virgin mother. I swore to tell the whole truth and nothing but the truth so help me God. I glanced up then and saw the herbalist. The sun shone down from the window, on him and his cream suit. His hair was cut close to his head; his skin looked tight across the bones of his face. He stared me down, his eyes blazing. He was dressed as he was the day he arrived in our town, but he didn't look the same.

Sergeant Deegan was first to take the stand. There wasn't a sound, not a cough or a sniffle, in the courthouse.

'The accused did unlawfully use an instrument on the person of Emily Mary Madden for the purpose of . . .'

The judge slammed his hammer. 'Anyone with any decency will now leave the court.'

There was a mighty long pause and then the people began to move. One by one they each took one last gawk, their greedy eyes pecking at my face and body, my unlawful body. It was ten minutes before the benches were emptied. There was only one woman left. Alone in the middle of the last pew sat Aggie, solemn as a mourner.

Sergeant Deegan continued, casual as you like, as if he was reciting his tables, '. . . and did use an instrument on the said person for the purpose of procuring a miscarriage.'

How did the accused plead? The accused pleaded not guilty. The burden of proof lay with the prosecution. They'd found all the proof they needed in a squalid wooden box. It held instruments, bottles containing liquid, jars containing powders and boxes of pills.

An important doctor took the stand and gave his medical opinion. He had snow-white hair, a bulbous nose and a bow tie. He said there were eighty-six medicines on the accused's premises, some poisonous, but most of a type that he 'couldn't determine'. There was also the matter of a speculum whose blades had been made from two shoehorns. The good doctor told the jury that this instrument would be effective in opening the womb. 'To let the light in, so to speak, gentlemen.' There was laughter in the court.

There was also a probing instrument, a rod. In the doctor's opinion no other instrument would be necessary. In the doctor's opinion, there would be death in one out of four cases.

'Excellent evidence, thank you again for travelling, Doctor Morgan,' said the judge.

Charlie was leaning against the wall at the back of the courtroom, and he had begun to weep.

The judge turned to the herbalist.

'Do you know Miss Madden?'

He nodded.

'Can you identify her for the record?'

He lifted his hand and pointed at me, holding his arm out longer than need be. I thought of the hula girl and the snake hiding under his crisp white shirt, of the way he banished his demons, of the way he'd kissed my skin. He said something, but I couldn't hear. I felt my legs begin to shake and couldn't stop them.

'Let the record show that the accused identified Miss Emily Madden.

'Miss Madden will now give testimony.'

And I had to say it all over again, the things he'd done to Rose. How many times she went to him, where he touched her, the instruments he used. Had they no shame, asking such questions? Words like that coming out of a girl's mouth in a room full of men. Telling me to speak up when I faltered, when I thought – how could he? How could he be this thing? Where was the other man, the one who had called me Cleopatra?

'And who was the father of the child?'

I almost told the truth but stopped just in time. If I mentioned Doctor Birmingham, my case – Rose's case – would be thrown out. So I said different, said a name they would have no trouble with. I raised my arm and pointed at the stranger.

'It was the herbalist; it was he that ruined me.'

I could feel the herbalist's anger; I could almost hear him hiss from across the room. I hung my head. This to me seemed the most shameful part, but I don't know why. I was cross-examined by the herbalist's barrister, Mr Butler.

'Didn't you tell anyone about the trouble you were in?'

'No.'

'What about your mother?'

'Mam is dead.'

'Were you keeping company?'

'No, sir.'

'Did you go to a proper doctor?'

'No, sir.'

'How long has this man been carrying on with you?'

'Since the beginning of the summer, sir.'

'Why did you let him?'

'He said that we would travel away together, sir, he said that we would marry.'

'And you believed him?' The barrister smirked.

'Of course, sir, why wouldn't I?'

I could see what he was thinking, that I was a half-wit.

'This man made a fool of you. Did you ask him to do an operation?'

'No, I didn't.'

'But you let him?'

'What else could I do?'

'Could you not confide in your priest?'

'Are you mad? What country do you live in?'

'What?' Mr Butler leant in – he'd long lashes, like a girl's.

'I didn't confide in anyone, sir,' I said, 'because I was very foolish.'

He seemed happy with that. By then I just wanted to go home.

The jury were back in a matter of minutes. Guilty, they said.

'Eight years' hard labour,' said the judge, 'for the crime of procuring Miss Emily Madden, a woman not being a common prostitute of known immoral character, to have unlawful carnal connection, and for eight counts of using instruments to procure miscarriage.'

Agnes Marian Reilly, known common prostitute, of known immoral character, clapped till she was removed from the court.

I felt shame heat my cheeks as I left the courtroom, but at least I felt something. Not like Rose.

The square was full of people when I went outside. There was a hush when they saw me, even amongst the children, who stood elbow to elbow on the wall by the river. Every hawker was still, arms crossed on their chests at their stalls.

I stood on the step of the courthouse. Old women in black shawls and young women in headscarves seemed to surround me. I'd known them all since I was a child, and they all knew me. Their eyes glittered with hatred. The silence was broken by an awful sound. The women's mouths gaped, and they squawked over and over again, louder and louder. They wanted something. What were they saying? Spit dressed their chins as they moved closer, and closer. What were they saying? I could almost smell the meat between their teeth.

Someone scooped me up and carried me back into the court-house. It was Garda Molloy. He shut the door. I put my hands on the wood. Their chanting buzzed my palms. What were they saying? A stout short man smiled at me, patted my back.

'Better stay here till they settle down.'

The voice was the judge's. I hadn't recognized him without his white wig. He was let out and there was a break in the shouting. We heard the motorcar take him away. The herbalist was being brought down the corridor towards us. Sergeant Deegan guided him by the elbow; he was handcuffed.

'Maybe we should wait, boys,' Deegan said.

'Wait, my arse,' was Molloy's answer; 'let him face the music.'

I felt the herbalist move from behind me, to beside me and then past me. I kept my eyes closed. I sensed nothing, no message. There was no last word between us, just the sound of the door being unbolted. I looked at him, but he didn't look back. I felt a river breeze and heard the crowd begin to bay. This time I knew what they were saying. 'Hang him. Hang him.' The women's voices soared above the men's. The guard shut the door behind the sergeant and the herbalist. I stepped foward.

'Don't follow him. You'll be killed,' Molloy whispered. 'They'll have him hung, drawn and quartered.'

At first I could hear Sergeant Deegan shouting at the crowd to get back, then I couldn't hear his voice any more, just a roaring like at an All-Ireland football match. 'Hang him. Hang him.' And then there was a deathly quiet. I fainted.

I came to with Charlie rubbing my hand. We were on Aggie's barge. She was lying on her settle with her old black shawl tucked around her. Men were singing out in the street. There was the sound of glass breaking, and a big cheer.

'We showed him,' he said.

'Showed who?'

'Him, we showed him and all like him. We showed him for what he was. A trickster. A savage. A killer. You should've seen it, Em: farmers brought pitchforks topped with lit turf, and we drove him and the sergeant all the way to the station house. We smeared him with tar. Saw what he really was without the white suit, without the flash smiles – he was a cloven-hoofed devil.'

'It's beneath you, Charlie, to be acting like that.'

'It was for Rose.'

'It was for you.'

Charlie dropped my hand, and went out to join the other boys.

'I'm afraid, Aggie. Can I stay here tonight?'

'You can't. I'm of no use to you, not any more.'

Aggie looked terrible; she was shivering and part of her hairline was clotted with blood. She must've been at the drink, for she kept rambling. Said she'd seen an omen, a red-haired woman the spit of herself. That she was soon for the next world. I knelt beside her, promised I'd be back in the morning. She clasped my hand and gave it a squeeze. I smelt gin off her breath.

I made my way out into the night. Young lads with lanterns and lit pitchforks sang in the square: 'He'd fly through the air with the greatest of ease, that daring young man on his flying trapeze.' There was an older crowd on the steps of the town hall.

'Mind the thatch!' one of them shouted to the boys.

That made me afraid – what if they set light to a house and one thing led to another and the whole town was burnt in their beds? It didn't feel safe. Charlie came over, a bottle of stout in his hand.

'I want to go home, Charlie.'

'Come on, come on, then.' He linked my arm and we began to walk.

A pebble hit me on the back of the neck. Charlie was gone in a second, his coat thrown off. Would he ever learn? He lambasted the boy he thought had hit me, while others circled. I couldn't see, didn't want to. I leant against the wall, melted into the shadow of the town hall – the brick was so cold. I wasn't worried about Charlie, he could hold his own.

I was worried about tomorrow. Was I to live like a shunned sow, like the Carver sisters in their flour-bag dresses, eating only from the land, and living like animals? I began to make my way home;

there was no sign of Charlie coming. I felt like all the windows of the houses were eyes narrowing at me as I passed. Kelly's shop was in darkness.

A stick hit my thigh. It was a woman all in black with a black headscarf. It was Birdie: she looked so small and bent since Veronique had passed. I missed the old her, the old sparky Birdie with the halo of white hair.

'Is there anyone in your house tonight?' I could barely hear her.

'I don't know, Birdie, but I'll be all right.'

'Stay at mine.' She hit me again, this time across the arm. 'Come on.'

So I stayed in Birdie's spare room, where everything was ornate and the sheets were cold with damp. She had no hot-water bottle for my feet, so she gave me a long black fur coat and a grey cat. The cat curled up on my feet straight away, obviously used to second jobbing as a foot warmer. I thought of the herbalist: he would sleep between the same four walls for the next eight years. He would never step across the town square in his white suit again. Where was Doctor B, where was the man who had planted the seed? He would never be punished. Why did I feel sorry for the herbalist? He was a monster. Yet I remembered him disappearing through the courthouse door and into the crowd, his hat yet to be knocked off, and felt the pity you'd feel for a lamb thrown to the wolves.

I shouldn't have felt sorry. He got hard labour, but I got life. If I was a nobody before the trial, I'd be a leper afterwards.

You found me, Aggie, you found me.

I knew I would, love, knew I would.

I was a good girl, Aggie.

I know, Rose.

Didn't go out on my own, averted my eyes around men and only went to the pictures with Mam. Sorry, no. Mother. I forgot: not Mam, Mother. 'Mam' is common. So is Charlie, but he's beautiful. Not like my father. My father didn't go – to the Picture Palace, that is. It's a low-class thing. Low-class things are so exciting.

Low class, my arse – that dada of yours thought he was royalty; gadding about town with his black bag, pushing up his spectacles and looking down his nose.

That wasn't his fault, Aggie. He was a doctor because he had to be – he was born to it. My poor father didn't have a say-so in the matter. He was a very busy man, worked all hours, tending to all and sundry. Mother made a sad face about that, but I know she hated it when my father was under her feet in her drawing room. She hadn't designed it with him in mind.

Your dada was a bastard.

Aggie, how could you! It wasn't him. It wasn't really. My father had a twin. Not many people know that. A not-so-nice a man as him. They were alike but smelt different. He used to barge into our house very late at night – he'd no right. Mother put on her visitors' voice, all polite and light. I'd listen to them talk, to their voices going up and down – my father's twin and Mother – thinking, 'He shouldn't be there. If my father knew, he wouldn't like it at all, at all.'

The maid always came up before him. Take your milk, then. Warm milk and whiskey. The new maid was a bit simple. Voices. The simple maid. Warm milk. Whiskey. My father's twin. That's the way it went.

Mother would say – 'night now – with a catchy kitten in her voice. And he would come up the stairs.

It started the day of the goldfish. I was carrying it home from the carnival. Rushing to get out of the sun; had got a notion the water would heat and boil the fish to death. 'Look at the girl's dress!' someone hooted. I stopped. There was blood on the back of my skirt, like a poppy. Mother told me to run.

She screamed when she got home. Who saw! Who saw! I was twelve years old and counting. To bed with no supper. Later I heard the door clatter, the thick voice, Mother telling tales and laughing. Well may they have laughed, she and my father's twin. When they were tired of laughing, he came up and did his sin.

It was the stain, you see. 'You showed me you were ready,' he always said. But I can't answer when he blows my mouth full of air, I can't answer.

I know, I know. Shush, I know. I have you now, I've found you.

How did you know where to find me?

Sure I'd seen you, Rose. Saw you every night since the one Seamus and myself set you on the road to that big grey house. Saw you hang over the river like a low moon, all alone. Heard you too in other places, crying by the shed for your child, searching the reeds; in the folds of the day, you were everywhere I lay.

Where are we going now, Ag?

To another river, different but the same as this one. It's not far at all now, around the next bend. Look, it's just over the horizon.

Three years later . . .

Are there more spiders weaving in September, or is it just me? The Holohans' shop front is grey; the window bald and dark, as mucky as the river, with nothing in it except for my reflection – a pale figure floating in a rectangle of glass as if I was the ghost, as if I was the one that torments this place. My hands leave prints on the dusty glass.

I think back on the impressive straight-backed couple that I once knew, so nice and well-to-do. Dan and Carmel, their respectable faces, their polite voices. How I wish that impression had stayed true. I can see them still, Dan drawing plans for shop improvements in a copybook and Carmel reading banned novels, drinking tonic wine.

I can't believe Dan went back to Tipperary, that he just abandoned the shop and everything in it. Finbar wanted it so much that he hired solicitor after solicitor to find a loophole in the will. And there was Dan, not wanting it at all in the end. So much for those who say it was the only reason he married Carmel.

The church bells clang, calling the town to attention. In the alleyway, young children skip rope. Soon the path will fill with people making their way to Mass. Not many would recognize me. If they did, they'd think me a vulture, skulking around to see what's left.

The herbalist would know me. I almost felt him when I walked into the market square, felt his knuckle graze my neck, lift a Marcel wave from my newly set hair, to peer past the pan-stick and eye shadow, past my carefully drawn womanhood.

Emily, he'd whisper, *Emily, is that really you?* Sometimes I confuse what I knew with what the townspeople said afterwards, so that even in my dreams he becomes just another smooth-tongued devil. 'A peasant Irish girl,' he once called me. To think it was me caused all that trouble. Skinny drab Emily. Lover of the next ruler of the Western world, the medicine king himself. Believer of all

305

his promises, waiting to be sent down the river on a raft, to be washed in milk, bejewelled with gemstones and adorned in silks. Something had to be done, but sometimes the cure is worse than the sting. A bad man he was, but I miss the sweetness of his fingertips, and the grand dreams he gave me.

How that crowd of bitches chased him in the beginning, flushed and powdered, perfumed to high heaven. Pushing their bosoms into one another's backs in their rush to get near his market stall. 'A great man to have. Aren't we lucky he came our way? You know he wasn't going to stay only for the great welcome we gave him?'

Fools, did they really believe that was it? The few pence they spent on invigorating tonic?

We were in love, I thought. *I'm a woman now, and soon we'll leave together and go to Brighton, where we'll marry. And he'll make a fortune as a medicine man with his cure-alls. He's a saviour, a great help to all.*

The herbalist always gave out about me and my big gob. Said girls were dangerous because of what's between their legs and what comes out of their mouths. How right he was. What came out of my big mouth got him prison. I did it for Rose. True. But I did it for him too. Well, it was better than being buried alive in the bog. That's what Charlie had in store for him.

Wasn't it funny? The herbalist sentenced to hard labour, considering the nature of his crimes? I can hear Aggie laugh at that. It's strange, but Aggie was right about not having long to live. She passed away the morning after the trial. Seamus found her and had her taken to the morgue. When he came back, the boat was gone. *Biddy* must've come undone – a badly tied knot no doubt, for it was last seen by Ned drifting in the current of the high river towards the leafy bends. Ned claimed there were two women in it, one old and one young. Everyone agreed that Ned was seeing things again. But the boat was never found.

I miss Aggie's dirty laugh, but I'm glad she got to see me make my confession. The way that judge looked at me. *Poor girl of the lower classes led astray, set upon.* He looked at my top button, moved his mouth like he'd like to set upon me himself. Wanted details, he wanted every detail, to better imagine me violated, offended, up against it.

It wasn't the herbalist that got those girls in the family way in the first place – everyone forgets that. And everyone got it wrong: he and I – monster that he was – we were equals. Not in the beginning, and not in the end, but during the most important time, when he was my love and I was his empress.

Kelly's shop was shut, in darkness and deserted. A window display of Jacob's tins held tight to their crumbling biscuits. No one dared enter. No one dared creep up those stairs. It was nonsense, a child's tale, but youngsters said that Carmel was there still, roaming around, peering through windows, lamenting. The grown-ups laughed, but no one went in. If they did, they might have seen the peeling wallpaper and the cracked plaster beneath it. The clothes that hung limply in the open wardrobes, the family photographs that lay smashed and greasy on the floor, and underneath – a five-pound note. They'd have to push open the heavily cobwebbed doors first, except for the one upstairs – that one was sealed shut.

The day Carmel drove out the gossiping women and slammed the door behind them was the last day Kelly's shop ever opened. She hid indoors during the herbalist's trial and after. Didn't work, didn't eat, didn't answer the knocking out front. A lot of people called in the beginning, but that fell off after a week or two. Birdie kept it up the longest. Finbar never showed his face, not once. The townswomen gathered outside and discussed her – what were they to do?

Carmel went upstairs, shut her ears, but she couldn't shut them out – *The girl was up to no good with Carmel's husband. Oh, the pity of it, the poor woman!* The town crowed with pity and delight. Carmel felt their words beat the roof at night.

The girl Sarah all but disappeared. The herbalist was taken off before harm was done – at least Carmel didn't have that on her conscience. Whatever evil had possessed her was gone.

Then Grettie B came to call, pushed her way in. Shoved and rattled the back door till the lock snapped. *To rescue me, from myself,* thought Carmel, but she thought wrong. Grettie came to return the five pounds she had borrowed. 'It bought death for my daughter. Have it back, go on. I'm making amends for my sins.' She threw it towards Carmel and left. It fluttered and lay on the floor. Carmel never touched it, never picked it up. The realization hit her fully and straight in the gut. Rose died, and Rose's child had died, and Carmel's five pounds had paid for their deaths. There would be no end to her torment now.

Carmel gathered what was left of the rope from the shed and went upstairs. She sat on the rocking chair, and listened for Samuel's cry to tell her when it was time. When he came, it wasn't as a cry but as a soft light, a blur in the corner of the room, and she knew that his soul had come to meet his mother's, so that they could make the journey together.

Sarah worked with letters, names, wrote in copperplate. That much didn't change. She often thought, *I'll write it down for him, I'll write it down for Ben*. But would she really want him to know such a sad, sad story? What good would it do for her brown-eyed boy? It would be her need, not his. Let him go on blindly and happily with his life. He'd go on better without knowing of certain incidents.

After the first couple of weeks, no one came looking. Sarah had been terrified that they would. For a time she had suffered nightmares about the herbalist and her ordeal in his house. But of course nobody came. She was just a stranger who had worked in the town for a summer and then disappeared.

Matt, it turned out, had saved her, but not through lies and persuasion. A silver tongue will only get you so far. No, he just showed simple human kindness and provided her with a side-altar marriage and a roof to grow strong under. What started out in name only soon became love, and the man who preferred to be alone became a fine father and husband.

She had never imagined how much comfort and loving a baby could bring. She adored Ben – who wouldn't? She loved that his hair was the colour of toffee, that his skin was flawless, and that his stout little nose was like a knob of butter. She watched as his chubby hands grew more capable, his body more sturdy. He was two now and loved to babble, to curl up on her lap. She'd never known a child so affectionate, never known she had all those hugs in her. The other day he was on her lap after supper. They were sitting on the wooden stool by the fire. He pressed his face on to her cheek, and with his own innocent impression of a kiss made a big smacking noise. 'Love you, Mam,' he said, 'love you.'

❧

Once upon a time, a few years ago, in a town not far from here, a stranger flung open the half-door of the late Veronique Chase's shop, set an easy chair out on the pavement and smiled. She was a young woman, elegant, straight backed. She removed all the yellowed newspapers and mouldy sweets from the low window and arranged hats in their place. Hats of all shapes and sizes, each on its own wire stand. Berets, straw, bonnets, cloches, and one she called a chapeau. She transformed the shop front, had it lovely. It made a great impression.

Inside, the shelves brimmed with ribbons, buttons and patterns. And all kinds of fabric – not just plain, striped and checked, but florals of all sorts. Reds, mauves and yellows, if you don't mind. The cloth came all the way from America.

She was well-got all right, this dressmaker girl – you'd know by her gait. She wasn't from these parts. The orphan daughter of a gentleman. Half French she was, you could see it in the way she waved her hands when she spoke. Fine boned, pretty, with her hair all done up in an elaborate chignon.

What had made her move to their small town? She'd wanted, it was said, a change of air.

The women adored her. Counted themselves lucky to have such style in their little backwater. She had a word for everyone, could mend or make anything, no job was too small or too big. You should see the dresses she created from almost nothing. Millie, they called her. Miss Millie can do anything. She's nothing less than a magician.